For Howard and Katie, always.

" A modern magician to make the semblance of a human being, with two laths for legs, a pumpkin for a head &c—of the rudest and most meagre materials....At the end of the story, after deceiving the world for a long time, the spell should be broken, and the gray dandy be discovered to be nothing but a suit of clothes, with these few sticks inside of it. And so this wretched old thing shall become the symbol of a large class."

—NATHANIEL HAWTHORNE, STORY IDEA, *AMERICAN NOTEBOOKS*

Chapter 1

*"It is dangerous to look too minutely into such phenomena.
It is apt to create a substance where at first there was a mere shadow...."*

—HAWTHORNE

Where no sound should be, Coral Rigby heard the papery rustling of new green leaves.

On this night in the latter week of May, no sea breeze ventured inland to the cottage colony. A starless sky lay close over the profound quiet of the Wonderstrand night. She paused in her work to listen.

More rustling.

She gathered herself into stone, not a hair astir.

The hulk of dog did the same, but a growl launched itself from deep in his chest.

Dickon! Silence! She didn't speak, but the dog understood.

Both heard the *ting* of a button or a watchband striking another surface in the man-high thicket. A human intruder then, not a raccoon or coyote.

She and the dog waited. A footfall, the frail snapping of fallen pine needles on soft ground, not the crunch of the oyster shell path. So a stranger was easing in, shunning the straightforward route. The dog's spiked hackles and her own instinct filled in what her ears didn't. A thief? Perhaps, but what was worth stealing here? Someone looking for her, intentions hostile? It had happened before.

Then the snapping and rustling inched west, farther from her cottage, nearer another. For a moment, she was relieved. Let her neighbors look out for themselves. Coral took great pains not to endure them, not to have to chatter and nod like a bobblehead.

Back to her work. She adjusted the little Canon that hung from a strap around her neck, for she'd been photographing her finished creations for her records.

Outside, a branch cracked sharply, like a bone. She tensed again. The threat was still too intimate, too near home.

Move! As quick as the thought, she and the dog sprang for the door. Out they galloped, the dog ahead of the woman. The camera banged against her breastbone, so she lifted it. A click and it flashed, revealing the true green of the shrubbery, bleaching the path to full moon whiteness. It also highlighted a small crowd of figures, their heads upright upon wide shoulders, arms outstretched, but Coral turned the camera away from them. With the next click, she saw the silhouette crouching among the shrubbery. One more crash of light hit a face dead center.

The man covered his eyes and snarled. The dog was already there, circling him, teeth bared.

"You," she said. Then came her smile, the combined effect like the scrape and flare of a match.

The man glowered, sinking lower into his collar. One hand dropped to the front of his trousers.

"Tumescent!" Coral aimed the camera and clicked again. "So you haven't changed a bit. If you keep doing that, you're going to go blind."

The man raised his arm, and Dickon leaped, pinning him to the dirt where he lay, legs flailing.

"Serves you right." Eyes now adjusted to the dark, she studied his position relative to the nearest cottage. Its shades were up, and a small lamp illuminated the room on the side facing them.

"Of course," said Coral. "I understand now. It's little Piety you want to see. Poor old pervert, your prey isn't at home. Hear that, Dickon? The great man's got himself busted, and for nothing. Oh, what a pretty irony. Might as well let him up, but keep him in reach of your jaws." She snapped several more photos.

The dog retreated, allowing the man to fumble to his feet. He had yet to utter a word, but now, towering over the woman (for he was a large and solid citizen), he summoned up his outraged dignity.

"See here, I have every right to be on this property." His voice was thick and rich, heavy as gravy. Yet she recognized the vibrato beneath the accents of entitlement.

"See here yourself. You've no business in the cottages at this hour of the night." Forced to face upward to meet his eyes, she didn't retreat; rather, she leaned forward, crowding him.

He stepped back. "Cousin," he said. "What do you want from me?"

"Stick to our agreement."

"This isn't the time or place to discuss ..."

"Damn the man! Couldn't I say the same to you? Is this *your* backyard? Is that your bedroom you were gawking into? But no, you're right. It wasn't real estate that was on your mind, it was your cock. And I've got its picture, right in here!" She hopped up and down, flourishing the camera like a tambourine.

"Why don't you just go online? There are all kinds of peep sites. Chat rooms. You could make like-minded friends! Or if you felt the need for a little night air, you could just take your laptop outside." Her voice became wintry. "Don't interfere with my home, or I use these pictures."

They faced each other, deadlocked.

Just then a crash issued from the opposite end of the cottage colony. The man recoiled.

"Oh, don't worry. No danger from that quarter."

"What was it?"

"Nothing. My tenant. He's oblivious. He'd never think to investigate—unless I screamed bloody murder, of course."

Coral continued in a conspiratorial whisper. "But someone *else* might appear at any minute, back from her evening out. And here's you, exposed for all the world to see." She squinted at his crotch. "Zip up your fly. You seem to have forgotten." As he reached down, she snapped one more photo.

"I wasn't interfering with you," he said.

"A matter of opinion. Indulge yourself someplace else. I don't trust you wandering around here at night."

"All right."

"Again?"

"I said all right."

Coral was silent for several beats, mulling it over.

"I keep my word," he added sourly.

She snorted. "And I've kept your secrets, God help me. But you owe me more than one good turn. Best to remember that. Now go back to your own place." Another laugh. "And your wife."

The man made a motion to seize the camera, but the dog lunged, slavering.

Coral waved the animal away. "Look sharp, Mr. Jeffrey Goodman Brown."

He flinched at the sound of his name, then turned to face her, as if an invisible hand gripped his chin.

She dangled the camera between them, meeting his eyes. Now the man's arms hung limp at his sides. He couldn't reach, couldn't make his fingers curl around the strap. Spitting and muttering, he retreated through the woods from which he'd come.

"I can hear you," sang Coral. "Better not hurl insults."

The rustling in the undergrowth grew louder. The man had begun to run.

"Humiliation is the devil's own rocket fuel, don't you think, Dickon?"

She turned toward home, her head aloft and her back straight. The dog preened, lifting his paws high. They marched past the little crowd of stationary figures she'd seen briefly in the camera flash—a crowd to hail the returning heroes. She stopped, as if to shake hands with a well-wisher, but instead reached out to adjust a long nose that had fallen askew. Poor scarecrows, she thought. Sticks and rags. If only my darlings had the powers of sight and speech, what allies they'd be.

Once back in her own cottage, she headed first for the kitchen, the dog padding after her. She peeled a slice of roast beef from a deli pack in the refrigerator and tossed it to him. He snatched it from the air, his mouth wolfish, then licked his lips, his face returning to bland dogginess. A glimpse of the ancestor, thought Coral. We all disclose our pedigree in our unguarded moments.

Cousin Jeffrey, for instance. His history, entwined with her own, made him dangerous. Bloodlines mingle, freshen, mingle again. Old family characteristics are sublimated, then reborn at the oddest reaches of the genetic tree, in different forms. Certainly she and Brown shared a dark view of humanity. If she possessed his secrets, he likewise knew hers.

Her triumphant mood began to fade. Promises and bargains? Trust belonged to the naïve. She hadn't heard the last of Jeffrey Goodman Brown.

Nevertheless, the crisis was over for tonight. She uploaded the pictures and transferred them to a flash drive. Technomagic. These were great days for socialphobes, when almost anything could be obtained without the slightest human contact. All one needed was a credit card. If not for groceries and supplies for her creations, she'd hardly have to go out at all.

She labeled the flash drive and gave the dog, dozing nearby, a nudge with her foot. "You! Make yourself useful."

Dickon stretched, then padded window to window, raising himself on his hind legs and poking his muzzle behind shades and curtains to look out. He sniffed at the doors, front and back, then satisfied, lay down again.

Comfortable in knowing she was unobserved, Coral dragged a chair to the fireplace and lifted the ugly portrait that hung there. Its heavy frame, ornate with scrolls and curlicues, was backed by a thick wooden panel into which she'd constructed a sort of pocket, just deep enough for secrets. She pushed the flash drive inside, and replaced the picture. "Sorry for the disturbance," she told it.

Coral had found the portrait moldering in an outbuilding on the property, long since collapsed, had cleaned it up and made it useful. Its subject, a woman, stood with her hand draped over the back of a half-shrouded empty chair. She was dressed in deep mourning, unornamented by lace or embroidery. The style was from the late nineteenth century, but the apparent coarseness of the cloth and the woman's stoic plainness suggested that her dress was neither new nor fashionable. Her face was utterly without beauty, though it may not always have been so. Coral could tell by the compression of the mouth that the woman had many missing teeth; that, combined with who knew what other pain, may have aged her prematurely.

The hands were large, the fingers blunt and scarred. The brightest thing in the picture was the glint off her wedding band, worn on her right hand. Why? A mark of widowhood? Of private rebellion?

Coral liked her. A flesh-and-blood woman would have jabbered out her life story, however boring or distasteful, but the portrait hung there, keeping its own counsel. Odd that anyone had bothered to have the likeness done. Surely its subject was free of vanity. And yet if Coral looked closely, she could see traces of gold leaf still clinging to the frame. Funny that it had turned up in an outbuilding with the damp and the insects.

Oh, well. Why speculate about one of the nameless people who'd shed the bits of skin and hair that became the dust still hiding in the cracks of these old floorboards? Coral herself was alive now and full of energy.

She tugged a bulging trash bag from a closet and dumped the contents on the floor, a snowstorm of white grocery sacks broken here and there by a tan or pink one, even a few orange from Hallowe'en promotions. Freed from their restraint, they expanded, puffed themselves like birds; some floated playfully on air currents. The dog roused when one settled over his nose; his breath blew it away. Coral had gathered the bags by handfuls from the bins at the recycling center. They made excellent scarecrow stuffing, for they weighed less than paper and didn't mildew like hay. One by one, Coral shook them, examined them for vestiges of leaked food. Receipts sometimes tumbled out, even small items forgotten in unpacking: batteries, greeting cards, envelopes of taco seasoning. She was never surprised by what people left behind, at the detritus of their lives.

After sorting, she crushed the good bags, again one at a time, pressing the thin plastic to the smallest possible compression and stuffing it into a muslin shell she'd sewn that afternoon. When she was finished, she had a solid but lightweight oval, about the texture of skin-covered cartilage. A head. Not her favorite type—she preferred dried pumpkins and gourds—but the easiest to shape, to personify.

The dog raised his muzzle around two a.m., hearing the grind of a poorly tuned car, then a step he recognized, unhurried, probably a little drunk. There's Piety, thought Coral. And not a soul to see her. She chuckled. If the dog found nothing amiss, neither did she. He yawned and lay down again, sighed, and slept.

Too tired now to work any more, Coral downed a jigger of dark rum against tossing and turning. She washed it down with water from a special jug in her kitchen. Safe now in her solitude, she toddled off to bed.

Halfway down the forearm of Cape Cod lies a tangled and rock-strewn wedge of land known as Wonderstrand. Bastard child of the town of Eastham, it was abandoned on the doorstep of the Atlantic in the eighteenth century, when the largest parish on the outer Cape split itself into independent towns, Wellfleet to the north, Eastham in the middle, Orleans to the south, and Wonderstrand tucked away where nobody much cared.

It merits neither post office nor zip code, nor has anyone ever seen fit to install a Welcome To *sign, information booth, or streetlights. Only a five minute ride from Route 6, and abutted in part by the National Seashore, it nevertheless is unknown to most tourists. If visitors weren't looking for it—and why would they?—they'd miss it altogether. Not a few native Cape Codders have lived three score years and more without feeling any need to locate it on a map. Its year-round population would barely cause a traffic jam even if they all decided to haul up on The Old King's Highway at once.*

Its very name is an irony. The early Viking explorers called the nearby stretch of spectacular Atlantic beach "Wonderstrand," but the little plot of land that uses that name today hasn't any beach at all; it merely creeps down to sea level through woody lowland and marsh. Through the centuries, the surrounding area has scrolled through other names, bestowed by the various occupants and invaders—Nawset, Mallebarre, Slut's Bush, Olde Eastham. But the old Viking name clings only to this corner.

Scrub oaks and pines grow freer here, dappling the days with shadows. The nights are said to be the darkest on the outer Cape. Will-o-the-wisps dart through the marshes, blue fires flicker among decaying trees, and wraiths glide along the beach road at night. History and legend hover over it like fogs, reeking of saltwater. The fireside corners of the houses are as full of whispers as those in Romantic tales. Readers fond of the sort of books usually left to dust and silverfish, should they happen to find themselves in Wonderstrand, might imagine that the seeds of Old Salem Village had been blown across Massachusetts Bay and two and a half centuries to settle and take root. Here you recall the tales you read as a student, of ancestral secrets, midnight gatherings and blood curses, of mocking demons who appear at your side, plying you with intimate conversation.

On a Wonderstrand bystreet stands a fenced cluster of ill-matched wooden cottages, like dozens of other such colonies built for the post-World War II tourist boom. Two or three small rooms with kitchenette and bath, they once offered vacationers their own little box of paradise, the illusion of belonging, at least for a week, an August, a long-remembered summer.

But Wonderstrand Colony isn't the ocean-view-and-lobster-stew of Patti Page; it's of another era. Its signpost has been swallowed up by nettles, wild roses, and raspberry bushes; its scrub oaks and pines close in over the irregular rooflines. The neighboring marsh, with its primeval scents, its turtles, birds and foxes, seems closer than it was half a century before.

The few cottages still occupied have become year-round dwellings, housing a mixture of old comer and transient, people whose lives fit a smaller scale. In making Wonderstrand my home, I found myself drawn to be its amanuensis.

—Prologue to *Wonderstrand Tales*, by Guy Thomas Maulkin

Chapter 2

"If not the thing itself, it is marvelously like it, and the more so for that ethereal and intangible quality which causes it all to vanish at too close an introspection. Take it, therefore, while you may."

—HAWTHORNE

Guy Maulkin had seen a sign, a flickering Eureka. It had come at the witching hour, midnight to the very minute. Anyway, he was pretty sure it had. His watch always ran fast, or slow, or not at all.

He'd been deep in his research, enfolded by books and papers when he'd seen it, a *plink* of light at the outer edge of his vision. By the time the image had tunneled into his busy brain, it was only a memory on the inside of his eyelids. He looked up, made an effort to focus. The window's rectangular ghost appeared once more on the ceiling and was gone.

He waited.

No thunder. No sound at all.

Yet there it came again, a flash that lit the low cloud cover, that touched the underbranches of the trees quicker than an indrawn breath and was gone again.

Guy knew signs. Guy knew about enchanted roads, the kind that unroll in front of you and lead to glory unimaginable. He knew about the glimmers of truth behind legends.

Outside, the night blazed again.

Me?

He leaped up, knocking over a pile of books he'd been using as a footrest. They hit the old hardwood floor with a crash that rippled into the stillness. He stumbled over them and reached the window.

There it was once more. Near the marsh, but too explosive for *ignis fatuus*, too contained and intimate for lightning. He felt a thrumming and twitching in something that was probably his soul.

Though he'd watched and waited, the light didn't come again. That didn't matter. He'd recognized the call.

Now he sat awake, by the light of a single candle, dreamy and restless. He swept his glance around the room. Haphazard piles of dusty volumes and documents lay on every surface, even the bed. Every night he pushed them aside to sleep, then replaced them the next day with new piles. His few sticks of furniture were supplemented by cardboard cartons containing individual packages of chips, crackers, cookies, and candy; he made his simple living servicing a vending route. These also served as his larder. When the packages became too stale to sell, he brought them home and, to save the trouble of shopping for anything better, ate them.

But he didn't live by snack food alone. He had loftier things to sustain him. He'd been writing his own book, a history of sorts, tales from Wonderstrand's past, some set in the cottage colony itself. He hoped someday to support himself with his pen, and besides, writing about the place where he lived would fill his head with tidbits of history, surely fascinating to other locals. This he was sure would ease him into conversations and camaraderie.

Now he laughed at the thought. He clicked on his laptop and read the page on the screen.

An oaken board screeches when torn loose from its fittings, a sound a crow might make to protest the presence of a straw man in a cornfield. A pile of similar boards lies off to one side, and a tin bucket holds the iron nails pried from them. An old house is coming down, not the first to rise and fall on this bit of land. Nothing salvageable will be lost, not wood nor iron, not stone, brick, or brass—all these scraps will be reanimated in the next structures to emerge in the midst of these turnip fields, long fallow. Any given shingle, by being more or less weathered than its neighbors, betrays itself as having been stripped from a different wall.

Poor patchwork things, these cottages. Rehashed and artificial, like the corn chips he stuffed into the machines, like his book itself. Life until now had been lacking in opportunities for transcendence. No more. He touched the palm of his hand to his head. "Something is *in* here," he whispered. "Something great. And here!" He smacked himself on the chest.

Funny. When the Illumination came, it had never occurred to him to venture out into the night to follow it. So much had he lived in his mind, in his books and musty documents, that a sign bursting indoors through his windowpane seemed right and just.

But how to respond?

He wished he had someone to talk to, but truth was, he didn't know anybody. The vending route was lonely. He had no family. He'd worked two jobs to finance U Mass Boston, and in the decade since college, lost track of his few acquaintances there. He'd moved a lot, looking for a place that felt like a home.

He'd found it one weekend when he'd been camping nearby. Wandering, a bit lost, he'd drifted out of the National Seashore and chanced upon this cottage. A miniature cape, its shingles buckling and curving in places, its shutters coated with mold, it nevertheless looked solid enough, and a For Rent sign stood propped in the window. He could just make out the faded phone number. When he called, he had to fidget through a dozen rings before the phone was picked up with a crisp "What?"

Guy managed to get his query across with a minimum of stammering.

"You don't want it. It's a mess."

"I don't mind."

"Of course you don't. All right, I'll leave a key on the windowsill tomorrow. Be there at eight a.m. I'm taking the key back by nine."

He called her back by 8:15.

"It's Guy Maulkin? About the rental?"

A groan. "Don't tell me. You want it. Oh, hell, I could use the money. Come back this afternoon. I'm going to leave an application tacked to the door. You'd better have references. Good ones. There's a three month trial period. I live right on the other side of the trees, and if you bother me, you're out."

Gobsmacked by his good luck, he was sure he was forgetting to ask something. Something important. He began to perspire.

"Hey! Are you still there?"

The phone, slippery from his hand, hit the floor with a rattle. He winced to hear the tinny obscenities rising from it, like the diatribe of an angry squirrel, as he scrambled to pick it up.

"The rent! That's it! I forgot to ask about the rent."

"Five hundred. Whatever I am, I'm not a thief."

He'd managed to scrape up references from his snack food supplier and a librarian who knew him because of the books he ordered every week. The rental contract informed him that his landlady's given name was

Coral, though he doubted he'd ever use it. Nearly a week passed before he actually saw her, loading something unwieldy and wrapped in brown paper into the back of her truck. White hair hung wild around her shoulders, and her face showed the light crosshatching of late middle age, but the way she handled the large parcel showed muscle. He waved, but she must not have seen him.

Besides the two of them, the colony boasted a third tenant, but of that person, he knew nothing at all.

He'd loved his new home. A furnace equipped the place for year-round occupancy, though it shrieked and banged when he switched it on. The walls showed wood rot, the plumbing leaked, and the outlets sizzled when he plugged in a lamp. But there was a fieldstone fireplace, chipped green shutters that could be closed against storms, and pleasing odd angles where the tiny bathroom and kitchenette had cut into the square shape. Most of all, it stood in Wonderstrand, with the sea, the woods, the marshes, the centuries of accumulated tales free for the taking.

Now both his cottage and Wonderstrand seemed small, dim, and lonely.

He'd always found social discourse the most daunting of activities. An orphan, he'd grown up in a series of foster homes where he was never exactly mistreated, but no one ever had time to listen. His temporary parents were harried, distracted by the parade of children who dragged the flotsam and jetsam of their troubled lives through each home, the endless visits by social workers, the appointments with court-appointed attorneys. Guy, they found, could be ignored. He was an ideal foster child, quiet, studious, tractable. Consequently he was often interrupted, brushed off, had his sentences finished for him.

Now he longed for someone to hear him out, to help him untangle the meaning of the wonderful thing that had happened to him. The only person who came to mind was his landlady. Why? She'd hardly seemed friendly. But perhaps the impulse was the next signpost on his new path.

Yes, he would take the risk. He was unfulfilled potential, a seedling not yet above ground. Sharp of eye, deep of thought, Guy Maulkin would be the man who accomplishes much, who forges ahead. When he figured out where and how, he'd be ready.

Chapter 3

"Art thou of the brotherhood of the empty skull,
and demandest of me what thou shalt say?...Talk!
Why, thou shalt babble like a mill-stream, if thou wilt."

—HAWTHORNE

Coral rose early, just after dawn, eager to get back to her work. She lit a log fire against the cool spring morning. Hers was the outermost cottage in the colony, the largest, but nearest to woods and marsh, and she felt the sea-borne chill in her joints. That worried her. A woman who valued privacy couldn't afford to get old and vulnerable. She bundled up in sweater and shawl before she headed to the kitchenette to brew her usual coal-black coffee.

She'd resolved to start a new creature today, something fine. Often she liked a bit of grotesquerie in her work, but today she'd strive for beauty. Either way, the process had the same beginning.

First came the bones. A broomstick made the best spine, especially old wooden ones. She liked driftwood, too, or saplings left to dry in piles at the edges of cleared lots. Sometimes she found and employed scraps of PVC pipe left over from newly-laid water lines. Unusual good fortune might present a finely-turned piece of mahogany or cherry, salvaged from the wreck of an antique table; these added particular shape and character. In a pinch, she bought the cheapest remnants the lumberyard offered.

She pounded the bones together with nails or lashed them with wire or heavy twine, weaving round and round for stability. Perhaps today she'd begin with a simple cross, just two sticks joined at right angles. But why stop there? Study your fellows, she told herself. Freeze their emotions—fists raised, heads hung, backs turned. Assemble fear or arrogance, pose longing or a belly laugh. Make these creatures as human as possible. Still, whether her creatures' makings came from nature or the factory, the farm or the junkyard, she used what was at hand. One could only plan so far.

Foundation in place, she built upward. The human head is approximately one sixth of the body's height, but she liked to imagine something more capacious. She often played with proportion. Some heads ballooned above the bodies, others shrunk to mere broadening of the necks. Soft heads, of pillowcase or sculpted cloth, she stuffed well. Harder ones, of papier mâché, plastic, or the produce of the field, she cushioned well against shattering.

Faces might be painted, pieced, stuck on, carved out, two-sided, or blank and empty as a stare.

Last, she dressed the whole figure in tatters or lace—or even let it go naked into the world. A vast store of old clothing culled from thrift shops, eBay bargain lots, and even her own past life lay stored in her cottage and shed.

When she finished, if what she'd made didn't match her expectations, she could tear it apart and gather different elements. Make it over. It was all just a collection of scraps anyway.

She heard his approach along the front path, the clumsy hitch of his steps.

"Whose skeleton is out of its grave now?" she wondered aloud. The dog lay in a patch of sunshine, uninterested, so she didn't trouble herself. But then came the knock on the door.

She ignored it.

Silence for a beat or two, then her visitor called softly, "It's Guy Maulkin. Your tenant."

"Shit," she said.

The moment she opened the door, the thing glowing in his heart like a hot coal burst forward. She tried deflection, knowing all the while that it would be no use.

"I told you to leave the rent in my mailbox."

"No, I already paid my rent. Didn't I? Is it due? I mean, it's not that." He addressed all this to the scuffs on his shoes.

"I'm busy. Very busy."

He slumped, as if his bones had melted.

She resigned herself. "What do you want?"

He was an odd-looking fellow. Very deep-set eyes in a complexion fever-ruddy, every feature a little crooked as if carved by an amateur hand. A loose, flustered smile. Clothes ill-fitted and unmatched, worse even than her own wardrobe.

"Advice," he mumbled to the doorframe.

"Okay. If something's leaking, call a plumber. If something's broken, call a carpenter. If there are bugs, call an exterminator. Put the bill in my mailbox."

She watched his resolve stiffen. She'd talked to him once or twice since she'd rented him his cottage—what was it, six months ago? A year? An ideal tenant, she'd thought, geek-shy and therefore unobtrusive. Now for the first time, he looked her dead in the eye. His irises weren't dark at all, but very light hazel, almost yellow, a candle burning in those deep sockets.

He twitched, blinked, swayed a little, but didn't look away. "It's a special kind of advice," he said, in a different voice, his tongue and vocal chords had suddenly loosened.

Here we go again, she thought.

Coral had her reasons for keeping to herself, and she made a fine job of it. Nor did her reclusiveness escape notice in a narrow community like outer Cape Cod. People will have their prejudices. Whenever some psychopath grabbed a gun and started shooting, or got caught with dismembered bodies in the freezer or children half-starved in cellars, the same phrases were hauled out. Loner. Social misfit. Theories trumpeted; editorials speculated: What mental deficiency or moral deviance led someone to avoid his fellows? Those like Coral who preferred their own company were always suspect, no matter how stainless their lives; in fact, the loner was the one member of society whom it was perfectly okay to distrust. She saw it as the last accepted form of bigotry.

If her seclusion gave her an undiluted quality, a manner that stung the palate and scratched the veneer, so be it. The better you knew most people, the harder they were to like. She asked only to be left in peace.

She'd had her run-ins. Because of her draggletailed clothes, none of which had been manufactured since the change of millennium, and her unrestrained hair, she drew stares. From time to time, some credulous teenager, fed since the cradle on Hogwarts and the like, would hover about. Dressed in black and dangling pentagrams, they'd sidle out from behind the bread shelf at the Superette and tap her on the shoulder, or stroll down the lumpy road past the cottage colony twenty times in two days, hoping to bump into her. They hoped, even believed, that she was a conjure-woman, that recognizing them for kindred spirits, she'd prescribe philters for love or vengeance, would pockmark the prom queen, snap the ankle bones of the gym teacher. She *must* have ways to nimble their fingers on the guitar strings, to attract the attention of the handsome boy smoking Luckys outside the entrance to the mall. Surely she possessed sprigs of flame-berried bittersweet, gathered at midnight on All Souls' Day, or bits of mandrake root she'd dug under the full moon and stored in a red-glazed jar, ready to be cooked into wax figures or worn around the neck.

Alas, Coral did not. Here was her only witchcraft: being the repository of people's secrets. She had the curse of drawing out what people were trying to hide. People had told her that when she looked, really *looked* at them, they felt turned inside out, their souls splayed open. Uninhibited, as if they'd taken sodium pentathol. They began to *talk*. Why did they do it? Perhaps there was something of the priest's confessional or the psychiatrist's office in it. Like them, she offered no intimacies in return, but neither did she offer any expectation of absolution or cure.

She didn't want to hear. Didn't want to know. She felt herself wrenched wide to receive the pouring forth of their deepest selves. She hated and feared it, was bewildered that anyone would choose her as confidante. It wasn't as if she had a kind or friendly face. Her perpetual half-frown should have warned people off. The corners of her mouth turned down, not up. She betrayed no curiosity. And yet, they talked.

With the kids, the secrets were probably nothing more than a terrible adolescent vulnerability, maybe compounded by an undescended testicle, thirty extra pounds, or a hellish family life. But what was *she* supposed to do? Even if she had been able to work magic, it would have been in service of Coral Rigby. Any resources she had, she needed to protect. When approached, she turned away. If asked directly if she was a witch, she laughed outright and directed the petitioners to look elsewhere. Plenty of Wiccans lived on Cape Cod, but she didn't happen to know any. Witchcraft

was a religion, and like all religions, it made her feel like an intruder, ignorant of someone else's rituals.

Her petitioners didn't always take kindly to this brush-off. There'd
been tears and hurled vulgarities, nothing that hurt very much. But rumors
were embroidered and spread, and sometimes another kind of threat crept
forward. It came from the brazenly upright who took the mistranslation,
"thou shalt not suffer a witch to live" with seventeenth century literalism.
Once she'd found a small cross alight at the edge of the woods behind
her cottage. Another time she'd been awakened when a Bible, bound to a
rock, shattered her window. She'd kept the book. Its pages were crisp, its
spine uncracked. She already had a copy; she'd always enjoyed the classics.
But perhaps someday she'd use this spare one to accessorize one of her
creatures. Perhaps a Cotton Mather, though who would buy that? The
familiar bumper sticker, "COEXIST," lettered in the symbols of various
religions, could be profitably illustrated, though. Spangle a scarecrow with
a crescent, stars of various shapes, a yin-yang symbol, put the Bible in its
hand. The good aspects of all of these came from the same source as did
the bad; it was all one to her.

People became so angry when their source of hope was challenged.
They withered into dogmatism or despair, usually too lazy to look elsewhere. Too often, their doubt had to be fought by violence turned out-
ward. This was why small sounds alerted her, and why she required Dickon,
whose ears could pick up the whir of a beetle's wing or a squirrel's shifting
in its sleep.

The dog was her only companion, a godawful nuisance at times, with
his malodorous shit, his ticks and fleas, but he was a loyal and vigilant ser-
vant. She'd come upon him on an October afternoon three years past, in
the lower parking lot at Fort Hill over in Eastham. Coral had just turned
off her truck's ignition and was trying to decide whether to hike up the hill
for the view of the marshes, with the blue and white ribbon of sea in the

distance, or to walk the boardwalk through Red Maple Swamp's glorious leaves, a rare treat on the piney Cape. There was a wildness about the place, in spite of the audible swoosh of traffic on Route 6. The undergrowth was so thick that a fox could trot out of it and disappear before the leap in your heart settled. Once she had been amazed to see at least a hundred rabbits feeding on the hillside. She'd exclaimed, and they were gone.

Coral had tried to ignore the single vehicle sharing the lot, but it showed in her rearview mirror. A woman was yanking and tugging at something in its trunk, from which squeals emerged reminiscent of bad hinges or fingernails on chalkboards. The woman managed at last to lift whatever it was, dumping it hard on the gravel. She examined the interior of her trunk and swore; an odor wafted from it that reached all the way over to where Coral stood. With a slam of the trunk lid, the woman headed off toward the swamp, yanking at a leash that Coral could now see ended in a puppy. It resisted, leaving a continuous, attenuated puddle behind it.

The woman gave Coral a dirty look. Unusual, that. Local etiquette dictated that strangers meeting in places like this, both isolated and public, exchanged a perfunctory greeting or a nod. Adequate communication, as far as Coral was concerned. She glared back at the woman just long enough to show that she didn't care one bit about her or her pup. When Coral looked again, the woman had disappeared. After a safe interval, Coral started off on her own walk.

A path led to the opening of the woods, becoming a hard-packed dirt trail as the pines thickened. Farther along, where the ground grew low and muddy, the boardwalk wound among the fiery maples. A blind man could find his way from the scents alone, first grassy, then piney, then damp and loamy. But now she could detect an undercurrent of dog urine, and something else—was it ruthlessness? Treachery?

Damn.

And double damn, when she saw the woman coming back toward her, walking fast and alone.

Why had she interfered? It was preordained, that's all. She planted herself square in the woman's path and fixed her with a stare.

Late afternoon's sharp rays broke through the trees. The woman blinked as if suddenly dizzy, or blinded by the glamour of the reddening sun.

She began to talk.

"I'd have gotten rid of it here sooner, but its dam wouldn't let it go, and she's so high strung. The rest of the litter had the decency to be stillborn. I should have suffocated it. Or shot it, but someone might have heard. I did try to poison it with roach killer, but it wouldn't drink the milk I put the stuff in. This place is perfect. All that undergrowth, the coyotes…." The woman paused for breath.

Coral said nothing.

"It happened backstage at a show. All champions, the purest bloodlines. I was traveling without my husband, and, well, there was this other breeder. Norwegian Elkhounds. We went up to his hotel room just for awhile, you know, but downstairs, something went wrong with the catch on my dog's crate and there was this fool who let his Alaskan Husky get loose. It was horrible. Horrible. I'd have sued, but I'd have had to explain to my husband, if you follow me."

Coral followed her indeed.

"And look what resulted. What if other breeders found out? My customers? I passed it off to my husband as a genetic glitch, bad blood in the sire…."

So there it was, the lies and cruelty she kept hidden.

"But now you've told me," said Coral.

The woman blinked as if she'd just awakened. "Did I?"

"Uh huh. Now here's what I could do if for some reason I took a dislike to you. I could write down your license plate number, use it to find your husband, and spill the beans. I could call the police—there are laws against animal abuse. I could get online at some dog websites and start rumors. On the other hand, you could knock me off the boardwalk and run. But you won't because you're a coward and a sneak. Otherwise, you'd have crushed that animal's skull back at home and been done with it."

The woman, breathing fast, stared at her.

"Don't worry. I'm not going to put myself to any trouble on your account. Just remember, though—I know. If we ever cross paths again, if you even see someone who looks like me, or drive by this spot, anything at all that conjures up this moment in your mind—a little knife will stab your conscience. Or your ego. Or wherever your nightmares come from."

The woman opened her mouth, then apparently changed her mind. Glancing nervously from side to side, she hurried back toward the parking lot.

Coral found the dog tied up in a tangle of fallen branches, invisible from the boardwalk. It was cross-eyed, one brown and one blue, and black-tongued. The mottled gray and rusty brown of its coat reminded her of old scrap iron; every hair announcing its misbegotten status. Newly weaned, it was remarkably unappealing for its age, repository of exactly those qualities of its sire and dam that were most likely to clash. She had no special love for animals, let alone this drooling, peeing troll of a puppy, but one had to recognize the tokens one was offered.

At what she considered great personal sacrifice, she saw to its shots, its worms, its housebreaking, cursing every distasteful chore. It rewarded her by being always at her service, and more—the animal seemed to have a quick wit, an imp's sense of humor. She called it Dickon, a name with pleasant associations of something she'd read once and forgotten.

Acquiring the dog, though, had been an all-too-familiar instance of seeing people's dark sides. Knowledge like that had two edges, both sharp. It conferred power of a sort, for those who told their secrets put a weapon into her hands, willingly or not. On the other hand, shame could make them her enemies. She was unlikely to run into the dog breeder again, but others like her walked every sidewalk, every grocery aisle, burdened with blushes, cringing over matters that would simply have disappeared—of *course* they would, if only they'd stayed hidden. Coral had to be wary.

Now here she was with her moony tenant lurking in her doorway.

"All right," she said. "Spill it."

"I saw an Illumination."

"Good for you. Take drugs, do you?"

"No. Oh, no. This was real. It was a Light, a Calling."

She could hear the capital letters. Looking as pained as she could, she stepped aside and let him come in.

"But I don't know what to do about it. I've been wasting my life."

"Is that a fact."

"I've been a dilettante, a wheel spinner. Writing unpublished books. Studying. None of it was enough. That's what the Sign was telling me, that I'm meant for something more."

"Are you, now."

"Great things."

She rolled her eyes. "How old are you?"

"Twenty-nine."

"Everybody thinks he's meant for great things when he's twenty-nine."

"I never did. Until last night."

She believed him. For all his euphoria, low self esteem still clung to him, the way the odor of smoke lingers with reformed smokers long after they've kicked the habit.

"So what awaits you, according to this message of yours? Fame? Money?"

"Yes!"

"Why not romance, too? That's usually on the list."

"Is it? That, too, then."

Geez, thought Coral.

"After I saw this burst of light…I didn't know what the next sign would be, and then this morning I saw your cottage through the trees."

She interrupted. "Why do you think I can tell you anything about this pinnacle you think you're bound for?"

She saw him struggling not to answer. But the words came. "I heard people talking. At the post office, and another time at the beach. They said you're…that you have…ways."

"Assholes," she said. "Who were they?"

"I don't know. I was eavesdropping."

Coral laughed, not nicely. This was going to be more complicated than usual because he lived so close, and worse, because she could feel the heat from that hot coal in his breast. "Ways to do what? Did they say?"

"To make things happen. Or not."

"Ah, hell. Do I look like the Pope? The government? Does this cottage say luxury? That I could get anything I want? Look at *me*, for God's sake. Why don't I just conjure up eternal youth? Or whip up wealth, like an omelet? Why don't I turn that dog into a wad of fifties?"

"Why?" he asked.

She uttered something between *ha!* and *huh?*, a sound so rich in contempt that even he couldn't fail to recognize it. She'd slammed the hatch on his soul-baring.

But she'd seen what was there. Ambition like that was so Faustian, so dangerous for someone fragile, who looked like he'd collapse if a crabby cashier snapped at him. What would be the effect on him of disillusionment, rejection, failure? Why, stronger men than he….

She wanted nothing to do with it.

And then she had an inspiration.

"Maybe I *can* offer some advice," she said.

Maybe it was time she, too, had connections, someone out in the world to watch over her interests. "I might know a way to get you set up. But if I help you, you'll owe me."

He swept her a low, courtly bow. He lost his balance and wobbled a little, but the general effect wasn't bad. She might be able to make something out of him after all.

"This is going to take awhile," she said. "You look like hell and I've got to think how to make you presentable, make some plans. Sit down for a minute; you make me nervous flopping around."

He bent his limbs into a chair, settling in, sweeping his gaze around the room. He examined the row of figures, in various stages of completion, crowding the walls of the small room.

"Scarecrows," he observed, apparently to the table leg. He'd reverted to his old self, addressing his remarks anywhere but to her. "Jack-a-Lents. Tattybogles. Fawkes. Rye Hags. Colonel Bogies."

"Stop that mumbling. I'm trying to think."

She was digging through a trunk, occasionally emerging with an article of clothing. Periodically, she turned to scowl, assessing him and not liking what she saw.

"Those are some old names for...."

She brandished a pair of scissors, and he held his peace for several heartbeats, as long as he could.

"Why do you make them?" he asked, apparently expecting an answer from the lamp.

"They scare things away."

A genuine blush turned his skin even ruddier. "I meant no criticism. I saw some of them outside, but you don't have much of a garden, so I wondered why scarecrows in particular. You're an artist; they look almost like real people."

"The point is that they're not. If you must know, I'm testing materials out there, how they stand up to weather. Paints, fabrics and so forth."

Looking encouraged, he continued. "I recognize some of these figures. There's Boris Karloff. How'd you get his head all lumpy and mottled like that?"

"It's a Hubbard squash. They make good space aliens, too." She was especially fond of this effect and not displeased that he'd noticed. She didn't have to pay for the squashes, either, another plus. She was good at getting things free. Every year, when the fancier hotels and restaurants changed from autumn to Christmas decorations, she collected the gourds and pumpkins before they were thrown out.

"Wow. Don't they rot?"

"Not when I'm done with them."

He nodded sagely.

Pretty damned credulous, she thought. She'd had to try a dozen methods of preserving gourds before she'd found a combination of drying and sealing that satisfied her, had carted a lot of blackened, reeking produce to the dump. He seemed to think she just waved a wand. Even now, each scarecrow bore a tag about care and how to get a new head, if necessary, but no one had ever contacted her with a problem.

"Who's the one with the tattoos? Oh, I know—Queequeg. My favorite character in *Moby-Dick*. Wow," he repeated.

She smiled, but turned her head so he wouldn't see. So he was naïve and impractical, but not stupid. And he knew how to flatter.

"What do you do with them all?"

"I peddle them at flea markets and craft fairs." She worked hard to shape each of the scarecrows into an entity, recognizable or archetypal. She'd made Draculas, Mae Wests, Kirks and Spocks, Lennons and Jaggers. One beautiful, angry Jim Morrison, sold to an elegant woman of perhaps seventy, accompanied by her teenaged grandson. But classics sold best, pumpkin heads, Straw Men, anything that looked like it might have served on a farm. People seemed to crave the back-to-the-earth feeling the figures added to a suburban lawn. She was about to add that a couple of galleries had begun to stock them; she had once or twice half-wished for someone to tell.

Nope, she decided. Keep yourself to yourself.

"You should sell them online."

"I do sometimes." On eBay or Etsy, with anonymous screen names. She didn't want her own website. The awful exposure of cyberspace appalled her, the most intimate (and soporific) details of one's life being spewed forth daily. When she bought something, she didn't care to know how the seller spent his afternoon, so why should her buyers wish to know her private business?

She changed the subject. "See that Abe Lincoln over there? He's already sold, the third Lincoln I've made. History buffs buy them. Lincoln was a tall, gangly man, easy to suggest with a wooden frame. And I can get cheap stovepipe hats and beards from costume shops."

"That's Honest Abe, all right! Ever try President Obama?"

"I avoid contemporary figures. Too much mass-produced stuff available already."

"How about George Washington?"

"Not him, either. Everyone would expect the wooden teeth, and I've never found a good way to do those. Here's the thing about people—they look for certain superficial markers, then draw all sorts of conclusions from that. So it's easy to suggest a character from a couple of details." A pithy insight about smoke and mirrors began to take shape in her mind, but before she could get it to her tongue, he interrupted.

"Does it hurt? Letting them go?"

Instead of an insight, anger puffed out. Here he was in her house, pushing suggestions, and now getting into locked places. She wouldn't have it.

"Do you think there's a choice? Do you think I can live on the pittance of rent I get from you?"

He shrank back, abashed.

What became of her creatures? Did buyers fuss over them like Christmas trees, then shove them away with the Easter baskets and turkey platters? Did they leave them out in hurricanes? Allow children to maul them? It *did* hurt her to sell them, but that was her secret, and secrets were her stock in trade, not Guy Maulkin's.

She jerked the chair out from under him, making him stumble to his feet.

"I can't work with you hanging around. Go home. I need the rest of the day. Be here first thing in the morning." She gave him a little shove.

He allowed himself to be propelled toward the door, but paused at the threshold, evidently gathering courage.

"You won't change your mind?" he asked Coral's shoes, a ratty pair of high-top Cons.

"I keep my word," she said, and remembered the last time she'd heard that phrase. "Just a minute. This light of yours—was it an actual light? You weren't speaking figuratively?"

He shook his head so hard she thought it would fly off his neck.

She continued before he could go into raptures again. "I'll bet it happened around midnight, didn't it?"

His wide mouth gaped. "How did you know?"

"Lucky guess. Midnight's the usual hour for portents."

Once she'd gotten him out the door, she watched from the window as he marched his way toward his own cottage, tripping over nothing and scattering bits of shell. A murder of crows, outraged by the noise, took flight in a chorus of complaint.

"The mind just boggles, doesn't it?" she said to the dog.

An Artist of the Beautiful

Within the average colony, all the cottages tend to be of a cookie cutter sameness, simple bungalows or cabins. Each cottage in Wonderstrand, however, is unique. Today, only five of the original nine structures remain, ranging in style from the classic architecture of the peninsula, foursquare and solid, to Gothic Revival confections. They were built one at a time, mostly of reused materials, by Eustace Albright, the grandfather of one of the present residents and a descendent of the early deed holders of the land. His ancestral farmhouse was demolished in the 1950s, but the fieldstone from its chimney and its wide pine floorboards now form part of the very cottage I call my own.

Eustace considered himself a master of wood and plaster. His whim of the moment, as well as the materials at hand, dictated his designs. He scattered them about, caddy-corner and widdershins, as far apart as possible, as if structures so diverse would want nothing to do with each other. No two faced the same point on the compass. The largest, which still exists, could be mistaken for a fairy tale witch's house made of gingerbread and frosted with lacy woodwork. It boasts three gables to crown four tiny rooms. Today, sadly, its gray shingle suggests something other than molasses and spice—perhaps a sweet left in a tin too long and grown moldy.

Another, also still standing, resembles a tiny country chapel, built as it was from the remains of one. Its white paint is discolored, but the interior, with its heavy woodwork and plaster niches, still calls to mind the ecclesiastical. My cottage is a traditional half Cape, with a single window to one side of the front door and minimal trim aside from the green shutters. There's a saltbox, with a high slanted roof and oak beams, and one in what's called the railroad style, bracketed and braced, painted a thick, deep tan with wide brown trim. Naturally, a dismantled train station went into its construction.

Two more, another Cape and a Greek Revival, are now nearly collapsed and uninhabitable. Old photos also show a flat-roofed Bauhaus style, destroyed years ago by a fallen tree, and three more, the plainest of the cottages, are reminiscent of the chicken coops from whose remains they were constructed. These last had to be torn down to install the modern septic system.

Quite a delirious range of architecture, especially since none of it is visible from the road. How they came to be built, however, is a pretty standard story, condensing the history of tourism on Cape Cod:

A one-room shelter hard by an Indian trail grew into a farm, raising corn, turnips and asparagus, fertilized with fish heads and seaweed culled from the Atlantic. The farmhouse expanded sideways and up, allowing room for "paying guests," when tourists first discovered the area. Of course, in the age of the railroad and the great Victorian hotels, private homes received less patronage. Nevertheless, small scale hostelry proved a profitable supplement to agriculture. Rollaway beds and luggage stands covered the braided rugs, sometimes ink-splashed by American bards writing travel journals.

Then came the automobile, carrying a new clientele. Enterprising local residents sold homemade quilts, pies, and jams, as well as household refuse labeled as antiques—whatever tourists found quaint enough to pay for. This crop of visitors was harder to please with makeshift accommodations, so guest cottages built solely for the trade began to appear. Often, they were monuments to Yankee frugality, patched together with flooring from a farmhouse parlor, ornamental railings off the veranda of a seaside hotel, or crossbars from a billboard advertising fried clams and saltwater taffy. Nothing was wasted.

Cottage colonies enjoyed their heyday in the two decades after WWII, then slowly began to lose popularity. Tourists wanted larger houses with more amenities, or the new motels. By the turn of the 21st century, an age of Mcmansions, master suites with double sinks, and acres of granite countertops, some cottages were being sold individually as condominiums or three season second homes. Not a few have returned to scrap.

Some, of course, are still going strong. Equipped with cable TV, microwaves, and WiFi, they still manage to retain their rustic appearance. The proprietor of a colony in nearby Provincetown told me a story about a California man, owner of a designer shoe company, who wanted to film a commercial "with that Cape Cod ambiance." He asked whether he might film in "those shacks over there." My acquaintance informed the Californian, without waste of words, that the structures in question were not shacks, but fully booked vacation cottages, that he should familiarize himself with the Cape before he attempted to exploit it, and that no, he decidedly could not film his pitch for spike heeled sandals and tassel loafers there.

Why did Wonderstrand cottages fail to thrive? No doubt, part of the reason was their location. Then there was their very design. Whimsical though they might be, guests did not find them congenial. Eustace Albright felt constrained by the need to equip his creations with actual living spaces, appropriate for cooking, bathing, and sleeping. Necessities were squeezed in and uncomfortably placed.

Also, they were expensive to maintain. Uniformity was practical; it made for easier and cheaper upkeep, but Eustace's elaborate color schemes and trim were difficult to paint and repair. As he grew older, he had less strength to keep up with it all. After he died, his married daughters had no interest in the place, which in any case he'd bequeathed to his two grandchildren.

Finally, rumors attached themselves to the colony. Someone was supposed to have died in this cottage; orgies went on in that one; another was haunted by a weeping woman or a phantom animal. The

Wonderstrand Incubus, the infamous peeping Tom who plagued the outer Cape in the 1980s, was said to frequent the colony.

It's true the cottages have a lonely, cloistered quality distilled from years of isolation, that some of their foundations are heaved up by the frosts of many winters, that floors are humped and seams buckled with the years. There are woodworm and termites, damp rot and dry rot. At night, the death watch beetle ticks in the walls.

Still, compensations abound. I can hear the surf churning off to the east. Marshes thick with buttonbush lie nearby, home to flocks of red winged blackbirds in summer. Crows and squirrels, whippoorwills and mourning doves populate the woods. Their voices join in a harmony I've never heard elsewhere. Wonderstrand cottages are an insula ex machina, *apart from the world, a fitting backdrop for stories.*

—From *Wonderstrand Tales*, by Guy Thomas Maulkin

Chapter 4

"This night it shall be granted you to know their secret deeds...."

—HAWTHORNE

Jeffrey Goodman Brown came forth at sunset from his fine house on Pleasant Bay. No longer a youth, he was still full-bodied and virile, a strapping figure of a man scarcely past fifty. He hadn't troubled himself to exchange a parting kiss with his wife, a mere blur of pearl gray cashmere when he happened to pass her on the stairs. He wished he could put other nuisances so easily out of his mind.

Last night, for instance. Why hadn't he wrung Coral Rigby's scrawny neck? Under the cover of darkness, he could have gotten away with it. Could have sealed off forever that ammunition dump she called a mind. Still, for a civilized man such as he, what choice was there? He had *not* crept away; he had simply chosen the most sensible course of action. Anyway, dwelling on the confrontation merely ratcheted up his anger and (he was loath to admit it) shame. Be realistic, he advised himself. Wasn't he the one with the resources? The force of character? Soon he'd shift the balance of power back where it belonged. Meantime, there was much to please him.

The garage door hummed sweetly as it opened to reveal a springtime dusk, a stage on which an al fresco entertainment was about to unfold. His Escalade slid out onto the newly-sealed asphalt, black and smooth as fine leather. He paused halfway down his driveway to admire the expansive facade of his home, the sweep of lawn with the shimmer of water just beyond. But when he turned his head, another irritant jabbed his thoughts, the homestead of a neighbor whose view had been blocked by the construction of Brown's establishment. This busybody had written a spiteful letter to the editorial page of *The Cape Codder*, ranting slanderously about ostentation and lack of ecological responsibility. Why, Jeffrey Brown disdained showiness; anyone could tell you that. His face went red as he remembered one phrase in particular: "a distasteful architectural cocktail of Colonial mansion and beach hotel."

Well, the neighbor in question was a neighbor no more, having found it necessary to relocate. Brown cast his eyes humbly downward. A whisper or two here, a debt called in there—amazing what one could accomplish without making a visible fuss. Now a realtor's sign decorated the front of the empty house. Ah, the savor of subterfuge. Of power. He rolled the word about on his tongue, holding its flavor as long as he could.

Having cast off this second assault on his mood, he drew his thoughts back to the night ahead.

He'd selected an area of smaller residences, comfortably distant from each other on wooded lots that edged into conservation land. The streets were unpaved and unlit. Tonight's wind blew just right, enough to mask the odd broken twig or involuntary exclamation, should he be startled by a cat or fox on stealthy errands of its own. Rain threatened, so people were likely to stay inside, where he wanted them.

May was a fine month for voyeurism. October's fallen leaves crackled; so did December's frozen ones. Winter's snow left tracks. Summer bloomed thick with concealing foliage but brought bugs and crowds. Spring, however, gladdened him.

Years of experience had honed his requirements and preferences. He never made his forays near his home, avoided the upscale neighborhoods of East Orleans and Chatham. There his car might be recognized, no matter how carefully he hid it. Worse, he might risk having his eyes assaulted by the *dishabille* of a selectman he'd helped put in office, or the naked flanks of one of his fellow volunteers in some civic cause. How could he face these people across a committee table or church pew? There were images that could not be removed from one's head.

The towns with nightlife, like Provincetown and Hyannis, presented few opportunities, but elsewhere, working folks and retirees were usually in early. He liked the narrow part of the Cape best, north of the Eastham rotary, where the tide's percussive roar lay over everything, good to hide in.

He selected his nighttime wardrobe as carefully as his destinations. Its dark colors stood in contrast with the creamy camels and beiges of his daytime clothing. Garments had to be protective and easy to clean: he'd been sprayed by a skunk, scraped his knees and elbows, and picked off many a tick, managing to avoid Lyme disease. Shoes were vital, too; they must be lightweight, with grave-silent soles, and of course, free of glowing swooshes or reflective patches. He replaced them regularly, deeming it wise to vary the patterns of the waffled footprints he left behind. Lately he favored a pair of water-repellant Mephistos. Sneakers, he called them, not athletic shoes. No one could say Jeffrey Goodman Brown lacked a sense of humor.

He left his car in the crowded lot of Billy's, a sports bar on Route 6, and strolled to the corner where a Y-shaped intersection took him to Nauset Road. There, he picked up the paved bike trail, just another exercise buff late with his daily run. For the first hundred yards or so, the trail was visible to the open yard of an industrial gravel operation. Without slackening his pace, he pulled the hood of his sweatshirt up to cover his face—he'd seen trucks entering and leaving the place even at night. Its dilapidated-looking buildings recalled Friday night horror movies he'd seen as a lad. He half expected to see a white-coated Dr. Frankenstein emerging from one of the shuttered buildings with something arcane or unspeakable in hand. The unsightly yard didn't displease him. Brown respected commerce. Neither did the mad-scientist associations it generated. Nothing wrong with bene-fiting from a God-given skill.

After a few minutes of jogging, he veered off the bike trail and into the woods, slowing to a walk on the uneven ground. He didn't use a flashlight; it blinded him to the greater darkness.

From the deeper woods, he approached an open circle of sky. This told him he was near the stump pit, like a meteor crash site filled with the detritus of storms and cleared lots. Circling this, he next came to the grounds of a gun club, its sharp cracks and booms silenced until morning. Occasionally, he'd been inside, skeet shooting with the sort of business acquaintances who liked to see a man's skill with firearms. He picked his way slowly among the junk littering the woods here, much of it metallic: besides the usual beer and soda cans, he saw a car engine, a truck cap plastered with hunting stickers, a washing machine, several pretzeled alu-minum chairs. A celebration of tetanus.

From the gun range, a dirt road led to a residential area. The going was easy now. His anticipation swelled.

Paths crosshatched National Seashore property, some of them in use long before the first white settlers (including his ancestors, he thought with pride) appropriated them. Much-trampled byways led through the woods to motels and restaurants; dirt roads came to dead ends and dwin-dled into the trees. Following these gave him a pleasant sense of time indeterminate—a trail could have originated with the Nauset tribes, long before white men, or it could have originated with the Cub Scouts the year before last. Best were the little known trails, not favored by hikers or partying teenagers but as familiar to Brown as the cadences of a Sunday School Bible verse. Any pursuer would find these almost impossible to follow. Brown had a thousand byways that could take him safe and unseen to his car, then back to his own door.

He'd never been caught by anyone but Coral Rigby, who had the unnatural senses of the madwoman she was. On the rare occasions when he'd slipped up—accidentally overturning a rake propped next to a garage, walking into the path of a motion-activated light—he had easily eluded detection.

Funny how people react to an unidentifiable sound. The first thing they do is look out a window. Of course that was futile, and stupid. They could see nothing from their lighted rooms. Their next step would be to snap on exterior lights, but he expected that and knew how to conceal himself. In his preferred neighborhoods, he'd memorized every depression, every rock and flowerbed. After staring in a bright window, of course his night vision was compromised, but he could still detect the difference between sand and earth, or between an asphalt driveway and a paved street.

Seeing nothing, people usually cursed their own nervousness and got on with their activities. Often, they'd pull the shades. This always made him laugh—why bother, if they'd convinced themselves no one was outside? Perhaps there had been calls to police, who sent a bored officer to reassure the citizens that what they'd heard was probably the wind or an animal. Brown was never around to know.

Jeffrey Goodman Brown was a master of his craft. He inhaled deeply, breathing the night perfumes, and walked on. From the humped shadows of the deeper woods, he emerged into a brushy area adjacent to a backyard. He knew the place. Addresses meant nothing to him; brass numbers were daylight things. His landmarks were the fences and painted walls that stood out even in pitch dark.

An eight foot stockade fence separated his target from the house to its left. He settled himself beneath it with a clear view of a side bay window. This one was always clean kept free of the salt that often coated Cape Cod windows. A gray-haired couple stared out into the night, backlit by something with low wattage, a nightlight perhaps. He'd seen these people before. They often passed an object between them that he soon recognized as a pair of binoculars—old-fashioned heavy ones, judging by the obvious effort the couple needed to lift them. Brown, of course, possessed a pair of lightweight night vision ATNs that had set him back several thousand dollars but made him feel like James Bond. Still, he preferred not to use them. More satisfying to get in as close as possible.

The couple, far from being a threat, amused him. They weren't bird-watchers looking for owls. The spite fence, plus the close-set row of fast-growing aspens planted near another of the adjoining houses, told him their neighbors knew the score. He deduced that gathering local gossip was the object here. This couple wouldn't guess that anyone might be lurking in their own yard, watching *them*. They'd keep their sights trained on the street and other houses they could still see, not the shadows. Brown smiled.

For as long as he could remember, tableaus of other people's lives had fascinated him. As a child, he'd sneak out of bed at night to look into keyholes and later, the windows of his own house. As a teenager, he'd found how secret observation could provide titillation, intimate as whispers. As a grown man, he enjoyed watching women when they were unaware, unable to manipulate or make demands. Mainly, though, his little hobby offered another satisfaction: to confirm what he already knew; that mankind was basically corrupt, often crude and ugly. He'd long since been initiated into a midnight knowledge that changes a man's outlook forever.

What he saw put his own behavior into perspective. And unlike the couple he was now observing, he never talked about what he knew, thereby raising questions about the source of his information.

If in his night walks he met the devil, he also stared him down. Voyeurism provided its own justification. Sin involved the insertion of the manly organ into an unwilling orifice, the degree of wrongdoing determined by which orifice in particular. But merely looking? Why this was the very age of exhibitionism, what with reality TV, Facebook, Twitter, and the like. So why did he bother with his night journeys when young women kept twenty-four hour cameras in their bedrooms, when intimate lives could be accessed with a few key strokes, when one could witness the degradation of the human race without leaving one's ergonomic chair?

Because those things were what people *chose* to show, and they belonged to anyone who wanted them. Electronic phenomena lacked visceral reality. He saw the life that people lived when there were no witnesses. He enjoyed the comfortable paradox of being part of the scene and yet outside it.

As for any sexual satisfaction he might gain, Brown didn't subscribe to any nonsense about adultery in the heart. The heart could not ejaculate. After all, it was not as if he were always masturbating in the bushes. Why only rarely…and he hoped to render even that unnecessary before long. Brown shrugged. Watch people in secret for awhile, add the fact that no one was to be trusted, and you could justify any minor peccadilloes of your own.

Truth be told, what he saw almost never aroused him. He was used to seeing the itches people scratched when they thought they were unobserved, the dirt they sometimes quite literally swept under their rugs. He'd seen expressions of vitriolic hatred cast at the back of a husband by his bride of six weeks; had seen a screeching infant hurled into its crib like a football at the end zone. He couldn't count the times he'd seen people, finding themselves alone, chug from hidden fifths, pop pills, pull photos from under cushions and stare at them hungrily, or perform a hundred other things crude, illegal, or forbidden. Then they'd hurry back onto their sofas as if they'd been there all the time.

Occasionally, someone revealed nothing more than a profound dullness, but Brown was never sure if such people were as flat and blameless as they seemed, or whether he hadn't observed long enough.

More rarely, he found someone of such interest that watching took on another quality, like a craving. It hadn't struck him in years, but now, in his late prime, he'd felt it again. Piety. Last night's ill-starred venture, his foray into the risky territory of his wretched cousin's domain, had only been in the cause of Piety. He blamed Coral Rigby for the lesser thrills he would have to settle for tonight.

He decided to move on. Staying behind trees and sheds, he passed several unoccupied houses, second homes or summer rentals. A truck in the driveway of the next showed that someone lived there, but whoever it was had drawn the blinds. He cut across the unpaved road, attracted by the blue flicker of a TV in an upstairs bedroom, but he could find no satisfactory angle of sight.

His next stop presented a nondescript Cape where a family, parents and two boys probably under ten, were playing a board game at a kitchen table. Brown could just make out the silver Monopoly tokens. Nothing there at present, but time would tell. Wholesome families were little more than a pretty fiction. Brown didn't linger. There would be other nights

He next approached a property boasting so many honeysuckle vines that he could have found it blindfolded even now, a month before blooming season. It also bore a hillock of unruly hydrangea bushes, allowing him to crouch well-hidden near a promising window.

He eased forward.

In an ell off the living room, apparently used as a home office, sat a man in his late thirties. He bent forward toward a computer screen. Brown's position allowed him to see the man's face only in profile, though he had a clear view of the screen. From this distance, its colors were harsh, over-saturated like Technicolor movies. Brown saw naked bodies cavorting, writhing, some among them with coltish legs and thin chests. Early adolescents, if not precisely children. Brown had often witnessed things he might have reported to authorities, but doing so would require explanations that he chose not to produce. Why interfere?

Amongst the hydrangeas, he sighed. Piety's image rose before him. Granted, she possessed a kind of wide-eyed malleability, an innocence of sorts. Charming, that, though an occasional flirtatiousness in her behavior hinted that in the right circumstances, she might not be so aptly named. He allowed himself a little chuckle and began to make his way to the rear of the house, back in the direction of the woods.

No warning, everything going along fine. Then a slight misstep. In his distraction and haste, he tripped in a root hole, wrenching his knee.

Disappear, he commanded himself.

But he lurched from the pain, causing a clatter of pebbles against shingle.

Brown shrunk low against the side of the house. Predictably, the face of the man in the window appeared, just inches away. Brown's legs were cramped, his knee throbbed. He had to make less noise than a mouse's footfall, the leap of a cricket, and to be sure his muscles would obey. So he waited.

Then a blink, and a porch light washed over the night. Before the door latch clicked, Brown had shot across the lawn to reposition himself behind a row of trash cans. The door opened a few inches, slanting forth a brighter column of light; the creak of aluminum on weather stripping had seemed loud enough to rattle the can in front of him. Heart drumming, Brown shrank lower, slowly, slowly, one muscle at a time.

The streak of light widened, and the man's head emerged. He stepped outside, letting the door slap shut. Brown held his breath.

"What's going on out there?" a woman's voice called from inside the house, probably the second floor. Brown heard a baby begin to wail.

"Nothing," the man said, but he didn't go inside.

Suddenly, the night felt cold and alien.

Then, from another cluster of underbrush across the yard, a raccoon waddled forth, blinked at the light, stopped dead. Brown blessed his luck.

The man, seeing it, clapped his hands and stamped his feet, shouting, "Hey! Hey!" as if punctuating a hoedown. Affronted, the animal turned back to the trees.

"It's just a raccoon, " the man called over his shoulder. "Did you put the brick back on the garbage can?"

Brown couldn't hear the answer, but he heard the man mutter, "stupid bitch." Indeed, the brick was resting on the ground near the can. Brown could see it.

The man began to descend the porch steps, pounding the railing with his fist as he went.

All Brown dared move was his eyes; they scanned the yard wildly for an escape route. He saw none.

The screen door creaked and slapped again, causing his heart almost to lurch out of his ribs. A little girl appeared behind the man.

"I want to see the raccoon, Daddy."

Brown saw the man unclench his fists and turn to the child. "It's gone, dumpling."

"Where?"

"To its bed, I suppose."

"Raccoons stay up all night."

"Well, Daddy's girl doesn't. Come on, I'll tuck you in."

"Maybe it will come back. I want to wait for it." The child's voice rose.

"Nope, I'm sure it won't."

"Why?"

"Cause Daddy says so." He reached to pick up the child, but she resisted.

"Don't you want to make Daddy happy?" he asked.

The little girl didn't answer, but allowed herself to be engulfed in his arms. The man carried the child back inside. Just before he shut the door, Brown heard the woman's voice again. "What's this on the computer?"

The man put the child down and moved away from the door.

Had there been time, Brown would have wept with relief, but he was up and into the woods before he'd drawn a breath.

Back in the covered darkness, he forced himself to relax. He wished he could howl with fury and dismay, with the pain in his knee. Two bad nights in a row.

To hell with what he'd told his harpy of a cousin. What he needed was a community of his own design and control, a place where houses sat at convenient angles, where streets curved out of sight, and tall, generous landscaping flourished. A development with plenty of windows to peer through. Plenty of people borrowing mortgages, using credit cards, and generally acting in ways that benefited him. He could find a way to install Piety there, so until certain difficulties were worked out, he'd be able to gaze upon her unmolested.

Utopia. And he knew just the place to build it. Kill two birds, as the saying went.

On the hobbled trip back to his car, he was forced to stop frequently, to sit on the dirty ground or a damp log. At least resting provided time to think. He'd long wanted to make some use of the Wonderstrand property; to demolish the antiquated cottages and build something profitable. He might have sold the land to a supermarket or discount chain, anything he could push past the tree-huggers on the planning boards and the Cape Cod Commission. But his cousin insisted on living in one of the cottages, God knew why, and Brown had no legal recourse, thanks to the Last Will and Testament of their common great-grandfather Eustace, that demented old fool. After last night's ambush, she'd be even more of an obstacle, but he'd find a way to get past her. He drew himself up from the termite-ridden stump and forged on.

To hell with Wonderstrand colony.

Chapter 5

"*Its very garments, moreover, partook of the magical change, and shone with the gloss of novelty....*"

—Hawthorne

Sunlight slid through Coral's eastern window, tinting the morning red but bringing no warmth. Dawn, she reflected, no longer kissed her awake with "gentle lips of light." It body-slammed her. The old furnace burned slow and cranky, and she didn't want to take time to build a fire, so she stamped and shivered herself awake.

She'd begun to assemble the new Guy Maulkin.

"Now listen," she told him when he presented himself half an hour later. "It took me all day yesterday to put this stuff together." She indicated the garments draped on various pieces of furniture. "I want to get it out of my way. Don't slow me down."

In the center of the room, Maulkin stood blushing in his undershirt and a too large pair of khakis, occasionally offering comments as she circled around him, placing a tuck here, marking a hem there. Her only answer was a scowl, pins protruding from between her lips. His being there crowded her.

He lifted a leather jacket off the back of a chair. "Ralph Lauren? Isn't that expensive? I don't see how I can pay you for it."

She uttered a short bark of mirth. "Consider it my contribution to the cause of greatness."

He opened his mouth again, but she waved him to silence.

"Don't start stuttering. If you must know, I collect clothes to dress the scarecrows. Nothing cost much."

She'd once been the scourge of every thrift and charity shop on Cape Cod, had prided herself on finding the gems among the tattered finery. Lately, she'd come to prefer online auctions. No more inhaling that mildew, feet, and sweat scent common to thrift shops; no more passing the time of day with the brooch-bedecked, well-meaning volunteers who staffed them.

For Maulkin, she'd chosen the leather jacket, distressed just enough to make it fashionable, two pairs of classic Levis, trim khakis, some decent shirts, among them a barely worn Brooks Brothers oxford, and a black Armani v-neck sweater, pilled, but still a find. Garments of good material and cut, the sort that don't get tossed out when fashion changes, that only turn up because the owner has gotten too fat to wear them, or died.

At the last minute, she'd tossed in a Roosevelt-era fedora, its label from a long defunct Boston haberdasher. That would add panache. She'd intended it for a Humphrey Bogart figure she was planning, but she had a plan for Guy Maulkin, too, and was willing to sacrifice more than a hat to achieve it.

Maulkin gazed around the room. His angular body shifted with each turn of his head, putting her in jeopardy from his knees and elbows. He focused on the chorus line of scarecrows leaning against the walls.

"Hold still, damn it," she squeezed out of the corner of her mouth.

He swayed a little. "Sorry. Do scarecrows really work?"

"What?"

"Do they scare crows? There's a ton of folklore about crows, you know. Harbingers of death, bad luck. That might be because they're carrion birds."

"It's not their fault."

"Then there's Jim Crow, discrimination, segregation."

"Don't blame evil on the birds or the scarecrows. They were both around long before that. Long before this country even existed."

"I know. I just enjoy symbolism. These are the sorts of things I wrote about. Do you know how to tell a crow from a raven?"

"No. Sometimes a bird is just a bird. We're not all ornithologists, any more than we're all racists."

"But do they really keep birds from eating crops?"

She let the question hover in midair, unanswered.

He went on unfazed. "There used to be a law around here that was supposed to keep down the number of blackbirds and crows. Every farmer had to kill a certain number. Then the town decided that every bachelor had to kill three of them, or some sources say six, before he could get married."

Lord, how this man could talk if you let him get started.

"Thoreau wrote about it. You know, the author of *Walden*?"

She spat out the pins. "You think you're the only one who ever read a book?"

"I didn't mean to imply...," he apologized to the curtains.

"Don't overdo the academic talk. It won't get you where you want to go." She retrieved the pins, lining them up in the sleeve of her sweater.

Still he wouldn't shut up. "People don't think of Thoreau as funny, but he jokes sometimes. Same is true of Hawthorne. He's my favorite."

"And I suppose you include yourself among all these misunderstood Romantics."

His complexion took on that pumpkin color, but he gabbled on. She had to be this close to him, had to look at him to alter the clothes, but the resulting conversation was hard to tolerate. She tried to work faster.

"Thoreau said he often mistook the scarecrows in the fields for men."

Coral paused in her work for the first time. "I remember that. "

Maulkin brightened. "What do you think of it? That crow law?"

"It strikes me as bloodthirsty." She thought of the birds' limp corpses, their feathers dulled.

"Me, too. If someone just couldn't bring himself to kill, do you think he really had to stay single? The men must have thought of it like slaying a dragon. A heroic task for love."

"Nothing heroic about it," she said. "Look at the times. It was the cradle of America, for God's sake, selectively breeding out the squeamish. Explains a lot, if you think about it. Besides, the gentle maidens could have pitched in if they wanted a husband badly enough."

"What do you think would be the equivalent today?"

"Of what?"

"Killing six blackbirds or three crows."

"Can't you shut up? I'm trying to work."

"I'm just saying, most people wouldn't want to kill birds in order to get married. I think it should be something positive. Acquiring a fortune, maybe."

"Quite the little materialist, aren't you? What if everybody had to break three bad habits before they could mate? Or do reparation for three sins? Couldn't hurt, and might decrease overpopulation."

"Were you ever married?"

"What's it to you?"

"Some people say you're a widow."

"Well, I'm not." Coral poked him with one of the pins, not accidentally. "Another thing I like about scarecrows, they keep their mouths shut. Go change into that other pair of pants, the ones on the hook in the bathroom. I'm finished with these."

That was the trouble with the Cape. Gossip everywhere, like a country village. For her, it wasn't just the witch nonsense—that would probably die down if she'd join a yoga class, wear knits from Talbot's, get her hair styled—something ordinary. But much of the talk about her stemmed from Jeffrey Brown. In the course of their long relationship, he'd planted plenty of rumors: She'd been a call girl. A gangster's moll. Had served time for prostitution. Had worried countless men right out of this troublesome world.

Only the last contained a grain of truth.

There had been men years ago, at the darkest time of her life, when she'd exiled herself from Wonderstrand. She'd rented a room in Danvers, clerking at a dry cleaner's to pay the rent. A tailor who worked on the premises taught her to sew a straight seam and predict the drape of a fabric. He was much older than she, humble, gentle. When he ran his hand along her bare arm as if it were a length of fine raw silk, she didn't bother to resist. What did it matter?

On Saturdays in Boston, she furthered her education by wandering alone to quiet places, the lectures, gardens, and sanctuaries that attracted other solitaries. There was a Buddhist (he'd cooked delicate vegetarian dishes, but his belief in reincarnation, in having to go through life again, depressed her); an Iranian, (seventh son of a family now living in France, and very handsome with his silky beard and olive skin), an Alabama-born Evangelical (the guilt made him impotent), and a classics professor (who shouted vulgarities in Latin when they were in bed). They'd all been happy to proselytize, and she'd let them. But as men, they left her empty, as if she'd taken a deep breath expecting fresh air and instead inhaled the solvent fumes she'd breathed at the dry cleaner's.

The last of them had been a bland, blond man who worked at a small factory that made fiberglass curtains. He'd come home from work with tiny bits of the stuff sparkling in his pores—and in his lungs, though they didn't know that then. One night in his apartment, as he passed her on the way to the shower, she noticed a sparkling halo circling the skin of his behind, like one of Saturn's rings—the result of sitting on the factory's toilet seat, where the dust settled between uses. It was the only sparkle he'd ever had, poor boy, and it killed him. He'd already begun to cough by the time she left him. Years later, she read a short obituary in the *Globe*. A sad story, but that of a stranger, and she couldn't weep for him. She'd long since stopped weeping for anyone.

She hadn't loved them. They were only ways to get through the days, the weeks, to dull her senses. Romantic love, primal love, that cocktail of biological urges and devotion to a false ideal—it all seemed cheap and ugly, like those souvenir shop rings that turn your finger green.

She'd loved only once, and that had been here. She'd driven that man, if not out of the world, at least out of Wonderstrand. But she wouldn't think about that.

Of all people, Jeffrey Brown had been the cause of her ending her exile and returning to her cottage. A letter from a law firm reached her informing her that Brown, as the co-owner of the property, wished to make new use of it, suggesting that since she was no longer in residence, her consent should be quickly forthcoming or would be assumed. So after five years, dead years, she'd come back. Perhaps, for that, she should thank him.

The rundown isolation of the cottages suited her. The colony contained some locus that was neither here nor another place, neither familiar nor strange. She clung to her share of it, even if she now found it necessary to put up with this garrulous tenant.

Coral straightened her back and rolled her neck.

"Hurry up in there," she called, loudly enough to make two of the scarecrows along the wall topple into each other. "I want to get this over with."

Luckily for him, when Maulkin emerged from her bathroom wearing the second of the two outfits, he'd switched topics as well as his pants. "Spacious cottage," he commented to the tape measure she held at his sleeve.

"Plenty of room when the dog and I are alone." She stressed the last word.

He went on, oblivious. "So you own the colony?

"Only half. My cousin...," she jerked the two ends of the tape measure as if she were tightening a garrote, causing Maulkin to jump.

"Don't twitch, damn it. My cousin owns the other half interest. He rents one of the cottages to a woman, what's her name, Polly, Phoebe, or something." Coral knew Piety's name perfectly well, but didn't want Maulkin to get the impression that she mixed much with neighbors.

"I haven't been lucky enough to meet her."

"What a shame."

"Smaller than the typical cottage colony, isn't it?"

"There used to be nine. Some were destroyed. This was only a sideline in the old days, anyway. It was all built on one of my grandfather's turnip fields."

"Ah! Did you know that this area used to be the turnip capital of the whole country?"

"I hate turnips." She didn't, but that was her affair.

He seemed cast down by this. "Asparagus, too," he offered.

"Look everybody knows this stuff. Every tourist magazine has a Good Old Days article, in between the fish-and-chips coupons and the real estate ads. If this is what your book's about, you're not adding much paint to the local color."

"It's just background. I was really interested in legends. People and legends."

"Same thing. She flipped up a cuff, and inserted several pins.

"I didn't want to write just a history, you know," he said to the dog. "I wanted to *create*, to take the people and facts and legends and mix them up into something new and…and highly significant."

"Hm," she said.

"Shakespeare did it. Hawthorne did it."

Behind his back, she rolled her eyes.

"I'll miss that in my new life. The history books. The old letters, diaries, newssheets." Wistful, he appealed to the sofa.

"There's plenty of that junk lying around here. You're welcome to it. The property used to have a bunch of storage sheds, but when they collapsed, I put the salvageable stuff in that new one behind my place."

"Oh? I wish I'd known sooner. Now I'll be too busy."

"So you said. You never know what you're going to need, though." She pulled the last few pins out of her sleeve and dropped them in a little tin box. It sounded like crickets.

She grasped his elbows and spun him around. "You'll do," she said. The clothes were just funky enough, just classy enough—a mixture of past and present. Respectable and confident—just the note she was seeking. Too bad she couldn't do anything about shoes, an item her scarecrows didn't require. He'd just have to shine up the standard-issue brown ones he was wearing.

That reminded her. "Don't move," she said. She reached for the camera and took a couple of photos.

He looked confused.

"Something on your mind?"

"Well, I wondered why you wanted a photo now, with the pins showing. I could have tried everything on after it was all finished."

"I just wanted to get an idea. Are you sure that's all that's bothering you? It wasn't the flash?"

"No." The word came out as two syllables, as if he wasn't sure how she wanted him to answer.

"Okay, just checking."

"I do appreciate…."

"Look at me when you say that. The dog had nothing to do with it."

"Sorry." He snapped to attention.

"Better," she said.

Coral's scheme was simple. Jeffrey Brown, rich, unscrupulous, and connected, was just the sort of man Maulkin would expect to launch him toward glory. She knew her cousin, his ego, the way to his heart (or whatever organ served in its place). Her tenant, silly as he was, could be shaped into just the creature to win Brown's confidence.

Maulkin had exposed to her the gaudy extremes of his ambitions; he'd come to her for help and she'd provided it. That should secure his loyalty. She'd be planting a living, breathing scarecrow in her enemy's corn patch, a spy who would report back to her. She would secure Wonderstrand Colony.

The Widow's Portrait

These cottages stand on land inhabited for many generations. Consequently, an accumulation of old furniture, family Bibles, letters, diaries, and keepsakes, left behind by residents and visitors, yield stories never told beyond hearth and home till now. Here's one I've pieced together from a small bound journal and certain letters that were stored with it.

In 1830, a fifteen-year-old girl recorded in childish handwriting the visit of a handsome stranger to her family's farmhouse. The first page bears the heading, "Anna, Her Life." No last name is mentioned. Educated in a rural way, in subjects appropriate to females at that time, she nevertheless had plentiful access to books and frequently alludes to stories she's read. Shy and fanciful, she often played at being the heroine of these, courted by knights and pursued by villains.

Guests weren't uncommon in the household, for distant cousins and friends often stayed with the family to help with the harvest or attend a wedding or funeral. Strangers sometimes rented one of the spare bedrooms while they pursued local employment or convalesced in the salt air after an illness. This visitor, however, impressed Anna more than any other. Though as shy as she, he paid her the courtesies of a grownup lady and seemed interested in what others dismissed as childish prattle. She describes him as "wondrous fair, with black hair but no beard, a smooth complexion like milk, and a high, noble brow." Her diary never gives his name, describing him at first only as "our boarder," and later not even bothering to specify whom she wrote about, for only one person absorbed her interest.

To her wonderment and joy, he was a literary man, what he called a "scribbler," and was indeed the author of a novel, though he confided this had been published at his own expense. He entertained her with tales of classical myths, older, he said, than Massachusetts or even England, where so many of her favorite romances were set. Someday, he promised, he would write down his own versions. Quiet and reserved with the other members of the household, he spent the hours after supper in conversation with Anna, while the younger children slept, the men smoked their pipes, and the women occupied themselves with darning or embroidery

He stayed for nearly a fortnight, and when he departed, the girl was bereft. In her diary, phrases like "heart torn asunder" and "bitter agony" blur together, presumably from tears. The diary ends in September; whether others followed it and are lost, or Anna never again felt her days worth recording, I don't know. With it, though, I found a series of letters, signed by people who must be Anna's relatives. The contents mainly concern other business, but here and there I found passages about Anna, sometimes patronizing, sometimes pitying, and sometimes downright spiteful. Taken together, they sketch the unfolding of her life:

"Our Anna persists in writing to that young fellow who boarded here this summer past. He has answered once or twice, no more. Nothing sinful occurred between them, of course. They were never alone. But she moons about like a lovelorn calf and sleeps with those thin envelopes under her pillow." This letter is dated 1831, signed Bessie. A sister, cousin, or aunt?

"Anna continues to fill her nieces' and nephews' heads with romantic nonsense, stories from her favorite authors, one of whom she claims as her Friend. Some say his work is well known in the city. I've no time for reading and can't speak for that. Better she should tutor them

in practical matters, for she has considerable skill in ciphering, a good memory for dates and names, and spells well." From Edward, maybe a brother, written in 1835.

"We fear daughter Anna will remain a spinster. She thinks on the characters in novels overmuch and gives no truck to the local lads. She is now nearly twenty-seven, too old to be so choosy, but she tends to the house and garden well enough, now that we are scarcely able." Signed Mother, 1842.

"With Father and Mother gone to their reward, sister Anna cannot stay alone on the farm, nor has she the right. Mr. G., a bachelor you met here at Ellen's wedding last spring, has offered her his hand, and is willing to make his home with her, sharing its produce with the interested parties, thus keeping the property in the family. He is not a polished fellow, nor much for light talk, but he is sober enough, and Anna's girlish prettiness has long faded." Edward, 1849.

"After many sulks and fits of weeping, Anna has at last consented to marry. My husband and I, with the other sisters, persuaded her that talk of eternal love and kindred souls is ridiculous in a rather plain woman of thirty five. Unless she's to starve, she has little choice, for the girls inherit their portion only on condition of their marriage." Amelia, 1850.

"Anna wears her wedding band, a cheap plain thing to be sure, on her right hand instead of her left. It's unseemly. Everyone knows that a vein runs directly from the ring finger of the left hand to the heart, binding the wearer to the symbol of wedlock. Anna will have none of this, nor will she explain." Bessie, 1850

"We have another newborn in the family. Anna has delivered her fourth, a healthy girl to be christened Phoebe. The mother recovers slowly, for she is much worn with childbearing and the work of the farm

and household. Her husband has no talent for farming, or indeed, much else. Bessie, 1857.

Only two more of the letters in the bundle refer to Anna, and these date from many years later. The first of these was penned by Amelia in 1864: "Anna has taken to wearing naught but black, as if she were a widow or bereaved mother, which she does not deserve. It is an insult both to the survivors of our heroes who perish on the battlefield and to her living husband! Now she has had a portrait made of herself. I chided her for the expense, but it seems that a lamed former soldier, who travels from town to town doing such work, charged her only a dollar plus a few days' food and shelter. Imagine my shock when I actually saw it—she's posed herself in full mourning!"

The last letter is dated 1896. "After Mama's funeral, we divided her few things among us, for Father has no need of them. We all chose one or two of her books, though most are quite old and worn. She had two cheap broaches, one with a broken clasp. These we gave to the oldest granddaughters, though I doubt they'll ever wear them. I took that old charcoal portrait, the one done near the end of the war. Poor Mama. She looks so old, though she was only forty-nine. The four of us owe her much. While I should not speak ill of Father, it was against his strenuous and often violent protests that she used her small inheritance to send us to school, insisting that even the girls learn history, art, literature, Latin and French. Without education, would I have attracted a man of the law, like my dear, erudite Charles? I shall order a fine frame for the portrait, and hang in the little sitting room off my bedroom. I've also saved a diary from her girlhood. A pair of old letters were folded inside it, but they were signed only by initials I didn't recognize, and contained nothing of interest, so those I consigned to the fire." Signed Phoebe.

I believe this very portrait hangs at the home of one of my cottage neighbors, a typical mourning picture of the period, a faded woman in widow's weeds, a half-drawn curtain, an empty chair. The ring is worn on the right hand.

From what I've read and seen, I surmise that Anna fell passionately and innocently in love at an age where she was first awakening as a woman, and that she never forgot the romantic writer she knew for only weeks. When he ceased to answer her girlish letters, she rationalized that he was too much occupied with greater matters. When he died, her one joy, her only link to the imaginative girl she'd been, died with him. She wore black for the rest of her life as a sign that, while she might be joined in the flesh to the lout she married, her heart would be joined to only one.

Now I must digress from Anna's story, but bear with me.

Unlike the rest of the Cape, where politicians, movie stars and rock musicians commonly vacation, Wonderstrand attracts few illustrious visitors. It boasts no luxury houses or charming B&B's. Even Thoreau, whose travelogue Cape Cod *included such powerful descriptions of the land and people, passed it by.*

Thoreau's friend Nathaniel Hawthorne, also fond of travel, may have visited the secluded coastline even earlier, though he never wrote about it by name. In many ways the more reclusive of the two men, Hawthorne might have found Wonderstrand quite to his taste. A few scholars speculate that his first visit may have occurred as part of a trip he took in 1830, on the way to or from Martha's Vineyard. I make no claims as a biographer.

But back to Anna. Perhaps her lifelong devotion, like any unrequited love, seems pathetic, but it sustained her. A few scraps of paper, ink, and charcoal are all we have to go by. We do know this, though: Nathaniel Hawthorne, handsome, romantic, master of old legends and tales, died in 1864.

—From *Wonderstrand Tales,* by Guy Thomas Maulkin

Chapter 6

"Thou hast a fair outside, and a pretty wit enough of thine own.
Yea, a pretty wit enough! Thou wilt think better of it,
when thou has seen more of other people's wits."

—HAWTHORNE

Guy looked straight into Coral's eyes. Time was when the superstitious considered green eyes to be unnatural, the eyes of changelings. Fragmented images flitted through his mind, cats and ladders, salt, the number thirteen. He felt a powerful urge to confess his boyhood belief in these things, to unburden himself of all the foolishness he'd ever thought or done. A cold sweat rose on his forehead, and he found it hard to breathe. He felt dazed, hypnotized, yet loquacious. He heard the words coming out of his own mouth sporadically, like puffs of smoke.

She brushed them away. "Pay attention," she said. "This is what you're going to do."

He shook himself alert.

"I'm going to tell you whom to see and what to say. There's an acquaintance of mine who can show you how to make fistfuls of money, introduce you around. You'll be so upwardly mobile you'll get dizzy. But you've got to do exactly as I say."

"Absolutely," he said. "On my honor."

"The man's name is Jeffrey Brown. Here's where to find him." She handed him a piece of paper with an address in the commercial section of Orleans, the larger town south of Eastham. "For God's sake don't tell him right off that I sent you. You've got to get your foot in the door first. Once you have his attention, you're going to give him this."

He took the small envelope, the kind that usually contained invitations or thank-you notes.

"What's inside?" he asked.

"Never mind. Just give it to him. When he sees it, believe me, he'll be ready to do you a favor or two. Don't get me wrong; he's not going to trust you once he finds out you know me. You'll just have to convince him you don't like me much. Shouldn't be that hard."

"But it would be!"

"You know, when the time comes to kiss ass, and it will come, you're going to do just fine."

This hurt. He'd never thought of his eagerness to please as a negative quality.

"Don't feel bad. Flattery's a great lubricant."

Was she reading his mind, or had he mumbled his thoughts without realizing?

"The trick is not to be obsequious. Make it seem like it's coming from *noblesse oblige*. That said, I've still got to think about what you could tell him about me."

"Why can't I just tell him the truth?"

Her laugh reminded him of a log fire crackling. "What might that be? You think you know?"

Did she say "damned if *I* do," under her breath?

"Beg pardon?" he asked.

More log fire. For some reason he couldn't name, he didn't care to pursue the subject of truth.

"Okay," she said, apparently reaching a decision. "Let's tell him this. He'll buy it—it's about money. Say I raised the rent on you when your lease ran out. You don't want to move; God knows why. We'll have to make up some reason."

She paced the room for a few minutes, and he was wise enough not to interrupt.

"I've got it, I think. Let's say you're still writing that book you were talking about. You've got to stay here because your magnum opus is set in Wonderstrand—you need to breathe the native air. So. You'll say you told me you can't afford more rent with your lousy job. I said tough cookies, that's not my problem. You tried to find better work, but no luck. Hell, everybody knows what the job market's like around here. Back you came, whining to me; I sent you to him. He's got fingers in a dozen pies, businesses all over the Cape."

"I understand," Guy said. "But...." He was going to have to be careful how he said this, not sound ungrateful. Nor obsequious, he reminded himself.

"But what?" she snapped.

"It's not that the clothes aren't just what I need," Guy said, indicating his pinned-up pants and unfamiliar shirt, "but if this man's so important? Shouldn't I wear a suit to meet him?" Hearing himself, he cringed; it must sound like he was asking for more. He added quickly, "I already have one somewhere. I think it still fits." In fact, it was left over from his college days. A bold plaid.

"I'm sure it's a doozie. But this is Cape Cod. Nobody wears a suit and tie to work except lawyers and funeral directors. As for Jeffrey Brown's being important—that depends how you define importance. Maybe he is to *you*."

Again Guy felt ashamed. She'd examined his values and found them wanting. All his life he'd felt empty-headed, embarrassed about his background. His orphan status had left him lacking knowledge and experience, both good and bad, that people with families took for granted. To compensate, he'd filled his head with facts, done everything he could to process them into something he could show. "Look at this university degree," he wanted to say. "This thesis. This book I'm writing." But once he was around people, such things shriveled up—he couldn't talk about them, couldn't find a practical use. Everything seemed futile after awhile.

And now? He'd yet to define this new idea of glory. Coral had mentioned money, fame, romance. Indeed, he intended to be more, much more than he had been. How that was to be accomplished, though, hadn't been explained to him yet. The mission she was outlining, this new contact, seemed to be the first step toward his future, and yet she didn't seem to like the man to whom she was sending him.

Guy didn't wish to invite more ridicule, would have suppressed the question had he been able, but he found himself asking her to explain further.

"Well, *he* certainly thinks he's important," she said. "Ever know one of those people who like the sound of their own names? Who use it as often as possible? Who repeat every compliment they've ever received, no matter how insincere or how hard they had to push to extract it? The sort who, if her name's Sally and she makes a pitcher of martinis, tells you everyone calls them 'Sally-tinis.' Everyone doesn't, but so what? She gets her name into every conversation."

"I've known people like that, yes." He'd always thought they must be universally loved and admired, on a first-name basis with more of the world than he could ever hope to meet.

"Well, Jeffrey Brown's one of them."

"Why do you suppose they do it?" he wondered.

"To inflate their own self images. Probably gives them a sense of substance. 'I hear my name, therefore I am.'" She squinted at Guy. "I know you're going to ask how I know him, so I'll tell you: he happens to be the cousin I mentioned, the one who owns half these cottages."

He *had* been going to ask. "Then you're not close. As family."

"As anything."

Guy understood better now why he had to get his foot in the door, as she had put it, and then to dissemble.

"Tell him I said he owes me one. That's when you'll give him that envelope. Got that? You've got to act confident, brassy even. A little brass can buy a lot in this world."

Confidence, he checked off mentally. Brass.

"Remember, people with inflated egos get taken at face value unless someone sees the inadequacy underneath. People who see themselves as inferior get treated that way, too. And for God's sake, try to look at the person you're talking to." She softened a little. "Here's a trick. Look at the middle of their forehead. Hold it a minute, then look away if you have to."

He tried this.

"It won't work on me, you dolt. I just told you about it."

He swung his glance to the floor.

"Let's see. What else? Ah, how could I forget?"

"Dickon! Water."

The dog trotted into the kitchen. A thump followed, something heavy hitting the linoleum, Guy jumped. Then the dog came back, pushing a glass jug of water with his snout. It rolled and gurgled toward toward Guy.

"Water's the source of all life," she said. "The elixir of the new century. Think of it as a fashion statement. 'No need of stimulants *here*,' it says. 'No green tea, no espresso, no Red Bull. My abundant energy comes from pure, clean water'."

He agreed; a water bottle did make the bearer seem perpetually fresh and robust, as if he or she had just returned from a bracing walk. Cold drink machines often stood in tandem with the snack machines he serviced. Though they weren't part of his route, he couldn't help noticing that bottled water had replaced soda in many of the slots.

"No need to put yourself to the trouble. I can provide my own water, at least."

"This isn't from the main well. I have my own source. And you don't want that bottled stuff. It just comes out of some tap somewhere. Try this."

With an effort, he hoisted the jug, twisted off the cap, and sipped.

"Delicious. Sweet, but tastes of minerals."

"It's clean, too. Don't worry about that. Now go put your own things back on. It's going to take me another day to make the alterations. I'll drop them off when they're ready."

Why did he put his faith in her? Guy wondered, back in his own cottage. Coral looked the way he thought a witch might. Not a Hallowe'en decoration or a pert Samantha, of course, but she had a windblown, "Night on Bald Mountain" appearance. And that odd dog. Weren't witches supposed to have animal familiars to do their bidding—cats, bats, rats...dogs? Imps to fetch fire for their hearths? The regional history he'd read was laced with tales of conjure women, of midnight necromancy and persecutions, of Cape Cod' versions of poor Goody Cloyse and Martha Carrier. Maria Hallett, best known of the locals, even had a street over in Eastham named after her. He'd written one of his tales about the Wonderstrand contingent.

But he didn't believe Coral could summon storms, read palms, heal or curse. He knew merely what he'd observed in their few meetings and what he'd heard. People noticed her, for good or ill, responded to her air of shrewdness and self-containment. Until now, no one had noticed *him*.

He'd been poor, awkward, rootless and alone until the Illumination had made him feel chosen. Now he was no longer the nonentity, lost in a crowd. The world would see his true self.

The next day, he returned midmorning from his vending route and sat down to wait, expecting Coral with the new wardrobe and maybe more instructions. He daydreamed, paced, lunched on broken pretzels, and daydreamed some more. Not a sound except the twitter of birds, broken occasionally by the *craawk* of a crow, to disturb the soft, cloudy noontide. In the hope that he'd see her coming, he opened his door to peek out.

There they were, the clothes neatly placed on hangers hooked over his doorknob. On the ground next to them, a gallon jug full of clear water. A Post-it stuck on the side read "For refills. Saves the landfill." A Stop-n-Shop bag held half a dozen empties of various brands, battered but clean.

How had he missed her? When had she come? But there was no time to waste in speculation. He put on a pair of the jeans, a crisp white shirt, and the leather jacket, the nicest and best-fitting garments he'd ever owned. His mirror was old and cloudy, the reflective silver chipping off the backing like mange, but his image came back sharp and quite dazzling. He added the hat. Why not?

Grinning, he jingled his keys into his pocket and went out, then remembered the little envelope and went back inside. While he was there, he gulped some of the water from the jug and filled one of the empties to take with him.

A fog had drifted in. Standing there, with the mist feinting and curtseying around him, he felt exhaled from a cloud. He noticed for the first time that the watery light brought out subtleties in the gray shingles of the cottage. The color wasn't flat at all; he could see undertones of sienna, rose, and celadon. The whole world was new. It was as if he had come into being right then, that very day.

Girded and ready, he set forth on his journey. That this amounted to a twenty minute drive diminished it not at all. A moment's doubt did assail him when he approached his ancient and unreliable Jeep, but his blood raced high and strong as he raced forward on the path of destiny.

The car started on the very first turn of the key.

Chapter 7

"A lone woman is troubled with such dreams and such thoughts
that she's afeard of herself sometimes."

—HAWTHORNE

Piety Rugosa carried a scent about her of cinnamon and vanilla, and also a note of the sour rag she used to wipe powdered sugar and spilled coffee off the counters at Deacon's Doughnuts. Her hair would be exactly the color of a dead mouse if she didn't buy highlighting kits from the CVS drugstore on Main Street and paint in blotchy streaks of fool's gold. Her boss, Mr. Brown, once told her she had a rosy, piquant little face. She remembered the remark because she'd mulled it over so much. Was she wearing too much rouge? By "piquant," did he mean bitter? Sharp? What? She always did that with a compliment, tore it to pieces and put it back together.

Another thing she had was a set of breasts she thought of as disproportionately large. These had once or twice come in handy in times of desperation, when she needed something and a man was in a position to help.

At three o'clock, the shop had only one customer, a perpetually unemployed type nursing a cup of coffee over in the corner. Mornings were busy no matter the season, but on spring afternoons, Deacon's trade mostly came from folks with nothing better to do than sit around in public places. Funny how the caffeine never seemed to perk them up.

When things got dull at Deacon's, she amused herself by experimenting on her customers. If someone sat too long over his decaf, she'd substitute some specially brewed high-test for his next cup. When a group came in with newspapers under their arms, ready for a political rant or a breast-beating lament over the Pats, Celtics, or Sox, they'd get the decaf. Some folks were just immune to her mood adjustments, though, which didn't surprise her all that much. It took more than caffeine to make her happy, too. Piety had long been devoted to antidepressant meds; just about every one on the market had been prescribed for her at one time or another. Some worked, some didn't. Lacking medical insurance at the moment, she was on pill hiatus, but she'd learned a thing or two about chemical therapy. If you asked her, that dude over in the corner could benefit from a little Prozac.

Who but lost souls would hang around here? The cops and other working stiffs went to Dunkin Donuts, where the service was faster. Kids from Nauset High tended to prefer the Chocolate Sparrow, which offered tall, whipped cream-topped espresso drinks as well as a big parking lot to socialize in. The artsy types had a couple of places with paintings hung on the walls and WiFi. All that was fine by her; she didn't want to bother with flavored syrups and steamed milk, or trying to figure out what some abstract painting meant. On the other hand, was being a *barista* more glamorous than being plain old counter help? It did sound sort of foreign and exotic.

"God, I'm bored," she said. The idler in the corner poked his head up, looking like he might offer to entertain her.

"Forget it, Hank," she said. He returned sadly to his newspaper.

She'd always been a loser magnet. Must be something in her pheromones. That wasn't old Hank's fault, though. She felt sorry for snapping at him, and carried the pot over to give him a free refill. Caffeinated.

"Thanks, Pie," he said.

"Don't call me that. And don't tell the boss." Mr. B. frowned on free refills.

"Where's he today?"

She shrugged and glanced across the street, where stood the neat storefront offices of J.G. Brown & Company.

"Whoa," she said. "Who's that?"

A man had stopped outside the office, checking the address against a piece of paper. He paused to sip from a water bottle, that individual size everybody carried these days, then slipped it back into the pocket of his leather jacket. So he was one of these fastidious types, his insides washed as clean as his hair or fingernails. He walked with a gait that might have seemed awkward had it not been so confident.

Hank peered at him.

"Look at the wicked swagger on that sumbitch, will you? Gotta be one of those summer people from New York or Jersey. Used to be they didn't show up until 4th of July—like the greenhead flies." Hank let go a chortle.

"You just crack yourself up, don't you, Hank?"

"Well, calling this the shoulder season's funny, ain't it? That's not the part of the anatomy I'd name after 'em."

"Oh, can it. Without them, nobody'd need to hire you to fry fish three months out of the year, would they? Then how would you buy coffee and tabloids the other nine? Anyhow, my tips sure show the difference when they're around—tourists don't leave a couple of nickels and pennies like *some* people."

She was sorry as soon as she said it. That was the thing about being off meds. She could never be sure if she was right or wrong, a bitch or a doormat. Instead of Prozac or Paxil, her bloodstream filled up with doubt.

"I left you half a buck just the other day. You think this is some fancy Eye-talian restaurant?"

She ignored him, concentrating instead on watching the stranger disappear into Brown's office. "Pretty good looking, isn't he?"

"Huh? What's so damn special about him?"

"He looks polished. See his clothes? They fit like they were tailored for him, but they don't stick out. That's taste."

"He's got on jeans, I got on jeans. What's the big deal?"

"You wear yours under your gut. They sag." Like a full diaper, she thought but didn't say. "Plus I can see grease on them from that doughnut you dropped yesterday."

"Shit. Give me those duds, and you'd think I was hot, too."

"Don't make me puke."

"You're pretty choosy for…"

"For what?" She felt a familiar sinking in her stomach; something ugly was about to happen, that would hang over her for days.

"For *you*," he said, and went back to his *Boston Herald*.

She stomped away, taking the coffee pot with her. How was it everyone could see right off that she was inferior merchandise? She wore *less than* like a uniform. Even coffee shop cowboys like Hank looked down on her. She wanted to tell him off, but if she did, he'd come back with a worse remark, words that might keep her awake for weeks. Whoever said anger corrupted the vessel it was in, or something to that effect, was right. Anger terrified her. When she let it out, it always seemed to come back to bite her on the ass. Or she waited too long and blew up. Or the person she was pissed at turned out to be the type who thought they had a God-given right to say whatever they pleased, and then went ahead and said it, cutting Piety all to ribbons. So she held it in.

She banged the metal racks around, combining the doughnuts that remained, washing the extra trays, making as much clatter as she could. Hank, that asshole, slipped out without her noticing. See if he'd get any more freebies from her. She went back to leaning on the counter.

Before her thoughts had time to sink too low, though, Piety saw Mr. Brown and the stranger leaving the office, and heading her way. The bell over the door, which drove her nuts when the place was busy, really did jingle her interest this time. The new dude's face, now that she saw it up close, was bright-eyed and smart. She liked it, and was disappointed that he didn't come to the counter. Instead he strolled toward the table Mr. B. indicated, the one Hank had just vacated. She wished she'd remembered to wipe it off.

Her boss's usual manner with her was chummy; he would join her behind the counter whenever he came in, chatting all the while. Today, he hardly greeted her, his smile chilly and locked in place as he ordered two coffees.

"What will you have in yours?" he called across to his companion, sounding as if he hoped it would be arsenic.

"Thanks, but I'm fine with this," said the newcomer, taking a dented Poland Spring bottle from his pocket.

Piety saw Mr. B.'s smile waver, as if a cloud had passed over a wintry sun. "Just one then, with double cream and three sugars," he said.

"Doughnuts?"

"No." He glanced toward the table to see if the other man had heard, but the attractive stranger remained unruffled and apparently not hungry.

So no free food. He was more foe than friend, then, maybe some kind of business competitor, or a tax auditor.

She was starting to feel distinctly less bored.

Mr. Brown rejoined his companion. He seemed to be limping slightly. "Did you hurt your leg?" Piety asked.

He turned a narrow-eyed look on her that made her recoil. "Pulled a muscle playing tennis," he snapped. Then he reassembled his features into something more benign. "Kind of you to ask."

The irritation returned to his voice when he addressed the stranger. Piety could just hear him say, "Now just what are you up to?" After that, the men spoke too low to hear.

She slipped a big metal spoon out of a drawer and tried to check her reflection. The scratched stainless steel didn't work very well. In the spoon's bowl, her face was upside down; on the back, it stretched into a horse face, elongated and distorted, her nose enlarged by the center curve. At least she could tell that some of her lipstick was still on. She hoped her hair was okay.

That morning before work, she'd been using a hand mirror to reflect the bigger bathroom one, so she could see the back of her hair. In the reversed image—and wasn't that the true one, the way other people saw you?—she'd noticed for the first time the hollowing under her eyes that meant her face was sinking into middle age.

A downer for sure. But, shit, she was barely past thirty, and right at the moment she wanted to look perky, not gloomy, in case that stranger happened to glance her way. He didn't. He stayed deep in conversation with Mr. B. Nobody was paying attention to her, which meant she could kick herself as hard as she wanted. She could always find some reason; if it wasn't getting older, it was money—or just life itself. Sometimes it seemed like feeling bad was her natural state. Pills, therapy when she had insurance to pay for it, books whose titles had "Joy" and "Happy" plastered all over the cover, none of it changing anything much.

Now depression, that had staying power. True, once or twice a year she'd feel a flash of something different. She'd stand on the beach, the mist softening and blurring the edges of everything; she'd notice what it could do with the colors of the sky and think, "Well, maybe not so bad." But her mind immediately stamped it "cliché." The sea and sky, for God's sake. Nevertheless, it was a Moment. She wished at those times she could just stop there, just plop down on the sand and that would be the end of it, her own little heaven or nirvana. But sooner or later she had to go home and go to bed and get up in the morning and sell saturated fat and white flour to people with clogged arteries and bad attitudes, and there it was, another day.

A few people drifted in and out; she served them and began cleaning up for the last shift. A couple of teenagers took over from four to six, when Deacon's closed, but Mr. B. liked her to clear the register—he didn't trust the kids, and left them only the minimum to make change.

"You want a refill?" she called to him. "I just made a fresh pot."

"Why, yes, Piety. I believe I will. And are there any chocolate frosteds left?"

So food was being offered now. "Just one. But we've got strawberry."

"Would you bring us some, dear?"

The boss looked less fidgety and pale. Piety put the doughnuts on a paper plate and loaded the pot of coffee onto a tray.

The stranger stood up when she approached; he even made a little bow. Now that was class.

Mr. B. looked a little taken aback, but he too stood up.

"Piety is my angel of the doughnut shop," he said to the stranger. Piety thought she picked up a little emphasis on the possessive. "And this is Guy Maulkin, the newest member of Jeffrey Goodman Brown's team."

She put the tray down and reached to shake his hand.

He kissed it. He didn't seem to notice her chipped, uneven nails or the red spots from the burns she was always getting from the coffee maker. The stranger, this Guy Maulkin, kissed her hand.

"An angel indeed," said the new dude.

Mr. B. laughed merrily, but his voice turned a degree or two colder. "Quite the charmer, aren't you?" He turned to Piety. "Of course, he won't be spending much time here. I have other plans for Mr. Maulkin."

"Nice to meet you," Piety squeaked, and backed away to her counter, forgetting the tray. Guy leaped up before she could return, and brought it to her. He had the brightest eyes she'd ever seen.

Then, as if nothing had happened, the men went back to their conversation.

So Mr. Brown had a new toady. Don't get ideas, she told herself. He's cute, sure, but look at him. Men like that don't run off with counter help. Counter help with cheap highlights.

Still…

She'd been in Jeffrey Brown's house last December. A holiday party for the year-round employees, most of them from the white collar businesses, plus her and the night baker, Marilee, who quit work at seven a.m. when Piety came in. The part-timers and summer help weren't invited.

The spacious rooms seemed to go on and on, half of them with huge windows taking in the view of Pleasant Bay. Heavy molding surrounded all the doors, the hardwood floors lay unscarred and glossy, the granite counters gleamed. Even the knickknacks looked expensive.

The house made her feel bad. No matter what she did, she'd never have anything this clean, this shining. If she let herself feel envy, she'd frizzle up like a hair over a flame.

Funny thing, though, the liquor served at that party was the cheapest brands, the kind of bottom-shelf, headache-inducing stuff she was sure the Browns never drank when they were alone. Good enough for employees—her hosts probably thought none of them would know the difference. Piety did, though; she'd done enough stints as a cocktail waitress. The employees were there to make the Browns look seasonally benevolent, to admire their bounty, then go home, talking about what a swell boss old Jeffrey was.

Well, he wasn't the worst she'd ever had, that was for sure. She shouldn't be so mean. Hadn't he found her that nice cottage? Rented it to her so cheaply? Even fixed it up some, with fresh paint and new windows so pretty she hated to cover them with curtains. She'd been practically homeless at the time, living in a trailer that wasn't zoned for winter use. She'd had to get out, and couldn't find anything else; even the smallest apartment in the shabbiest building was out of her range. Everybody talked about how working people had a tough time finding housing on Cape Cod, and it was true, though if you had kids, were old, or sick, you might be able to get help from some agency. But Piety, able-bodied and with no one but herself to support? You're on your own, honey. Take those big tits out there and find yourself a husband with a job. Or work two or three jobs yourself and forget about a life.

Mr. Jeffrey Goodman Brown had helped her a lot, all right.

But that party. What would she do if she had money like that? Would she serve Gray Goose and Balvenie? French Champagne? Who knew? She really had no idea how she'd behave if bounty suddenly appeared on her doorstep.

And odds were, it wasn't going to now.

Chapter 8

"There needed no other proof of his rank and consequence, than the perfect equanimity with which he comported himself...."

—Hawthorne

When the cocky stranger had appeared at the outer door of the offices, he'd occasioned a great flurry and flutter among the female staff. Brown heard breathy exclamations, the irregular clunk of pumps on Pergo, and the thud of hips bumping against desks and filing cabinets. Wondering what caused the fuss, Brown peeked through the little window in his office door. He could see only the visitor's back, but the noise apparently came from the staff's tripping over one another to be the first to help him.

Brown had been in his own inner sanctum, thinking about the way Piety looked when she leaned over to grab two creme-filleds from the rack, her dainty fingers hidden under little squares of tissue. She used two sheets, a wasteful practice for which he would have reprimanded anyone else.

So who was she, this woman upon whom he spied? Delicious speculation, but he corrected himself: he did not spy on Piety. He watched over. Observed benignly. He speculated about where she'd been that evening, now two days past, when he'd been accosted by the Rigby woman. The possibilities displeased him. Next time he saw Piety wasting doughnut tissues, he would rebuke her. He would.

Then he recalled the way Piety often looked when unaware of being watched, the world-weariness punctuated with sidelong glances full of sunshine. The sharp, sweet little smile, the slightly crooked lower front teeth. His irritation fell away.

He couldn't entirely pin down the reason for his attraction to her. A lesser man might have thought first of her chest, the way it rounded out the red letters of DEACON'S across the T-shirt that served as a uniform. The head of a black-hatted Puritan, Deacon's emblem, rested just above her right nipple, stretching his stern face almost into a smile. Anyone could see Piety's vulnerability; she flaunted it, he sometimes thought, displaying her downcast status like a handicapped parking placard. An opportunist might find that appealing.

He was not so coarse. Didn't he recognize the inner woman? She would appreciate the things he gave her (unlike his current wife, that barren and frivolous creature). Piety would be a business asset to him—a woman plucked from the gutter, as it were, would know the value of a dollar. Younger than he by a good many years, she might even produce a son for him. Jeffrey considered this. At first, of course, he wouldn't want to compete for Piety's time and attention, but when the ardor cooled a little, and her age climbed, well, why not? A hardy boy, strong and respectful, a boy with Piety's tough peasant genes and Brown's own canniness and strength. In time, a new sign over his offices, Jeffrey Goodman Brown and Son, and his youthful wife, still slim and hot, helping the boy keep up a healthy cash flow as he, Jeffrey, reveled in semi-retirement.

At this point in his reverie, the flurry from the outer office reached him. Irene, the tallest and heaviest of the competent matrons who handled his office affairs, had outwrestled her coworkers. Blushing and simpering, she conducted a young man to Brown's door.

"Jeffrey, this is Guy Maulkin. He wishes to speak to you about...." She looked momentarily confused. "What was it about again?" She smiled, a grandmotherly coquette.

Brown's lip curled. Why the fuss? he wondered. His firm performed a variety of services appealing to the rich and attractive—scouting out secluded and luxurious rentals, employing discreet household help, securing mortgages, negotiating local inspections, licenses and fees. Actors from New York, CEO's from Hartford, magnates from as far as Japan, many such had passed through the quaint clapboarded and flower boxed storefront office, so appealingly Cape Cod. He and his staff had eased numberless shell-strewn paths into summer homes and aboard yachts— and no one at Brown and Company had so much as fluttered an eyelid.

"He asked for you specifically," Irene continued. "Or we would have been delighted to help him."

"Just seeing your earnest faces brightened my afternoon," said the newcomer. "I'm sure your capable hands could have dispatched any business other than the present errand."

He winked.

Lewd, thought Brown.

Irene giggled.

Brown, who had often heard the woman's thin-lipped harangue on pornography, men in Speedos, and off-color jokes, noted with horror her hundred and eighty pound frame jiggling delightedly.

Was it possible that wink, that brief flash from his visitor's clear and sparkling eye, had charmed her? Brown filed this idea away, marshaled his bonhomie, and beamed at the stranger, whose manner and dress spoke of potential income.

"Thank you, Irene. I'll take it from here."

Dismissed, she backed out as if in the presence of royalty. Brown could see her rivals watching wistfully. The stranger grinned at them all, then withdrew one of those plastic bottles of water from his pocket, sipped, and replaced it. Normally, Brown might have found this rude, but the fellow managed it delicately enough

"Now, Mr...Mawkish, is it?"

A lift of the eyebrows said the stranger had gotten the shot. "Guy Maulkin, sir." He spelled the name out slowly, as if talking to a dull child. Parry and thrust. The gaze was straightforward; the voice full of assurance. Still, the "sir" showed respect.

They shook hands.

"How may I help you?"

"I'm looking for employment."

Brown hadn't expected this. "Employment? Of what sort?"

"That depends on you."

Something told Brown to be wary. "Have you a resumé?

"No."

Brown let contempt drip from his voice. "I regret that I have no openings."

"That's what she said you'd say."

"Who?"

"She said to give you this."

Maulkin drew forth an envelope and passed it over.

Brown ripped the envelope open, noticing from the corner of his eye that his companion once again sipped from and replaced the bottle. The Poland Spring label, he saw now, was bubbling, as if dampened and dried. Was it refilled or spiked? Was the man intoxicated?

Brown read the few words from the contents of the envelope and knew the danger was real, regardless of whether Maulkin's water was actually vodka.

"Who are you?"

"You know my name. Coral Rigby suggested I come."

Brown's whole body twitched with fury. "Are you and that woman trying to blackmail me?"

Out came the bottle again.

"Let me see that." Brown grabbed the bottle, sniffed it—no trace of alcohol—and hurled it across the room. "I don't know what your game is, but you won't put anything over on Jeffrey Goodman Brown."

Maulkin slumped a little. "Coral Rigby is my landlady." He paused. "A tyrannical one. She's raised the rent on me again. I, well, I'm an independent contractor. In the food retailing industry. Underemployed."

Brown sneered.

"Please understand—I have other projects. Ambitions." M a u l k i n spread his arms to corroborate the vastness of his interests. "Meantime, I need more lucrative employment."

"And what has that to do with me?" The stranger actually seemed to be fading before Brown's eyes.

"She said...she said it would benefit all of us."

"I fail to see how. Why don't you move if your rent's too high?"

"Because..." the stranger patted the pocket where the bottle had been and found it empty. "I'm writing a book. About Wonderstrand. I need to live there. And you know how hard it is to find year-round rentals...."

"Bleeding heart nonsense," said Brown.

"She said you had lots of businesses."

"I do. That doesn't mean I hire every indigent I meet."

Maulkin dropped his glance to the floor. "She said you would after you read the note."

Brown felt the crisp Egyptian cotton of his shirt growing damp at the collar and armpits. Why should his cousin care if this fool stayed in her cottage? For the money? No, he thought not. More likely, she saw this as an opportunity to harass him, to remind him that she had leverage over him. How he hated her.

The stranger rose and almost crept to the corner where his bottle had landed.

Brown, the taller of the two, rose as well.

"It's only water," his visitor said humbly. He took a sip, then pushed the bottle as deep into a leather pocket as it would go.

Brown harrumphed. "Awfully thirsty, aren't you? Diabetic?"

"No. But I'm told water is very good for you."

"So the health fanatics say." Maybe they were right. Maulkin was starting to look revived.

"Look here," Brown continued. "I'm a successful man. Yes, and wealthy. The Rigby woman is neither. She's jealous and spiteful."

Maulkin listened intently, which Brown took as agreement. The fellow had a certain presence. Perhaps he could be useful.

"I can only guess at her motives in sending you to me, but I'm willing, for your sake, not hers, to hear you out. What do you have to offer me?"

Maulkin pulled himself up straight. "Energy. Drive. Facility with language. I could write advertisements, do research, work late hours. What do you need?"

"I need adaptability. Loyalty. And most of all," here Brown pounded his emphasis on the desk, "I need fire in the belly."

"I can provide all that."

Brown looked him over.

A rustling and whispering in the outer office told him that the staff had not forgotten their visitor. "We should find a more private place to talk. I have a place across the street where we can get a cup of coffee."

There'd be few customers at Deacon's this time of day. Piety would be there, of course, but one set of eyes and ears was better than three, and he could handle Piety.

"Whatever you like," said Maulkin.

"We can go out this way. It will be quicker." Brown's office opened onto a small paved yard, closed in by the backs of other businesses except for a narrow driveway. He kept his car there and had the only key to the door.

"Handsome jacket," he said, as they stepped out. "Lauren?"

"Yes," said Maulkin. Then he whistled. "Handsome car."

"Classics never go out of style. It's an '88 Eldorado. Beautiful, isn't she? Chrome everywhere, 155 horsepower 4.5-liter engine. Can't be beat. Never given me a minute's trouble." Truth be told, the motor was a little sluggish for the size of the vehicle, but no need to mention that.

"You drive it all the time?"

"Of course not. I lease an SUV for utilitarian purposes, trade it in annually. My business interests require a lot of driving."

"I'll bet this one turns heads," Maulkin said.

"That it does." Brown made no effort to keep the pride from his voice. "I can't drive it as often as I'd like, even when the weather's fine. Those government bean counters who do the safety inspections keep records of mileage."

His companion had been circling the car, admiring it. "Does that matter?"

"Low mileage gets an insurance discount. Don't you own a car?"

"Not like this."

"I'm already a thousand miles over what they allow. The discount may sound trivial, but I didn't get where I am by squandering money."

"Ah, but *you're* the company. The company's profits and losses are yours."

"That they are."

"I can fix it," Maulkin said.

"I beg your pardon."

"The odometer. I can turn it back. Only takes a couple of simple tools."

"That's illegal," said Brown.

Did the fellow really think Jeffrey Goodman Brown would turn a screwdriver-wielding stranger loose on his beloved car? Maulkin gave no sign of being stupid; therefore it must be a calculated move. Brown was beginning to enjoy this chess game.

He turned from the car and walked around the building toward Deacon's. Maulkin just behind.

Brown chose a table as far from the counter as possible, positioning the chairs so only he could see Piety. For appearance's sake, he ordered coffee. Maulkin declined.

"See here. Why should I trust you enough to employ you?"

"Because you're a man of the world. You're really trusting your own instincts."

Brown liked the answer, but had by no means lost his suspicion. "Why were you willing to be her messenger boy? Didn't this sealed note ploy strike you as odd? Most people would make a simple phone call."

"She said it was a joke between you two."

Brown leaned back in his chair. "My cousin and I don't joke."

"I see that now, and I'm sorry for the false start. She told me about your success..." Maulkin's head dipped slightly in a subtle, respectful little bow. "I intend to be successful, too, on the greatest scale. Until now, I've wasted my time, but I intend to change."

"How so?" Brown wasn't sure why he continued to listen. That accursed message from the Rigby woman had trapped him, but still, he could have gotten rid of Maulkin by giving him a job somewhere up-Cape, some kind of manual labor in which they'd never have to cross paths again. And yet the young man had a natural aristocratic bearing that reminded Brown of himself as a youth. Most of all, he needed to see what his cousin had up her sleeve.

"You know the world, the ways and means of power."

Piety glanced up from the counter, but Brown was fairly certain she couldn't hear them. He reclined in his plastic chair, consciously taking the pose he'd seen kings and emperors use in movies, knees apart, head tilted back. "Perfectly true. But why should I share that with you?"

His companion took another sip of water. "I'm educated. I'm smart."

"So are most of my employees."

Maulkin leaned close. "I'm willing," he said.

Brown held his peace for a minute. He'd learned through many successful negotiations the potency of silence.

"That business with the odometer," he said finally. Where did you learn to do that?"

"I was orphaned as an infant. No relatives; the authorities checked. I grew up in foster homes."

"How sad." Brown studied his fingernails.

"This isn't a pity story. No tragedy, no abuse. But my childhood made me a self-starter." Maulkin sipped again. "I did have some colorful foster families. Some of their occupations were distinguished by, let's call it an everyday sleaziness. One operated a city pawn shop—guns, hot jewelry, you know the type—a fact that got passed over by Social Services. I saw how people in need behave. Another family owned a used car lot, where the specialty was altering odometers. I picked up odd skills along the way."

Brown kept his kingly stance for another pause. Then he leaned forward and clapped the other man on the back. "I think we can work together," he said, and shone forth a smile on his new protégée.

Just then Piety called over from behind her counter, offering fresh coffee. Brown nodded. He'd enjoy the taste of sugar on his tongue.

Maulkin stood up when she approached. Brown thought the bow a little overdone, even more so the hand kiss. He wished he'd thought of it.

He stood up, too. Not too early to establish territory here. Piety was *his* angel, after all. He watched her closely for any sign of recognition—these two lived in close proximity in those damned cottages—but he saw none. He wasn't really surprised. Those places weren't situated to encourage intimacy among neighbors. You could hardly get from one to the other without risking poison ivy or Lyme disease.

He introduced them, as a matter of form, but planned to keep a wary eye on both.

Brown watched Piety walk away, then turned back to Maulkin.

"Show up Monday with a resumé. We'll talk numbers then. As for duties, well, we have any number of options. My businesses do a little contracting, a little investment counseling, manage the properties I own. We'll see. Oh, and a word of advice: don't have any more involvement with the Rigby woman. You'll pay whatever exorbitant rent she demands and stay out of her way. Understood?"

"Certainly. Until Monday, then."

"And Maulkin? Bring those tools you mentioned."

Alone, Brown settled into his doughnuts and his thoughts. The lad was unformed, yes. Perhaps naïve. But not, it seemed, an instrument of Coral Rigby's. Even if he were, Maulkin's living so near the woman could come in very handy. A spy in the midst..

When Brown finished, he joined Piety at the counter. "Off to home in a few minutes?" he asked.

"Sure am."

"And how are things in your little cottage? Any problems?"

"Not at all. You can't imagine how much it means, your getting me the place."

"A pleasure," he said, basking. "I take it you've never run into Mr. Maulkin before?"

"No," she said, glancing out the window in the direction he'd taken. There was something about her expression that Brown didn't like. "Is there some reason I should have?"

He decided to leave well enough alone. "Perhaps it's time we consider some better housing for you."

"Better? Compared to that trailer, this is paradise! Why would I want to move again?"

"The place is run down. You must find it rather isolated, too."

"Well, those scarecrows everywhere—they creep me out sometimes. Like they're watching me."

"I should have warned you about that. Disgusting, pagan things. But there's nothing I can do as long as my cousin owns half the property."

"Really, I'm okay."

"Just between us, I'm making arrangements to develop that site. Houses, fine ones."

"Well that lets me out."

Two vertical lines, annoyance and worry, appeared between her plucked brows. He wished she wouldn't do that; someday, it would cost him plenty for cosmetic interventions.

"Don't worry. I take care of my employees. And you never know what the future holds, do you?"

She regarded him curiously.

He opened his mouth to say more, but just then the two teenagers who worked the four-to-six shift ambled in, pocketing their phones, shoving headsets into backpacks. Piety pulled her purse from under the counter and hefted it over one shoulder.

She turned and waved a goodbye at him. Was there a slow, sensual curve in that wave? A new interest in the way she looked at him from under her lashes?

Leave it to me, thought Jeffrey Goodman Brown, to turn dross into gold, to turn a dangerous situation to my advantage. He drew the note from the Rigby woman from his breast pocket, wadding its two words ("I know.") and crude drawing into a tight ball which he stuffed into his half-filled cup of coffee. He dumped the soaked and illegible contents in a trash container and barked at one of the teenagers to empty the bin into the dumpster.

All in all, it had been a good day's work.

Night Vision

Whisper just one phrase, The Incubus of Wonderstrand, and there are still those who'll shudder. Here's a tale that does not date from the colonial past. It plagued the outer Cape just a few decades ago, perhaps making it more urban legend than folktale. Certainly it's one of Wonderstrand's most troubling tales, rife with fear, accusation, paranoia.

Who were the victims? Women, usually young, on the Cape for summer jobs at restaurants and inns. Some were college students, mostly from the Midwest or other landlocked states, others came from Ireland, Jamaica, or Eastern Europe, but not so many as in later decades. Some were spending their summers with their families in rented homes—then as now, accommodations in Wonderstrand were cheaper than those in other towns. What the young women held in common was that they slept alone, near a window.

Imagine a nightmare so intense that it rivals the laudanum dreams of Victorian literature. The girls dreamed of a hazy figure that hovered near, watching them intensely or reaching to them through a haze of smoke, which some described as sweet, some as bitter. A few admitted the dreams had an erotic quality; others said quite the opposite. One or two, perhaps influenced by horror movies or religion, described visions of brimstone pits. An art student among them recalled Fuseli's painting "The Nightmare," the crouching fiend pressing the breath from a slumbering maiden.

All slept heavily, woke nauseated and headachy. Some awakened before dawn, crying out; others failed to hear alarm clocks and arose, disoriented and groggy, at noon.

One of the girls told another, and another. Rumors spread. Three of the girls went to the police. Parents and employers, worried about losing staff, did the same. The investigation began.

The screens on the girls' windows sometimes fit loosely, since many of the houses were old, the windows warped and bearing many layers of paint. Not once did anyone find a definite sign of entry beyond a tear in the screen, bent inward, unfolded like a flower, leaving an opening wide enough for a bird, or a man's hand. The following morning, a smell of smoke still lingered in the room, more pungent than tobacco. Demonic, said the superstitious. A party, said the police, the employers. They accused the girls of smoking marijuana or hashish, but most of them denied it with tears or outrage.

None showed signs of rape or physical injury, though a nightgown may have been slipped off a breast, sheets and blankets pushed to the bottom of beds. The real harm was psychological. Many developed insomnia, depression, or agoraphobia. All complained of a sense of being watched, never alone, never inviolate.

The police failed to catch the perpetrator in the act. Boyfriends were questioned, coworkers accused. Innocent men, out for a midnight walk, found themselves in spreadeagled against squad cars. One of the girls experienced a public breakdown at an outdoor concert when she smelled smoke similar to that which clung to the dream. Women refused to sleep in rooms with open windows, bought handguns, kept baseball bats next to their beds. Fear snowballed. Elderly widows left their beloved seaside homes to move in with children in distant cities. Little girls slept in their parents' bedrooms. Worst of all in some people's eyes, tourism in the surrounding towns began to suffer.

When no one was apprehended, some people called the girls liars. Others, less judgmental, pointed out that while dreams are immensely private, they are also readily suggestible. Unable to sleep or work, under suspicion by their employers, most of the victims left the Cape, perhaps tucking the experience away into the places we visit only in our loneliest hours. Eventually, the public's attention turned elsewhere.

Was the Wonderstrand Incubus supernatural, psychological, or criminal? Was it the product of a kind of hysteria, like what occurred in Salem in 1690? How can we ever know?

—From *Wonderstrand Tales,* by Guy Thomas Maulkin

Chapter 9

"He has lived the life of a perfect recluse till very lately—so diffident that he suffers inexpressibly in the presence of his fellow-mortals..."

—LETTER FROM MARY PEABODY, DESCRIBING HAWTHORNE

"Is that you?"

Coral looked up, annoyed. How does one answer that question? Amid the bustle of the marketplace on this sunny day, she picked out the speaker, who fluttered her fingers in greeting.

"It's me, Piety."

"Oh." Realizing that more seemed called for, Coral added, "Hello."

How she loathed these days at the flea and crafts market. The whole world seemed to pass through, an endless onslaught of people. She had to be pleasant, suffer fools in order to be wise enough to sell anything—on a good day she could make several hundred dollars. The market was held every weekend in the uneven terrain of a drive-in movie parking lot. Vendors set up their wares between the painted cement poles that held the speakers, their gray metal surface weathered to the granular smoothness of sea glass.

Few movie patrons actually used them anymore, since the soundtrack came through more clearly on a special radio channel. Sometimes on summer nights, Coral and the dog came here to watch a film in the privacy of the truck. She liked the old cartoons that came before the feature, and the ads resurrected from the fifties encouraging men to loosen their ties and take it easy in the comfort of their chromed, finned automobiles. Women could kick back, too, or so they were told— no need to change out of their housedresses. Coral remembered these from her childhood, utilitarian cotton garments that rendered the wearers faded and shapeless, though they'd been half the age she was now. Maybe she could find one to clothe a scarecrow. She'd put the hair in narrow rollers, tie an apron around the waist. Just for laughs, a girdle and one of those torpedo bras, if such things could still be found.

When the concession ads came on, Dickon yipped at the dancing hot dogs and hamburgers. The only downside to these drive-in movie nights was braving the lines outside the concession stand restrooms, their hot yellow lights jaundicing her face in the small cracked mirrors over the sinks, their surrounding armies of flying insects. She wished she could relieve herself in the bushes behind the screen, as the dog did.

In daylight, the drive-in lost its cinematic flair. The flea market drew eager hordes to roam among the bargain-priced T-shirts, handmade jewelry, and cheap ethnic skirts. Shoppers scavenged among dusty effluvia spaded up from attics and basements, as well as local pottery and woodwork fine enough to be called folk art. Here and there one might find an object that could legitimately be labeled an antique.

One Saturday every month, spring through autumn, Coral rented a slot for twenty dollars, piled a dozen or so of her creations into her old Toyota pickup, and headed out at dawn to set them up. The truck served as backdrop to her stall, plus shelter and storage. Sawhorses formed the sides, holding up two rows of scarecrows. A metal box for cash, a water bowl in a corner for Dickon, and her emporium was open for business. She priced high, bargained only when it suited her, and sometimes took deposits on special orders, to be delivered the following month.

Even on cloudy days, a wide-brimmed hat and aviator sunglasses circa 1980 protected her anonymity, but there always loomed the possibility of running into someone who recognized her. Ignoring Piety, Coral went back to the yarn hair she was applying to a stuffed head. The work kept her attention away from the crowd and passed the time while she waited for customers. Unlike some of the vendors, she didn't have to worry about shoplifting. With the potential for barked shins from broomstick backbones, head butts from shellacked pumpkins, whacks from outstretched wooden arms, no one could carry her creatures away unnoticed.

Piety, apparently in no hurry to leave, reached down to pet Dickon, who thumped his tail once. "I spotted the scarecrows before I saw you. So this is what you do with them."

"Sometimes. Want to buy one?"

"Well, no thanks. I'm not real worried about crows. I like this, though." She indicated a female figure in a green dress, the hem intentionally tattered into foliate points. A brown tapering shawl doubled the leafy effect. A hat the color of birch bark crowned hair of weathered rope, unraveled and cut to uneven lengths; atop that, a darker green veil obscured all but a suggestion of the face.

Piety ran her hand slowly through the fringe of the shawl. "She's spooky, but kind of sad."

That could be said about a lot of people, thought Coral. "Why aren't you at work? Board of Health finally close that place down?"

Piety frowned. "Of course not. It's a half day for me. I worked breakfast."

"Nothing personal."

"Actually, I've got yesterday's Day Olds right here." She rattled a paper sack bearing the Deacon's logo, the dour-faced Puritan who looked like he just came from burning a witch or flogging a Quaker.

Coral recoiled.

"I bring them to share with the vendors. You know, I give them a few doughnuts; they give me a discount. I get some nice designer knockoffs that way, really cheap. Purses and shoes mostly."

"Good for you." Sounded like little Piety was picking up her employer's entrepreneurial style.

"Would you like a doughnut?" She held out the bag.

"I'm not going to give you a discount."

"I didn't mean that. I was just offering."

"No, thanks. Sugar and sunshine, when you put them together, melt into a sticky mess."

Piety looked blank, apparently missing the jibe.

"Anyway, those things will kill you."

"Oh, no, Mr. Brown says we use pure vegetable oil!"

Coral laughed, knowing her cousin fully capable of re-labeling containers of lard. "Let's see what the dog thinks. Dickon! You want a doughnut?"

Piety cast her a dolorous look but pulled a plain doughnut from the bag and held it out to the dog. He came forward and sniffed it. He walked away.

"Must be watching his waistline," observed Coral. "Or maybe your boss's scent gets into the flour."

Just then, a couple in shorts and I ♥ WELLFLEET shirts detached themselves from the throng. "Oh, aren't these just adorable," trilled the woman.

Coral hoped Piety would leave, but she only stepped out of the way.

"Not bad," said the man. "I could make one myself, though."

"Not like this, you couldn't." With a sigh, Coral explained why her methods and materials were more weatherproof, more durable.

"She's right," the woman told her husband. "Besides, yours wouldn't look so nice. I want to put it in the front yard."

"Did you see what they cost?" He flicked a price tag with his thumb.

His wife ignored him. She seemed to be settling in front of the leaf figure.

"Wait a minute—look at the one leaning against the truck. Is it wearing a Sox shirt?" The husband stepped to the back of the stall. "If we're gonna get one, I want this."

"That costs more."

This is where it got tricky. They'd argue, and maybe buy nothing.

"I have to get the shirts and caps new," Coral explained. "Adds a lot to overhead."

"Could you sell it naked? I could use one of my own jerseys."

Coral was hot and weary. "I'll give you twenty bucks off if you buy both."

The man turned to his wife. "What the hell do we need two scarecrows for? We don't even have a garden."

"It's not a question of needing, stupid. They're decorative. We'll put one in the front yard, one in the back."

"Oh, Jesus. Make it twenty-five off and you've got a deal."

Coral took the pair of hundred dollar bills. She slipped off her sunglasses and propped them on the dash so she could see clearly to give him his change. The wife had wandered off to the booth across the aisle, which sold dried flower arrangements. The husband, pocketing his wallet, met Coral's eyes, paused, and said, "I hate her."

Coral looked away.

The man hefted the Red Sox scarecrow. Coral, behind him, gave it a pat on the cheek. "Bye," she said to it.

"Bye," grunted the man, shifting his burden to a more comfortable position. "Hey," he called to his wife. "You're going to have to carry one of these."

The woman put down a beribboned wreath and wove her way back through the crowd.

"This one's for the front yard," she whispered to Coral. Already burdened by a well-filled shopping bag, she lifted the leaf figure awkwardly, allowing the shawl and skirt to drag along the ground.

Coral seized the woman's arm. "Put her down. You're hurting her."

With an odd look at Coral, the woman propped the figure back on its base.

"Well, what am I going to do? Hulk Hogan here can't carry both of them." She turned to her husband. "We're just going to have to put these in the car now, one at a time, then come back to look at the rest of the booths."

"No way. I'm not going all the way back to the car—it's like half a mile away! I'm going to check out those military antiques in the next aisle, and I want to look at the baseball cards."

"My knight in shining armor." She turned to Coral. "Can we leave them here and pick them up later?"

"I'm closing." She was beginning to regret this sale; the leaf lady was one of her favorites. She was at the point of offering a refund.

Then Piety (Lord, was she still here?) stepped forward. "Come on," she said to the woman. "I'll take one end and you take the other. Then you can come back and catch up with your husband."

To Coral, she said, "I'll just leave my stuff here while you pack."

All the scarecrows were tucked into the back of the truck by the time Piety returned. Dickon had resumed his position in the passenger seat, his huge head emerging from the window.

Coral held Piety's imitation Vera Wang handbag firmly by its crooked seaming, but the sack of doughnuts she pinched with two fingers at arm's length, like a soiled diaper.

When Piety came back, Coral pressed the bags quickly into her hands. "I owe you one."

"No problem. You're my neighbor."

"Yes. Well. I'd better let you get to your shopping. It's late and a lot of people are closing."

"It's okay. I come here all the time. I can chat for awhile. We have some things in common, right, besides where we live? Like we both have weird names."

"How nice of you to say. For the record, yours is a virtue name. People liked them in the old days."

"Virtue name, huh." Piety looked skeptical, then apparently thought of a new topic. "So what's the man like who rents the other cottage?"

"We don't mingle much." In fact, Guy had come around to borrow a screwdriver and a small electric drill. When Coral heard why he needed them, and the rest of the details of his meeting with Jeffrey Brown, she'd been delighted. He was doing better than she hoped. No reason to complicate matters with other introductions.

"He's single, though, right? Is he good looking?"

"You wouldn't like him."

"Oh." Piety looked disappointed. "It's hard to meet nice men. I get tired of being alone, you know."

"There's nothing perfect about marriage, either." As obviously as she could, Coral busied herself packing up the last of her booth. She didn't want to hear tales of the lovelorn.

"No kidding. My mother...."

"Excuse me. You're in my way there."

"Sorry. Anyhow, I know what you're saying. Have you been single long?"

"I'd rather not talk about it."

"Too painful, huh?"

Her back turned, Coral didn't answer.

"Wouldn't it be nice to have someone to take care of you, though? I mean, it's so hard to make a living on the Cape."

"Gets harder every minute," Coral said. The implication didn't seem to bother Piety any more than the moldy smell of reused wrapping materials wafting from adjoining booths, whose owners were now packing up, too.

"There's this older man."

Coral stopped dead, and Piety took the opportunity to swerve her way around, face to face.

"He's married. But I think not happily." Piety's breathing became shallow.

"Don't." Coral said.

"I know, married men. But he's got a lot of money, and he's nice to me, and sometimes I think…"

"Don't tell me any more."

She scowled at the plaintive note in her own voice.

She'd been just a child when people started telling her things she didn't wish to know. Outwardly, she had been no more extraordinary than other shy kids, neither standing out nor quite fitting in. But as early as she could remember, there had been whispered confidences from unknown children in line at ice cream stands or at playgrounds. Stories told in Kindergarten corners. Secrets that made her want to hide, that drew her inside on summer days, kept her from Scout troops and softball teams.

Nevertheless, she was sometimes invited to other girls' parties and sleepovers. She brought overly elaborate gifts to these as compensation for never having parties of her own.

Her desire for solitude caused no ripple at home. An only child, she came from reclusive stock. Her parents had little to do with her, or each other, each sunk in inaccessible worlds of their own. Their great gift to her had been to leave her alone. They provided a roof, food, and clothing and that was that.

Nor was there an extended family. Her father's sister had a son, her cousin Jeffrey Brown, but they had disliked each other from toddlerhood. Holidays brought no tables seating twenty, graduation announcements went unmailed. Blood, among her kin, wasn't thicker than water; it was thinner than sea mist. Coral had the luxury of bringing herself up, free to find her own ideas and philosophies.

When she was fourteen, she attended her last pajama party. In a finished basement of one of the new ranch-style houses in Eastham, a dozen girls had piled their sleeping bags in a corner. Most of them sported their first bras, keeping them on even under their flannel pajamas The evening's entertainment was a supply of five-and-dime store makeup.

They all paired off to do each other's faces. A girl named Lynn volunteered to be Coral's partner. Lynn was the kind of girl who offered a cheerful hello to new kids, opened doors for the ones burdened with casts or crutches, and volunteered to drop off homework for absent classmates. She had sleek chestnut brown hair and a rosebud mouth, and lived in a house with a historic marker, full of Early American furniture that always smelled like lemon polish. There was even a barn with two horses, the envy of every girl in school.

Lynn's family was special in another way, too. Her father was dead. Everyone would have been nice to her because of that, even if she wasn't pretty and smart and good. Now she chattered as she applied blue mascara to Coral's lashes.

"I read in a magazine that blue makes the whites of your eyes whiter. Open them wide. Don't blink. That's it."

"Don't you think it clashes with the green?" Coral ventured. Lynn was everything Coral was not, sweet and easy to admire. Her opinion mattered.

"No, it contrasts. It's kind of interesting."

Lynn looked closely at Coral's eyes, smiling at first, then closer still, the smile fading. Suddenly she swallowed hard. She dropped her voice so it couldn't be heard against the chatter and giggles. "You know last year? When my Dad died?"

Still wide-eyed, Coral nodded.

"And everyone said it was a tragic accident? Then my brother Joey went away to that school way down in Connecticut?"

Lynn's hand fell limp, drawing a blue line down Coral's cheek.

"It wasn't an accident, even though everybody said so. My brother told me."

Coral mouthed an "oh," but no sound came.

"My brother shot him on purpose. My Dad made Joey go hunting. Joey didn't want to go. He likes animals. He wants to be a vegetarian, but my mom says it's not healthy. My dad killed this rabbit, and told Joey to skin it, but Joey wouldn't. So my dad said he'd kill Joey's hamsters if he didn't. He made Joey cry, and Joey never cries anymore—he's fifteen. Well, fourteen then. Dad said he was a baby and pussy, which doesn't mean a cat. So Joey picked up one of the rifles and he shot my Dad right in the chest."

Coral remembered going cold all over.

"He never even told my Mom. Just me."

Lynn tightened her rosebud mouth. "I'm glad he did it," she said. "My Dad was a jerk. Once he..."

Then someone put on a record, "Light My Fire," by The Doors, and the other girls all stood up and began to swivel their narrow hips, their makeup garish in the basement lights.

For a moment, Lynn seemed unsure where she was. Then she ran for the bathroom. Coral followed.

The door was unlocked. Lynn was splashing water over her face, now icy pale except for two bright red circles on her smooth cheeks. "I wasn't supposed to tell," she kept repeating. "Why did you make me tell?"

After that, Lynn avoided her. The other girls followed suit.

And Coral avoided them.

Still, she'd had to exist in the ordinary world, go to school, grow up. The next year, she stayed after class one day to catch up on an algebra assignment she'd missed while home with a cold. Coral couldn't even recall the teacher's name, only her neat maroon dress and tortoiseshell eyeglasses.

"So X equals three. Good job," said the teacher. She and Coral shared the brief, bored smile of people who have only the most mundane connection, but who have reached some goal together.

The glance held too long.

"X can equal twenty years," said the teacher.

Coral paid attention. She thought this was a math lesson.

"My husband is leaving me," said the teacher.

Coral shook her head to say she didn't understand. But really, she did.

"I'm forty-eight. We have a grown son."

Coral crammed the paper they'd been working on into her notebook, the notebook into her satchel.

"How am I supposed to pay the mortgage on one salary?"

"I don't know," said Coral in a small voice, but the teacher didn't seem to notice.

"He hasn't touched me in three years. Not once. Not even a goodnight kiss. In three years."

The heavy satchel knocked over the molded chair as Coral fled, the echo still audible when she reached the empty hallway with its smell of peanut butter and sneakers.

Next day, and as it turned out, the rest of the school year, there had been a substitute teacher for algebra. Even as an adult, Coral wondered what would have happened if she'd reached out and laid her hand, still chubby with childhood, on that teacher's, in the smallest gesture of comfort. What else would she have heard?

She got so she wanted to close her eyes, press her fists over her ears, avoid all sight and sound of other people. She was afraid she'd go mad.

Perhaps I did, Coral thought now.

Piety had the look of a stunned mackerel thrown back in the water. "Okay, you don't have to glare at me. I won't talk to you, if that's how you feel."

I hurt her feelings by cutting her off; now she wants to get even, Coral thought. But she turned her back. "I've got to finish loading."

Piety followed her. "Funny thing, my boss was talking about you just yesterday. I mean, I can tell you two don't get along, but it looks like you're going to do really well from that deal. Some people don't appreciate how lucky they are."

"What deal?" Coral stopped loading. A little kernel of anger began to heat up in her chest.

"Building his development."

Coral gasped. "He said this when?"

"I don't know, a couple days ago. Hasn't he told you about it?"

"Guy Maulkin, the one you were asking about, was he there when your boss told you this?"

"No, just the two of us, me and Mr. Brown. He seemed really excited."

The kernal popped. "Look, you did me a favor, so I want to tell you something. I know you like to go out to the bars at night. I know you're drunk when you get home. Fine. But pull your shades. You never know what's out there."

Piety stepped away. "What are you talking about?"

"Someone might be creeping around the cottages."

"Who? Did you see them?"

"Let's just say I've seen someone who gets excited when he shouldn't."

"Huh?"

"You need to be more careful."

"What are you saying—that I'm some kind of exhibitionist? A drunk? A slut?"

Coral, to her dismay, saw a tear slide down the other woman's cheek.

"I'm saying you need to exercise simple caution. What you do is your own business, but as you said, we're neighbors. I don't want you tempting anybody to…cause trouble."

"Tempting anybody?" Several more tears slid down Piety's cheeks.

"For heaven's sake, I'm just trying to help you."

Piety swallowed a shaky little sob. "You know what I think?" she said. "I think if anybody looks in my windows, it's you. I think you don't have any life of your own and you're an old busybody and you're mean to Mr. Brown." She sniffled. "You act like a witch because that's what you want people to think you are so you never have to be nice to anyone." This time, she let the sob out, a choking *huff*.

Dickon's head jutted out on the driver's side, near where the two women stood. He uttered a sharp warning bark. Piety flinched, clutching the doughnuts so hard that the bag split. Jelly and powdered sugar shot out, speckling both women.

Coral yanked open the truck's door, gave the dog a shove, and got in. Her sunglasses lay on the dashboard where she'd left them while she was packing. She slapped them on so hard it hurt, jammed in the key and gunned the engine.

Piety jumped out of the way. Wiping at her face and shirt, she snaked her way into the now diminished crowd of shoppers and was gone.

Coral gave the steering wheel a sharp rap with the heel of her hand. "See what happens when you try to help somebody?" Dickon licked some of the jelly off her arm, but she brushed him away, ashamed of the quaver in her voice.

Damn people, she thought. Damn relatives and neighbors. Not one had as much sense as God gave straw. Everywhere she looked, nothing but misjudgment and delusion. Damn the whole world.

Why the hell hadn't she checked up on that Maulkin fool? She'd been insane to trust him, to let Jeffrey Brown slip to the back of her mind even for an instant.

Sounding her horn at pedestrians, swearing, scorning the ten mile per hour speed limit, she made her way through uneven aisles of booths being disassembled, into the weekend traffic on Route 6 and home.

The Hand Mirror

In 1848, a Wonderstrand sea captain, Obadiah Snow, took a wife at one of his ports of call. A letter from the era names an island in the South Seas as her place of birth; another letter says South America or India. Both describe her as dark of eye and hair, with striking features, sure to be perceived as heathenish and strange by the standards of nineteenth century Cape Cod. She had learned the English language, but spoke it with an accent as pungent as an unfamiliar spice.

A man of strong opinion and independent spirit, Captain Snow was known as a hard master, but among the best at his trade. He owned the ship he sailed, and those who manned it came home far wealthier than the average sailor. Honeymoon or not, he continued his journey. His bride traveled with him for the first months of their marriage, during which they visited many ports, trading with the locals. In one of these, he bought her a silver hand mirror, encrusted with pearls and fine stones, and had it engraved with both their names.

When at last they began the voyage homeward, the ship was caught in a terrible storm. The captain, unwilling to sacrifice paying cargo, threw over items belonging to himself and others on board, barrels of provisions, clothing, souvenirs of faraway places. Among these were his young wife's trunks, including the one containing the mirror.

The ship and all aboard survived. They returned to Wonderstrand, where he made restitution to every soul aboard for objects lost during the storm. He installed his wife in a newly built house near a bluff over-looking the sea.

There, she did not thrive. "I cannot see myself," she lamented. The captain pointed out the new gilt hand mirror on her dressing table, the large framed one above it, the ornate beveled one that graced their front hall, but she only shook her head. "I'm neither in there," she said, "nor here in this windy, gray place. I can't see myself."

Her neighbors, too, acted as if she were invisible. None befriended her, in spite of her husband's wealth and status — or perhaps because of it, for she wore jewels and silks of an opulence not favored by the local farmers' and fishermen's wives. Nor did the chill winter, the snow and sleet, diminish themselves for this daughter of the tropics. When she looked for her reflection in the swells that lapped the shore below her house, she saw only the dark waters of the northern sea.

Within a year, she died in childbirth, along with her stillborn daughter, an infant dark-haired like her mother.

The captain, it's said, went mad with grief and remorse.

In due time, he went back to sea. For many months he never left his ship, but one day, his loneliness drove him ashore on a faraway coast. It was a market day, and he wandered through the stalls of colorful fruits and vegetables, dyed cloth and carved totems. He happened to stop at one that sold beads and other trinkets, and there, in the midst, he saw an ivory brooch he knew to have been among his wife's things. The old woman who ran the stand, frightened by his ferocious questioning, called her sons to protect her. Placated by many coins, one of them, who spoke a smattering of English, told the captain that his mother had found the brooch on the beach, that the whole village had found treasure strewn on the sand from a broken trunk that had washed ashore one morning. This was not unusual. All along that coast, people had found such objects and traded them with the ships that passed through.

From that day, Captain Snow sailed a roundabout course, visiting and revisiting any port where there might be a marketplace. At first, the holds of his ship were filled, but soon no merchant would trust him because he no longer delivered their cargo on time, no longer could be depended on to return with materials ordered. He became obsessed with one thing only, finding the mirror that he believed to have retained his wife's image.

Captain Snow was an educated man. Did he know that many cultures believe that an object may retain the soul of the one who possessed it?

Eventually all but a handful of the most derelict sailors abandoned him, for he could pay little beyond rum and gin. His ship became unfit to sail; probably it sunk somewhere near the coast of Spain. Again he survived, and signed aboard any ship that would take him to the ports he wished to visit.

Emaciated, ragged, unbarbered, he returned at last to his empty house in Wonderstrand, bringing with him only a knapsack filled with salt-encrusted trinkets. The taxes on his property had not been paid for years; only his former standing in the community had kept it from being taken over by the town. He sold most of the furnishings to pay the taxes and lived there alone, in the simplest way.

The few neighbors who saw him buying or trading for the few supplies he needed, or hunting fowl in the marshes, reported that he was much altered. Where in his youth he'd been stern, he now bore an expression almost beatific in its gentleness. The smile so few had seen before his marriage now never left his face. This they attributed to simple mindedness.

Several years had passed when the town was awakened by a red sky atop the bluff. Before help arrived, Captain Snow's house burned to the ground with him inside.

Did there lie, among the ashes and bones, a twisted, tarnished bit of silver, with shards of broken glass still clinging to it? No one recorded finding such an object, but I like to think they did.

It makes me wonder about the throngs who haunt the Cape's flea markets, yard sales, and antique shops. Maybe some of them, of us, share Captain Snow's belief, and seek that one object among all others that will provide us with what we most desire.

What, after all, is the logic that governs the irregular verb to seek?

—From *Wonderstrand Tales*, by Guy Thomas Maulkin

Chapter 10

"Our body to be possessed by two different spirits;
so that half of the visage shall express one mood, and the other half another."

—HAWTHORNE, STORY IDEA, *AMERICAN NOTEBOOKS*

Thunder and lighting blasted with Old Testament fury just outside his front door, or so it seemed to Guy. Leaping up, he dropped the real estate licensing manual he'd been reading, scattering the clippings and articles he'd tucked between its pages. A glance at the window revealed a clear sky. He pressed his ear to the door. Amidst the pounding and crackling anger, he recognized a voice.

Coral. He'd forgotten to return her tools.

Guy opened the door, letting in a wedge of fury he tried to stem with apologies. "Let me just get your drill and things…only take a minute… awfully sorry."

"Drill? Forget the damned drill. I've been trying to catch you for days."

He arrested his hand in mid-lift toward the tools, which lay on the kitchenette counter. Given the puffs of brimstone bursting from his companion, he half expected to see his appendage transformed into a toad's flipper or a pig's cloven hoof.

"I haven't been here much. I'm at work most of the time."

"At night?"

"Very late. There's a lot to learn. You're probably asleep when I get in, and I've been leaving early in the mornings, too. I have breakfast at the office or with Mr. Brown."

"What do you know about this project of his? Why haven't you told me?"

"Which project?" He sounded stupid, and it irritated him as it never used to. At his new job, he'd begun to feel quite competent and assured.

"Which do you think? What's that snuffling hypocrite trying to do to Wonderstrand? To the cottages?" Her words snapped like sparks.

"I haven't heard anything about it," he stammered.

"Well, you'd better learn faster. Your boss is planning to tear down my home. I didn't send you in there to let this happen."

"I thought it was to learn and, um, emulate."

"And report back to me, you ninny."

"But I can't tell you what I don't know." To his dismay, he'd begun to squeak and stutter like his old self.

"Haven't you gotten him to trust you yet? After all the pointers I gave you?"

With a mighty effort, Guy called forth the *savoir faire* he'd picked up lately. "Definitely. I'm pretty proud of the way I..."

She brushed his pride away like a greenhead fly. "Just tell me everything you saw. From the beginning."

His first week working for Jeffrey Goodman Brown had been a whirlwind, the most glorious of his life. Brown's wariness had begun to dissipate almost immediately.

"You're a quick study," his new boss had allowed. "Got that academic polish."

Guy accepted this truth with appealing modesty.

Brown squinted at him. "I'd even go so far as to say you have an aristocratic quality—as do I. But you have that young lean look while I (he patted his paunch) have substance. Not a bad working combination. You have a middle name?"

"It's Thomas. Guy Thomas Maulkin."

"Perfect. From now on, you're G.T. Sounds like a go-getter. Fire in the belly. Much better than 'guy'—that sounds like just anybody. Therefore a nobody. Not the image you want if you're going to play with the big boys."

"G.T." Guy rolled it over on his tongue and found it strange but not unpleasant. Like his new clothes, it could be made to fit.

"What you call yourself affects how people see you. Remember that. Take me, for instance. Jeffrey Goodman Brown's a name people respect."

Soon enough, they'll respect G.T. Maulkin, thought Guy.

He had a small office to himself, where he spent his first days studying up on Brown's various concerns. Under the adoring tutelage of Irene, the office manager, he learned to use the software and phone systems. Guy had the scholar's habit of taking careful notes; he listed all the steps in linear fashion, connected by arrows. By afternoon he felt acclimated enough to answer phones the rest of the day.

At this task, he triumphed. Without the worry of speaking face to face, of reminding himself constantly to make eye contact, his dulcet tones and suave manners charmed all callers. He orated into his new headset, drawing clients into the office as if they were conventioneers at an open bar.

Here Coral interrupted. "Who calls?"

"I haven't recognized any names."

"Well, keep a record. Get an idea what they're calling about. Listen for anything related to building and planning—architects, construction companies, permits."

Guy bobbed his head. "I'll try."

"You'd better do more than try. How much direct contact do you have with Brown?"

"He's in and out of the office. He took me to lunch on Thursday."

"Such a sweetheart. What did you talk about?"

"Well, the view, at first. It was a waterfront restaurant, and…"

"Don't be too impressed. It was deductible."

But Guy had been impressed. Brown had ordered for both of them, shrimp cocktails to start, then steak tips.

"Did he mention business?"

"Only in general terms. Except for the doughnut shop—he said that was his sentimental favorite."

Coral uttered a snort.

"He said that on Cape Cod, you're never far from a doughnut shop or a liquor store."

"Well, he's right about that. The only other thing you can find on every corner around here is an AA meeting."

"So he picked up on the trend, he said. He bought a liquor store up-Cape, but didn't enjoy it much, too many laws, too much interference. So he sold it and opened Deacon's."

"Yes, yes. Nothing about the cottage colony?"

Guy shook his head.

"All right. You seem to have worked your way into his good graces. But you need to be part of the planning. Upcoming projects. Inner workings. Don't forget I got you in there. You've got to do something for me."

"Glad to, of course." To his shame, he'd nearly forgotten Coral since he'd borrowed the tools to fix Brown's odometer.

"Be sharp. You never know what might be useful."

Guy considered this. "That's true. I didn't remember about odometers until that day I saw his car."

"Nice bit of work, that. Keep it up."

Guy basked in the praise and began to relax. His life fairly abounded in compliments lately. The whole world had come to appreciate Guy Maulkin.

Coral was looking at him closely, and he blushed.

"I'll check back with you—and soon." She spun on her heels and was halfway out the door.

"Wait," he called. "Your tools."

Her skirt had pockets deep as kettle ponds. She rummaged in them briefly, then tossed him something metal and jingling. It landed short; when he bent to pick it up, he saw an oversized paper clip linking two keys.

"The big one's for that shed behind my cottage. Put the tools in there. And while you're at it, take some more water. You'll find a couple of gallon jugs."

"That's where your private source is?"

"Yes. You'll see a pump. It's an old well, goes back to the colonists or maybe even the Nauset tribes. When the cottage colony was built, they drilled a new one. Better location or something."

"So this just serves your cottage?"

"If it's any of your business, all the cottages use the same well for their taps, including mine. I built the shed around the old one and keep it going for memory's sake. The water's sweeter."

He nodded. He'd become almost addicted to its smoky, deep-earth flavor.

Though they took the same path, she walked much faster. He heard her door slam just as he approached her cottage. The shed, capacious and solid, stood directly behind, a few yards from her back door. Inside, he clicked on the overhead light to reveal various scarecrow makings stashed everywhere, but in good order. Gourds drying, bits of plastic and wood sorted by size. The place smelled pleasantly of new lumber from the stack of scraps in a corner, and something else, a damp, mossiness with an undertone of minerals.

A circular stone wall, maybe four feet high, filled the shed's center. It looked just like the base of an old-fashioned wishing well, but the peaked roof was gone and the opening had been closed off. A modern pump rose from the top, incongruous against the old stone and mortar.

On the back wall, boxes filled a row of metal shelving. With a peek outside to make sure he was alone, Guy lifted the lids of one or two. They contained what he assumed to be more scarecrow supplies, clothing, yarn, unidentifiable odds and ends. He smiled, resolving to buy himself one of Coral's scarecrows on his first payday, maybe one of the historical characters. In his head, he could hear Jeffrey Brown mocking the waste of cash, so he wouldn't tell him. The scarecrow could stay inside his cottage to scare away dark thoughts, doubts and disbelief in himself. Like it or not, he had a kinship with the effigies. Wasn't he wearing garments that had been meant for their rigid limbs? Also, as Coral had reminded him, he owed her a debt.

Recalling his benefactress, he noted that the uppermost shelves were well beyond her reach, and he didn't see a ladder or stool. He wondered if these boxes, obviously of little interest to her, contained the old papers she'd mentioned, from the early days of the property. Stretching, he pulled one down and sat next to it on the cement floor, cold as a tomb even in June.

He brushed away a few web-bound remains of earwigs and made a cursory examination of the contents. Bills, receipts, lists, all in the careful, looped handwritings of other generations. Two or three bundles of folded stationery, tied with string. A couple of bound books might have been town histories, ledgers, or ships' logs. Yellowed newspaper clippings announcing wars, declaring peace, a few obituaries, accounts of local politics and petty crimes. The kinds of things people clip out, then forget.

He'd begun to read more closely when he became aware that his own breathing, fast and shallow, had become so loud that the shed seemed filled with it. He held his inhalation.

The panting continued.

He whirled around to see Dickon, black tongue lolling between strong teeth, watching him from the doorway. Coral stepped around from behind the dog.

Guy leaped to his feet, bumping his head on a shelf. "You'd mentioned some old papers, relating to the history of the colony, and I happened to…"

"Couldn't resist, could you?"

Together they looked down at the papers as if they might speak. The dog poked his snout around the side of her skirt.

An hour ago, she'd seemed so angry, but now? She seemed almost pleased.

"I wouldn't steal anything. It's just that old documents, even though they're not my real work anymore—I can't help being curious about them."

Coral raised her free hand in a weary gesture he took to mean that no apologies were necessary. She was his friend. She'd understand.

"It's like I touch this old paper, and my fingers draw the stories out. Like ghosts."

Why did he feel compelled to tell her how dust still enticed him like perfume? That even though his career, his very identity, was now rocketing toward the stars, he still thrilled at the touch the dry leaf-smelling pages?

As he unburdened himself, in terms he thought quite lyrical, he saw her foot slip out from under her skirt to poke the dog.

The animal, taking a cue, set up a howl that echoed through the shed like a choir of demons.

"The dog has to pee," Coral said. "As for that junk," she indicated the papers, "knock yourself out. Take it all with you. Now give me the keys."

Guy regretted having to stop talking. Clever insights about himself lumped up on his tongue. Nevertheless, another part of him twitched with cupidity. "How long can I borrow them?"

"I don't much care."

"And can I use them?"

"I'd expect nothing less of you. But didn't you say your authorial career was over?"

He opened his mouth, shut it again.

She waited.

"I just wondered if there were private papers, family documents...."

"People see precisely what I intend them to see. As for my valuables, I keep track of them." Something that might have been a smile curved her mouth, adding to his confusion.

"Don't forget the water."

"Water," he repeated. He needed a drink of it very badly all of a sudden.

When he returned from carrying the first load of cartons back to his own cottage, Coral had gone. Dickon lay just outside the shed, his mismatched eyes following every step. Last, Guy filled the gallon jugs to the brim, along with some other containers he'd retrieved from his kitchenette. His arms loaded, he turned to see Coral emerge again, this time to lock the shed. He called goodbye and thanks.

She returned that same odd smile. He congratulated himself on working through a delicate situation. His personal charm seemed to have increased tenfold in the past two weeks. From his orphan status, he now had all the mentors anyone could ever want. As for Coral, he felt a tenderness toward her that was almost filial. He vowed to pay closer attention to anything that might relate to the colony.

Back in his own cottage, he couldn't resist picking through the cartons. He found a diary with a old-fashioned bucolic landscape on the cover, a number of letters filled with tiny handwriting, filling the pages front and back. They'd take time to decipher, though, and the hour was growing late; he had to get up for his new job tomorrow. Snapping his priorities firmly into order, he stored the cartons with the discarded remains of his book and went to bed.

On the following morning, Jeffrey Brown strode into Guy's quarters. "Let's you and me go for a spin in the Eldo," he proposed.

As they drove off, Brown beamed at the odometer, which now read just over 50,000. "Time we move out into the world a bit," he said.

As they rode, Guy found it was easy to let his boss do most of the talking.

"How well do you know Cape Cod? Washashore, aren't you?" Brown continued without waiting for an answer. "Well, don't worry. Few of us true natives around these days. You've got to be smart to flourish here, you know. Not easy to make a decent living. Without the tourists, what do you have? Fishing? Messy, dangerous. Construction? Not much building land left, and if you do find some, you're buried in regulations."

He spread his body into his kingly pose. "But it's like anything else; the cream rises to the top. I can tell you what you need to know about Cape Cod. People call me a pillar of the community; I expect you've heard that. I'm a churchgoing man, naturally, and a tireless volunteer. I was three times a selectman—three times! Had to resign, though. Demands of business."

"Understandable," Guy offered.

"You know I've got a lot of rental properties, commercial and residential. They bring in a nice income most of the time, but a couple of them give me trouble. That's where we're going now, to check one out. This first one had a good rental history until last year. Not a lot of bites for this summer, though."

Perhaps here was just the sort of opportunity Coral had told him to look out for. Field experience.

Brown parked in front of a half-cape on the bay side of Wellfleet. A dull rain made the place look dismal, but Guy had lived in a lot worse. It was run down enough to have some real age to it, but he found it hard to tell an antique cape from newer ones. The exteriors didn't vary much. Old shingles weathered from tan to gray, but an eighteenth century structure might have been reshingled last year. Likewise, windows might have been replaced, additions built, roofs retiled. And reproductions of lots of venerable New England classics got better all the time—he'd even seen slate tombstones, those mainstays of colonial cemeteries, their winged skulls and draped urns effaced by vandals and weather, replaced by cast metal ones. One ringing tap and you knew the difference, but from a few feet away, who could tell?

"I'm thinking of selling," Brown said. The place used to bring in close to a grand a week, but this year I could only book it for the first half of August. Not worth it. Still, it's a buyers' market now. Bad time." He pulled out a set of keys and let them in.

A wall of odor made up of moldy linoleum, old mattresses, warm refrigerators and ill-treated bathrooms hit them. Brown pressed a crisply ironed handkerchief over his nose and mouth, gesturing toward the door and front window. Guy propped the door open with a rock, then struggled vainly with the flyspecked window. It refused to open. Brown stepped over, gave the frame a hearty blow with the heel of his hand, loosening it; the two of them working together finally forced it up. As both men leaned into it to gulp the outside air, it crashed down again, nearly taking their noses with it.

"It's the damned tenants," Brown said. "They destroy everything."

Guy, remembering the lack of upkeep landlords had lavished on some of his college apartments, said nothing.

"I've got half a dozen places like this. Don't know if they're worth the bother. I hang on to them because even though they look small, they can sleep a lot of people. Come on, I'll show you."

There were indeed beds for a dozen, three doubles in a warren of small bedrooms, two convertible sofas in the living room, and a selection of folding cots and cribs.

"Built in the sixties?" Guy guessed, noting the avocado green metal cabinets in the kitchen.

"Yes. Been a rental ever since. I picked it up cheap on a foreclosure."

Guy opened one cupboard. They'd been cleared, but a desiccated clump of brown fur that in livelier days had been a mouse rested in one corner. Brown looked it at it a second too long, blinked, and turned away, moving down a hall to the bathroom. Guy closed the cupboard door gently, then followed.

In a bathroom, a shower curtain blackened with science fiction-worthy vegetable substances undulated in the breeze from the open front door. Throughout the house the husks of insects lay thickly, accumulated over the fall and winter.

"So what do you think?" Brown asked, mopping his brow with his handkerchief. Though he'd touched nothing with it except his own face, it looked soiled. "Sell? Hold? It's paid itself off; question is now, will it make a good profit after repairs, upkeep, and taxes?"

Guy knew he was being tested, so took his time to answer. He flipped open the notebook he was carrying and scribbled a few lines on a fresh page and passed it to Brown.

Remember those Cape Cod vacations when you were a kid? The cottages that smelled of the beach, where you could get sand on the floor, and no one minded? Where you could eat a Popsicle without worrying where the cherry-red drops fell? This year, escape from the hum of electronics, the tyranny of décor. You have that at home, right? Give the gift of a real old fashioned summer to your own kids—and to yourself.

"G.T., my boy, I think you've hit on something." said Brown. "Pull in the GenXers. They'll buy any old junk that reminds them of their childhood. Turn a liability into a draw."

"Exactly!" Guy said. "You've seen those ads in the *Globe*'s travel section, 'Cape Cod—a short trip to far away'? We play on that, sell this kind of house as a short trip to nostalgia. "Then finish the ad with the usual: 'Room for the whole clan, bike to bay beaches,' and so on."

"Excellent. No need for a lot of repairs, as long as it passes inspection. And I can deal with that." Brown winked as he handed the notebook back to Guy. "More of these places will be on the market now. Recession and all that. A man with some means can pick up foreclosures for a song. The trick is unloading them again. Can't rely on renting them all. There's another way your skills can come in handy, I think."

"How's that?"

"Well, a man gets laid off, right? To cheer himself and his family up, he takes a cheap weekend at his cousin's place on the Cape. Looks at a real estate flier. Sees a property half the size of his house in Boston or Hartford or wherever, realizes he could trade it for his equity. No mortgage. He thinks 'Maybe I could open up a little business, live here all year. Goodbye, daily grind.'"

"Sounds great. I could play on that in the ads."

"Exactly. Places like this could be made to appeal to a man like that, and I, or we, could make a good buck out of it. Trouble is, it's not quite as simple as it sounds. First of all, foreclosed properties might come cheap, especially if you happen to know the lender involved, but it's a tricky business. Lowlifes don't pay their mortgages, then think they have a right to resent it when the bank is forced to step in. People don't want to face reality. Take the kind of person I mentioned, the one who sells out and comes down here to live. He finds out that little business he started takes up more time than he put in at his job. Then after a couple of years, it fails. He followed his dream and now he's lost that, too. He's angry. He's disillusioned. His family thinks he's a failure. Bitter people don't bother to leave the places broom clean, if you follow me."

"And you don't want a lot of expense to fix the houses up."

"Of course not. But there are worse things. People won't get out until they have to. They don't care about upkeep if they don't own the house anymore. They rip down the sheriff's notices and unroll the sleeping bags. Sometimes we have to insure that they're gone, once and for all. Think you could handle the personal side?"

Guy visualized himself, black-coated and mustachioed, driving widows and children out into the street. To relieve a sudden nausea, he pulled out his water bottle and drank.

The image dissolved. He saw a family waving goodbye, telling him it was all for the best because Grandma had that big place in Vermont and she was getting on, so it was a blessing for everyone if they moved in with her. In his vision, Guy scooped up a toy left behind and placed it in the arms of a grateful toddler.

"I could certainly try."

"You, sir, are going to be a valuable asset. Your winged prose will make the most mildew-scented hovel sound like a palace, and you aren't afraid to get your hands dirty." Brown rubbed his own hands together with gusto. "Now how about some lunch?"

This time, Brown chose a trendy place in Orleans. "Lobsters all around," he told the waitress. "Two pounder for me. Same for you, G.T.?"

Guy agreed but felt his confidence slipping. Though he'd lived near the East Coast his whole life, he'd never eaten a lobster before. His foster families certainly hadn't served them, he'd never been able to afford anything marked "Market Price," and no one had been in the habit of buying him meals before this. How did one work his way through that hard red shell? Know which parts were supposed to be eaten and which not?

When Brown ordered two Jack Daniels on the rocks, Guy interrupted. "Put mine in a tall glass, if you don't mind," he told the waitress.

She and Brown both lifted eyebrows, but neither commented.

When the drinks came, Guy pulled out his bottle of water and filled his glass to the top. "Whiskey and water is my drink," he explained, as if he drank it all the time. "I'm as particular about the water as the whiskey."

Brown looked pointedly at the faded Poland Spring label. "Ever tried Evian? Or Pellegrino? Oh, well. We all have our unique tastes, don't we?"

Guy drank. When the lobsters arrived, he had a plan. He watched everything his boss did, then followed suit. No projectiles of shell and flesh assaulted neighboring tables; the strange gray lungs lay discarded with the carcass. And the meat was delicious, like sea spray licked from the lips on a sunny day, but sweeter.

"So tell me," Brown said, "about this book you were writing."

"It's nothing, really. No money or recognition in it."

"Probably not. Who has time to read fiction?"

"It wasn't fiction exactly. More like history, I suppose. I was retelling some of the local tales."

"You mean like Black Sam Bellamy, that sort of thing? Nothing wrong with local color, of course. Tourists like it. But you're right, it won't get you anywhere."

"Well, these tales were specifically from the Wonderstrand area. Pretty much forgotten."

"Like what?"

"Old laws. Mysteries. Landmarks. Odd characters."

Brown's eyes glazed over. "Hmm. I'm not a literary man. More practical minded."

"Well, I've moved beyond that. Wonderstrand's a strange place, though. That's what drew me there."

Brown's face brightened. "You think all this historical stuff makes a place desirable? I'm talking an upscale clientele now, of course."

"Oh, definitely. I was reading the other day—might have been in *The Wall Street Journal*—that people pay extra for the haunted bedroom in certain hotels. The Lizzie Borden murder room's part of a bed-and-breakfast now, and it's always booked way in advance."

"The hell you say!"

"Really. It's the old 'George Washington Slept Here' panache. If George haunted a place, that would be even better."

"But to buy, to live? Not to take the kiddies for an educational outing?"

"More so, maybe."

"You know, you're right. History's always been a selling point on the Cape. The Mayflower and all that. People with money, and they're still out there, recession or not, that sort wants Jacuzzis and maybe solar panels, sure, but that's not all. They want to look out at cranberry bogs from the custom window over that Jacuzzi and visualize Olde Cape Cod. More fools they. You think this book could glamorize Wonderstrand?"

Guy considered. *Wonderstrand Tales* would certainly appeal to people like himself, but which self? The book-sodden loser who subsisted on stale snack food? Or the snappily-dressed tiger dining on market-priced crustaceans? "I think it might bring Wonderstrand to your—our—best clients' attention."

"That would make a change, all right. You know, G.T., I think you ought to finish that book. Make it charming. Picturesque. With just enough violence to show that men were men. Page turning stuff. Think you can do that?"

Guy squared his shoulders. "I can try."

"Do more than try, my boy. That's how you succeed." Brown swallowed his last mouthful of lobster. "Always save the claw for last. Best part. Now listen, there's one more thing I want you to do for me."

These days it seemed Guy had so many things to do. There was another mission he was supposed to keep in mind, but in the sensual pleasure of food, drink, and newfound confidence, he couldn't quite recall it.

"I've got a specific deal in the planning stages." Brown leaned forward, his voice low. "I'm going to need to depend on you."

By now Guy had observed Jeffrey's behavior among people. To those who wanted something from him, he behaved like a benevolent king, granting (or withholding) alms. He was ever ready with a *tut* or two at someone's bad luck, a quick insincere compliment at someone's good fortune. With those from whom he wished a favor, he was less jovial.

Guy knew what was expected. "Absolutely," he said.

"The worst piece of property I own is that cottage colony in Wonderstrand. The very one where you live, but don't let that concern you. You'll be moving somewhere better before long. That place is a white elephant, an anachronism. Ripe for development."

Development. In a rush, Guy remembered his other mission: to report back to Coral.

"Of course what I'm saying to you here goes no further. Is that understood?"

Guy swallowed hard. Now what? He couldn't serve two masters. He looked down at the lipstick-colored carapace of his lobster. He could still taste drawn butter and whiskey.

"I'm with you," he answered.

Chapter 11

*"I need monotony...an eventless exterior life—before
I can live in the world within."*

—HAWTHORNE

Coral woke to a gray sky, the clouds thin as gruel. Weary of her anger, of the battle with her cousin, she could see no alternative but to fight. Without knowing the details of Jeffrey Brown's plan, she nevertheless heard the bubble and hiss of trouble brewing. The walls of her cottage, her refuge, seemed less dependable by the day. This involvement with other people had taken its toll.

She'd managed Guy Maulkin well enough. He'd followed exactly where she'd led, seen just what she'd wished, though that triumph was spoiled by the bitter aftertaste of her encounter with Piety Rugosa. "Mean to cousin Jeffrey" indeed. If the little fool knew the truth, she'd change her tune.

Why did people refuse to see what was in front of their faces?

It irked Coral to admit a kind of empathy with Piety. Apparently, the younger woman had passed the wide-eyed ingénue stage and begun to take a serious look at her options. She might be teetering on the verge of repudiating romance in general. The beginning of wisdom, Coral thought. People mate for all sorts of reasons once cynicism sets in: lust, practicality, avarice. She couldn't quite suppress a curiosity about which of these most guided Piety.

Of course, some of the disillusioned chose solitude.

Had the situation been reversed, Coral wouldn't have listened to her own advice, either. She knew the sound of her own voice, the sharp notes, the language, abrupt and profane. Put her on a city street and she'd be taken for a muttering bag lady. She probably looked the part, too. Far more care went into the clothes she put on her scarecrows than what she hung on her own back. She combed her hair every morning without looking at it, hadn't even had it cut in decades. When she brushed her teeth, she rarely glanced up at the mirror over the sink. The last lipstick she'd bought had melted into a sticky mud-colored clay.

Today she happened to be wearing a pair of full black trousers that flapped about her legs, and a navy blue cape with a hood, probably once part of some uniform. No wonder she'd been called a witch. Once, like Piety, she'd worn clothes that made men turn their heads and smile, had deepened the green of her eyes with liner, sweetened her lips and cheeks into ripe peaches. But where had the effort gotten her? Why do we do what we do in youth? Or in maturity, for that matter. Our hearts are broken, our dreams disabled, and we wander in directions all wrong.

"Maudlin," she jeered at herself. "Stop it."

Dickon looked at her reproachfully.

"Not you. Go away and let me think."

He ambled off to another room.

Her relations with her two neighbors seemed to come down to this: interfere only for worthwhile cause, and worthwhile meant Coral's own. Enough do-gooder nonsense. Guy was useful, but the other people had to manage their affairs as they saw fit. As long as they didn't get in her way, or God forbid, tell her about themselves, it was none of her business. At least dark glasses kept people from looking into *her* soul.

Satisfied with that resolution, she nevertheless felt dry and empty as a beached clamshell, even on this damp day. She needed the outdoors, the cathedral of the sea and sky. If there was a God, a great spirit able to confer balm to the soul, to clear stony paths, he (and what folly, attaching genitals, male or female, to the ineffable!) made his home there. Yes, a walk in relative peace. She supposed she owed it to the damned dog.

She parked at the Little Creek lot in Eastham, clipped on the dog's leash, and crossed the street. A path through the woods, then a wooden bridge over the marsh, would take them to the beach. The rain fell more softly under the trees, tapping at the last year's carpet of dead leaves and new green seedlings. She watched a ridge like an unfurled ribbon rise underneath, something small and mysterious fleeing. A snake? A field mouse? Or just the tail of the wind?

She would have liked to speak to this invisible presence, to say that she and the dog meant no harm. Wasn't it better to talk to wild creatures, to the rustling in the trees, to the logs that squeaked and snapped in her fireplace, even to her scarecrows, than to people? But why burden some poor mouse with her thoughts? Best just to be silent.

From the top of the short boardwalk through the dunes, Coral plotted her course. While the chilly temperatures weren't unusual for June, the misty rain left the beach nearly deserted. Just to the north, a surfer, clad head to toe in a black wetsuit, sat mourning the flat seas, his board stuck in the sand like a tombstone. Two, no, three solitary walkers were visible in the same direction. To the south, a couple huddled under a waterproof blanket; a surf fisherman a quarter mile or so beyond them. Like herself, these people were drawn irresistibly to the sea on this dreary day. Experience told her to expect one of two responses from those she passed: they'd be eager to chat, to share their troubles, or they'd wish to hunker down in their private thoughts, wouldn't even look her way if she gave them a wide berth.

The couple had each other, the fisherman his poles and lines. The surfer and walkers presented the greater risk. She tightened the hood of the cape and headed south.

The dog tugged on the leash, no doubt believing he'd been patient long enough. He stopped every few paces to claw the sand with his shovel-like paws, sniffing at whatever he found with the discrimination of an epicure. A half tide falling exposed a stretch of heavier, darker sand. At its scalloped boundary, Dickon unearthed bits of debris, some of which disappeared into his capacious mouth.

"Don't swallow anything! I don't want you puking all over my floors."

He answered with a grin-like contortion of teeth and black lips, inky tongue lolling.

They walked on. The gloom suited her.

As Coral passed the blanketed couple, she saw the man cup his hand around the cheek of the woman as if her face were a rare bird, perched for a moment that might never come again. His companion gazed up at him with equal wonder.

Coral turned away. To her own confusion, an emotion akin to loneliness sank over her. She shook it off. She was behaving no better than Guy Maulkin, with his delusions, his prophetic lights and dreams.

Once she and the dog had passed the fisherman, who faced the sea like a pillar carved of driftwood, she paused to watch the tiny flittering plovers, dashing at the sea on their spindly legs, pecking at miniscule creatures, then racing back. Even today's waves, little more than ripples, could engulf them. She looked at the opaque sea and shivered.

A jerk at her arm told her the leash had gone taut; the dog had come to a dead stop behind her. He sniffed at the sand, then commenced digging again, but daintily this time, with the tips of his paws. He clasped something in his front teeth and trotted over to her.

"Now what?"

He dropped what he held in the sand at her feet, revealing a slice of deep blue, pure as a summer dusk, curved as the dome of the sky. She bent over and picked it up. She'd never seen a piece of sea glass so fine.

"Oh," she said. Then again, "oh." She had few words for wonder, even fewer for gratitude.

With a twitch of his tail, the dog galumphed forward to the end of his leash.

When the salt spray and the mist began to sink into his coat, making him stink terribly, she didn't complain. When he barked unmusically at the gulls in his path, she never told him "hush."

The drizzle at last began to diminish; the brightness to the west grew. Against the gray flannel sky there now lay ropes of gold. Coral felt the pull of a smile against the muscles of her face before she recognized the impulse. Pure joy, that. Quick to emerge and quick to fade.

They walked until Nauset Light came into view, then turned around. The sun now shone intermittently. Wisps of fog swept along the shore. "Time to head home," she told the dog.

The brightening sky had drawn more people out. Coral kept her gaze down as she approached the path off the beach.

Where it joined the boardwalk, three teenagers jostled her, two boys and a girl. Coral's ankle bent sideways in the sand, causing a shot of pain. The dog growled. Coral regained her balance, held him back. "You bite one of them, the animal warden comes knocking," she warned him.

Nevertheless, she felt her temper rising, gathering, where caution would be more appropriate. Only days had passed since the last high school shooting, somewhere out west. Only a few months since the one before that. Where had that been? She couldn't remember, but an angry teenaged boy had shot several people. Elsewhere, a stabbing by a twelve year old. Danger might lie behind the most innocent faces.

The kids moved on a few steps. All she could see was their backs. The boys were obscured under baggy pants and T-shirts, could have been weight lifters or beanpoles. One had the twisted golden curls of a cherub or a druggie; the other had a buzz cut, a style that suggested head lice or neo-Nazis. The girl had long dark hair pulled through the hole of a base-ball cap, and wore a gauzy skirt so long that it swept a trail in the sand, blurring the prints of her bare feet.

Then the boy with the curls turned. "Sorry, ma'am," he said. The other boy added, "Yeah, sorry. We all had our heads up our asses." The girl slapped at him. "Show some manners," she said.

Ordinary kids. Visitors, probably, carried away by the unfamiliar head-iness of sea and shore. Coral made an effort to look pleasant, to show she understood, probably failing. Was she becoming the kind of woman who took offense at every bump, every slight, real or imagined? She didn't get her jollies from other people's secrets, the way her cousin did, but like him, she expected misdeeds and trouble behind every face, in every heart.

She and the dog trudged up the walkway. Storms had eroded the dunes around it more with every season. So much was washed away, every day, every year, so much laid bare. Yet the walk seemed steeper. They continued past the old Coast Guard Station, now decommissioned, then on to the viewing platform with its panoramic view of sky and sea, where permanent displays enlightened tourists about the power of storms. A tall woman, heavy set and red-faced, stood there already, facing the beach. She grabbed Coral's arm.

"Can you believe that? Delinquents, that's all they are!"

Coral yanked her arm loose and huffed at the woman, who didn't notice; her attention was fixed on a cluster of activity maybe a hundred yards to the north, opposite the direction from which Coral had come.

Most of the beach now lay in sunlight. The kids who'd bumped Coral had formed a semicircle around what at first looked like a log. Squinting a little, Coral made out that it was actually a baby harbor seal that had hauled up above the tide line. The girl in the skirt dug in her backpack, pulled out and unwrapped something, and waved it near the seal's nose, trying to entice the animal toward the water. It raised its head, but stayed put.

"They're not supposed to do that!"

The big woman was right. Anybody who read the signs posted near the beaches, who'd ever sat through a naturalist's lecture on a school field trip, knew you were supposed to leave the seals alone. But the woman's gleeful self-righteousness, her mottled face and loud mouth offended Coral.

"Lighten up. They don't mean any harm."

"Oh really? You must not be from around here. I've been on nature tours and lectures at the Natural History Museum. Twice." She poked a finger in Coral's face. "Do *you* know why the seals come out of the water? To rest, that's why. To warm up. They don't want to go back in, that's whales. Outsiders don't understand.."

Born on the Cape, Coral detested this sort of clannishness. Besides, this woman's hard *r*'s betrayed her as being "not from around here" herself. A poseur. Before Coral could fashion a reply, the woman let out another yowl.

The boy with the curls rolled up the sleeves of his shirt over his elbows. He and his friend began to push the seal back into the surf.

The woman stomped off toward the beach, the boardwalk shaking with her every footfall. "I'm calling the help number," she shouted. "I'm calling the rangers." She lifted a cell phone, dropped it, retrieved it. The kids didn't seem to hear her over the breeze and lapping of the surf.

At least Coral had no part to play. The big woman thrashed along in pursuit of the kids, brimming with righteousness. She'd set them straight, by God.

As Coral watched, the kids did manage to return the seal to the ocean. None of them seemed to have gotten themselves bitten. The animal, apparently healthy, swam off in sinuous ease, so unlike its ungainliness on land. The kids high fived each other and punched the air.

The "help number" indeed. Who was most in need of protection— the seal, living in a world overrun by humans, or the kids, naïve but kind and well-intentioned? What tribunal chooses the most sympathetic character in these everyday dramas? That smug know-it-all had usurped the power to decide.

Best just to be an observer, Coral thought. Keep my powder dry.

The dog gave a short bark to remind her of her inconsistencies.

"Keep your opinions to yourself," she said.

The kids continued along the beach, the big woman puffing along after them but losing ground. Coral found herself hoping that the kids would escape, that they'd learn the truth some way that wouldn't drown their innate goodness.

She and the dog, both tired now, made their way back to the truck, then home. As she was turning into the rutted main road through the cottages, she caught sight of a black car, an expensive import, driving away.

She could have sworn she saw Guy Maulkin slide down low in the passenger seat. Then she saw the driver.

So she hadn't been deluded. The strange mood, the miasma of memory and regret that had pulled at her all day had been as real as the wet dog next to her. Signs had arisen everywhere. At last, she read them.

The past had come back to Wonderstrand, and what was she going to do now?

A Fish Tale

Wonderstrand was once home to many who made their living by the sea, and many local superstitions arise from nautical sources.

One man, native to the place, held the position of first mate on a whaler. The ship was docked in Nantucket, due to set sail the following morning. This sailor had a burning wish to see his betrothed before he departed and so consulted a local wisewoman who had a reputation as a witch. A coin changed hands, and he was given the power to become a great fish for one night, though terrible harm would result if he told so much as a single soul about the magic.

He swam back to Wonderstrand in a few strokes of his mighty tail. There he saw his beloved walking by the sea. In his joy, he leaped from the surf, causing a huge splash.

She screamed like a gull, angry as a harpy because her pelisse and bonnet were soaked with brine and fouled with seaweed. She spied a broken bottle in the sand and cast it at the fish, striking him in the left eye. He sank to the ocean floor with the lobsters and the drowned ships, from there to make his painful journey back to Nantucket. In his true form, he set sail at dawn, but he wore a black patch, for his left eye was blinded.

Months later, when he returned to Wonderstrand, he refused to marry the girl on the grounds of bad temper, pride, and vanity.

"Nay," he said, "I'll not marry one who puts such store in dress; her vanity will cost me a pretty penny. Nor will I marry a lass with a temper so hot—'tis only a matter of time before she puts an iron skillet to me head. Or worse, a pointed boot to me jewels."

The girl wept into an embroidered hanky. "When have I ever said a cross word to you?" she demanded. She did not remove her cream-white gloves, lest she be tempted to scratch him. "When have I showed a passion for worldly goods?" She did not tell him that she'd already tatted yards of lace for her trousseau. "When have I so much as glanced in a mirror while in your company?" She did not tell him how she loved to catch her reflection in the parlor windowpane, the surface of the tide pools, the side of her grandmother's silver teapot.

The sailor remained adamant and refused to say more.

Not so very long afterward, the girl married the butcher's son. She spent many a waterlogged hour scrubbing blood and offal from his aprons. Her hands became rough and red, her dresses faded.

The sailor married the town slattern. Rumor had it that she delivered something much worse than a boot to his jewels, for he died an early death of the pox.

Those who knew them debated over the moral to their story. The pious said only evil came to those who consort with witches. The romantic said that couples shouldn't keep secrets from one another. The rest just shook their heads and said marriage was a risky business. As for the witch, she kept her own counsel.

A Wonderstrand tradition arose that lovers should never cast glass into the sea, for they never knew whom it might cut.

—From *Wonderstrand Tales,* by Guy Thomas Maulkin

Chapter 12

"...I have business on earth now, and must look
about me for the means of doing it."

—Letter, Hawthorne to George Hillard

"**G**ood man," said Jeffrey Goodman Brown. Putty in his hands, this G.T. Pleasant quality in a subordinate. He'd made the fellow practically volunteer to do the dirtiest chores in the business. Getting him to betray the Rigby woman wouldn't be as challenging as he'd feared.

A waiter arrived to clear the table, and Brown ordered espresso.

"The problem is," he continued, "I don't own the whole property. Your landlady owns half. I'm going to figure out a way to...persuade her to cede control to me. Sell out, I hope, based on current value, of course, not potential—and there's plenty. You with me so far?"

G.T. nodded.

"I'm going to be adding a partner on this, both as investor and planner. Man with a lot of experience. Does golf communities where you can get a luxury condo on the ninth hole, that kind of thing. And those developments that are built to look like New England villages, with the narrow streets and the picket fences."

"Someone local?"

"Not anymore, but he's from this area originally, knows the people and the way things work. Now here's what I'm going to need from you: We've got to get him in and out of the cottages without arousing any suspicion. Can't run this project all on paper; he's got to do some field work. I don't want the old harridan raising a fuss until I have a real handle on the plans. Gives me time to pull a few strings. And this new man—name is Wakefield—can give me an analysis, get his people to lay out a design."

Brown allowed his companion a moment to take this in. "I won't turn a blind eye to your cooperation. I'm prepared to offer you a five percent interest. Wakefield's in for forty; I of course retain the rest."

"That's very generous."

The squeak in Maulkin's voice assured Brown that he'd hit home. The offer *was* generous, if Brown said so himself, but more importantly, it was enough to suck Maulkin deep into the project. And if anything went wrong, he'd would make a perfect scapegoat.

"Consider it done, then. Ah, here's our friend now."

He watched Wakefield scan the room and settle on their table. Only then did Brown rise to greet him. Never look too eager.

All their recent dealings had been by phone and email. Now he sized up the man before him. He must be around sixty, Brown supposed, but with the flat belly and muscled arms that spoke of an active life. His clothes had a big city cut, but were quiet in a way that Brown approved.

"You haven't changed much," Wakefield said by way of greeting. Brown wasn't sure he liked his tone.

The other man stood an inch or so shorter than he, so Brown made it a point to exaggerate his reach downward to shake hands. Wakefield countered by prolonging the handshake just long enough to keep Brown's back bent awkwardly.

Touché, thought Brown. Strength and confidence would be handy in this partner, but Wakefield carried himself like an alpha dog. Have to watch that.

"Sorry you couldn't join us for lunch."

"No time, I'm afraid. I landed in Boston, took Cape Air to Provincetown and rented a car. I stopped at my hotel on the way, but my room wasn't ready, so I picked up a sandwich there."

"My new lieutenant, " Brown said, indicating Maulkin, who had stood up when Wakefield approached and remained standing, hand outstretched, wavering like a reed in the breeze.

"Guy Maulkin. Everybody calls me G.T."

"Doane Wakefield." They shook hands.

"Doane's an old Cape name," said Maulkin. "Family?"

"In another century." Wakefield opened a briefcase (Coach, and well broken in, Brown noted with approval), extracted a laptop and flipped it open.

Brown beamed. "We've been nursing a midday libation. Care to join us?"

"Sounds fine."

"Jack Daniels?" Brown held up his glass.

"Scotch."

When the round of drinks came, Maulkin performed that ridiculous operation with the water, but Wakefield didn't appear to notice. Brown tried to telegraph his amusement, but no response came. Poor sense of humor, Brown concluded, but that hardly mattered in a business relationship. Cash, resources, ability—that's what counted here. Plus a bit of useful history.

"It's been a long time since you've seen Wonderstrand," Brown said.

Wakefield didn't look up from the screen, which now showed a map.

WONDERSTRAND TALES | 141

"Not much change, you'll find. More weeds, more ticks, more coyotes. The cesspool of the outer Cape," Brown chuckled.

Wakefield listened. Did the man ever smile?

Brown worked a little harder. "Of course the potential is enormous."

"I suppose it's been a hard sell for realtors because so much of it is unfit for building." Wakefield pointed at a spot on the map. "Over here, it's protected National Seashore territory, and north of that most of the acreage is marshy."

"Yes, that's been part of the problem, but now we've got our hands on one of the best sections. A few loose ends to tie up. I still have to get full title to the land. Expect to settle that soon. Some structures have to be condemned, tenants informed. I'll handle that side of things."

The lunch crowd had trickled out, leaving the restaurant quieter. Brown wondered if the few remaining diners might tune in on their discussion. "Wouldn't it be better to take this back to my office where we can talk more freely?"

"I'd rather get a look at the site today, before we talk specifics."

"As you please." Brown chose to capitulate for now. He'd picked this public setting for their first face-to-face to make the other two feel that the project belonged to them all. Subsequently, he'd make sure they knew Jeffrey Goodman Brown held the biggest spoon in the pot.

Wakefield turned the computer so the others could see.

"Here's what we do," he said, pointing at the screen with a pencil. "Keep it heavily wooded, edging all the way up to the marsh on this side. These houses will have a nice view from the top story; we're going to design them so they have balconies off a sort of second floor sitting room. That's an extra space we include—people seem to love these behemoths with too many rooms. Course we may have to keep the number of bedrooms down—septic laws and zoning. But we can pad the design this way."

"But these marshside balconies won't have a view of the other houses, or the street?" Brown asked.

"Correct."

One of Brown's earliest memories was watching a house being torn down. He was only a toddler at the time, and no one he knew had ever lived there, a nice bit of land in Truro with an ocean view. He remembered the windows, like the dead eyes of a manikin, and the way the walls collapsed on themselves. He remembered, too, seeing the big new house that took its place and wondering if it had eaten up the little one. He smiled, recalling it.

"Excellent. These babies will go for top dollar," he said.

"Will we find enough buyers in that price range?" This from Maulkin. Neither he nor Wakefield bothered to answer. They'd find the buyers, even if certain strings had to be pulled for mortgages. Less of that going on these days, perhaps, but still possible.

Brown decided to venture out on a limb here. "Not too many folks left in Wonderstrand who remember it back in the day," he said. "One or two holdouts."

The lead on Wakefield's pencil snapped. He brushed the black speck aside and wound out a new point.

"We're going to need to throw in some so-called affordable housing," Brown added with distaste. "It gives us some leeway on restrictions. Maybe even a subsidy."

"So you said. The cheaper ones we'll put over here." Wakefield pointed at the area closest to the road.

"We'll pitch it as a service to the community." Brown turned to Maulkin. "You'll see how this works. Phrase a thing the right way, and they'll believe it. Address people with authority, frown a little. You can't appear to be beholden. Oh, and cheerful condescension works nicely, but don't use it when you're lying." Brown winked. "Fudging," I should say." He treated them to a merry laugh.

Wakefield kept a poker face. Maulkin grinned uncertainly.

Brown hoped he wasn't going to have trouble with these two. "Relax," he said, allowing a little irritation to creep into his voice. "They'll buy it. They'll buy anything."

Wakefield looked at his watch.

No, thought Brown. I'll decide when this meeting is over, not you. He extracted a cigar from his pocket and tapped it on the table. "Don't you miss the days when a man could light up one of these with his post-prandial drink?" He directed the question to Wakefield.

"Not particularly."

"Hmm. Don't care for cigars? Oh, well. To each his own." He leaned back and gazed at his companions benignly.

"You haven't said much about what you've been doing lo, these many years."

"Working," said Wakefield. He didn't elaborate.

"My associate here has been writing a book."

Wakefield turned to Maulkin. "Really? May I ask what it's about?"

Addressed by Wakefield for the first time, Maulkin haltingly explained.

Brown assumed an expression of enthusiasm. "I've already told my young friend that his literary efforts could be a boon to our little project. Give panache to the area."

"It's certainly worth pursuing," Wakefield agreed. "I remember hearing some interesting stories when I was a kid."

Maulkin fairly glowed with earnest interest. "I understand you were born here. A genuine native, like Mr. Brown."

Don't overdo it, thought Brown.

"That was a long time ago."

"What's drawn you back?"

"This project."

"But you must have bigger fish to fry elsewhere," Maulkin said. "I hear all the growth's in the Sun Belt."

Brown kicked him under the table. The fellow had to learn when to shut his mouth.

Wakefield, however, half smiled at last. "Call it nostalgia."

"Ah, the Cape's changed so," Brown began.

"Oh? Didn't you just say Wonderstrand's the same?"

"Well, yes, but Wonderstrand's never been typical. It's more dilapidated, of course, but look at Route 28, or Hyannis. They've become…"

Wakefield interrupted him. "I'd like to see your manuscript," he said to Maulkin. "I've worked on plenty of community projects, and I have a feel for spin."

Maulkin hesitated. "It's not finished." He was hedging, a useful skill no doubt picked up from Brown himself, but the lad hadn't yet learned when to employ it.

"Is it in readable shape?"

"Of course," said Maulkin, showing backbone.

Funny that the fellow was so proud, even defensive, about his literary efforts. No skin off my nose, thought Brown. He liked his subordinates to excel in skills that didn't compete with his own.

"He'd be delighted to show it to you." Under the table, he aimed another kick.

"Delighted," Maulkin echoed.

The waiter brought the check, and Brown tucked a credit card into the folder. While they waited for the receipt, they settled that Maulkin alone would accompany Wakefield on a quick tour of the site. Brown had no intention of running into Coral Rigby.

"There's work waiting for me back at the office," he began, prepared to demonstrate the vastness of his empire and the accompanying responsibility.

But just then a low ring came from Wakefield's pocket. He pulled out a cell phone and glanced at it. "I'll need to take this," he said, stepping away from the table.

For a better signal? Privacy? Brown didn't care. This was just the opportunity he needed to speak to Maulkin alone.

"If the Rigby woman's truck is gone, take him into the colony. Otherwise, make some excuse and just look over the surrounding area. Agree with whatever he says, but tell him you have to talk to me before you commit to anything. As for that book of yours, I think the man's just being polite. Busy people don't want to read fairy tales. All the same, have it ready."

"You said it would add panache. Be a draw." Maulkin's voice spiraled up into the higher registers.

"For the *buyers*. The ones putting the money out, not those of us creating the show." Honestly, sometimes the fellow acted as if the brain had been hollowed out of his skull. The waiter brought the receipt, and Brown signed it, calculating a fifteen percent tip to the penny and noting "business" at the bottom of his copy.

As he did so, Wakefield returned. "I'm ready when you are," he said.

Back at his office, Brown found himself unable to concentrate. He resisted the urge to phone Wakefield or Maulkin, not wanting to look overanxious. He had a deep desire for a cup of coffee and a doughnut, but it was too late; Piety would have left Deacon's for the day.

He allowed himself to become lost in a daydream until Irene knocked on his door to say she was locking up out front.

"Lovely afternoon after all," she chirped.

She was right. The day had emerged bright and sunny. The night would be clear.

He kept to the paths anyone might use. His dark blue Sox cap, the kind owned by half of Massachusetts, was pulled low. He looked anonymous, not like Jeffrey Goodman Brown, Just another person out walking, enjoying the warm evening. Only when he was sure the path lay clear behind and in front of him did he pull out his binoculars. For tonight, he would be satisfied to use them.

June wasn't the best month for his observing. The first influx of summer people offered new obstacles as well as temptations. Freshly arrived in paradise, they wanted to spend as much time in the honeysuckle-scented outdoors as they could, often getting in his way. The Cape's population swelled like a tick every summer, an inconvenient if lucrative reality. But his urge was powerful, and Brown felt strong. His annoyance with his business associates had dissipated with his first breath of night air.

He turned his attention to some waterside properties in Truro. He would pass an hour gazing in on people utterly unknown to him, would witness their trivial doings and celebrate his own coming good fortune.

Sadly, he was ill rewarded. People were too happy, this warm night. Too many of them lounged on patios and decks, where they were more likely to notice him, less likely to show their hidden selves. Brown kept his binoculars sheathed. Several times he returned to his car, moving into different neighborhoods. That each of these lay to the south, closer to Wonderstrand, was only coincidence.

At last he acknowledged that the circle had narrowed to its center. He found himself panting.

A jogger passed him, trotted back, stopped. "You okay, buddy?"

Brown made a point of wiping sweat from his brow. He pulled the bill of his cap a little lower. "Fine, fine," he said. "Great run. Five miles. Just cooling down."

The jogger bounced away.

Brown realized that continuing to deny himself might become as great a risk as being seen in Wonderstrand. Once, a close call like this would have sent him scurrying towards home, expecting a police car to screech into his path any minute. No more. Now he would simply backtrack to more familiar territory.

He veered into a deserted backyard with a swimming pool, newly uncovered and filled for the season. He tested the gate of the surrounding fence, gently so as to avoid squeaks. It was unlocked, which was illegal and should be reported. Scofflaws. He urinated into the chlorine-reeking water.

Then back once more to his car to change his base of operations. As he drove, he mused again on his little hobby. Where was the harm? No pain, no injury, no foul. He didn't buy this psychological trauma nonsense. People indulged their emotions too much. Bootstraps, he thought. He used them; let others do the same.

He stashed the car, then skirted the woods and marshes. A patch of light through the trees set his pulse racing. Sometimes, it's true, he mistook a high, lighted window for the yellow moon. The opposite could happen just as easily. No, he *did* see a light in the cottages, but it wasn't Piety's. He cursed. It belonged to the Rigby woman.

And still, he couldn't resist. He'd just begun to edge toward Piety's cottage when a hand fell on his shoulder.

Chapter 13

*"Let us content ourselves to be earthly creatures,
and hold communion of spirit in such modes as are ordained to us."*

—HAWTHORNE

"I refuse to end up like her," Piety repeated. "I won't, won't, let that happen to me." She sat alone at a booth in Billy's, rehashing her clash with Coral Rigby for maybe the hundredth time. "Old crank. Nasty as medicine."

Billy's Sports Bar had an air of catering to the downward spiral. Its sign, standing on unpainted posts near the street, offered the first hint of diminishing returns: the big block letters spelling out the bar's name, once red, had now bleached to a dull pink. Below that, a smaller sign boasted FOUR (4!) LARGE SCREEN TVS. BEER. CLAMS. Some trick of weathering had scraped away the white paint around the last word, surrounding it in a rough, dark circle. No wonder the regulars called the place "the bearded clam." Almost at ground level, dangling from a pair of chains, hung a final square of plywood informing passersby, "Voted! Best fried clams on Cape Cod!"

This hand-lettered afterthought had never convinced Piety. No one knew where, when, or by whom the honor had been awarded. She'd heard speculation by the sad little crowd who stood around the entrance, puffing at cigarettes—Billy's clientele had never quite recovered from the restaurant smoking ban. Occasionally, some defiant type still lit up inside and had to be shooed out by the bartender. There the smoker would join like-minded others to discuss serious topics of the day such as climate change, a new municipal sewer system, gun rights, and who actually liked Billy's clams enough to cast a vote in their favor.

Still, Piety came here often. The place was close to Wonderstrand, so she didn't need to drive far if she had one too many. It was familiar and more or less safe. She'd already been here an hour and was now sipping at her second kir royale, the classiest drink she could think of. Amazing that a dump like this even offered it, but then they made green apple martinis and gooey Mudslides for the tourists, so why not stock some cassis? The Champagne they used was strictly bottom shelf, and often kind of flat from having been recorked, but the drink looked pretty. She never ordered beer in a bar. Let a man see a woman alone sipping a Bud, and he made certain assumptions.

She'd gone straight home after work to change clothes, then come here. One more hour in that Deacon's T-shirt and she might have gone insane. She was tired of being on her feet all day, tired of making payments on a three-year-old Dodge Neon that still had four more years of installments and made a noise like whooping cough every time she hit the accelerator. Tired of crabby neighbors who spurned her offers of friendship. Tired, too, of feeling guilty for blowing up.

She'd always been one to keep her feelings inside where no one could see, but since the incident with Coral, she felt like a fissure had opened and something unfamiliar was seeping out. She kept thinking of boiled eggs. Their shells were so smooth and pure, but if you dropped one too hard in a pan of water, it would crack, maybe just a hairline, so you could hardly tell. Then out would come the inside of the egg, hardening it into lumpy, clinging attachments.

When she was a child, Piety had always thought these watery translucent tails looked like ghosts. She'd felt happy for them, escaping like that, but frightened of them, too. Her mother had always said she wasn't going to waste an egg, broken or not, but Piety would slip the cracked ones into her pocket and go hungry rather than eat them.

For the last couple of weeks, whenever people annoyed her or insulted her, she kind of exploded. Just today, a couple of women had come into Deacon's. They'd lingered over their decafs and shared a bear claw between them, tearing bits of it off with their long nails. Both used polish the color of dried blood, ugly to Piety's taste, but somehow more empowered than her own choice of Cotton Candy. Once they had their order, she'd forgotten about them; a stream of customers had come in and out and she'd been busy. Then the shop emptied just about the time the two women ran out of gossip and noticed her.

One of them had thick steel-gray hair and an old-fashioned nose job, the kind that turns up at the end, stretching the nostrils upward into perpetual scorn. Maybe that was useful—her forehead was pulled so tight that frowning would be impossible. The other was dark haired and leathery thin, wearing a pair of bright yellow flats with the pointiest toes Piety had ever seen, so extreme that they had to be expensive.

She'd felt their eyes on her even before she heard them.

"It's the same, no matter where you go, isn't it?" one said. The other tittered.

"Really, here on the Cape, Manhattan, La Jolla, Boca—they all look the same. It's like they come from central casting. Bad bleach job, big boobs, triple pierced ears."

"Wonder if the boobs are real?"

"Doubt it. She probably got them done on a time-payment plan, like in those ads."

Piety felt it then, a ghost trying to escape. She knew that if it got out, it would cling to her, on the outside. Maybe these women would complain to Mr. B. Maybe she'd get fired. Images of her boss, not all bad, rushed through her mind. Maybe it wouldn't matter, after all, if they complained.

She turned to the first woman. "They're real," she said. "The very ones God gave me. Which is more than you can say for your nose. And you," she said to the other. "When you stick your finger down your throat to upchuck your half of that bear claw, make sure you do it somewhere else. Sound carries in that restroom, and no one wants to hear you puking."

They'd called her "sleaze" and "trash," but left fast, so Piety knew her shots had hit home.

Mr. B. hadn't come in during the rest of her shift, so that had been okay. But she was so very tired.

And she felt like drinking.

She recalled these outbursts, just like the boiled eggs, as both exhilarating and scary. Maybe she was getting touchy, a sourpuss like you-know-who. She tried making a mental list of the parallels between herself and Coral Rigby. Both women, living alone, almost in the same place. Both pretty close to the bottom of the economic heap. Then the rebuttal: she, Piety, was a hell of a lot younger. And a hell of a lot cuter, she hoped, even if she said so herself. But she wasn't eighteen anymore, or twenty-five. If she didn't shake her life up soon, the couple of decades separating her from wrinkles and crabbiness would fly by.

Coral was probably about the age Piety's mom would be, if she hadn't eaten herself to death when Piety was nineteen. Her mother. Now there was another appealing option. Mom had a husband all right, a man with a skill, roofing. A steady job, good for the down payment on a ranch house on the edge of Hyannis. Of course, he also had a taste for betting on horses, dogs, football, or anything else his bookie had going. Mom didn't know about the second mortgage, or the lapsed insurance, so when Dad took a header off a colonial in Yarmouthport, she was pretty well screwed. So much for family life.

Not alone for long, though, not Mom. She'd gained a lot of weight when she was pregnant with Piety, a fact she never tired of repeating. Mom had squeezed into tight shorts and halter tops for long enough to score herself another husband. Say rah rah for security; raise a cheer for lifelong companionship. Of course, husband number two had a little trouble holding down a job, but they got by. Until Mom's weight hit the two-fifty mark and the diabetes set in, then love-the-second-time-around bloomed a little less brightly. Stepdad disappeared before Piety hit middle school.

Her high school years meant coming home after an early dismissal to take care of her mother, whose health steadily deteriorated. Sometimes, her mother settled in front of the TV, Piety managed to slip out with one or another of a series of loser boyfriends. Tom was inconvenienced when the police spotted him sitting on a South Yarmouth sidewalk with a needle in his arm. Dick happened to mention on their third date that he had three children by three different women. Harry headed off to the men's room near the end of a Meg Ryan movie, she'd forgotten which, never to be seen again. When the credits rolled, Piety found her purse open and her wallet missing, also never to be seen again.

"Face it, Pie," her mother said shortly before she died. "There's no security, nowhere. Not in love nor money. Marry a hard worker, work hard yourself? Won't help. You still end up scratching and scraping at the end of the month."

She, Piety, intended to find another option. The curtain with the big prize behind it.

She was on her third kir royale now, which had begun to taste a lot like Robitussin, when she spotted the new man from Jeffrey Brown's office. Guy. She'd tucked his name into a safe place in her mind. He looked even hotter than he had before.

He was standing at the bar, his back to her. The bartender set a shot of something and a tall glass of ice in front of Guy, who turned his head left and right, deciding where to go with it.

As much as she usually hated to be looked at, tonight the booze made her long for company. She willed him to glance her way.

He didn't.

"Hey!" she shouted.

His wide, loose smile cheered her. She gestured, palm open, to the empty side of the booth, and he slid in, sweeping off the hat. She noticed the glass of ice was full of liquid now, slightly tinted. He must have had it filled with water and added the shot before he left the bar.

"Remember me?" she asked.

"How could I forget sweet Piety?" He lifted her hand from the scarred tabletop and kissed it, just like he had the first time they met.

Billy's must have opened some fresh Champagne for that last kir because she felt a definite effervescence, especially between her legs.

"I haven't seen you around Deacon's since that first time," she said, a little breathlessly.

"Mr. Brown prefers to get the coffee for the office," he said.

"He doesn't pay for it. That's probably why."

"Ah. Owner's privileges."

"Privileges. Yes."

She opened her purse on the seat, where he couldn't see, and peeked into her pocket mirror. She didn't look too tipsy. Not much lipstick left, though, most of it now forming kisses on the rims of the empty glasses. Was it okay to retouch lipstick at the table, in front of a man? She thought she'd read an etiquette column a long time ago that said it was. Eyes lowered to the mirror, she drew a glossy pink mouth, taking her time, looking up through her lashes once or twice to see how Guy reacted.

He'd followed the slow progress of the lipstick the way some men looked at a Mercedes roadster. He was definitely not going to complain to Miss Manners.

Piety blotted her lips together with a little smack. She remembered where she'd seen that hungry expression before: Jeffrey Brown wore it when she reached over him to fill his cup, or leaned down to pluck a French Cruller from the bottom rack. *Married* Jeffrey Brown.

She felt sober all of a sudden. "You're not attached, right?"

He looked confused.

"Not married? In a relationship?"

"Oh. No. Not at all."

"Me either. Not just at the moment, that is. I mean, I have been, of course. In relationships, not married." She pointed to his now empty glass. "Are you going to have another one of those?"

He nodded hard. "May I get you one of those amethyst-colored drinks?"

"Why, yes, I believe you may," she answered.

He went to the bar again—at Billy's, if you waited for someone to come to you, you'd die of thirst or sobriety—and came back with two more.

She thanked him sweetly and took a hefty gulp. "So how's the new job?"

"Not so new anymore. And quite rewarding."

"What do you do, exactly?"

"Well, today I showed an out-of-town investor around some of our properties. Nice fellow."

"At least you get out. I'm stuck behind that counter." She took another swig of her drink. "I had a crappy day, actually."

"I'm really sorry," he said.

Did he mean it? These polished, continental types flirted with everyone. But he listened so intensely, to her every word; he didn't just pretend while he was really scanning the bar for other women or looking past her at the Sox on one of the bar's TV's. She decided he was sincere.

"I had a fight with my neighbor a couple of weekends ago, too. She's related to the boss, and she doesn't like him. I kind of stuck up for him."

"Mr. Brown?" Maybe she was imagining it, but Guy looked a little funny.

"Yes. Now I feel really awkward if I run into her."

"I can understand that," Guy said.

"Anyhow, this neighbor's really strange. When you look at her, it's like, did you ever happen to notice a light bulb, just before it burns out? There's a twitch—you can't really say if you hear it or see it—then the hundred watts or whatever is multiplied for an instant, a tiny little burst. Well, it's like being in the bulb. You're surrounded by this glare; your whole mind is illuminated. Then you start to talk. It's like time stops. Then the bulb goes black and there you are."

"I know what you mean." When he didn't say anything else, she went on.

"Plus she makes these scarecrows, really fancy ones, and sticks them up all over the place. They creep me out—I always feel like they're staring at me."

Just like Guy was, right now.

"Do you happen to live in Wonderstrand?' he asked.

Piety narrowed her eyes. "Why?"

"Because I do, too. In the cottage colony."

She shook her head to clear it. "That can't be. Only three of the cottages are occupied, mine, Coral Rigby's and...wait a minute. You're *him*? The guy in the other cottage? Word on the street was that he's a real geek."

Guy seemed to fade.

"Oh, shoot. I meant, you're not a geek at all, so I didn't think you were the same person...you know what I mean. How come I'd never seen you before?"

"My previous employment took me on the road. In my free time, I was occupied indoors, with, um, scholarly pursuits."

"What's that mean?"

"I was writing a book."

"You're a writer? Then why do you work for Mr. B.?"

"Well, I haven't published anything. Not yet."

Piety's buzz flattened into gloom. He'd looked so classy, so successful. Now it turned out that he lived in a rundown cottage, just like her, and drove the wreck that was parked in front of it. Same old, same old.

Guy talked on, apparently oblivious. "I'm in a new phase of my life now. Bigger and better. I'd actually given up the book, but Mr. Brown thinks it's going to be worthwhile, so I'll be working on it in my spare time."

Maybe things weren't so bad after all. "What's it about?" she asked.

"This area. Local legends and tales. Folklore."

So he was writing about Cape Cod. Him and half the other people on the sandbar. Plus the dead ones whose work gathered dust on "For Library Use Only" shelves. She wondered how it hadn't all been written down already.

"The Cape's still rural, beyond the elbow. So self-contained. It reminds me of places in books. The coast, the marshes, the sea."

"I guess I have trouble seeing that. I mean, parts of it are pure honky-tonk. And a lot of neighborhoods look like any suburb, anywhere. All of it's a madhouse in season."

"But not Wonderstrand. The past is still there. I kept thinking of Nathaniel Hawthorne and Salem. Not the city it is today, of course, but as it was then. And before his time, the way he imagined it. Do you like Hawthorne? I do. His work's half real, half romance. That's the way I see Wonderstrand."

"I'm not much of a reader," she said. "I read *The Scarlet Letter* in high school, but I don't remember a lot about it except it was depressing."

"You probably have little time now for books. Someone so lovely must be constantly in demand."

He did have a silver tongue. "It's not that. You writers never seem to notice the same things I do. So I quit reading."

"For example?"

"Well, that an ocean wind, when you inhale it on a damp day, tastes exactly like fresh oysters. And that's sad."

"Why sad?"

"Because I love oysters, but they're a buck apiece in fish markets and maybe twice that in a restaurant. And don't tell me to dig my own. I can't afford the license."

He pulled the grubby menu from behind the napkin holder. "Do they have a raw bar here? I'll order you some."

"Not a chance, but you're sweet to offer. You know the last time I had oysters? It was last fall. Mr. Brown gave them to me. He heard me say something about them at work, and the next day he brought me two dozen to take home. I had to shuck them myself, and I'm not very good at it. My hands were all bloodied up, and the oysters were kind of gritty from bits of shell. They were still good, though." She recalled their cool sweet saltiness, sliding along her tongue.

"He can be very generous," Guy agreed.

"He can afford it. It was a nice gesture, though." And one of the reasons she didn't discourage the way Brown looked at her. She lifted her glass and was surprised to find it almost empty again.

"So what else do you notice? I'd like to know."

She laughed. "That's just the drinks talking. But okay. Here's how the beach sounds to me. You know the way all those multicolored wet pebbles rattle when the tide recedes? That reminds me of a full vial of Vicodin. I like that because I get bad headaches, and it's nice to know I have plenty of relief on hand." She liked pills for the filter they put between herself and conscious thought. When the dentist prescribed Tylenol with codeine or the doctor gave her a scrip for her headaches, she was never one to have leftovers. "I suppose you think that's silly."

"No, I don't."

"Really? Well, it's not as pretty as what you were talking about."

"Please go on. I'm interested."

"Well, there's a downside to the Cape, but you probably already know that," she said. "It reeks of vacation. Of fun. That can make you feel really bad if you've got to go to work instead of the beach, and you've got to pay bills instead of dropping a hundred bucks on souvenirs."

"Did you grow up around here?"

"Yeah, up Cape. You?"

"No. Around Boston, mostly. You must have a lot of family nearby." He sounded wistful.

"Actually, not a soul. I'm alone in the world."

"Amazing coincidence." He went on to tell her about his orphan's life.

"Maybe you were better off. My mother wasn't crazy about me, and she didn't have a pretty death. I spent a lot of time with her in hospitals when I was a teenager. That kind of sets you apart from the summer beach crowd, you know?"

"It must have been hard."

"Yeah. A lot of young people hate the Cape because there's not much to do here off-season. Not me—I was always working, so it didn't matter. It's cool that you got an education and all. Me, I wasn't motivated that way. I guess that's why I'm still stuck slinging doughnuts while you...."

"You have a natural wisdom," he said. "Everything about you shows that."

She resisted an urge to dig out her pocket mirror again. "Thanks. But I always feel, you know, insecure. Especially this month. I hate June. The stores are all pushing graduation and wedding stuff."

"I've felt like that at times, too, but not anymore. To me June is the month of Midsummer Night. Enchanting."

Somehow he made it seem that he was talking about her, not the calendar.

"So how come you're at Billy's tonight and not working on your book?"

"I just didn't feel like going back to my cottage. Actually, I'd prefer not to run into our neighbor, either."

"I hear you."

"Or perhaps this was simply fate."

"Let's have one more," was all she could think of to say. "I'll buy this round."

"No way." He slid smoothly out of the booth.

Honestly, she was falling in love, here. She stood up to get the bartender's attention. "Hey, Nick. Don't give my friend that cheap stuff. I know you've got some single malt back there. Don't try to kid a kidder."

Nick scowled at her, but she watched him stretch to pull a bottle from an upper shelf, and was satisfied.

This time, she invited Guy into her side of the booth. She liked the weave of his jeans against her knees, her thighs. Premium denim. She liked the way his eyes glowed, too, and his courtly manners. He was what she thought of as "book smart." Such people knew where to find the sources of the clever phrases that ran through her head sometimes. She'd thought of men like him as impractical, but maybe she'd been wrong.

"You want to get out of here and go over to my place?" she asked. "I don't have any Scotch, but I've got Sam Adams and some white wine. Are you hungry? I've got cheese and crackers, too. Better than the crap they serve here." She hoped he was hungry. She wanted him to see that she had nice cheeses, not Velveeta or even Cracker Barrel, but imported stuff like Brie.

"I um…" he said. From his pocket, he withdrew a bottle of water and tipped the contents into his empty glass. Only a few drops came out. For a moment, he looked dumfounded.

Then he said, "That would be very nice," for some reason addressing the greasy salt and pepper shakers. "I have to stop home first, though."

"Okay. You know where I live. Just walk on over."

He held the door of her car as she climbed in, helped her disentangle the seat belt, brushing against the bare skin just under her collar bone he did so. She felt another fizz inside, but it flattened when she realized he was looking everywhere but at her. Did he intend to ditch her?

Well, nothing ventured, et cetera.

With all the windows lowered to get the fresh air, she felt sober enough to drive the short distance. She'd done it before. After a deep inhale, she shifted into drive. Just once, she looked back.

He stood waving to her, looking a little dimmer, not so polished. But that was probably just the glare of Billy's parking lot lights.

Chapter 14

Hi!" *said the blackbird, sitting on a chair,*
Once I courted a lady fair;
She proved fickle and turned her back,
And ever since then I've dressed in black.

—"THE BIRD'S COURTING SONG," TRADITIONAL

The touch on his shoulder, though light, felt like an explosion. Brown's heart leaped up and clogged his throat. He whirled, palms raised. "What the devil?"

Then he recognized his assailant, and his heart settled back into his chest. Maulkin stood there gaping at him.

Brown heaved a deep breath. "What a happy coincidence," he said through gritted teeth. "May I ask what you're doing here?"

That the question made him look ridiculous, Brown realized too late. He'd have to seize control, and fast. "Oh, of course, you live just over there." With his best show of disinterest, he indicated the cottages. "I suppose you're wondering why I'm here. Was having a jog on the Seashore trails—healthy body, healthy mind, you know—when I became a little lost. Saw this familiar landmark, and used it to orient myself."

Still his employee held that annoying silence. Brown squinted at him and sniffed the air. "Been imbibing?"

Finally Maulkin worked up a sentence. "I'm on my way back from Billy's, up on Route 6."

Even in the dark, Brown could tell the man's face colored up like a candlelit pumpkin. So. Maulkin too had something to hide.

Brown drew his lips back in a smile. "I see. And you're on foot? Wise policy."

Maulkin hemmed and hawed, raising Brown's hackles a little higher.

"Perhaps you're on your way out again?"

"Yes, I…have some business to attend to."

"At this hour? What business might that be?"

A gritty scratch was his only answer as Maulkin scuffed his shoe back and forth in the dirt.

"I see. A personal matter." Highly suspicious, this reticence, but under the circumstances Brown didn't see how he could press further. "Well, I have my bearings now. I'll just be on my way."

His employee wished him a good night.

Brown jogged away, in case Maulkin was watching. Then he doubled back, found a good hiding place, and settled in. Early crickets and frogs brought the night to life. Mosquitoes whined too, but didn't alight. Brown smelled the gasoline-like traces of DeepWoods Off rising from his heated skin, and congratulated himself on his foresight, but he detected something beyond himself, too—June's panoply of fresh leaves, flowers, warmed earth.

Summer's advent always cost him a pang.

Many years ago, there'd been a summer or two when he'd dared so much more. Reached out. Reached in. The occasions when smoke masked the green scents of summer. Brown breathed faster, recalling the thrill of one hand stretched to his privates, one to theirs. Then the fear, the publicity.

Ridiculous.

There were no victims. What woman, if she were honest, hated the flattery of desire? Nevertheless, he'd been halted. Shut out. Forced to limit himself to the visual.

In his hiding place, Brown shifted, writhing as quietly as he could against the unfairness of life.

His summer wedding, too, came to mind, no more pleasant to recall. Those banks of hothouse roses and lilies, redolent of refrigeration. His bride had insisted on carting several vases full to the hotel for their wedding night. Among their funereal perfumes, Brown had watched her undress. Pleasurable, that, but ultimately dissatisfying. Each white garment she removed promised to reveal the wicked heart he knew was there, but it evaded him. He couldn't fight what he couldn't see.

Watching her had been what got him married in the first place. After the fuss in the newspapers, he'd limited himself to girls he dated; if they caught him outside their windows, he could invent some excuse. He'd claim he'd been about to tap on the glass to get their attention. Once he said he'd been planning to serenade, and the girl had believed him.

"How romantic," she'd sighed, and offered herself to him.

Recalling this, Brown laughed softly.

In this same way, he'd stalked the woman he'd married, but she wouldn't be romanced. Would accept no excuses, no fantasies about love songs in the moonlight. She knew she wasn't the first of his targets but made it clear that she'd better be the last. Indeed, his fiancée was perfectly open about what she wanted, and at the time he'd found that admirable. She foresaw that he'd be rich someday, was already accruing money at a handsome rate.

She planned a life for herself of golf and heated pools, letting him picture her toned thighs in Lily Pulitzer capris, ankles crossed neatly under a patio table. She could describe the cut and weight of the flawless solitaires that would grace her ears and left ring finger.

She suggested, coyly, that such a marriage might be better than, well, what she might tell her girlfriends. And her lawyer father.

So he'd married, and a period of peace followed. Then Coral Rigby returned to Cape Cod after years of wallowing in gutters elsewhere. She'd settled into her half of the property they'd inherited from their grandfather and established herself as a thorn in his side.

"Do you really think it quite fair for you to move in?" he'd asked. He'd been quite civil, even made a lighthearted joke about The Prodigal Cousin. "After all, your tenancy would block other use of the property."

Her response had been anything but civil.

Coral Rigby had been saving up her venom like a spider. His memories drifted back still farther, no longer summery but autumnal, in a lonely place. There'd been a night when she'd tapped his shoulder much as Maulkin just had. Brown's mind blurred, but he seemed to recall words torn from his soul, flowing unstoppable. Not a confession, perhaps, but too much.

He hadn't been able to look away from his cousin, his memory was clear on that point. "'The whole earth is one stain of guilt,'" he'd quoted, he knew not from where.

"You would know," she said.

"Are you so different?" he challenged her. Didn't she understand that they were joined in a brotherhood of sin with all humanity? "I'm no worse than the next man," he'd said, or thought he had. He might have wept.

He cringed to remember it

Not a word of comfort passed her lips. She merely stored his words away.

So he'd conceded. He'd let his cousin take over Wonderstrand Colony, though her being *in situ* made the place hers more than his, as if his partial ownership didn't matter a whit. Still, he'd vowed that in the future, his concessions would be few, both to his cousin and his wife. He'd become an unyielding businessman and a businesslike husband.

His fortunes grew. His wife met his carnal needs. The first remained exciting; the second staled quickly.

There'd been a son, dead days after birth. His wife had blamed Brown because he'd refused to be present at the delivery, but he'd been firm. Some things he did not want to see, and birth was one. Blood, pain. She'd acted as if these things were the consequences of his actions, and he should witness them. Nonsense. Eve's burden, not Adam's. Relations between them had ceased.

Nevertheless, Jeffrey Goodman Brown was a man of honor. He'd had admirably few dalliances over the years. A call girl at a convention, perhaps. No more. He'd employed many women in semi-menial work, counter girls, receptionists, sales help, all of them interchangeable, none worthy of a second glance. If he engaged in innocent flirtation, it was only with friends of his wife or professional women, the sort who understood light social amusement. Women not unlike himself. What he truly wished for in feminine company was someone to applaud his deeds, melt under the warmth of gifts bestowed. A woman neither very shrewd nor very simple.

Then came Piety. He longed to witness her blossoming into the life he could offer, to see her don silk instead of nylon, step into marble tubs instead of plastic showers. With appropriate awe and appreciation.

Of course, the Rigby woman had spoiled that dream, too, by forcing him to curtail his nocturnal admiration of Piety by attacking him again, just last month.

He was beset by philistines.

When Brown had settled into his hiding place, Maulkin was still in the same spot where they'd parted, obviously waiting to be sure he was alone.

Then sometime during Brown's reverie, his employee had begun walking again, in the direction of Piety's cottage. Her door opened, and Maulkin went in.

Brown gnashed his teeth. How did Maulkin dare? How could Piety behave so? Then from a distance he heard a sharp *woof*, neither indoors nor out, so probably at an open window. The Rigby woman's cur.

With an effort, Brown gathered his wits.

He decided to risk staying put. From Piety's windows came the flicker of candlelight. Just as he resolved to peek in, the shades snapped down, one by one. This was not an insurmountable obstacle; he knew well enough the gaps left between window frame and cheap shades.

To an observer, the scene might have seemed lascivious and perverse, but that was the view of the ignorant. Brown alone felt its poignancy. He inched forward, then hesitated. What did he expect to see? He sickened at the notion that a glimpse of their intertwined limbs, their contortions, might give him pleasure. That he might witness their bodies from the unlovely angles never seen by the partners themselves, that their glistening sweat and spotted sheets might never be erased from his memory.

Women are temptresses; of this he had no doubt. It was as true of Piety as of any other of her sex. So why was she special to him? Why did observing her make him feel like a romantic fool, gazing at a virgin goddess in a tower? Piety was no innocent, with her tight shirts and mascaraed eyes. He recognized the cynicism and cupidity that lay beneath the sweetness. Nevertheless, when he saw her, his heart turned over.

At the dog's second bark, more insistent, and the distant click of a door lock, he was almost relieved. In haste, he retreated silently, a lover betrayed.

Later, at home, he tossed in his bed, sleepless but sharp of mind. Piety, he would forgive. Spared the sight of her face *in flagrante*, he didn't need to replace the image of her he held. When she was his, she could repent at leisure.

As for the rest, he would kill two birds with one stone.

He would destroy Guy Maulkin and Coral Rigby both. No hurry. He'd play them out slowly. Before summer sloped into autumn, before the outgoing tourists jammed the Bourne and Sagamore Bridges come Labor Day, his enemies would know the wrath of Jeffrey Goodman Brown.

Chapter 15

"A love-scene should be laid on such an evening."

—HAWTHORNE

From the moment Guy saw Piety, silhouetted in her doorway against the light of a multitude of candles, he forgot the anxious drive home, his thirst, and worst of all, the encounter with his boss.

The jittery walk from his cottage to hers had taken Guy through the seedlings and chokeberries and past a phalanx of Coral's scarecrows. Some of these appeared to punch the air, miming congratulations and encouragement, while others seemed to wave him back, scowling in Puritanical rebuke. Just the breeze in their clothes, he assured himself.

While he'd been guzzling Coral's well water in his own cottage, then talking to Jeffrey Brown, Piety had showered and changed into a silky tank top and shorts. In the flickering light he could see the dampness at her hairline, the condensation at the folds of her arms and in the hollow between her breasts. It brought out not just the perfumes from her soap, but the smell of her skin, with the ever-present hint of cinnamon and vanilla.

Unable to speak, almost unable to breathe, he watched a drop of water collect at the tip of a curl over her ear, growing slowly heavier until it had to fall, and yet it didn't. At last it slipped down, landing on the silk just below her right collarbone, spreading into a darker spot, smoothing the thin cloth against her body.

He reached forward and traced the path of the droplet, circled his finger over the spot.

Piety lifted her face.

In college, where the concentration of youthful hormones made sex accessible even for geeks like Guy, he'd had several fumbling encounters with women. All had been students like himself, with less time for romance than their primary sources or problem sets. The sex had been as cramped as the narrow dorm cots, as flat as the second-hand futons. Since then, he'd been celibate. Small wonder.

This would be different. He knew it even as he bent to kiss her.

Tonight he and Piety were the pounding Atlantic, the calm freshwater ponds, the tidal pull of the Bay. Tonight he hit all the right spots. They perfumed the roses, the honeysuckle, the pines. Even his own body seemed attached to his brain in a new way.

Guy knew signs. Guy knew about glory. The night glowed again, as it had on that momentous occasion not so long ago. Now the illumination seemed to say, *"See, I told you,"* but this time the light, softer, issued from inside the room where he and Piety lay. Everything he'd dreamed of was coming to pass.

They woke in the wee hours, folded together. He reached across her bed and lifted the shade to see the sheerest wash of violet in the east.

"It's the first day of summer," he said, as much to himself as to her. Summer. The word tasted of lushness and bounty. Of heat.

She stretched. In the guttering glow of the last of the candles, her arms were pale and sinuous, heron's necks. She wrapped them around his neck. He ran his hand along one, shoulder to wrist, pressed his palm to hers.

With her other hand, she pulled the shade back down, then turned to him. "But doesn't that mean the days start to get shorter now?"

He buried his face in her hair, wanting to tell her every day was going to be endless, perfect. She kissed his cheek before he could speak, and was up and off to the bathroom. When she returned, she drifted back to sleep almost immediately.

He didn't mind. She was in his arms. He watched the light at the edges of the shade grow until he, too, slept.

The Crow Law

In the published records of Old Eastham, to whose government Wonderstrand owed its limited allegiance, one finds several references to a peculiar local law of the seventeenth century. It required all landowners to kill six blackbirds or three crows, those accursed despoilers of the harvest, and to do so before he would be permitted to marry. Probably the most amusing version is Henry David Thoreau's, in his book Cape Cod. I like to picture him entertaining his friend Hawthorne with the anecdote, as the two shared a mug of spiced ale at some snug fireside.

At least one tale survives describing the law's effects.

In 1715, an Englishman named Ezra Brown immigrated to the New World. He settled in the Wonderstrand, where certain kin of his were already established. Though he prospered as a householder, he remained, to the consternation of his neighbors, a bachelor well into middle age.

"'Tis the only family he'll ever father," folks said of the numerous scarecrows that protected his fields. Why? It seems Ezra refused to fulfill his legal duty and kill his quota of blackbirds.

But one Mehitabel Snow, the daughter of a nearby farmer and a maiden of thirty-two, sought to alter Ezra's bachelor state. Through gifts of apple pies and beach plum jam, she gained his confidence and thus the key to the man's stubbornness.

In his youth, Ezra had been employed by the English East India Company, in whose interests he'd traveled to that exotic land. There he'd acquired not only a comfortable fortune, but a personal philosophy.

He'd met up with men who worshipped strange false gods and goddesses, who ate no meat and drank no spirits. At first, he'd treated them with the disrespect accorded to what was considered, in those benighted days, an inferior race.

One evening, while walking in a lonely place, he was bitten by a viper. He thought he was doomed, but just then one of the heathens emerged silently from the shadows. Ezra recognized the fellow as one who had lately been beaten by a white man, a traveling companion of Ezra's, in a drunken fit. Expecting retaliation, Ezra tried to draw his knife, but pain and poison made him weak. When the heathen wrested the knife from him, Ezra hoped at least to die quickly, but to his surprise, the heathen used it to make two quick cuts near the bite, and proceeded to draw out the snake's poison. Ezra's life was saved.

In his gratitude, Ezra made it a point to know the man, to learn a few words of his language and study his ways. He came to realize that many of these heathens were better Christians than the civilized men at home. As a tribute, Ezra made a vow never to kill another warm-blooded creature. He ate no meat, and wore no leather, even going so far as to fashion boots for himself from boiled wool with wooden soles.

In Massachusetts Colony, this was an aberration. Men hunted to survive. They killed to destroy predators and protect their crops. They set bone-snapping traps to gather furs against the New England winters. But Mehitabel let it be known to their neighbors that Ezra's strange behavior was the result of a pledge to God. The man was sober and upright, and a good farmer, so the community listened to her and let him be, as long as he broke no laws. A vow must be respected.

Mehitabel, however, had made no vow. She grew weary of her maidenhood. Though there were widowers aplenty who might have taken a bride of her mature years to wife, she wanted children of her own, not a passel of brats borne by another woman.

One sunny morning she shouldered her father's rifle and marched into the fields. One by one, she took down the quota of crows, plus an extra, a sort of avian exclamation point. Witnesses reported that each time *a bird fluttered to the earth, she uttered a laugh rather too coarse for one of the gentler sex.*

Mehitabel delivered the crow's bleeding corpses to the town fathers in the name of Ezra Brown, but first, she plucked a long tail feather from each. Three of these she displayed in the ragged hats of the scarecrows that dotted Ezra's cornfields. And the fourth? Legend has it that she wore a black plume in her bonnet on her wedding day, as another bride might have sported a posy. Some said a single circle of red held it in place. A garnet pin, bestowed by the bridegroom, or an everlasting drop of blood from the breast of a fallen bird?

If Ezra had any qualms about Mehitabel's massacre, they are unrecorded. It is on record, though, that he died a mere decade later, leaving her a rich widow. They also produced a pair of sons, Sylvanus and Ebenezer, and descendants of the Brown family live in the towns of the outer Cape to this day.

—From *Wonderstrand Tales,* by Guy Thomas Maulkin

Chapter 16

"The blackbirds, however, still molest the corn. I saw them at it the next summer, and there are many scare-crows, if not scare blackbirds, in the fields, which I often mistook for men. From which I concluded, that either many men were not married, or many blackbirds were."

—Henry David Thoreau

The dog yapped, pulling Coral back from sleep, from dreams of the face she'd recognized behind the wheel of the black car that had passed her on the way back from the beach. As the driver turned toward her, she called out, but her words were lost as soon as she awoke.

She groaned. Dickon had probably heard Piety stumbling into her cottage after a night out. After a few minutes, though, he barked again. The dog was not one for idle talk, so she untangled herself from the sheets and quilts and went to him. He stood on his hind legs with his paws on the windowsill, nose to the screen. Coral opened the door and peered outside, feeling too dispirited to investigate. She was glad when

Dickon dropped back to the floor, turned around a couple of times, and settled himself on the rug.

"Sure, fine for you," she said. "Pitch a fit every time a coyote trots by. Don't worry your pretty head about me."

For Coral, any chance of sleep had decamped. She pulled on trousers and a shirt, then busied her hands with the construction of a new scarecrow to mark the summer solstice. When she was young, she'd celebrated these universal turnings, but now change loomed ominous. The scarecrow, offspring of her mood, turned out so ugly and frightening that it would be better suited to Hallowe'en. The head she chose could hardly be recognized as a gourd. The preserving process had gone awry, producing a blackened oval whose lumps and valleys formed the semblance of nose and eye sockets. She painted on lips, contorted into a rictus of pain and sadness. After some consideration, she took off her own clothes and dressed the scarecrow in them, covering her nakedness with a plain terrycloth robe. Finished.

Poor hideous thing. It reminded her of Guy Maulkin, not in appearance but in its air of being misbegotten. Last time she'd seen him, he'd been slumped down in the passenger seat of that black car. No wonder he'd been slinking in and out of his cottage, avoiding her, offering her no intelligence on her enemy. She'd stopped fooling herself with the notion that he was only being discreet, that he would be useful eventually. He disappeared like a puff of smoke whenever she went looking for him. Clearly, he was no longer her creature.

The young idiot had signed himself into league with the devil.

At dawn, Coral let the dog out, then hiked the finished scarecrow over her shoulder and carried it outside. She didn't want this one staring at her in her own living room. Propping it against a tree, she fetched a shovel and dug a narrow hole to steady the backbone, twisted it in, then braced it with stones. As she stepped back to admire him, a crow flapped down from the trees and settled on one of the outstretched wooden arms.

"Everyone's a critic," she said.

The crow cocked his head at her and stayed put. Another swooped in to join him, then a third. They pecked at the gourd with avid interest.

"I've got no quarrel with you," Coral told the birds. "Let's agree to call this 'scarecrow' tag a misnomer, shall we?"

The birds puffed their feathers, hunched their wings, then directed their attention back to their own affairs.

"People," she muttered on her way back inside. "There's the threat. Not the damned birds."

Guy Maulkin had been nattering about crows, the day she'd fitted him up for clothes. Something about that colonial crow law, about what a modern equivalent of killing them might be. Something positive, he'd said. Perform some set number of symbolic acts to secure your heart's desire. Atone for three mistakes? Maybe. Break five bad habits. Perform six good deeds. But good deeds hadn't gotten her anywhere. Look at Maulkin. Hadn't that been a good deed of sorts? As for bad habits, others might criticize her, but all her ways served a purpose. Mistakes? That was different. She closed her eyes and saw that black car skim past again. This time, the driver turned and looked at her accusingly. Something ached way down in her soul.

She knew him, all right. Doane Wakefield. So long ago, but the effect of seeing him was as fresh as yesterday, when she'd been pulled into his riptide. Why on earth was he here, tooling around with Maulkin, Jeffrey Brown's new toady?

She closed her eyes. Exhaustion, that's what was causing these dreams and visions. A reaction to this tumult of guilt, old pain and betrayal. She lay down on the sofa, the curtains drawn against the sun, which now rode high.

Just as she began to drift, the dog recommenced his racket. Up rose the crows like tattered black rags, bickering and guffawing in their metal-scrape voices.

She was none too pleased herself. "What is it this time?"

He'd had good reason to bark. A van was just leaving the colony driveway. Even with the trees and shrubs in full leaf, she could see enough of the lettering on the side to recognize it. A surveyors' firm.

"The liar!" Her fist on the sill rattled the window. She whirled and stamped in her fury, knocking down backbones, scattering unfinished heads.

Three crows. Six deeds. Twelve acts of vengeance. Choose the magic number.

She fumed. Then with an effort, she arrested her wild dance, the better to think clearly.

"Let's keep it simple and go with three," she said at last to the dog. "Very potent. Think of the Threefold law, Holy Trinity, and so on."

She brewed coffee, anthracite in a mug. The time for drowsiness had passed. She toasted the grim faced woman in the portrait on the wall, then put down her mug, slipped the heavy frame aside, and took out the flash drive of Jeffrey Brown photos. How to proceed? She had little use for social media, so even if Brown had a Facebook page, or more likely a profile on Linkedin, she wouldn't have known how to post photos on it. And possibly he could delete them before anyone saw them. Best to take a more direct route. She made sure the dates and times were clearly stamped, selected and printed half a dozen that showed the background well enough to identifying their location. She shoved them into an envelope and addressed the packet to his wife.

Waiting had been a mistake. Time to fire the cannons.

Deed number one.

"Registered mail for this," she said to the dog. "Want to take a ride over to the North Eastham post office? There's a Ben and Jerry's in it for both of us."

By noon, she'd completed the second deed. A cluster of new padlocks shone from the shed. Bright new nails sealed the window. On Guy Maulkin's door, an eviction notice writhed and bellied between restraining thumbtacks. Held beneath it was a second sheet, handwritten: "You broke our contract. Get out. You have thirty days."

A breeze pulled harder against the sheets of paper. She pushed the tacks again with all the force she could muster. A pale, tingling circle remained impressed on the pad of her thumb. As she regarded it, a thin crescent of blood appeared at one edge. C for crow. A witch's mark. A stigma.

"I should have brought the dog along," she said aloud, but there was no one to hear. She was entirely alone.

And the third task is always the hardest.

Chapter 17

"Is not this consummate discretion? and am I not perfectly safe? ... I look at the matter with perfect composure, and see all round my own position, and know that it is impregnable."

—HAWTHORNE

Jeffrey Goodman Brown hummed "Yankee Doodle" to himself, aglow with the spirit of the Fourth of July. After a few bars, he burst into full lyric. "And with the girls be handy..."

How easy it had been, after all.

He'd come home from the office early the previous Friday, satisfied with his accomplishments for the day. They'd included sending Maulkin off Cape with a list of appointments, carefully arranged to keep him away as much as possible, and, as a bonus, requiring him to traverse the tourist-jammed flyovers and bridges at peak hours.

"And don't forget that book of yours." With a great show of bonhomie, he gifted Maulkin with a top of the line laptop. "Work in your hotel room at night. During meals. Every spare moment, that's the ticket."

In another fine inspiration, he'd even offered his young scribe some material, filling in Brown family history, telling how his strong stock had migrated to Cape Cod in the early days of this great nation. "That should give you a tale or two. Plenty of heroes. Legendary feats. You might need to spend a little time at the library to put it in historical context. You'll have evenings and weekends for that."

Maulkin would never suspect his motives, but just in case, Brown added a little misdirection: "Can't let Wakefield down, you know."

Next, Brown fired most of the summer help at Deacon's Doughnuts and offered Piety double time to work the extra hours. Anything to keep her away from Maulkin while he laid his trap.

The day's chores done, he entered his home though the double front door, as was his habit. The master didn't use the kitchen door like a housemaid.

He was surprised to find the tables in the vestibule stripped of their pewter candlesticks, china statuettes and crystal vases. An Early American still life that had hung opposite the door was missing. Instead of the nineteenth century Hereke runner that lay in the hall to the living room, he saw the bare parquet.

In the living room, his wife sat dead center on the sofa. She wasn't flipping the pages of a magazine, nor chatting on her cell, nor listening to her MP3. She was merely waiting. For him, Brown presumed. Her posture was as upright as a church steeple, as alert as prison guard's.

"So here you are," he said, assuming an air of pleasant curiosity. He gestured around the room, as denuded as the hall. "Redecorating?"

"You could say that," she said.

It was then that Brown noticed the photographs, spread into a fan on the coffee table. He was reminded of the casual but artistic arrangements of *Architectural Digest*s in upscale furniture stores.

"A friend of mine came by this morning, at my invitation." His wife smiled slightly. "She works at one of the nicer auction houses in Boston."

He waited.

"Did I mention she came in a van? With crates? The proceeds, of course, will go to me, as will half the proceeds from the sale of this house."

Still, Brown held his tongue. Best to let his wife play her hand first.

"These are enlargements, of course. Lovely, no? My lawyers have the originals."

She arched a neat eyebrow. "I always knew you were a pervert, Jeffrey. But masturbating at windows at your age? Really!"

"Let's not be hasty," he began.

"Hasty? I've wanted to get away from you for years. Do you think this hurts me? I'm so happy I can barely stand it."

Brown, disoriented, plopped down heavily in a damask-covered chair.

"So I'm going to make it easy for you."

"Easy?"

"For both of us. Why should I make this public? Have people start wondering about me, too? They might think like attracts like, Jeffrey."

He began to realize what was really happening. His attention honed in on the issue that most touched him about the end of his marriage. "But financially...."

"Oh, I'm not as stupid as you think. I know you've been looking out for yourself, and that you won't take as big a hit as you might pretend."

Again Brown hesitated, unsure whether a denial would enrage or amuse her.

"Stop opening and closing your mouth, Jeffrey. You look like a fish. Which reminds me—I'm sick to death of Cape Cod. I'm tired of fog and baked scrod and cranberries. I'm not amused by town meetings. I'm sick of people who wear shorts and flip-flops to restaurants at night. I'm going to New York."

She stood up, ascended the curved staircase. He took in the room, stripped of its gewgaws. How light and airy it felt.

The next sound he heard was the *clunk, clunk, clunk* of wheeled suitcases being dragged down the stairs. This was repeated several times. Then the garage door hummed.

And just like that, he was free.

"Yankee Doodle keep it up," he sang.

He still wondered at the irony. All this time, he'd believed that if his wife learned of his pastime, he'd be ruined, but now things were going to be fine—as if he cared about a few scraps of wool and glass, a daub of paint. The Wonderstrand development would bring in plenty of money, and long after his wife had any claim to it. Brown chuckled. The Rigby woman probably thought she'd had him by the testicles. So much for her.

His cell chimed. He glanced at the ID—Wakefield—snapped it open, and listened for a minute before answering.

"Didn't I suggest it was imprudent to send surveyors in there too soon? If someone has vandalized the stakes, we'll just have to replace them—maybe find something more impervious."

He listened again briefly.

"No. I think it's time I went over there myself."

After all, he had nothing more to fear.

He longed to stop off at Deacon's, but the Orleans parade had blocked the main road. Piety could wait. Business first. As he circled the town on his way to Wonderstrand, he could hear the drums and trumpets of the middle school band through his open windows. In years past, he and his Cadillac had sometimes participated in the parade, honking his horn behind an antique fire engine or crawling along behind the Coast Guard Auxiliary as they marched and waved. Town selectmen or other local officials often rode along with him, basking in the crowd's goodwill. Next year, perhaps he'd do it again, Piety in the seat beside him.

Humming Sousa now, he pulled into the cottage colony and parked in full view of Coral Rigby's cottage.

He was surprised when she didn't come storming out immediately. Her rattletrap truck was there, and that demon of a dog was raising a racket loud enough to bring down the walls. Fine. It would spare him the expense of demolition.

Holes still showed where the surveyor's stakes had been. Brown made a show of pausing at each one, shaking his head. When he heard a door slam behind him, he slipped a pair of sunglasses out his pocket and donned them. He borrowed a smirk from Jack Nicholson and turned to face her.

"I just stopped by to thank you," he said.

"What are you talking about?"

"Why, the pictures you sent my wife. They've driven her from my bed and board."

"She'll drag your sorry name through the mud."

"On the contrary. You've played right into my hands."

Her narrowed eyes revealed her confusion. To think he'd been afraid of her. His smirk widened into a grin. She looked like a ragbag with a face.

The dog, emerging from behind her skirts, growled. Brown didn't even flinch.

"My wife has decided, most wisely, that her own interests are best served by divorcing quietly. She's not as easily manipulated as you thought."

"She married you."

"Now, now cousin. No more hurling insults. Accept the inevitable. Take a page from her book and walk away with what you have. I'll give you market value for your half of the colony—*current* market value. You could buy yourself a little place in Salem. That should be to your taste."

"I'll send those pictures to the police. The media. Post them online."

"And I'll say I was relieving myself in the bushes. In the dark, on property I own. What man hasn't? Crude, yes. Criminal? For a man with a record as pure as a hymnal?"

"Hymnal my ass. You and I both know the truth."

"Answering the call of nature is proof of a crime? Hardly."

"It will raise suspicions. Get them watching you."

"And you! Have you seen what happens to whistle blowers? The spotlight falls on them, too. Police, reporters, TV cameras, YouTube—you'll be a media superstar. What will happen to your precious privacy then?" He paused. "You're perfectly happy to have someone else stir up a scandal, but you don't want to hold the spoon, do you? Dear cousin, you're a hypocrite."

"I'll show Piety."

Brown had expected this. It was an attack he'd have to head off. He ambled toward his car.

"My offer stands. Don't wait too long, cousin."

As he pulled drove away, he could see her glowering at him. Fired up by his triumph, he rejoiced with song: "And there was Captain Washington, Upon a slapping stallion, And giving orders to his men, I guess there was a million."

Chapter 18

"It is a heavy annoyance...that so much of the mean and ludicrous should be
hopelessly mixed up with the purest pathos....
Life is made up of marble and mud."

—HAWTHORNE

Piety listened hard to what Jeffrey Brown was telling her.

The post-parade crowds had departed to cookouts or the beaches, and Deacon's was closed for the day. As they talked, she folded and refolded a paper napkin until its edges were feathered like small birds.

He sat with his hands squarely on the Formica. "The divorce will be quite amicable. Now I'm free to admit that I've long desired to speak openly to you."

He went on to say how he wouldn't have compromised his reputation (or hers, he added a blink later) by stating his feelings while still in the bonds of legal wedlock.

Piety was touched. His formally announcing his intention to court her was kind of endearing.

He reached across the table and put his hand over hers. A diamond sparkled at twelve o'clock on his wristwatch when it caught the light.

She gently disengaged her hand. "But you're still married."

"That's true. It would be imprudent to be seen openly quite yet. But this is the Fourth of July, and I wondered, if you don't have plans?"

Here was a dilemma. She'd had plans, with Guy. They were going to Provincetown, walk Commercial Street, watch the fireworks. But then late yesterday he'd had to go off-Cape on business. She'd probably spend the night watching the Boston Pops on TV.

Already she'd begun to think of herself and Guy as a couple. She'd stopped her solitary trips to Billy's and the other local bars. Would it be cheating to go out with someone else?

"I did have a date," she said.

He raised his eyebrows.

"You don't believe me?" Her old buddy insecurity seeped in. Did he assume no one else could be interested in her, that she was a recluse like Coral Rigby?

He raised his eyebrows a little higher.

"Actually, I'm seeing someone." She knew she sounded defensive.

"Young Mr. Maulkin."

"You know that?"

"I'm an observant man. But isn't your beau out of town today?"

She blushed, caught in a lie.

"And you two aren't yet engaged, or, shall we say, committed."

"Well, no. Not exactly."

"So I have reason to hope?" His voice remained smooth, but hope wasn't the message she was getting here. She was reminded of the way a wolf looks when the meat's right in front of him. But Mr. B. didn't tear in. He could wait. She found power like that exciting.

Still, she worried about what exactly he knew and how he'd found out. She recalled her first night with Guy, the hookup in the bar. He'd seemed so straightforward. Sophisticated, but kind of innocent, too. Told a certain way, though, the story of that night could lose its sweetness, could be made into a nasty, between-us-boys chuckle. Would Guy do that?

She'd been wrong about men before. In love and money, you had to be wary, not limit your options too soon.

And here was Mr. Brown, catching the light with his wristwatch.

"Hope springs eternal," she said.

"Excellent. I have an acquaintance who'd be happy to lend me his boat—very nice, a thirty-nine foot Wellcraft. We could watch fireworks from the water. You'll want to go home and change."

He was right. She had to get out of her Deacon's t-shirt or she'd feel like an employee all night. Her mind raced ahead to what she was going to wear. The new sundress from T.J. Maxx? She'd been saving it for her next date with Guy.

He went on quickly. "I'll go and pick up some delicacies, a bottle of wine or two. Meet me at the Sesuit dock around seven."

He'd already stood up. What's the dividing line between confidence and arrogance? Yet he was so jovial, so disarming. So rich.

Where was the harm? "See you at seven," she said.

It rained. A fish-scented drizzle washed the fireworks right out of the sky and drove celebrations under awnings and umbrellas.

She was having a pretty good time, though. They'd pulled out of the slip and dropped anchor just outside the harbor for privacy, then sat there and talked. He'd brought a well-stocked hamper. Lobster salad. Oysters, so many she couldn't count, and he shucked them for her. She didn't like the pâté, which tasted like liver, but the wines were lovely, nothing like what he'd served at that Christmas party at his house.

So she was special. Not one among a horde of employees. Piety kept her guard up, but he'd touched her exactly once, taking her hand to help her step onto the boat. Even with a couple of empty bottles behind them, he remained a perfect gentleman.

"I should get myself one of these," he said, indicating the boat. "Grew up with them, but haven't had the time lately."

"It is nice, Mr. B." She settled back onto the cushions, listening to lapping waves.

He walked over from the galley, where he'd been pouring more wine, and loomed over her. "I think it's time you called me Jeffrey, don't you?"

"Okay," she agreed. "Jeffrey." She'd have to practice; it wouldn't come easily.

He handed her a full glass, and she sipped. "Believe it or not, I haven't been in a boat—even a rowboat—more than half a dozen times in my life."

"That's unusual for a native."

"Not if you don't come from either fishing people or money."

"You've lived here all your life?"

"Yeah. But all over the place. Not like you, with ancestors and houses and stuff."

They talked about how Cape Cod had changed, that omnipresent local topic.

"We're at the mercy of tides and weather," Piety said. "Nothing stays the same."

"You're right. And the cost of progress is high. More people, more regulations. I remember when a man didn't have to lock his door at night. There were no hours posted at the beaches or the parks. You could come and go as you pleased."

"I guess there's a lot more crime now. Drug trafficking. That model who was murdered in Truro. Now I hear there are gangs in Hyannis, same as in big cities. I like Wonderstrand because it's so quiet most of the time."

"But that's the quiet of decay. Of anachronism. Just as bad in its way."

She couldn't help seeing the contrast between Jeffrey's and Guy's ideas of Wonderstrand. Jeffrey saw potential in it; Guy saw it as full of ghosts and dreams. He'd shown her parts of the book he'd been working on, and it reminded her of fairy tales. Things from long ago and far away, but to Guy they were still part of the landscape.

"So all the history and stuff isn't a big deal to you?"

"Oh, in its way. Don't forget history has its dark side, too. Plenty of murders on the Cape before it got so developed. There was a nasty one in Onset, way back in '46. Or did you ever read about the Lady in the Dunes, back in '74? Murder, mutilation, just as grotesque as what goes on today."

This was depressing. Piety wished they'd change the subject.

"Nostalgia is all well and good," Jeffrey continued, "but like it or not, no point in hanging on to the past for its own sake. Especially when there's still land that can be put to profitable use."

"I suppose you're right."

"Have you ever heard of the Wonderstrand Incubus?" There was something funny about the way he said it, like he'd been saving it up. He was studying his hands, reminding her a little of the way Guy talked to inanimate objects sometimes, except that Jeffrey was more focused. She followed his glance, noticed the stripe of paler skin where his wedding band had been.

"Sure. When all those women were attacked at night."

"The incidents could hardly be called attacks."

"Not the way I heard it."

"Tabloid nonsense. Gossip and innuendo. Finger-pointing." He hurled the empty wine bottle into the water and watched it sink.

"I don't think it was nonsense. I knew one of those girls. She was a lot older than me—I was a little kid when it happened, so this was quite a few years afterward, but we were in this group therapy thing. I couldn't afford private. Just women, all different ages. Anyway, she hated to be touched so much that she couldn't function. Stuff like getting back change when she bought something—the money had to be on the counter, not handed to her directly. And she couldn't stand being stared at; it really freaked her out. I can understand that part. Staring creeps me out, too."

A dark look she couldn't quite read filled his face, then disappeared.

"Why on earth did you need therapy?" he asked.

"I was miserable."

"Waste of time. Quacks."

If that was his opinion of shrinks, she could guess what he thought of her for seeing them. Deficient. Weak. Crazy.

"People have a dark side," he went on. So what? It's human nature. Can't be talked away."

"Talking can make you feel better."

He chuckled. "You're naïve, my dear."

His air of amused indulgence annoyed her. She yanked a hoodie over her sundress and ventured out on deck. The rain was now little more that a spattering of drops, pocking the surface of the water. She breathed in deeply and felt steadier.

He followed her.

"There are other ways to deal with problems. I could make you so comfortable…."

He trailed off, seemed to be waiting for her to speak.

It was a long time before she knew what she wanted to say. "That girl I was talking about? She made herself an object of curiosity because she couldn't stand to be looked at or touched. People stared more because she acted weird, or they kept patting her and hugging her to make her get over it."

"Perhaps that's what she really wanted."

"Oh, please. It was just the opposite."

"Not everyone is sure of her true desires."

"I heard she killed herself, a year after that group therapy."

The rain had soaked through the hoodie by this time, reaching her skin. She turned to go back in the cabin, but Mr. B. held her back.

"I have a confession to make. It has to do with the very incidents we were discussing. The man I've chosen as partner was once a suspect."

The cold sea seemed to rise up suddenly and wash over her. He must mean Guy.

"You'll ask how I can associate with such a person."

She swallowed hard. "Yeah. I will."

"Then let me explain. It's my belief that we have a moral duty to stand up for those who are accused, but not proven guilty."

"That's real righteous of you."

"We're all sinners." He was breathing hard, seemed barely contained.

"Let's go back to the dock," she said.

"Not yet. Not until you've heard me out."

She shook herself loose. "Do you have any idea how a woman feels when she's watched, judged, liable to be pounced on at any minute?"

"It might be troubling to a personality that's already unbalanced. Someone morbidly insecure. But the average person should expect...."

This evening had been a mistake. What did *she* expect? "What about being touched against her will, like when she's unconscious?"

"Hallucinations. Never proven."

"It all depends on who's telling the story, doesn't it?" Cold and tired, she went back in the cabin and switched on the light in the neat little bathroom, the head, whatever it was called. She flipped her hood down and tried to smooth her hair. In the mirror, it looked frizzed from the dampness and way too gold. She checked her teeth to see if anything was stuck in them. Nothing was, but their slight crookedness seemed more obvious than usual. Unlike most of her peers, she'd never had braces. She closed her lips, emphasizing little hollows below the corners of her mouth. Her face showed every minute over thirty.

Wait a minute. Was Guy a partner yet? He'd never called himself that. And that Incubus thing happened a long time ago. Guy was a year or so younger than her; he'd have been a kid then, too. Mr. B. must be talking about that consultant, the one from off-Cape.

She laughed aloud in relief. The wine must have been getting to her.

Mr. B.'s reflection, reddened and tight, appeared behind hers.

"You laugh?" he asked.

A threatening note in his voice made her wonder whether she could take the boat back to the dock herself if he wouldn't. Was it like driving a car? But a last glance at her image made her want, first of all, to get out of that harsh light. She certainly didn't want to be seen in it by anyone else, friend or foe.

She escaped to the softer lamps of the cabin, settling down among the cushions, stacking them around herself on three sides. Their surface felt hard and slick, a protective plastic coating for her body like the packing in a box of drugstore candy. The thought made her feel less jumpy for some reason.

"You're talking about that new man from out of town, right?" she asked. "What's his name, Wakefield?"

"Yes."

"He seemed so decent."

"As I said, he was only a suspect. Never prosecuted."

Wakefield had certainly *acted* nice, the once or twice he'd come into Deacon's. At first, she'd marked him as one of the Quebec people that often vacationed here, maybe because of his Frenchy coloring, but when he spoke she heard Cape Cod. All the same, she saw mystery and maybe tragedy in that handsome, craggy face, in the tight lines around his mouth. Aging came so much easier to men. The kicker was that he'd left her a five dollar tip on coffee and a cruller.

"Okay," she said. "What's his story?"

Mr. B. sat at one of the built in benches, facing her. He was a hefty man, not tall and thin like Guy, and his size shrunk the cabin.

"We weren't friends. He was older, closer to certain members of my family than to me. Actually, Coral Rigby was one of those who brought his name up in connection with the Incubus investigation. She had reason to know he was often out late at night near the areas where the incidents occurred. Do I need to be more specific?"

"He was her lover."

"You could call it that. The police talked to him and let him go."

"Maybe they were like you and didn't think there were any attacks to begin with."

"Perhaps. Anyway, my cousin blacked the poor fellow's name until he felt it necessary to leave the Cape. Whatever substance there was to the Incubus story, I personally never believed Wakefield had any connection to it. I know my cousin's spite too well. He carried on with her for a while— men will be men—then broke it off. Her way of getting revenge."

In some corner of her mind, Piety couldn't help taking the side of the women involved, even Coral Rigby, though she had seen the sharp side of her neighbor's tongue.

"So you really think he got a raw deal?"

"I do."

"But like we were saying before, everything's changed. A lot more people live here now who weren't around when that happened. It's not like everybody's going to remember and give him a hard time."

"When a man's reputation is compromised, he doesn't forget." Mr. B. pulled himself up straight. "I came across his name as one of those qualified to do the job I needed and felt it was my duty to offer him the opportunity. He's been quite successful in the interim, so not only was he interested in the work, he became an investor."

"Did he feel uncomfortable, coming back here?"

"He hasn't said. Really none of my business."

"So why are you telling me all this now?"

"Don't you know?" His face softened into Hallmark sentimentality.

"You didn't want me to hear it from Coral."

"Exactly. She'd have found a way to make both me and Wakefield look like villains. Make you feel nervous and frightened. Don't you know how much I value your good opinion? Your peace of mind?"

Did he? She allowed a little smile. "But I still think something happened to those women."

"I concede the possibility. People are capable of great evil. But the true danger, as I see it, is copycat crime. Impressionable minds hear these tales and act them out. What starts with a nightmare or the effect of an evening's revelry assumes a life of its own. One or two girls, perhaps mentally ill to begin with, fabricate a titillating story. Equally unbalanced males expand on the story, and real crimes result."

"Yeah. I suppose an incubus is more interesting than a peeping Tom, the same way a vampire in a black cape is more glamorous than, well, a real man that bites."

He hesitated, then laughed. "People will romanticize things. In any case, the rumor gets rehashed every few years, while Doane Wakefield has been away from the Cape for decades. The man deserves Jeffrey Goodman Brown's trust."

"I hear you," Piety said.

"I'm glad. And now it's quite late. It's time we got back to the dock."

While he steered the boat into the slip, she packed up the remains of their picnic and straightened the cabin.

Just before they stepped off the boat, he kissed her goodnight, a real kiss. She felt enveloped. It wasn't bad.

As July progressed, Piety saw less and less of Guy. She said nothing to him about her little Independence Day boat trip, and the secret weighed on her. She had other chaste outings with Jeffrey—she'd finally gotten used to calling him that—though she wasn't sure how she'd react if he wanted to sleep with her. On his part, he seemed to be holding back for reasons of his own. Sometimes his erection pressed against her stomach as they exchanged those goodnight kisses, but he never acted on it.

Guy, even when he wasn't away on business, was inattentive and strained. Often she gazed from her window through the trees at his cottage lights, burning long after midnight as he worked. Less often, they spent the night at her cottage. These times together stuck with her like nothing she'd experienced with any other man, but she couldn't quite put her finger on why.

Then the next morning, he'd be dim and faded. Piety would go off to work where Jeffrey Brown shone over her, hotter than the tourist season's sun.

It seemed she had a choice here. One man was cute, romantic, and just starting out. One was a lot older, and loaded. In the time she spent alone, Piety thought a lot about her future.

Near the end of the month, she went along with Guy on one of his library visits. Some work on local family histories, he said, for one of those tales he was writing. While he buried himself in yellowing sources too local and obscure for Google, she browsed through the philosophy section hoping he'd find her there when he finished.

"Did you think I'd be reading *People?*" she would ask, and he'd laugh and tell her how smart he thought she was. He'd say it to her directly, not to a piece of furniture or his shoes, as he did more and more often lately. Then the little compliment would lead to a discussion of how much, how truly, they had worlds in common.

Of course, that's not the way it happened. She finally got bored and went to find him at the big wooden table near the front entrance. She picked up one of the free local adzines stacked at the door, and that's what she was reading when he finally found her.

Still, she'd learned a few things in the stacks. Wisdom, pleasure, virtue. That's what mattered, according to some of the ancient Greeks, and they were the experts. But all of these qualities were hard to define, and highly personal. One woman's idea of virtue was another's idea of bad behavior. The bottom line seemed to be that we all need to figure it out for ourselves. The responsibility made her head spin.

She followed Guy out of the library and spent that night at his place. It wasn't great. He was jumpy, distracted by every sound. He'd told her that Coral, that witch, was trying to evict him, but he didn't want to leave. She hoped it was because he liked being so close to her, but he didn't say so. The next morning he headed off Cape again, and she went to Deacon's where she knew just how Jeffrey Brown liked his coffee.

Chapter 19

"Pure, fresh, almost sparkling, exhilarating—such water as Adam and Eve drank."

—Hawthorne

Guy tipped back his bottle, sucking out the precious drop or two that clung to the polished metal. He was down to his last jug of Coral's well water. He'd been rationing it since she'd cut him off, limiting himself to sips when he most needed them, to work on his book or spend the night with Piety. He tried not to waste it when he was off Cape. Strange that his work these days was almost never local. Often, he found himself with hours to kill between errands in Springfield, Providence, Nashua, errands whose objects seemed pointless, easily handled by phone or email.

Feeling too lethargic to write, he often employed these empty hours away in wandering around malls and gallerias. Money had lost its novelty. He bought new clothes, though they never seemed to fit as well as those Coral had given him. When his refilled disposable bottles grew too dented, their labels shredded, he replaced them with high-end models of stainless steel, as if his dwindling water supply would be more substantial if better housed. He even found one equipped with an LCD display that monitored the bearer's hydration needs, a feature he hardly needed, so overpowering was his thirst. He bought it anyway. These shopping trips distracted him only briefly; the worry always returned.

Of course, he'd long since recognized the restorative quality of the water. He'd attributed that simply to its being purer, though why that could be, he had no idea—a single aquifer provided most of the water for the whole Cape, and the Colony itself drew from the same groundwater. But what came out of his tap had no unusual effect. Neither did the stuff on the shelves at Stop-n-Shop. He speculated that Coral's little well might emerge from some isolated bit of glacial rock, a subterranean anomaly rich in some healthful mineral, or the opposite—such a high content of arsenic, nitrates, or some mutant bacteria, that any enlivening effect was a symptom of disease, like a fever rush. He even wondered if she added some drug. He paid a lab in Cambridge to test a vial of it. The report showed the usual parts per billion of the usual elements, both good and bad; nothing differing greatly from the average.

He knew the little well predated the main water supply by centuries, but not why that should matter. Did ancient spirits inhabit it? So many mysteries under the land and sea, so much he couldn't explain. A new strain of bacteria can kill a thousand people or save a million. A drug cures a lifetime's depression or creates an addict. One person has an allergy that makes a peanut lethal while another thrives on a diet of pbj's. Science? Magic? The fruit of prayer?

He was always left with one thought, irrational or not: the water was the liquid avatar of that Eureka he'd read in the sky all those months ago. Without it, was he cast into utter darkness?

The more diminished his supply, the harder he rationed and the greater his need. Thoughts of water consumed him. He couldn't pick up a newspaper without reading an article that urged everyone to drink eight glasses a day. If he turned the page to local politics, polluted ponds, fluoridation, and coastal erosion dominated the discussion. Click on the TV and he'd hear a chiropractor, rosy and limber, hold forth about how water kept the body lubricated, purified the bones, the blood, the muscles, the brain.

To add to his difficulty, July was the busiest month of his life. Mr. Brown filled ten and twelve hour days with work, but paid him accordingly. Guy traveled everywhere over a Cape redolent of fried seafood and onions. Drives that took ten minutes off-season stretched to an hour. Against the onslaught of kayak and bicycle-laden vehicles, a simple left turn became an adventure. Then the full moon brought the bloodthirsty greenhead flies, driving people off the beaches. Folk wisdom predicted they would disappear at the next full moon, but Guy found no one who really believed that. The hardiest of them would remain until September, diving in from nowhere to raise welts that would itch for days.

Yet all this he might once have enjoyed as the essence of summer. Now it made him shudder and sweat. He longed for respite, but Wonderstrand, the eye of the tourist storm, brought him no peace. Even in his beloved cottage, he felt like an animal driven to cover, for he dreaded running into Coral.

Traveling back and forth over the clogged Bourne and Sagamore bridges, he was offered frequent reminders that the Cape is a peninsula, at its narrowest point spanning only a scanty mile between ocean and bay. An island, if you counted the Canal as a body of water. But those surrounding horizons of saltwater couldn't quench his thirst. He tried concentrating on the road rather than the scenery, but in large letters on each side of the bridges, the Samaritans' signs asked him "Desperate?" But wouldn't those whose answer was "yes" find it hard to jump, with those inward-curving metal strips at the top, like claws?

Guy tried other beverages. Every variety of coffee and tea, performance drinks with ginseng, Red Bull. They made his hands shake. He miscalculated, made typos, sent unstamped mail, deleted files. He was slipping back more and more from G. T. to Guy with each passing day.

Piety noticed, he was sure. She rolled away from him in bed as if she'd reached for him and found empty space, even when he was right beside her. He saw her stiffen with irritation when he asked her, sometimes twice, to repeat a comment she'd made just a moment before. He longed for her, knew himself to be in love for the first and only time in his life, but felt too languid and dull to tell her. Besides, how could she ever care for him if she knew his old, his true, self?

Even the weather mocked him. Since the 4th of July, Wonderstrand had lain in the midst of a summer draught. Dust coated the trees, dulling the leaves. Reeds poked themselves higher every day from the shrunken ponds and salt marshes. Animals crept out of the woods at night to lap at lawn sprinklers.

Desiccated as he was, he would have done the same if it would have helped.

He dared not ask Coral for more. He'd gone to the shed, but found it double locked. Even the small cloudy window had been nailed shut. Peeking in, he saw that the well itself had been boarded over, and no filled jugs stood waiting. He longed to rip off the locks, pry the boards away from the well, but when he considered himself in the role of a common burglar, arrested, handcuffed, his glory days ended forever, his courage failed him. He walked away. As the deadline on the eviction drew nearer, his panic increased. Homeless, cut off forever from his elixir, what would he do?

Near the end of the month, Jeffrey Brown sent him to a house in Danvers, to "settle something," as his boss phrased it. "I bought the place from the bank, but I let the deadbeat former owners stay on as tenants. Not surprisingly, they didn't pay rent any more regularly than they paid the mortgage."

With a heavy heart, Guy approached the property, an aging Craftsman style on a street of well-kept, small lots. A child's plastic wading pool, molded in neon blues and greens and apparently freshly filled, contrasted sharply with the browned grass. Nearby stood a For Sale sign.

Guy parked across the street but couldn't bring himself to leave the car. His own eviction notice lay heavily on his mind. Through a screen door, he saw people moving within the house, could hear a jingle from a TV commercial. He sat in the car for so long that he felt the sun through the window began to burn his skin.

Guy grasped his handsome stainless steel bottle, unscrewed the cap. Less than an inch of water remained, a swallow or two. He'd been saving it for a night with Piety, but he couldn't face this without it. He tipped it and drank.

A man not much older than himself answered the doorbell, asked Guy what he wanted.

"I represent the property owner. I'm here to…"

"Put me and my family out on the street," the man finished. "You a cop? From the sheriff's office?"

"No, nothing like that. I've just come to remind you that you were notified quite awhile ago, and you're going to have to leave. If you don't, law enforcement officials will be here next, sooner rather than later."

"You work for that bastard Brown, do you? Well, you ask him where we're supposed to go. I've been a mechanic for fifteen years, but the dealership I worked at closed. You think it's easy to find another decent job? My wife works at McDonald's, like that would meet the rent, plus food, diapers, gas, utilities. I've got two kids, man. We don't even have a phone anymore."

"I'm sorry. But it's *my* job. I really want to spare you future unpleasantness." This was not precisely what Mr. Brown had told him to say, but it was true.

"This is my home. Can you understand that?"

Guy did, and he couldn't think of anything to say.

"I used to own this place. Well, me and the bank."

"I know. Your situation must be difficult, but the current owner has rights, too, and he's been generous."

"Generous? That's a joke. You don't know the sonofabitch you work for very well, do you?" The man stretched his fingers, rubbed his knuckles. Then he seemed to lose all his fight. "Hey, I know you're just following orders. I shouldn't take it out on you." He shook his head, swallowed. "Look, I just need a couple of months. I had two interviews last week, and both look good. I could get on my feet again before long. Maybe even buy the place back."

From the front step, Guy could see two children assemble behind their father, both strangely quiet. This wasn't the first such scene they'd witnessed, Guy was sure. He fumbled for his water bottle, then remembered it was empty. There was something else in his pocket, though, a folded envelope. His paycheck. The biggest of his life.

In a flash, he'd pulled it out and endorsed it. "Use this for your rent. It should cover the rest of the summer."

The man's jaw dropped. "You serious?"

Guy pressed the check forward. The man looked at it, shook his head. "No, you're crazy."

"Take it."

"Jeez. Wow. I don't know what to say. Who are you, some kind of guardian angel?"

"That's my name on the check, but you can call me G.T."

"Thanks, buddy. I mean, G.T. Give me your address, too. I'll pay you back, I mean it. Honest to God. Wait till my wife hears about this. She's going to cry. Honest. I feel like crying myself. You're a prince, you know that? Never seen anyone like you."

Guy gave him a business card, declined his offer of a beer or soda, and returned to his car for the drive back to Wonderstrand. The older of the two children accompanied his father to the street, where they stood waving until Guy's car turned the corner.

Halfway there, the warm glow faded. He wasn't worried about the loss of the salary. In spite of his spending, he had some money left over from the last two months in Jeffrey Brown's employ. But what about the next such errand? What about his conscience? This sort of work wasn't what he envisioned when he saw himself as rich and successful. Plus there remained his troubles with Coral. Had he misplaced his loyalty? He longed to seek comfort from Piety, but would she agree with what he'd just done? He wasn't sure.

He'd let Coral down; he couldn't deny it, but didn't he see his boss make similar choices every day? She'd promised to point him toward all his dreams, had sent him to Jeffrey Brown in the first place, and he, Guy, had tried to be a proper apprentice. If he hadn't told her all he learned, had taken Brown's side instead of hers, it was because…and here he stumbled. He couldn't explain his betrayal; even self justification eluded him. His thinking was as muddled as if his head were stuffed with cotton balls.

Chapter 20

"In an old house, a mysterious knocking might be heard on the wall, where had formerly been a door-way, now bricked up."

—HAWTHORNE, STORY IDEA

August was the month of spiders. They snuggled into angles and cracks, hid behind picture frames, leaped out of laundry. Tiny ones, the size of pinheads, burrowed into the scarecrows' stuffing. Huge ones, making their way across sunny windows, cast shadows the size of ripe peaches. Strands of web floated from ceilings and trees. Overnight, angular rags of lace appeared in corners, with sometimes the carapace of an unwary earwig dangling within.

Sweep though she would, Coral couldn't eliminate their traces, nor would she kill them, artisans like herself. Nevertheless, they troubled her.

Once while she was asleep, a spider wandered over her face. Her head must have seemed mountainous, her hair a dense, gargantuan forest, the smoothness of her skin easier going. Perhaps provoked by the movement of her eyes as she dreamed, it chose her eyelid for its bite. The swelling and itching lasted for days. Still she couldn't blame them. Their venom was their only defense, as was hers.

Spiders had their purpose. They preyed upon things even more unpleasant. So she carried them outside, enfolded in tissues or astride sheets of paper, trying to be careful not to crush them or break any of the eight legs. Sometimes she failed, and afterwards felt guilty. She wondered, do I love you or loathe you?

By now she'd seen the results of her first two deeds, undertaken with such bravado.

Jeffrey Brown flourished. The destruction of the colony went forward. Though not a shingle had fallen, she felt her home's dissolution as if it were her own flesh. Signs and omens multiplied. Cars stood parked in the road with paper cups of Deacon's coffee cooling on their hoods. Strangers carrying laptops and cell phones slipped into their cars and away before she could catch them.

An unusual spate of assaults on her hermitage, a warlike barrage of knocking, began about this time. Once or twice Guy tapped softly, like a drumbeat far away. She knew what he wanted. If she felt qualms about locking the shed and boarding the well, her anger at his betrayal was stronger. It was as if one of her scarecrows had lifted his straw fist and shaken it at her.

Apparently, he was ignoring the eviction notice she'd posted, and she hadn't summoned the energy to pursue it, but that didn't mean she had to do him any favors. She never had to wait long to hear him slump from the implacable closed door. Glimpses of him passing between his cottage and Piety's showed that he still grasped at the pearly oyster of his world, but his face had grown haggard.

Another day, a luckless engineer came, clacking on the door with the edge of his clipboard.

"Just wanted to warn you I'll be taking some specs around the property today," he said when she opened to him. "Sometimes folks get alarmed when they see a strange face in the area."

Coral, with Dickon's slavering, snarling assistance, issued a friendly warning of her own. Whatever the man's business, he either failed to accomplish it or did so with amazing haste; Coral never saw him again.

The following morning, another knock, brisk and businesslike. The dog uttered the growl to show he recognized no immediate threat, but was ready to exhibit his best impersonation of a rabid pit bull if necessary. Coral opened the door to see a pleasant-faced woman in her late forties, carrying an enormous florist's box.

"There's no one home at your neighbor's cottage across the way. Would you mind signing for these?"

A strong reply rose in Coral's throat, then she thought better of it.

"Let's see the card."

The woman's arms were too full to prevent Coral's snatching the small envelope taped to the top.

Coral pulled out the card and read: "To my Piety, with warmest regards, Jeffrey."

"Hell," she said.

The woman shifted the box, as if it had grown heavier. "Sorry to bother you, but can you take these? The man who ordered them made a big deal about their being delivered today."

Still thinking about the card and what it meant, Coral didn't close down her own gaze fast enough.

The woman eased her hip against the doorjamb, settling in. "I'd hate to waste another trip out here to Wonderstrand. This is my son-in-law's shop, and I only work there to help my daughter out. He's too cheap to hire help, so if I don't handle the deliveries, my daughter would have to, and drag the baby along. I told her, if that husband of hers can't...."

With an upward sweep of her hand, Coral urged the woman away from her doorjamb.

"You got the wrong address. There's no Piety around here."

The woman's confused face disappeared behind the slammed door.

Behind it, Coral shook her head. Poor gullible Piety. What fools we are when we're young.

Her cousin was recruiting everyone to his side. She could almost see the boards of her cottage protruding from a dumpster, could hear the nails that held the floor beneath her rattling as they struck metal. Nothing would be salvaged.

The cannonade of knocking continued.

A girl of perhaps fifteen or sixteen, appeared, her knuckles muffled by lacy fingerless gloves. The dog's hackles lay low, but he pricked up his ears to show he was alert and curious. Coral cracked open the door, and the girl pulled her hand back as if burned. She wore black and gray striped thigh-high stockings and leather ankle boots in defiance of the late summer heat, baring a couple of inches of thin leg below a brown taffeta skirt and black camisole. The girl's bowler hat was studded with tarnished metal—elaborate keys, clock gears, watch faces, a tiny compass. Two pairs of Victorian filigree earrings dangled from each ear and an industrial looking stud pierced one nostril.

Coral heard herself say, "Nice outfit." She kicked herself behind the door. Should have just slammed it.

The girl looked up from under her lashes. Tears had streaked her thick eyeliner and mascara down her pale cheeks all the way to her chin, giving her the appearance of standing behind a barred window. "You being sarcastic?"

Her tone was defiant, but the girl's eyes were pleading.

"No, I like the Goth thing. You've given me an idea for my next scare-crow." Lately, words had rattled out of her when she didn't want to speak, her own unwelcome gift turning back on her.

"Yeah, I heard you make them. I saw a whole bunch on the path. I'm not Goth, though. I'm Steampunk."

"What?"

"*Steampunk.* Like old time mixed with time travel. Past and future together. You never heard of it?"

"Do you want to buy a scarecrow? Because if not…"

"Crows are a sign of death. They're these things called psychopomps. Guides to departed spirits. To the underworld. I suppose that's why you make scarecrows?" Her expression mingled hope and challenge.

"Look, kid…"

"I heard other stuff about you, too," interrupted the girl. She wrapped her arms around herself, straitjacket style. "I have all these issues, you know? All this unbelievable shit. My parents suck and my ex-boyfriend's an asshole and everybody at school hates me. My shrink thinks she gets me, but she's so far off. They're gonna lock me up; I just know it."

Suddenly, the girl unclasped her arms and grabbed Coral's hand. "Please, can't you give me a spell or something? Or a charm, a potion, whatever?"

Coral shook herself free, but not before she saw the scars, crooked lines like broken spider legs, on the girl's skinny arms.

"Or maybe you could show me how to disappear."

Coral groaned. "That's not easy. Believe me."

The girl brightened as if she found this answer encouraging. "Can I, like, come in?"

"No!" A tart dismissal began to take shape on Coral's lips, but stuck there. She seemed to have lost all control these days. Plans went wrong; habits failed her. A feeling she preferred not to identify, akin perhaps to loneliness or empathy, began to sting like saltwater on a blister. It was the same in her dealings with Guy and Piety. Perhaps they couldn't help their needs, their foolishness. But she hated the traces they'd left in her life.

The girl still stood there, limp with disillusion.

"Hold on," Coral said. "I have just the thing you need. "

Several finished scarecrows stood handy. She grabbed the closest, a female figure in a 1950s party dress, frothy with yellow tulle. "This is the one. Yes, perfect. An amulet to ward off evil. Protect you from everything."

"But how can you tell?" said the girl in a small voice.

"I thought you said you'd heard all about me."

"Yeah, but…"

"Well, then. True, every word of it."

The girl wavered visibly between hope and skepticism. "I've only got about ten bucks."

"That'll do. Special discount, just for you. But in return, tell everyone you know that those tales about me are bullshit. I only have so much to go around, so you tell them I'm a harmless old lady. Even better, a nasty old lady. Whatever works."

The girl nodded, blurred eyes wide.

"Here, take it. And don't come back. It's all up to you now, not me. Put your own power into it. You believe in powers, don't you?"

The girl passed over a wadded bill and took the scarecrow.

"Do I have to put it outside, or can I keep it in my room?"

"That's for you to decide. Me, I'd keep it where I could see it."

Coral closed the door and slumped to the floor.

The dog, who'd waited quietly for instructions, trotted to the window and put his paws on the sill, nosing the shade aside. Soon he let the shade fall and walked away. The past and future child was gone.

After that, Coral stopped answering the door. When any knocking came, she curled into her smallest self and hid in the most protected corner of her cottage, an angle of the hall with no sightline to any window. At her command, Dickon accompanied her. As she cowered there, hating it, she made a mental list of who might be at the door. She could tell general categories by the dog's behavior: stranger, enemy, or acquaintance. There was no one who could be considered a friend, no one for whom the dog might utter a friendly bark of welcome.

Then in the midst of one of those searing sunsets that dyed the very atmosphere red, there came another knock. This one echoed in her chest, like a heartbeat.

The dog did nothing.

"Dickon!"

Still he uttered neither bark nor growl, but merely waited, his bicolored eyes on her.

No command came to mind.

A second knock, louder. A third. Finally, silence.

She let go the breath she now realized she'd been holding.

She knew who it was. How long, how many decades, can one be haunted? But who was the ghost, she or Doane Wakefield? Or was the ghost the past itself? Regardless, it was more threatening than a dozen Jeffrey Browns armed with wrecking balls.

If need be, she'd never open the door again.

Chapter 21

"Some of those who create Scarecrows believe that a face
with an expression is an important factor in deterring predators;
others are content with more abstract forms."

—COLIN GARRATT

On a rare day when he hadn't been sent off-Cape, Guy sat in his office trying to concentrate on his computer screen. He jumped as the phone buzzed in the outer office, banging his knee in the desk, then did it again when the call was transferred. He heard his boss answer in his usual hearty manner. Odd, he thought. Mr. Brown usually kept his door closed.

"I'm extremely sorry to hear it. He forgot to include the damage deposit? They flooded the whole bathroom? Yes, yes, I know—if it's not in the contract, the renters aren't liable. Let me see what I can do."

A pause, then in a wounded tone: "You know I never let a client down." Another pause.

"Again, I apologize. This isn't the first mistake? He listed the wrong number of bedrooms? Omitted the outdoor shower? You should have let me know sooner. Of course, no one likes to complain. Drug problem? Certainly not! Jeffrey Goodman Brown doesn't hire addicts. You've known me many years; how can you ask…yes, yes, I understand. Most likely he was merely tired. Don't we all get tired sometimes?"

A laugh, warm with forbearance. "No, I can't disagree with you there. The young man is…." The sentence hung unfinished.

Guy slumped lower in his office chair as Brown's plummy laugh boomed again.

"I'll handle your properties personally from now on. You have my word on it."

The conversation tapered off, ended. Guy heard the squeak of Brown's leather chair, felt the vibration of each step as he left his own office and headed to Guy's.

What explanation could Guy muster that wouldn't sound ridiculous? Was he to go back to his vending route, back to stuffing crackers into machines? Was he to invite Piety to share repasts of broken pretzel sticks and squashed Snickers bars? Homeless. Helpless. Hopeless.

But to Guy's surprise, his boss's face exhibited no anger.

"How's that book coming?" Brown asked.

"Book?"

Brown raised his eyebrows.

"Oh. The book. My book. Very well." Guy addressed the carpet; he couldn't seem to help it.

"Indeed?"

Guy kept his gaze down. Industrial carpet, beige nylon.

"You haven't found yourself overworked, between that and the travel? No? Quite sure? Not everyone is meant to be out in the field. I have some work coming up for you in the next few days that's a little closer to home."

"Sounds good," Guy told the desk lamp.

"In the meantime, this book of yours. Did I ever tell you about my paternal grandmother, Faith Brown? No, I don't think I did. Here's a tale you might be able to use."

The boss made himself comfortable, and Guy opened the appropriate file.

"Faith was named for a great grandmother of her own—several 'greats,' I forget how many. This ancestress was one of the residents of the Massachusetts Bay Colony. Salem, actually. Don't you love these little tidbits of family history?

"Anyway, the modern Faith, my grandmother, married a second cousin, also named Brown, but was widowed early. Times were hard, but she was resourceful. Something has always come along to keep us Cape Codders afloat and solvent, as you know." Brown ticked them off on his fingers: "fishing, whaling, wrecking, salt works, cranberries, shipping, tourism— and now real estate and development." He stressed the last as the epitome of achievement.

"For a few years, there was one other profitable industry, and that's where Faith Brown found her opportunity. Can you guess?"

Guy, trying to type, could not.

"Why, rum running, of course!" A vulpine smile creased Brown's face. "No shame in that. A poor widow has to make a living. Of course, if you choose to write this tale, you wouldn't use real names."

"Oh, of course."

"In Wonderstrand, like the rest of the Cape, the Eighteenth Amendment wasn't viewed as entirely a bad thing. Private imbibers, and, in a commercial way, smugglers, found our vast coastline hospitable. My ancestress sold and borrowed everything she could to buy a boat, then made a tidy fortune employing it during the evening hours.

"She rented the barn of a local farmer as temporary storage for the cases of liquor waiting to be trucked to cities on the mainland. She trusted this man, her employee as it were, and paid him well. But he grew sloppy. Perhaps he was dipping into the stored goods. He bragged of his new-found income in public once too often, and government agents found and seized a large and valuable cargo.

"Of course, the man was arrested. He named Faith Brown as the source of the liquor, but my grandmother knew how to cover her tracks. In every other way, she was an upright citizen and a pious woman, so in the end, the farmer was blamed for the whole crime. He'd made things difficult for her, though, and she didn't forget that. While the farmer was serving his jail time, his wife and children struggled to keep the farm going, but one night, just after harvest, they awoke to find the barn in flames. The fire spread to the house and even the fields. It was a dry year, and all was destroyed."

"What happened to the family?" Guy asked, perspiring.

"Ah. Forced to go away. Dispersed into poverty and anonymity. The farmer died in jail." Again, Brown displayed that fox's smile. "I believe a bank and a medical building stand on that property now."

"And your grandmother?"

"Oh, she was forced to abandon her rum running, but the repeal wasn't far off, and she'd tucked away a tidy sum. Eventually passed down to me." He patted his paunch. "Jeffrey Goodman Brown."

"Remember, G.T. my boy, every tale has a moral. A scholar such as yourself won't miss that." Brown rose and stretched. "Much will be required of us all in the coming days."

He turned to leave. "Oh, by the way, something odd came to my attention recently. Your last paycheck was cashed in Danvers, and dou-ble endorsed. Your financial dealings are your own business, of course. I thought you'd like to know, though, that our property there is free and clear. The tenants decamped the day after the check was cashed. Left the rent in arrears, of course, but at least they're gone. Out of state would be my guess, but they left no forwarding address."

Alone again, Guy closed the computer. He knew he wasn't really intended to write up Faith Brown's tale or include it in his book. Its moral was meant for him alone.

Chapter 22

"Is truth a fantasy which we are to pursue forever and never grasp?"

—HAWTHORNE

A light knock, then pounding.

Coral poked the dog. "Growl, you fool. Bark!"

Dickon stretched and spread himself out on the rug.

"Judas!"

The dog opened one eye, the blue one, but otherwise ignored her. There'd be no help from that quarter.

From outside came words spoken close, meant to carry through painted wood and more: "Open the door."

She knew the voice.

She raised her own, parrying his. "Go away."

This time, Doane Wakefield didn't retreat. "It's been long enough."

"Too long. Too late."

"I'll break it down."

"Very dramatic. But don't even try."

He rattled the doorknob.

"Go away."

A heavy thud. A mumbled "shit."

"Stop it. You'll hurt yourself."

Another thud.

"I'm calling the police."

"No, you're not. Not this time."

He was right. As if watching herself in a dream, she slid back the bolt, flipped the lock, and let him in.

Here he stood at last.

His body had softened, but not much. His face was crosshatched and creased. His hair had thinned, with streaks of pure white making the black stand out like charcoal strokes.

He was still beautiful.

Coral knew how she looked. Hair the color of bone. Cheeks and eyes hollowed by years of solitude. A woman appearing to be alive but flat and cold to the touch, bleak as winter. For the first time, she was ashamed.

"Living here, don't your memories eat you alive?" he asked.

"And you? Conspiring with Jeffrey Brown. How does that serve your memories? Your conscience?"

This very cottage had been their favorite trysting place. Here, Coral Rigby and Doane Wakefield loved each other with all the sweetness of youth.

It made no sense. Both were of private natures, solitary habits, without siblings or close friends. Both preferred the company of elemental things, the sea, the sky. If at night, they turned their faces to the full moon, the communion was private. Both enjoyed the way their blood raced and their hair whipped about in a northeast wind, but they walked alone, requiring neither company nor witness.

Both had grown up on the Cape, though in different towns, different schools. Probably their paths had crossed over the years, but they'd never glanced up. Then like two wild creatures, surprised to encounter another of their species, they recognized each other instantly, hungrily. Curling together in sheltered dunes, pine groves, graveyards, abandoned dune shacks, they made one world, one flesh. They shared their childhood haunts, those isolated stretches of beach and woodland where they'd never taken another living soul, and each place became as fresh as the first time they'd seen it. Sometimes they ventured south to Monomoy, north to the Provincelands, ferried east to the islands. But in the end, they always returned to the cottage in Wonderstrand.

Until Doane, this place was the only thing Coral had ever loved. She came from mean, sly people, and knew it. Conceived in the intoxicated jubilation at the end of the Second World War, she caused the union of a couple who had never meant to pass more than a summer weekend together. Thus blighted, her parents found variable outlets for their surplus misery. One week, they vilified banks and bankers as the scourge of working folk; the next they raged about welfare cheats. If a recently arrived neighbor replaced the poverty grass in his yard with a real lawn, they said washashores were ruining the Cape with their suburban ways, but the native who refused to remove his dinghy from a beach now declared private was an inbred local. They became equal opportunity misanthropes.

Coral, they largely ignored. Her name had been chosen by her eight-months pregnant mother, nostalgic for better days. She was strolling through Wonderstrand's cemetery when she saw the name on an old tombstone. It recalled to her a necklace she'd bought for herself before she was married, and the coincidence pleased her. Coral's father, though eager to veto his wife's choice, traced someone by that name in his ancestry. He chose to view it a tribute to his own family genes.

In the rare time they spent with their misbegotten daughter, each parent treated her to a copious narration of his or her side of things, thus indulging their one shared pleasure—playing people against each other. Her mother informed the child that she couldn't have a bicycle because her father had spent the money on fishing equipment he was too lazy to use. Her father told her there was only peanut butter for dinner because her mother blew the grocery budget at Bingo.

Though her parents came to loathe each other, they stayed together for the bit of family money that had come down to them, sufficient to keep them afloat together, but not if they lived separately. Nor was it enough to keep their small house in repair or buy a dependable car. It did allow them to avoid working most of the year. Her father took summer jobs, bartending or scooping chowder; her mother did some typing or cleaning now and then. October to June, they stayed at home and annoyed each other.

At what point in her childhood did she realize her parents were liars and sneaks? She could hardly recall. By the time she was in elementary school, Coral had grown expert at hiding the five dollar bills she got for her birthday, and even more, her thoughts. In her early teens, she recognized the satisfaction of local gossips and estranged relatives when they favored her with contradictory versions of her parents' stories. Jeffrey Brown, then a nasty little boy, took special delight in laying embarrassing truths before her. Among them: the bar owner who had supposedly refused her father a job for the winter had in fact never heard of him. Her mother's quarrel with the neighbors hadn't been because their dog dug up the Rigby's yard; it had been because her mother sneaked next door at night and stole their ripe tomatoes off the vine. Jeffrey never said how he knew these things, but they always turned out to be true.

One night when Coral was eighteen, her parents, probably in mid-argument, hurtled their jalopy over a cliff that dropped seventy feet onto the sand. It rolled over once and into the sea, killing both. Coral pitied their unhappy lives, but couldn't mourn them. She was left with an over-mortgaged house, a collection of frayed sofas, chairs with uneven legs, a liquor cabinet filled with half-empty bottles, and no money. She did have an excellent education in trusting nobody, plus the half interest in the cottage colony left to her by her maternal grandfather. She moved in there.

Doane Wakefield's parents, on the other hand, enjoyed their only son, born to them late in their lives. His father had a small construction business, more additions and remodeling than building houses; his mother answered the phones and drew up the invoices. Snug in the house they'd put up themselves during their first year of marriage, they were the sort of native Cape Codders who never crossed Sagamore Bridge from one year to the next. His father had served with the Pacific forces, and vowed he'd seen enough of the world; his mother had waited stateside for her young husband and wished never again to be anywhere he was not.

Consequently, until Doane had a car of his own, he'd never seen a game at Fenway, eaten at a restaurant that didn't serve chowder, or traveled on a road with more than four lanes. Later, he and Coral would climb onto a dune near a beach parking lot or sit at the back table of some clam shack and watch for cars from far away. One night, they counted fourteen different states, including, unaccountably, Hawaii.

He told her how they were going to go these places together.

They never did.

When his parents moved to a retirement community in Barnstable, Doane rented a room in a boarding house, got a job with a builder in Hyannis.

"What makes you such a loner?" Coral asked him once. "Your family's nice."

"I'm not a loner. I have you."

She touched his cheek, liking the roughness. "Before that."

"My parents never needed anyone but each other. I mean, they were good to me, but I guess I grew up thinking there'd be one person you'd trust with everything."

"Don't you find that frightening?"

"No. Should I?"

"But what if...?" she began, then hesitated.

"It's not frightening. You'll see."

"Well? Are you happy now?"

"What?" She realized his voice wasn't coming from her memory. He was there beside her.

"Are you happy because you were right? You always said it was crazy to trust anybody. Here's your chance to say 'I told you so.'"

"What a horrible thing to ask."

His laugh scalded. "And what you believed about me? That wasn't horrible?"

"You wouldn't listen, wouldn't wait."

"You shouldn't have needed proof."

"You shouldn't have disappeared. All these years and not a word. Then you come back here, working for my worst enemy. *Your* worst enemy."

"I don't work for him!"

"Don't shout at me." Normally, Dickon would have been in attack mode at the sound of raised voices, but the damned dog dozed on. He took his commands from her, yet he there he lay, unconcerned. Was everything in disarray?

"It's an investment. Brown's a blowhard, and I don't like him. If anyone's in charge, it's me."

He hated her that much? Coral felt her knees weakening under the blow. She put a hand against the wall to steady herself. "You must be so proud."

He ignored this. "But he's not my enemy any more than any other cutthroat I've done business with."

"Oh, God. You don't know, do you?" She'd been alone so long that her memories seemed the only ones.

"Know what?"

But she shook the question off. "Why did you have to come back?"

"Oh, just another boomer longing for his childhood home."

"Liar." Her head was spinning. From the blur of past and present, she grasped for words and was surprised at what came out: "Did you ever see all those places? The ones from the license plates?"

After a long pause he answered. "Most of them. Why not? I was an exile, thanks to you."

"So you've come back here to get even with me?"

Silence clotted around them.

"Well, did you?"

Another harsh laugh. "Can't you make me tell you? Unload all my darkest secrets, the way you did that other time?"

They'd been in bed, all the cottage windows open to a spring breeze, the glow from the fireplace reflecting on their skin. They talked lazily about the day now passed, the week ahead, plans for the summer. She'd been telling him about a man she'd encountered that morning.

"He kept talking about his son, that he's some kind of delinquent. That he tried to beat it out of him, and the kid ran away. It was awful. I don't know why people dump their private lives on me."

"If I'd been there, I would have gotten you free of him."

"I wish. But why do they do it? It's not as if I care."

"No?"

"You think I do?"

"Maybe."

"I don't. Except about you."

He grinned. "Then why do you get depressed when people tell you about bad things?"

"I suppose it's just envy. It's so easy for them."

"Envy yes, empathy no? If you say so. But I know you better than you do." He wrapped a leg around hers.

Her joy rose so strong it was akin to pain. To him, she wasn't a misfit, cold fish, a misanthrope like her parents.

"Most people like to talk about themselves," he continued. "You don't, so you listen. Who wouldn't grab the opportunity?"

"You're saying I draw them out? The confessors, the horn blowers, the braggarts, the breast beaters, the soul barers?"

"Maybe some of them need you."

"No one needs me but you."

"Let's see what happens, okay" He faced her, almost nose to nose. "Here, look at me. That's right."

"This isn't working." She was having trouble keeping a straight face.

"It's not funny. Stop screwing around. Concentrate."

"I can't help it. I feel like we're having a staring contest." She gave up, rolled over on her back. "It doesn't work with you."

"We've told each other all our secrets already. That's why."

"You're the only person I trust."

"Me, too."

She curved herself into him. "But everyone has an inner life that they keep to themselves, don't they?"

So long ago, and she'd been right. "I don't want to make you tell me anything," Coral said now. How many unwelcome truths could she bear?

"Ah, you want it to be voluntary. Reveal nothing yourself, but expect answers."

He took her by the shoulders and made her face him straight on. She flinched, but allowed it. To her shame, her eyes started to burn. No one had touched her in years, and her flesh seemed to rise to meet his hands as if it had broken free of her will. She hadn't shed a tear in years, either. Two forgotten sensations.

"Now what is it that I don't know?"

He was turning her own witchcraft back on her. She began to speak. "Do you remember that conversation we had once? She stopped, swallowed. "About swimming naked in the ocean...."

His grip on her shoulders tightened.

It had been the anniversary of the day they'd met, and they'd gone out for lobsters. Now they lay on a blanket on the beach, iced Champagne propped in the sand. They'd forgotten glasses, and were drinking from the bottle, foam cascading over their chins.

"You really think we've told each other all our secrets?" she asked.

"Are you still worrying about that? Well, I suppose there are always new ones."

"See what I mean?"

"If not secrets, then fantasies. Things that aren't really about you, but, I don't know, imagined."

"Lovers share fantasies. Willingly."

"Then are you going to tell me one?"

"Probably not." She laughed.

"That's not fair."

"Is so. 'People like to talk about themselves,' remember? I listen."

"You said talking to me is safe."

"Okay, okay. Here's one. I'd like to swim naked with you, in the ocean. At midnight."

"Easy. We can do that tonight. Come on; there must be more."

"I want to make love in the waves."

"I was hoping. It's a quarter to eleven now. How about a trial run?"

She loved the way their laughter rang in the big hollow of sea and sky.

Then all was silent again, and she told him the rest. "I want to conceive our child like that, in the sea. On a wild night, so wild that everything I've been until that moment gets lost in the water and the wind."

He made a sound in his throat and tried to pull her closer, but she shook her head

"Now you. This was your idea."

He sat up.

"Okay. I can't get enough of you. When I'm not with you, I want to picture what you're doing. Sometimes I imagine I'm looking at you, and you don't know I'm there. You're thinking of me. You run your hands over your body, and I can see you sigh. Maybe you're in a clearing in the woods, in the moonlight. Or in the cottage, alone, by firelight. I slip behind you, but you don't hear me or see me, and I put my hands where yours were and you shudder. And we make love, but you never see me. I'm invisible, but you know I'm there."

She sat up, too. "You'd be a mystery then. The real you, I mean, not the one in my head."

"But you wouldn't be a mystery to me."

They listened to the waves crashing. One, then another, then two at almost the same instant.

"I'm chilly," she said lightly. I don't want to swim after all. Let's go home."

Within a week, everyone was talking about the Wonderstrand Incubus.

"I had a ring in my pocket that night," Doane said now. "I was going to ask you to marry me. After we left the beach, the time seemed wrong, so I decided to wait."

Coral wondered what would have happened if he hadn't waited, then chopped off the thought. What use was it?

"Before I left the Cape, I threw the ring in the ocean."

"Let go of me," she said.

He ignored her. "How could you have suspected me?"

"I heard things."

"What, rumors? Gossip? You of all people should have known better."

"No, not rumors. Remember, that summer I worked at that big inn in Chatham as a chambermaid? So did this corn-fed kid from Ohio or somewhere, just out of high school. One day I was passing in the hallway while she was supposed to be doing one of the guest rooms. She'd left the door open and I could see her hunkered down in a corner, sobbing.

"I closed the drapes and locked the door before someone came along. She wouldn't move, though; she said that corner was the only safe spot in that room because it was hidden from all the windows. No one could get at her there, she said.

"She'd been trying to make the bed and just freaked out. Every bed, every window reminded her. She could feel a hand scrabbling at her. It wasn't as if she'd been raped; people might understand then, and sympathize. But this was so dreamlike, so fanciful. She hadn't rested for days. And I knew how she felt, that awful distrust that never goes away, that sense that the ground could collapse under you at any moment."

"You thought I did that to her?"

"What you told me...it was so like the attacks."

"That was about you. Only you."

"But the coincidence."

"You *knew* me." His voice turned bitter. "Oh, but we never *really* know anybody, do we?"

"Stop it. Just stop it."

Finally he let go of her. "You were my world."

"Damn you! Why didn't you stay, then? Give me a chance! How faithless…"

"You dare to call me faithless, after you went to the police?"

"What?"

"They stopped short of taking me to the station, but clearly I was a person of interest."

"So you picked up and left? Didn't you think that would make them more suspicious?"

"I didn't care what they thought. I felt the most terrible anger," he said slowly. "You can't imagine."

"Oh, yes. I can. And I never went to the police!"

"Then who did? Not the victims, because I had nothing to do with the attacks."

"Oh, God." Coral sunk into a chair. "Here's what you didn't know— nor did I, until later. It was Jeffrey Brown, all Jeffrey Brown. After that girl talked to me, that same day, I ran into him, and he made a snide remark that I should be keeping better track of my boyfriend's late night where- abouts. That fantasy of yours, and the girl's story—it all came together. I couldn't think. You were so angry. By the time my head cleared, you'd disappeared."

"Jeffrey Brown," Doane said very softly.

"He probably dropped a hint to some family connection in the police force. And there's more. I know, I can prove, that he's a voyeur."

"He's a fucking peeping Tom?"

"I have pictures."

"Christ. So he did the attacks?"

"I'm sure of it."

"And you've let him get away with it?"

"No. Until recently, I thought he'd stopped. We had an arrangement."

"The cottages."

"Yes."

Mutual accusation hung between them.

"They meant more to you than I did?"

"You were already gone, God knew where. I went away after awhile, too. I suppose I had some notion of finding you. Then I got notified that Brown wanted to tear everything down. Of course, he couldn't without my permission. I came back and never left again. I pieced together a life."

"So did I. A fake life."

The atmosphere in the room had turned to ice. Coral pressed her hands together for warmth. The scarecrows lining the wall seemed to huddle closer together.

Then like a man awakening, Doane seemed to take in his surroundings for the first time. He half smiled, but there was little mirth in it. "Do you remember the scarecrow that always stood against the back of that barn in Eastham, the one facing Route 6?"

"The old Brackett farm. It's a bank now."

"Yes, I noticed. You always believed scarecrows kept bad things away. Seems you were wrong."

"Not just about that."

"I could say the same."

For awhile, neither spoke.

Doane found words first. "Brown will pay."

"Don't go off all crazed again. You should have learned."

He took his time responding. "If I come back tomorrow, will you let me in?"

"Why?" She felt so sad, so tired.

"Don't we both have scores to settle? We still share that, at least."

"But old scores aren't my biggest worry now. He's trying to take my home—with your help, I might add. I can't make any more mistakes."

"I'll be back."

"No." She remembered the waiting, the expecting. Only a fool would plunge back into the undertow after almost drowning.

In the wake of the slammed door, the scarecrows along the wall bowed their heads like a row of penitents.

Chapter 23

"My journey, as thou callest it, forth and back again,
must needs be done 'twixt now and sunrise."

—HAWTHORNE

The shelves of Jeffrey Brown's Sub-Zero shone clean and orderly since he'd stripped them of his wife's yogurts and celery sticks. His own stock now lay in easy reach: two bottles of Chardonnay, one of Grey Goose, a pound of thick-sliced ham, a jar of imported mustard, and a wrapped package from Crowell's Fish Market. He removed this last and emptied its contents into a cooler filled with ice.

Next he pulled out his cell and pressed the screen.

"Ah, you're at home. Excellent. And I see it's nearly ten o'clock—I didn't wake you? Sorry to call so late, but I've just run into a friend of mine who went oystering today. He gave me a couple of dozen, and I know how you enjoy them. Problem is, I can't drop them off in the morning. Breakfast meeting at Chatham Bars. Glad you understand. I've got 'em on ice, but I'm tied up at the moment so I can't say when I'll get there. Suppose I just leave the cooler by your door so you won't have to wait up. Fine. In the morning, there they'll be, nice and fresh."

He listened for a few seconds, then laughed merrily. "Can't say I'd fancy them for breakfast myself, but you go right ahead. No, no—always glad to do what I can."

With an endearment and the slide of his finger, the call ended.

Now let anyone question his reasons for being at the cottages tonight.

He'd insisted Maulkin meet him in the woods half mile or so from the cottage colony. If the young pup thought that odd, too bad. One small dilemma was choosing the best place to leave his vehicle, the SUV this time, not the Caddie. Later on, he wouldn't want his behavior to look clandestine. If he parked near his destination, Piety might wonder why he hadn't just driven up to the cottages; besides, he'd want the car accessible when the evening drew to its finale. On the other hand, he didn't want to draw attention to the length of time he'd been in the vicinity. He decided to leave it on the road outside the colony, but back a ways, where the Rigby woman, even with those hooded lizard's eyes, probably wouldn't notice it. If anyone asked, he'd say he wanted to avoid the lumpy, unpaved driveways that served the cottages themselves.

A waxing moon hung low, obscured now and then by thickening clouds. Employing his usual caution, he wound his way on foot among the trees. Not far from one of the paths stood a colonial stone wall. Brown had appointed this spot for the rendezvous, and arriving first, had time to muse. Probably one of his ancestors had stacked those very stones to mark his property, through the sweat of his brow protecting what was his. Some of the stones had fallen and lay embedded in the soil, but the wall still rose up from the land, gently curving like a sleeping woman's spine, the individual rocks like vertebrae. Brown seated himself at the foot of an old tree, well shadowed.

He was proud of his ancestry, but not unrealistic. Certainly, he had what Piety would call "baggage." As a crooked ring finger, widow's peak or harelip reoccurs in some bloodlines, so the Brown family had produced its share of melancholics, tyrants, and lunatics. They married acrimoniously, or not at all. On his mother's side, the Albrights had been just as bad. His grandfather, Eustace, was responsible for that white elephant of a cottage colony.

Genealogy didn't trouble Jeffrey. Several centuries of marriages, remarriages, abandonments, new identities, family schisms, disinheritances, illegitimacies and even misspellings had diluted the line—if a stonecutter left out a letter or two on a tombstone, it was cheaper to adapt than to order another stone. Clearly, the worst of the genetic code had landed with his mother's sister, the Rigby woman's mother. His father had told him that branch was descended from some old crone in Colonial Salem, reputed to be a witch, who fled here after an incident involving a rich man's daughter. Jeffrey didn't doubt it.

It wasn't unusual back then for people to migrate east to rural Cape Cod, where life was less restrictive than in the Massachusetts Bay Colony. The Browns had done the same, finding that religion sometimes crossed purposes with their own. Jeffrey's own mother had told him, after one of her acrimonious quarrels with his father, that the Browns were scions of the most miserable man in old Salem, his misanthropic nature formed by nights spent in the forest with disreputable company. Still, it had all worked out, and he, Jeffrey Brown, was the proof of that.

At last Maulkin stumbled into sight, letting out a cry of alarm when he spotted his employer.

"Calm down. It's only I, nothing to fear. Let's just wait here a minute and catch our breath, shall we?"

He handed over a flask. "Brandy. Have a sip."

Maulkin gulped, made a face.

"You're probably wondering why we're here. I'll be direct. Coral Rigby refuses to budge, and stronger measures are called for. This is my plan. If the cottages are condemned as uninhabitable, she'll have to get out. It's that simple. We're going to implement a few tricks tonight to ensure her departure. Don't trouble your tender conscience, though—she'll get her share of the land's current value."

"But why does it have to be done at night?"

"Need you ask?" Brown indicated the tool bag.

"Is Doane Wakefield coming with us?"

"Haven't heard from him today. Called and got voicemail. More discreet if it's just the two of us, anyway."

Brown had no intention of including Wakefield. Maulkin's question reminded him, though, that the man hadn't come through that afternoon with some expected estimates. He wondered briefly where he could be.

"I'm not sure this is a good idea," Maulkin ventured.

"What, scruples now? Don't lose your courage this late in the game." Brown seasoned his tone with camaraderie and just the right amount of threat. "Be a man, G.T."

"Is it, um, completely legal?"

"The law's a flexible commodity." He aimed a hearty pat on the back, causing Maulkin to cough.

"For heaven's sake, get hold of yourself. Here." Brown passed the flask.

Again Maulkin swallowed. The film of sweat he was sporting grew to pendulous drops.

"Why all these nerves? Many a businessman before you, both upright and ungodly, has made these nighttime journeys, I assure you. Anyway, I need you there mainly to act as lookout. You can manage that, can't you?"

He could see Maulkin pondering. All daydreams, all tales from books, no substance or action. When they'd first met, the fellow had seemed sharp. Strange how he'd deteriorated with further acquaintance, but it was all to the good. Surely Piety was beginning to see through him, too, and Brown would blot him out of her mind soon enough.

Maulkin sat up a little straighter. "While we're there," he began, then hesitated.

"Yes?"

"There's something I need in Coral Rigby's shed."

"Oh?" Brown was interested now. "Something of yours you left there accidentally?"

"Of mine, yes." Maulkin was a poor liar. "Since she and I haven't been speaking lately…"

"Hardly surprising."

"I'd like to get it back." He eyed the tools.

"So you'd like to break the lock and slip in?"

"Not to take anything of value, honestly. Just to…"

"To get what's yours. I understand completely. Might be a bit of a risk, but once we finish our task successfully, I don't see why we can't… retrieve your property."

Maulkin's relief rushed into the air between them, almost palpable.

"Give as well as take, that's my motto." Brown rose. "Tell you what, I'll fill you on the rest of the plan as we walk."

He was careful to keep the details sketchy in places, specific in others. Whatever Maulkin knew about odometers, he was ignorant about construction, so Brown stirred up a mélange of vagueness worthy of a politician. In a disorder sure to confuse, he fired forth terms like compromised foundations, underpinnings, and carrying sticks. He mentioned the chisels, hammer, and crowbar in the canvas duffel he carried, and how they might be used.

Of course, Brown could have paid someone to do damage in broad daylight if he'd really wished it. A simple septic check by a hired acquaintance of his, a little wadded cloth stuffed in the right place, the system backs up a week later, the cottages are polluted beyond fixing, and who'd know why? If he met any further resistance, that could furnish a *coup de grâce*. This little journey with Maulkin, however, promised much more far-ranging payoffs.

When at last his companion managed to insert a question, Brown had only to admonish, "Keep your voice down. We're drawing close." And that was that.

Beautifully handled, if he said so himself. He almost wished they could perform Maulkin's little burglary so he could see what the Rigby woman had stashed away. But even Jeffrey Brown couldn't allow himself *every* delight.

They began at the unoccupied cottage farthest from the Rigby woman's, just as a drizzle began to fall. Brown made a show of measuring, testing, tapping softly at the foundation. "This is a bit louder than I anticipated," he said, though in fact he'd made almost no noise at all. "You need to go see if anyone's noticed."

Maulkin crept along the wall, poked his head into the open and glanced around.

"No one's outside. I don't think they heard."

"Good. I suppose that hellbeast of a dog would have barked if he had. But I still need to know who's home."

"There are lights in both cottages."

"They might have left them on. Lots of women are afraid to return to a dark house. Are their cars there?"

"I see Piety's but not Coral's truck."

Odd, that. The woman rarely went out. Her absence was a mixed blessing, though. She wouldn't be around to interfere or to force them to rush, yet he would have welcomed, for once, her being a witness.

"Does Piety ever walk out? Perhaps to the local tavern? I'm sure you'd know." It irked him to acknowledge the familiarity between her and Maulkin, but it wouldn't last much longer.

"Sometimes. She might."

"I'll need to be sure."

"I could call her, but she might not pick up."

Why the hangdog air? Brown wondered. Had there been a lovers' quarrel? This might be easier than he expected. "No, you have to go over there and see. Are her shades up?"

"What?" Maulkin turned to look at him oddly.

A misstep. Brown had to tread carefully here. The fellow was a fool, but he knew the local tales. "Can you see if she's in there?"

"Not from here."

"Then you must go find out. No, wait. This is complicated work, and it might be better if we hold off until people are asleep. The Rigby woman isn't home at the moment, so we'll do that little business with her shed first. I'm sure Piety is used to the dog's barking; it won't draw her out. And getting your property back, whatever it is, will put you more at ease."

Of course, Maulkin liked this plan.

"But we can't risk Miss Piety's noticing us. First we really must know if she's home. One minute, though. Hold these tools while I check something."

As Brown had hoped, Maulkin scarcely seemed to noticed that the tool bag was now slung over his own shoulder.

Brown stooped, pretended to be examining something on the foundation, then stood up. "All right," he said. "Go now and check on Piety. Quickly. I'll meet you at the shed."

Two or three minutes should be about right for Maulkin to creep through the shrubbery and get into position. Brown waited. Standing nearer to the road than Maulkin, he could make out the sound of a vehicle drawing close. It turned onto the driveway to the cottages, rumbling along slowly, its headlights contained by trees and bushes. Brown thought he recognized the outline of Coral Rigby's truck. Yes, there it was, bumping over the potholes and hillocks, still a good distance away.

Perfect timing.

Chapter 24

"*You speculate on the luxury of wearing out a whole existence in bed, like an oyster in its shell, content with the sluggish ecstasy of inaction, and drowsily conscious of nothing but delicious warmth. . . .*"

—HAWTHORNE

Oysters. Piety's mouth watered. Jeffrey's call that morning had come at a good time. Tomorrow was her only morning off this week. She'd have coffee, lie in bed for awhile, then around eleven shuck the oysters and eat them with a glass or two of wine. Maybe a nap afterward. She'd be a lady of leisure.

Alone?

Pop! The old needle teeth of depression chomped her pink balloon.

The phone still in her hand, she started to press Guy's number. Was that wrong? They were Jeffrey's oysters after all. She cancelled the call.

Alone.

She pressed Guy's number again. Jeffrey was the founder of the feast; she wasn't forgetting that, but after all, he wasn't available in the morning.

"Piety." Guy grasped at her name with such apparent longing that she just melted. All the lovelorn resentment over his recent neglect fell away like dry sand. "You want to come over," she asked.

But he wouldn't. Couldn't, he said. In fact, he was just on his way out.

"Out where?"

"Just a business meeting."

"Bullshit." How crude she sounded. Maybe that was the problem. No class. Who wouldn't get tired of her?   "You look down on me, don't you? You think I'm just a hick."

"What? Look down on you?"

He sounded genuinely incredulous, but still she felt shriveled. "I hardly ever see you anymore. And when I do, you're all distracted."

A sound on the other end. A whimper? Or a sly little laugh? Then dead air.

She shook the phone. "Hello?"

He was still on the line, beginning to stammer out variations on the theme of "busy."

Tomorrow morning, then? But no. She grabbed the words back before they escaped. If he didn't want her tonight, he damned well wouldn't have her by dawn's early light, either.

"If it's over, just say so," she said instead.

An earful of denials. She held the phone at arm's length. Promises became distant, meaningless chirping. When she caught the words "after tomorrow" and "destiny," she brought the phone to her ear again.

"You tell me that, but you seem so unhappy. You don't even look the same. When I first saw you—well, you just glittered. The way you wore those cool clothes like you weren't trying. I thought you must have been born confident. Now it's like you're all faded. Because of me?"

Another of those odd sounds. Then he said, "Coral gave me those clothes."

"Huh?"

"She found them and made them fit."

"She dressed you up like one of her scarecrows?"

"Pretty much."

This time the dead air lasted a lot longer, and again she was the one who broke it.

"You're not real, are you? Like everything else in my life, you're make-do. A shoddy substitute."

He offered no defense, though she waited until it began to seem ridiculous, then she tapped "end" and let herself weep like the lonely loser she was. Piety had to admit it: even Coral Rigby couldn't be any more pathetic.

After a nice soggy cry into a dishtowel, she found herself thinking of her mother, to whom the towel had once belonged. Piety remembered it hanging over the stove handle in her mother's kitchen, its pattern of strutting roosters almost as washed out and stained then as now. Probably this wasn't the first hail of tears it had soaked up. Her cheeks felt taut and dry from the salt as she ran her fingers over her forehead and felt the lines, deepening every day, just where her mother's wrinkles had been.

She had her mother's hips, too, or at least the potential for them. She wasn't overweight, not yet anyway, but she knew what poverty and misery could do. She remembered her mother saying that when you're "large" (her mother never used the more clinical term "obese" or the ugly word "fat"), the people behind you are always looking at your butt and laughing, even if you can't see or hear them.

That was one thing her mother had right. A critical presence always lurked somewhere, unseen but ready to make you feel bad. Just as well Guy wasn't coming over, or Jeffrey either. All puffy, her makeup cried off, she was better off by herself.

She regarded the dishtowel with disgust. Her inheritance. A twenty-year-old rag. New dishtowels were the sort of thing Piety never wasted money on—why buy linens for a four by six kitchenette? She remembered Jeffrey Brown's kitchen from that Christmas party, roughly the same size as her whole cottage. The granite, marble, stainless steel, the appliances with brand names out of *Better Homes and Gardens.*

Damn it, she had options.

Be practical, she told herself. Remember who's supplying the damned oysters.

But maybe Guy really did have to work tonight. Maybe.

Face it, Piety. That's love talking.

Her face crumpled all up again and she scrabbled for the soggy roosters. Her mother had claimed she'd been in love with the various slackers who followed Piety's father. Look how that worked out.

She stamped on the pedal of the garbage can so the lid slammed against the wall. In went the roosters, which disappeared with a *clang*.

A dozen steps and she flopped down on her bed. The shade was still up, the window open to admit a rising wind. It ruffled her hair, like a lover's hand.

So, what was her heart's desire? She had to figure that out, and soon.

Love? Oh, sure. But was it more important than having nothing to worry about? Than knowing that her clothes were good enough, and her hair had been cut a strand at a time, and her manicure was fresh. That she could spend her afternoons at the gym and never have her mother's hips. That no one could find anything about her to call *less than*, even if they stood behind her and whispered.

Her experience of love hadn't been all that great, anyway. The teenage groping, the sentimental trappings of immature romance, the wham-bam losers when she was older. And family love? Even worse. Sometimes she thought about a baby of her own, but children grew up, despised you. Not one person she'd ever met admitted to a happy childhood.

It didn't matter that Jeffrey was so much older, not really. Or that he scared her a little sometimes. Maybe that was because he had substance. A solid surface always offered resistance. It could also be something to lean on. How lovely it would be just to lie back.

She lay back against the pillow, then sat up again.

Jeffrey was not Guy.

Somewhere in the distance she heard a grumble of thunder, so she lowered the window. The black rectangle of glass threw her own image back at her and with it, a thought chilling as a ghost at noon: what if somebody could see her? The idea of people witnessing all this blubbering and tossing around....

She yanked the shade down, too.

Then realized what had been underneath that silly reflection of herself.

She lifted the shade again and screamed.

The Sailor's Theft

Some of these tales are gleaned from the oral tradition, others have contemporary written sources to back them up. While many may be fanciful, or altered in the telling, in this case, I myself have read the very letter mentioned below.

In about the year 1850, Enoch Atwood, a young man of Wonderstrand, was spurned by his lady love, one Abigail Knowles. He took his broken heart to sea. When word arrived that his ship had foundered, his friends assumed he had perished. This news caused Abigail to repent her hardness. She retrieved from her drawer the silver locket he'd given her, the twin of one he possessed, and clasped it around her neck. It held within a curl of his brown hair, as his held one of her cornsilk yellow locks. After that, she abandoned her sewing and knitting, neglected to feed her chickens, and left her mother and sisters to cope with the household chores without her. At chapel on Sunday, she uttered only one prayer, for his return.

"He lives," she said. Neither her family, the reverend minister, nor the local medical man could convince her otherwise.

Seven years passed. Her sisters married, her parents grew gray, and still she pined for Enoch. Then one day, she saw him approaching on the sandy road. She fell on her knees and begged his forgiveness, which he granted. They wed the following month with much rejoicing, and moved to a small farm adjacent to the one where she'd grown up.

On their wedding night, long before dawn, her parents were disturbed by a loud banging on their door. On the threshold stood Abigail.

"Cold as fog," moaned their daughter. "Bring me wine. Heap the fire."

They did these things, and chafed her hands and feet until she ceased shivering and her teeth stopped rattling.

"What ails you?" asked her mother.

"Cold as fog," she answered.

"Why are you wandering in the dark? Of course you're chilled."

"The night is clear and warm enough," answered Abigail. "Tis my bridegroom who chills me to the marrow."

"You didn't complain of that when you were courting," said her father. "And he seemed hot blooded enough when the two of you danced at your wedding."

"Cold as fog," she repeated.

"This is unseemly," her parents said together. "You were too long a virgin and that by your own choice. Warm yourself, then return to your lawful husband,"

Abigail begged, but as her only charge against her husband was one of temperature, they sent her on her way as the first rays of the sun broke over the Atlantic.

The next night, the same thing occurred. This time, her father accompanied her home at dawn. Enoch paced before the door, apparently wild with worry. He wrapped his wife in his own greatcoat, and led her inside. Abigail's father had a word with the man, after which they shook hands. The bridegroom's hand was chill, as one would expect after he'd been pacing outdoors, but firm and steady.

The third night, Abigail was back.

"This must stop," her parents told her. "You have a sacred duty." They took her home without waiting for morning, warned her never to try her foolishness again.

Thinking it was best to leave the young couple alone, her mother didn't visit the newlyweds for a fortnight. She found them apparently well and satisfied with each other. Her daughter had a lividness around her lips and on the tips of her fingers, but she uttered no more complaints.

In due time, Abigail gave birth to a daughter, but the child came blue from the womb, never drawing breath. Another year passed, and a son was born, blue like the first infant, and again, he never drew breath. The following spring, Enoch himself grew ill with a strange fever, the like of which the local doctor had never seen. At the crisis, when Abigail was most busy with nursing her husband, her mother brought a letter addressed to her daughter, but wrongly delivered to their house. Abigail had no time to open it.

Enoch died and was laid out in their parlor. His wife sat up alone with the corpse on the night before his burial, allowing no one to share her vigil. In the stillness after midnight, she remembered the letter and opened it.

In it she found a locket, the twin of her own. The letter read as follows:

> To Miss Abigail Knowles,
>
> I am among the few survivors of the schooner Adamant. It foundered on 8 December these ten years past. Mr. Enoch Atwood, my shipmate, drowned then, as I did nearly. I know not where he lies, but I admit to my shame that I picked his pocket as his body lay on the rocky coast where the sea left him, and those of my fellow sailors. This locket I could not bring myself to sell, as I did most of the objects I stole from my shipmates. It has haunted me all this time, for he often talked of his great affection for you. In the typhoon that made us lose our way and brought us down, he swore that neither wind nor water would prevent his seeing you again. I saw him washed overboard, those words scarcely uttered.
>
> I have not known a moment's peace since I committed these crimes. Death is upon me, the wages of Drink, and I took it upon myself to find you, since I knew your

name and the place of your birth from Enoch's conversa-
tion. I hope this finds you well, and that you will forgive
a sinner and a false sailor.

The signature was heavily crossed out, as if the writer's courage
couldn't extend quite that far. Only an "R" or "B" could be deciphered
at the start of the surname.

In the morning, when her family and neighbors came to bear Enoch's
coffin to the burying ground, they found Abigail frozen where she sat,
her hair strands of ice, her fingers blue as those of her dead infants, but
still clutching the letter. Around her neck hung two lockets on a single,
salt-caked chain.

—From *Wonderstrand Tales,* by Guy Thomas Maulkin

Chapter 25

"For what other dungeon is so dark as one's own heart?
What jailer so inexorable as one's self?"

—HAWTHORNE

As if in the lee of a vast wave, Coral struggled to regain the surface of her life. Doane's presence, then his departure, seemed like images rising out of her memory, gaining flesh and stature. The past churned around her, all mixed up with the present.

Of course, she'd been pregnant. Isn't that always the way? An old story, she'd heard it herself more times than she cared to remember.

Unable to distinguish one pain from another, Coral had scarcely been aware that her breasts ached. Her nausea she attributed to sickness over fate. By the time she accepted that her periods had stopped, she was four months along, then another passed while her situation forced itself into focus.

Oh, she'd been foolish; she'd been negligent. Her muscles tightened with shame. The days since Doane's disappearance had been airless, thick and heavy as an algae tide, swallowing her. At first, she merely waited, hoping he'd come back. She analyzed every word, every incident and bit of innuendo until her head pounded.

When at last she roused herself to see a doctor, she chose a stranger, near the hospital in Hyannis. He examined her, had the nurse draw blood, then ordered Coral to dress and talk to him in his office, a room filled with photographs of him and a numerous family posed under palm trees, waving from a sailboat, pointing to the Arc de Triomphe. The leather chair facing his desk was cold and stiff against her skin.

"Didn't you notice the signs months ago?" he asked. "What is it with you unmarried women? You're old enough to have known better." He tapped his pen on the desk. "It's too late to terminate the pregnancy, so you'd better make some plans. Do you have insurance?"

She shook her head.

"I didn't suppose so." He slapped some pamphlets and Xeroxed lists in front of her. "Contact one of those agencies." Off he went to his next patient.

How long she sat motionless, she couldn't say. At last, she stood up, and with a sweep of her arm, sent the photographs, paperweights, and telephone crashing from the doctor's desk. The receptionist, a woman of all one hue, the same beige as her cardigan, came running at the sound. She met Coral's eyes, hesitated, then returned to the hallway, where the doctor and a nurse had poked their heads out of examining rooms.

"It's okay," she called. "A patient dropped something. I've got it." Back in the office, she closed the door and leaned against it, blocking Coral's way out.

"Look, the front desk's on the other side of that wall, and I'm not deaf. Honey, I've gotta tell you, I know just how you feel. Working in an OB's office and all, I don't spread this around, but I've been where you are. You were crazy about him, right? The father? Me too, about my kid's daddy. So when I got knocked up, I said to myself, 'If I don't have him, I'll still have his baby.' My son's fifteen now. A little wild, but he'll grow out of it."

The receptionist grew misty. "Someday his father will meet him. I think about it all the time. He'll see what a good job I've done, and he'll be so sorry he'll..."

From the front desk, someone shouted, "Is there anybody here?"

The receptionist ignored it. "Me, I was only eighteen..."

Another call from the waiting room.

She knelt and began to pick up the photographs, setting one down so hard that the glass cracked. "And I believed him when..."

"Stop." Coral covered her face with her hands. "Please. No more." She grabbed her bag, pushed the receptionist aside, and fled the office, ignoring the stares of the crowd around the check-in window.

Coral saw the truth. Lovers abandoned you. They made other lives. They didn't come back, strewing compliments and bouquets. "At least you have his baby"? Oh, sure. Here was the child she'd longed to conceive in the midnight sea, growing in her belly, fed by the twin poisons of fury and regret, lullabied with her weeping.

Outside at last, she leaned against the wall of the building and vomited.

She would never love another human creature.

She did not want this baby.

When she could walk, she found her car, fumbled the key into the ignition, and drove, scarcely seeing the road. The early autumn dusk was closing in when she arrived back home. As she approached her door, she noticed a figure slipping around the corner of one of the other cottages, distinguishable only by his motion against the fixed background. Jeffrey Brown. If she hadn't recognized his shape and bulk, she might have thought he was a shadow, so quickly did he disappear.

By then, the colony was descending beyond seediness. Hers was the only cottage occupied. The few summer renters, able to afford nothing better, had long gone. No others replaced them; stories about the Incubus clung to Wonderstrand, keeping away all but curiosity seekers, and even they preferred accommodations with reliable plumbing and roofs that didn't leak. No one, certainly not Brown, bothered anymore to mow the weedy grass, make repairs, or sweep away the leaves and needles. His presence meant no good, probably a scouting mission for some plot, but she couldn't have borne dealing with him.

She fell into her bed and for the first time in weeks, slept deeply.

She awoke with a start in the hour of the wolf, deeper and darker than the witching hour, when everyone is most alone, when the gloomiest thoughts plague insomniacs, and the dying give up the ghost. Instead of worry, though, a blue-white burst of insight made her gasp. The stealthy way Brown had disappeared around a corner, so quick, so practiced. The veneer of manners over the insinuating curiosity he'd exhibited even as a child. How could she not have guessed?

He'd ruined her happiness, and Doane's. She would have revenge.

She called none of the agencies, saw no more doctors. She watched Jeffrey Brown, followed him, lay in wait to trap him. Hard as it was with her growing bulk, she learned to make herself inconspicuous, ignoring the demands of her body, walking miles at night when she should have been sleeping, eating only when she remembered. With the remains of her savings and the small income from the few summer rentals, she bought oatmeal and canned soup, paid for gasoline and a little heat and light for the cottage.

Sometimes, when the sun came out or a breeze caught yellow leaves and sent them fluttering, fantasies came unbidden. She'd prove to the world that Doane was innocent. He'd come back, and they'd forgive each other. But these daydreams left her with nausea worse than morning sickness.

She was as deluded as the doctor's receptionist. Better to turn every whit of her attention to Brown, and so she did.

Late November. A day when the sea and sky were indistinguishable, the somber gray of a slate tombstone. Damp, unseasonable warmth filled the gaps between gusts of wind. Her anger turned the fog to steam; her woolen coat smothered her, yet without it she shivered. Since dusk she'd followed him, unable to rest, catching sight of him, losing his trail, spotting him again. She was swollen and ill, as if the burden she carried was her fury at Jeffrey Brown, Doane, and herself, not the weight of the child.

With autumn, souvenir shops and clam shacks closed for the season, the streets emptied, and she had to work harder to keep from being noticed. She tried to blend with the weathered shingles, the sere landscape, her presence dwindling to almost nothing. Brown at that time was still a bachelor, newly engaged to a socially connected girl from Sandwich, but not yet ensconced in the trophy home on Pleasant Bay. From various doorways near his Orleans apartment, Coral could watch his comings and goings, her car close at hand on side streets. Around ten o'clock one night, she followed him to a parking lot in Brewster, and from there on foot to a wooded neighborhood of imposing houses set well back from the street. At first she thought it remarkable that he failed to notice her, then she realized that her methods, her camouflage, echoed his own. She'd become his mirror image.

As she brooded in the shadows, she had much time to think about the power of a peeping Tom. Why is it so sickening to be watched when we don't know anyone is there? Maybe it explained why people are troubled by haunted places, and why children are frightened when parents tell them Santa sees them when they're sleeping, knows when they're awake. Even a child understands that what we do when we're alone should be between ourselves and our own consciences.

Yet there she stood, watching him watching others.

That night he planted himself near a window where a young woman passed back and forth. Two men entered the room. One of them grabbed her breast and laughing, pulled her close. He gestured to his companion, who joined them in what might have been construed as a group hug. The first man seemed to be cajoling her to do something, but she shook her head. The second man joined in. She continued to resist, sidling away from them toward the window and, gazing out. Brown crouched lower; Coral too moved deeper into shadow.

While the young woman gazed out the window, the men shared a thumbs up behind her. With a slow smile, she turned back to them and began to take off her blouse. The men stepped aside to let her pass, already beginning to unfasten their own clothes.

Jeffrey Brown turned away then, but the light from the window caught his face just long enough for Coral to make out the smug satisfaction, in which lust played only a small part. She'd already decided the gratification he gained wasn't wholly sexual. In November, and with the Wonderstrand Incubus story still being told, he could no longer risk reaching in, touching, but he could still pleasure himself in the bushes. The catalog of human folly before him tallied well with his avowed estimation of his fellow man; this apparently aroused him.

Following him, Coral witnessed it all, too. From her womb came a kind of settling, like a sigh. Wait, she answered. Let me do this first, then perhaps I can do better for you. Give me more time.

But she felt something give way, just as she stepped into his path.

The cramp in her belly scarcely registered now that she faced her enemy. In his gaping shock, she read the boundaries of his courage. He wouldn't run, postponing the confrontation, nor would he kill her, which he could easily have done in that deserted place. She wasn't afraid.

"Jeffrey Brown," she said.

He gasped but recovered quickly when he recognized her. "It seems we share a habit," he said.

"We do not. You disgust me."

"Oh? You're here, aren't you? Say what you will, to whom you will; you'll still have to account for that."

She couldn't deny it.

"We both see only the evil in people, cousin," he continued.

"You seek it out. I have it forced on me."

"Really?"

She wanted to claw him, to tear his hair from its roots, pound him into food for the crows. Perhaps a taint in their blood did link them. She hated him the more for that.

Then his voice became crooning, cajoling. "Everyone's a sinner; this much I know. The stain of guilt is on us all. You, me, your decamped lover. He won't be back. Blame me or not, you're the one who drove him away. You would have found another reason if I hadn't given you one. You think to ruin me, but based on what? You won't get far with the law. Look at you, in the last stages of pregnancy, traipsing about dark places on a cold night. Unwed, distraught. Which of us would appear deranged?"

He was talking faster and more freely now. "Maybe you think you could cause a scandal. I suppose you imagine talking to my fiancée. Don't bother. She's aware of my habits. She caught me watching her. Weren't you in attendance that night? Too bad. I think she rather liked it. Oh, I don't think she suspects me of the Incubus business. She believes that I prefer to look at her in particular. Perhaps her ego is bigger than her intellect. Anyway, she knows where her bread's buttered and that we'll make a good partnership. Perhaps you could plant doubt in her mind, but would that be wise?"

Coral didn't answer. Better to let him trap himself in talk.

"No. You and I could be partners of a different kind. You're in dire straits. It would be to your advantage to keep my secret. In return, I'll leave you alone with your cottages. Scrap any plans to profit from them. I'll even see to it that any suspicion attached to your lost lover disappears if that still matters to you."

She steeled herself, determined to give nothing away.

"I can do that. I have certain connections."

Another pull from her belly made her wince.

"You're not well, Cousin. Why don't we make an agreement and go our separate ways? I swear to you, I'll stop these activities that you find so objectionable."

The pain ebbed. "How did you manage it?"

"The logistics? I should think you knew, after following me."

"I know how you slip around unnoticed. Not the rest."

"What kept the girls from waking, you mean?"

"And the smell of smoke that was reported afterward. What was that, brimstone?"

"Opium." He said it with a tinge of pride.

"My God."

"Quite a risk, yes? Both in the possession and the obtaining. I'd inhale it, not for long, then exhale into the window. It felt like I and those girls were breathing together. Were in the same dream. But I'm not some hippie. I don't giggle; I don't lose perspective; I don't hallucinate, though it does add a certain surreal quality. I miss it sometimes." A spot of saliva had begun to gather at the corner of his mouth, threatening to drip down his chin.

She knew she couldn't let him look away. She needed more. "Move back behind those trees."

"Why?"

"We'll need light. It won't be seen there."

Face to face, like partners in a dance, they edged into deeper cover, mutual distrust stiffening every step.

She clicked on a small flashlight and rummaged in her bag for a piece of paper. All she found was a page of prenatal instruction given to her at the doctor's office, but the back was blank.

"You write down what you did. And sign it. I won't reveal it unless you force me to."

He scrawled half a page and signed. She read it and nodded. Of course he blamed the drugs for what he'd done: he wasn't himself, he'd been young and foolish, and so forth.

As he wrote, the flashlight illuminated a bulge in his jacket pocket. It revolted her to touch him, but she burrowed her hand under the flap and seized a plastic bag.

"Give me that."

"Don't come any nearer." She held him with a stare he couldn't break. His eyes on hers were almost bewildered.

A terrible weakness took her then. She closed her eyes, braced herself against a tree. The spell broken, Jeffrey Brown uttered a curse or a laugh; she couldn't tell because of the roaring in her ears.

"All right. We have a bargain," he said, his voice a rasp. "Don't cross me." He paused, as if to contemple his options. She half expected violence, but when she raised her head, he was gone. Like most bullies, Brown was a physical coward.

After a safe interval, she slowly retraced her own path. Someone had drawn the curtains in the window they'd been watching.

With difficulty, she made it back to the cottage. The bag from his pocket turned out to contain a small metal pipe, with a black, pungent lump in the bowl. So he'd still hoped to find an open window, a sleeping woman. The residue could be tested; the pipe would have his fingerprints.

She put it, with the sheet of paper, in her secret place behind the portrait, and lay down on the bed. By moonrise she began to bleed.

When the pains twisted her, she thought she would simply allow them to kill her, but compelled by some animal urge, she called an ambulance. Was this how Jeffrey Brown had felt earlier that night, disconnected, powerless?

The EMT's did their work, cool and efficient, as did the nurses when she reached the hospital.

"Who should we contact?" one asked.

"No one." She saw them exchange glances. They left her in a room alone.

Time lost all meaning. One nurse, kinder than the others, tried to tell her how to breathe to ease the contractions.

Coral tried, but before long doctor appeared. To her dismay, she recognized the one whose office she'd visited. She could see that he knew her, too. He regarded her with distaste, as if she were doing some vulgar personal act in public.

"What's all the heavy breathing?"

The nurse began to explain. "I'm teaching her some techniques to help with the contractions."

"Bit late," he said. And to Coral, "Stop that puffing and panting."

After a brief examination, he and the nurse stepped away from the bed. Coral heard them muttering. When they returned, she felt a scalding stab in her spine, followed a smell of antiseptic. The pain eased; time folded in on itself. A confusion of blood, through which came no infant's cry. Then oblivion.

Out of a haze, the doctor appeared again. She was in different room, where a thin daylight filtered through blinds. Her belly was sunken, and the drugs and fatigue still lay heavily on her. "Your baby was a girl," he said. "I regret to say she didn't survive."

A frost, hard and killing, began to grow inside her, spreading with each pulse.

"Do you want to see your baby before arrangements are made?"

She turned away. "It's my fault."

"What do you mean? Did you do something to induce premature labor?"

She'd done much. Falsely accused Doane. Failed to love their child.

"Did you do something to yourself?" he repeated, louder.

She thought of the long, cold vigils, the scenes she'd witnessed, the anger and hate. Sins of omission and commission. "Yes. I suppose I did."

"You're a waste of my skills. Women like you. Selfish. Promiscuous. Unnatural. "

"Then bring me a scalpel," she said. "Or a vial of morphine."

He jammed a needle into Coral's arm.

"Tomorrow you'll be transferred to the psychiatric ward where you belong. Think of it as God's judgment."

She had indeed been mad to talk to this man. Had she hoped for comfort? Absolution? She made another vow, another "never again."

The doctor dropped the needle into a receptacle. "Tell anyone what I've said to you and I'll say you were dreaming because of the anesthesia."

The only loose object she could reach was a plastic pitcher of water on the bedside table. She hurled it at him. Then she began to scream, every obscenity she knew, rising to a wordless shriek, and didn't stop until a nurse came with yet another needle. She lost consciousness almost immediately.

She awoke, surprised to find herself still in the postnatal ward. Night had come again. All was still except for a woman moaning in another room, a baby whimpering. Coral put on her stained clothes and walked out of the hospital, unseen as a ghost. She found a taxi to take her back to the cottage, where she threw away the bloody sheets and towels, packed a few necessities and the contents of the secret place behind the portrait. She locked the door, never even turning around to say goodbye to Wonderstrand.

Five years of exile followed, of meaningless work, of nearly forgotten men. Then came the letter from the attorney, informing her of Jeffrey Brown's intention to raze the cottages. She slipped easily into the role of recluse, local oddity, the weird woman who made scarecrows.

An hour earlier, when Doane had stood in this very room, they'd spent the whole time clawing at each other, seeking answers. All they'd acknowledged was an enemy, Jeffrey Brown, the only part of their pasts they could talk about, but she'd been torn open just the same. Now it was her turn to pour out her secrets. They were Doane's, too. She had to tell him.

Coral looked down at herself. A man's shirt, spotted with paint and glue, a pair of jeans two sizes too big, rolled three times at the bottom. A ragbag of a woman.

What possessed her? She showered, washed her hair, put on a soft flowered dress she'd meant to use in her work. She wondered briefly if the paint she used on gourds and cloth faces would suffice as makeup; she hadn't bought eye shadow or powder in years. In the end, she decided not to cross the line between improvement and artifice.

A tinge of rose lingered in the west when she steered the truck out of the colony, but the clouds hung thick, racing and colliding. The air crackled, rendering the landscape sharp-edged and vibrant. For so long, she'd left home only for the most practical and familiar errands. Now Wonderstrand's trees and few houses seemed new to her. The shops, miniature golf, and restaurants on Route 6, then the rotary curving into Orleans, seemed like landscapes from a dream long forgotten.

In the lights of the town, she recognized faces, people who probably thought her mad or a witch. Trapped at a traffic signal, she found herself next to the flower delivery woman, who glared at her from her car. Coral almost turned back. She wasn't sure she could bear coming to life again.

Then at a crosswalk, she saw what looked like a giant daffodil. It was the Steampunk girl, accessorized with the same hat, gloves, and stockings, dangling the same amount of metal, but now wearing the scarecrow's frothy yellow dress. A young man lifted her off her feet and whirled her around. The girl laughed, then spotting Coral, waved. Coral lifted a hand in response just as a pattern of raindrops hit her windshield. They spread into a starburst and flew away as she accelerated.

The security chain rattled against the hotel room door as Doane slid it aside.

"I want to explain," she said, before he could ask why she'd come.

He gave her a hard smile. "Is this where we look into each other's eyes, overcome by a need to confess? Why now? Why not when I was with you earlier?"

"It's one of my blackbirds," was the only answer she could think of.

"The old Crow Law. I remember." He rubbed a hand over the stubble on his cheeks. It had grown even in the short time since she'd seen him, and now showed more gray, making him look older.

Suddenly she was sure she was right to be here.

"Yes. I've reinterpreted it. Three powerful deeds, I think it means." She didn't say deeds of vengeance now. The notion no longer seemed to fit.

"I see." He stepped aside so she could enter.

A laptop lay open on the desk, with a yellow pad and a pen next to it. His suitcase hadn't been unpacked.

"As you can tell, I've been working on my own deeds. At the moment, the old way of removing pestilence from the community has its appeal for me. Bloodshed."

She sat in the desk chair, swiveling it into the room. The only other place to sit was the bed. He remained standing, arms crossed. She told her tale, calmly, steadily, as if it had happened to somebody else. She'd already pulled these things out of their hiding places in her mind, lined them up so she could face them. He listened without interrupting, though his jaw was tight.

When she'd finished, she handed him the confession written out so long ago by Jeffrey Brown. He read it, then turned it over and looked at the other side.

"Jesus God almighty."

She reached for the sheet of paper, stuffed it into her pocket. "I made a deal with the devil. I wanted to live in peace, so I kept his secrets. Even after I knew what he'd done, I blamed you for leaving." She remembered then that she'd blamed Guy Maulkin, too, for his own devil's pact with Brown. Her own hypocrisy stunned her.

"I blamed you, too, and myself," he said. "For my pride, my hardness of heart. I couldn't come back, though. I suppose I wanted to suffer."

"Me, too. I found some purity in isolation. Made my own company."

"Scarecrows."

"I came to think of myself as some kind of holy hermit."

"I came to think of myself as a man of the world. I never settled any-where. Plenty of travel, plenty of women. But there was no joy in it, no dignity. I never loved anyone again."

"Neither did I. There were men, once. I made do, that's all." She hesi-tated. "Did you marry? Have children?"

"I thought about marriage a couple of times, for practical reasons, shared assets and so forth, but never went through with it. No children. I couldn't have imagined a connection that permanent with anyone after you." He ran a hand over his face. "It's funny, in tales people fall irrevoca-bly in love; when they're forced to part, they live on in total celibacy. That's not how it works, is it?"

She shook her head. "The day comes when someone, anyone, is just standing next to you, and you say what the hell. It gets you through that hour, that night."

"The times when it seems no one's alone but you. Holidays. Tragedies."

"That's why I came back to the cottage and never went away again. I was alone, but there was…."

"The past."

Neither spoke again for a long time.

"So now I've come back, too," he said finally.

"For revenge."

"I didn't know."

"Do you now?"

"Coral," he said.

She rose from the chair.

The joy of skin on skin after a long absence of human touch. Bodies with decades behind them don't grope and pound, they ease into each other. If a hand passes over a mark of age, it still feels the beloved face beneath. Perfect fit, never altered.

She lifted her head from his shoulder. "I've heard some people say this is what dying feels like. As if you're turning to light, dissolving."

"Yes. But we're not dying. Quite the contrary."

"Life. That should be frightening, but it isn't."

"I thought I wanted revenge, but I only wanted to come back. You were always the only thing that kept me from turning to cinders." He turned his gaze to the room. "This is an awful place. Hotels all smell like furniture polish and Windex. We need to go to the cottage."

"It's almost midnight."

"A good hour for beginnings."

They took both cars. He brought his suitcase, his computer and brief-case. They didn't discuss this.

She never lost sight of his lights moving behind her on the now deserted roads back to Wonderstrand.

Chapter 26

"*Do you remember any act of enormous folly, at which you would blush, even in the remotest cavern of the earth? Then recognize your Shame.*"

—HAWTHORNE

On the other side of the glass, Piety's screams carried out into the night. Guy watched her run from the room and realized why: she'd seen a face staring in at her, its expression jumpy as a thief's, voracious as a predator's. His face, full of desperation to get past this part of the evening's work. "Piety!" Her name was a supplication. Had she recognized him? He attempted to rush around the cottage to her front door, but his feet wouldn't work, as if he were in a bad dream.

At just that moment, Coral Rigby's truck pulled in, and another car behind it. Both drivers reversed and skewed to a stop, throwing oyster shells and pine needles. Coral jumped out, leaving the truck running.

Guy cowered. He couldn't just come creeping into the scene now, tools in hand. He needed to explain to Piety alone.

Coral was pounding on the door.

He heard it open, then Piety's voice spill out. "...a man looking in at me! Right in my bedroom window. I couldn't make out his face, but he was carrying some kind of bag over his shoulder. He was going to get in, I know it!"

"What the devil?" Doane Wakefield emerged from the other vehicle.

Coral's voice: "Doane's with me. It's okay."

"But that man—he's got to be around here somewhere. Go get your dog..."

"Slow down. Come over to my place. We'll lock the door and call...."

Guy made himself step around the corner of the cottage. The one nearest her bedroom. The tool bag caught the headlights, a handle or two jutting out.

Piety whirled to look. For a moment she just stared. Then she began to wail, "No no no no...."

Nearby, Dickon, frenzied at being locked in, began to howl, too. The wind had risen, weaving the dog's and Piety's combined laments through the colony in a Doppler effect.

What was wrong with him? Why couldn't he speak up?

A third car approached, stopped. The three sets of headlights lit the scene like a prison break.

Jeffrey Brown rolled down a window. "Is there a problem here?"

Guy was surprised that Brown had appeared by car, when a few minutes earlier he'd been standing just a few yards away, but he forgot that in his relief to see him. Brown would explain everything. They hadn't actually done anything wrong, not yet.

Piety pointed to Guy and let loose. "What were you going to do? Break in when I was asleep? Why? You could have just come in the front door. I invited you, and you turned me down." Her voice climbed steadily. "Is that how you get your jollies? How long have you been sneaking around like this? I see now how you understood so much about me. I thought we were soul mates. I thought...." She crumpled into sobs.

Guy tried to protest but his tongue clove to the roof of his mouth; his legs were wooden.

Jeffrey Brown stepped forward resolutely. Surely now he'd tell them all that Guy was only doing his job. Brown was carrying a cooler for some reason. He put it down and instead of explaining, instead of taking Guy's part, he wrapped an arm around Piety. He murmured to her, things Guy couldn't hear.

She didn't resist.

Guy blinked. Didn't she see that Jeffrey Brown's outrage and concern couldn't quite mask his glee? Didn't anyone? But Guy's quivering, his gasping like a caught fish—these things, he realized, were obvious to all.

"Has anyone alerted the authorities?" Brown asked.

Guy stood alone. Slices of light fell on the trees, the ground, and him, creating wild geometrics. He saw his own silhouette, broken and distorted. A gush of accumulated water, released from the foliage above, drenched his hair and face. When had the rain become so heavy? The bag of tools slipped from his wet hand to the ground.

Behind Piety's back, Brown raised his cell and snapped several photos of Guy, in the pose of a guilty man.

Guy blinked. Something about the camera flashes was greatly familiar. The way they reflected off the underbranches of the trees.

Wakefield approached and picked up the bag, examined the contents.

"Be careful—these perversions often bring out violent impulses," warned Brown.

Guy backed away, shaking his head. He understood now. There had never been any sign, any incandescent message in the sky, any portent of glory. Just Jeffrey Goodman Brown's machinations, and Coral, hers too. G.T. was just shorthand for goat. He was once again the old Guy Maulkin.

His future had at last announced itself in mere camera flashes, showing him that he was a greater fool than he could ever have imagined. All his pride and confidence had been marsh lights, ignis fatui leading him further into trouble.

His soul flew to pieces.

He threw up his arms, and in a voice of agony and desperation, he called Piety's name again.

The three syllables expanded and filled the night before they faded.

Then he turned and fled.

Chapter 27

❦

"By the sympathy of your human hearts for sin ye shall scent out all the places—whether in church, bedchamber, street, field, or forest—where crime has been committed, and shall exult to behold the whole earth one strain of guilt, one mighty blood spot."

—HAWTHORNE

"Not to worry," Jeffrey Brown assured Piety. "He'll be caught." He turned to Wakefield. "You see why this place should be condemned? It's a moral cesspool as well as an eyesore."

Predictably, the Rigby woman jammed her two cents in. "This is your doing."

"Oh, dear," said Brown. "An incident like this could get the community up in arms, couldn't it? How difficult for you, cousin. Police, media, curiosity seekers. Just imagine."

Wakefield stepped forward. "Don't be a jackass, Brown."

Brown bristled but kept his hold on Piety. "This young woman has been assaulted and needs to tell the police."

"We aren't even sure what happened yet," Wakefield went on.

Piety lifted her tear-stained face. "I told you. Guy was watching me when I didn't know he was there."

Brown tutted. "Piety, pay no attention to these two. They're not on your side. We're wasting time."

"Are you positive it was Guy you saw?" This from the Rigby woman.

"Yes. Now I am. But...."

"No 'buts.' We all saw him hightail it out of here. Hardly the act of an innocent man."

His cousin laughed nastily. "You would know."

Brown kept his self control. He remembered an occasion years ago when he could have killed Coral Rigby. Now he wished he had, but the impulse confused him. He hated the woman; she blocked him at every turn, yet was he, Jeffrey Goodman Brown capable of putting his hands around her throat? Squeezing? That long ago night had been colder than this one. Recalling it, he had to suppress a shudder. He would display nothing that looked like cowardice.

"How could Guy do that?" Piety went on, to no one in particular. "He always seemed so, like, sweet. He never did anything creepy. I mean, he always looked into that little window of Coral's shed when we walked by, but don't we all like to see into other people's lives sometimes? To if our stuff measures up to theirs?"

She was rambling. Time for him to close this deal. "My poor girl, you're a nervous wreck. We'll go where it's quiet, where you can rest. Then we'll decide together what action to take."

"You conniving hypocrite!" began the Rigby woman. "I could tell her...."

Wakefield lifted a cautionary hand. "Not yet," Brown heard him whisper. He regarded the two of them with suspicion. Odd that they'd arrived almost simultaneously. What was Wakefield doing here at all? One thing at a time, he decided.

"You know what he told me once?" Piety went on. "His favorite writer believed violating the sanctity of another human heart was the unpardonable sin. Funny, huh?"

Brown happened to meet the Rigby woman's glance just then. Both turned away.

"Come," he urged Piety. Slumping under his arm, she allowed him to lead her to his car. He inhaled deeply of her scent as he buckled her in.

He had to get her away before the Rigby woman could start shooting off her mouth again. It didn't matter much where they went, so he headed to Deacon's, a shorter drive than to his house. Besides, he'd stashed a surprise for her there, intending to give it to her after her next shift.

He unlocked the door, deactivated the alarm system, and switched on just the back room lights, leaving the front of the shop in a blue dimness. With his own hands, he brewed a whole pot of coffee in the big commercial machine, and damn the waste. He poured two mugs and put one in front of Piety, who sat at one of the tables staring at nothing.

"Drink this. You'll feel stronger."

"I don't want to call the police."

"I'm disappointed in you. Don't you realize what he did is criminal? Remember the Wonderstrand Incubus?" They were alone now so he could safely play this card.

"Guy had nothing to do with that. It was years ago."

"I'm not saying he did, but the fellow's a scholar, or so he likes to think—he knows these local tales. It's a typical copycat crime."

When she looked doubtful, he added his trump. "You owe it to other women like yourself." A laughable sentiment, but Piety wouldn't think so.

"Yes. I guess that's true, but on the other hand, the worst thing you can do is claim you're a victim if you're not. Doesn't crying wolf just make it harder on the women who really are assaulted?"

Brown's patience was waning fast. "You're not 'crying wolf.' Of course it's hard to accept that you've misjudged someone so badly, but that's no reason to gloss over what he's done. Once they start, these behaviors are never fully eradicated."

"Maybe I should talk to him first. Not alone. Maybe Coral could be there."

"Her? She wouldn't help you. She's no friend to anyone, and mad besides. You know she dabbles in the occult, right? Some delusion about witchcraft."

"But she knows Guy, plus she doesn't take any shit."

He aimed a mighty kick, toppling the empty chair next to hers. The crash shook the empty shop. Piety leaped up like a nervous deer.

Brown struggled to regain his composure. "Terribly sorry, so clumsy of me. Just what you don't need with your nerves all shattered. Tell you what, I have a gift for you. Would that cheer you up?"

She cast him a bewildered look, but sat down again.

Moving quickly, he retrieved a large beribboned box, emblazoned with the name of one of the boutiques in Chatham, from the cupboard where he'd hidden it before he'd gone to meet Guy. He put it in her hands, smiling broadly. Jeffrey Goodman Brown knew how to influence a woman.

Chapter 28

"There is a fatality, a feeling so irresistible and inevitable that it has the force of doom, which almost invariably compels human beings to linger around and haunt, ghostlike, the spot where some great and marked event has given the color to their lifetime."

—HAWTHORNE

Guy found himself circling Wonderstrand's dead ends and cul-de-sacs, fearful of being followed, but unable to head for Route 6 and escape. The rain, heavier by the minute, pooled in depressions, overflowed drains. It obscured the landmarks he passed, houses where sea captains and drowned sailors had dwelled, the graveyards, glacial rocks and bogs. Nevertheless, he knew they were there, the source of his tales.

When he decided his circling might itself appear suspicious, he took a back road into Eastham, toward the ocean. The car went dead not far from Nauset Light Beach; he let it coast onto the shoulder. Out of gas. Not so long ago, he'd been planning to trade in his jeep on a new car, so he hadn't bothered to fill the tank; after that he'd simply forgotten, or not cared. He sat there for a while, watching the lighthouse beam revolve, the way it dyed the rain red, then white. Fire to ice, in an endless cycle.

If only he'd resisted Jeffrey Brown's call and spent the evening in the arms of Piety. If only he'd recognized himself and those around him for what they were before he was swept into this maelstrom. He got out of the car, and began to walk toward the sea. Though he could barely stand against the rising wind, hissing and growling among the trees, he didn't have far to go. The few houses on his way, summer homes mostly, were closed up for the night. No children romped in the yards, no vacationers sipped margaritas in the screened porches. He passed the Three Sisters, former lighthouses themselves, now beheaded where once they'd shone the only triple beacons on the coast. He passed the entrance booth where carloads of impatient vacationers lined daily up in July and August.

This close, the surf's roar swallowed the voices of the wind and rain, a fiercer beast than they. At the top of the staircase to the beach, he leaned over to look down, almost overbalancing. Nearly high tide, he guessed; waves foamed almost to the cliff. In such weather, the rangers sometimes closed off the stairs, which had more than once collapsed, but tonight no one had bothered. Who but he would be idiotic enough to venture onto the beach in such weather?

Now he could make out the rattle of the rocks and pebbles at the edge of the receding waves. Piety had once told him she liked that sound; it reminded her of full pill bottles. To Guy, it sounded more like rattling bones, but she had a point. He wished he had a fatal overdose of some sleeping potion. He could just lie down and let the rising tide take him. Drowning was slow and painful, or so he'd heard, but how much worse could it be than this exquisite ache of knowing what the world held for him?

How many people had stood right here, recognizing the sea below as the sure refuge within their reach, having arrived at their own moments of truth: the lover is never coming back; the diagnosis is right; the debts can't be paid. Without the nectar from Coral's well, he, Guy, faded to nothing. Piety would never speak to him again. He'd be evicted from his cottage in a few days, and he had no job. He might even be arrested. Worst of all, he'd seen himself for the fool he was, and nothing could change that. Oh, God, what a joke to be Guy Maulkin—a man made up of smoke and mirrors, a little education and a lot of imagination, held together by old clothes and books.

Then came one of those oddities that occur with nature's extremes. The moon persisted, high and full under the heavy cover of roiling cloud. An edge of it broke through, sending a thin finger of silver over the opaque water. It seemed to point directly at him. "J'accuse," it said. Then the sky closed, as if the moon had snapped down a window shade.

What would be the easiest way, then? A knife? Those in his kitchen were dollar store cheapies, dulled by use; they barely cut a sandwich. A gun was quick and sure, but of course, he didn't have one. Yes, liquor and some pills would be best, then just to walk into that delicious cool opacity. Surely if he could make himself drunk or drugged, the sea wouldn't hurt so much as it filled his lungs. But he had none of these comforts, these facilitators, and now no transportation to go get them.

A note would have been nice, too. He wished he'd left one, a masterpiece full of lofty phrases and pathos. As if he had the capability of finding the right words, or saying anything worthwhile. Nevertheless, he'd have liked to explain to Piety. Suicide gets more complicated if you're connected to other people—maybe you don't want to saddle them with guilt, leave them with their own source of misery. On the other hand, staying alive for their sake adds another burden to your own.

Guy imagined utter and complete peace. "To make of his ponderous sorrow a security." Where had he read those words? He couldn't remember, no longer cared.

A gun or drugs wasn't necessary. He would have courage.

He climbed down the wet stairs, feeling them tremble with each blow from the elements. What if he could be transformed into something elemental, something strong and potent, his bones turned into rocks and sand like the cliffs, his blood the tidal rivulets? When the waves retreated, he reached down and gathered a few fist-sized stones, loaded them into his pockets. Then he stepped forward.

Chapter 29

"*The very woman whom he pictured—the gentle parasite, the soft reflection of a more powerful existence—sat there at his feet.*"

—HAWTHORNE

Piety slipped the pink ribbon off the box, but her mind wasn't on presents.

When she'd stood in front of her cottage, with those headlights on her and everyone shouting, she'd felt as if her heart had fallen out and lay in the dirt. She dropped to her knees as if she could pick it up and try to put it back. It would never be clean again; blades of grass and pine needles would always cling to it and stab her. She could see now why Coral Rigby didn't trust anyone.

She parted the layers of tissue. Jeffrey had bought her a dress, a white sheath from a shop she'd never had the nerve to enter. The tag was still on it, several hundred dollars. Probably would have gone on sale soon, as the season wound down, but then the cost was no biggie to him, she supposed.

"Do you like it?"

"It's beautiful." She let it slip back into the box.

"You can try it on in the ladies' room."

"Now?"

"Why wait?"

"I'm a mess."

"Please. For me."

She didn't have the energy to resist.

The dress was a size too small, pulling across her breasts, cupping her behind. Now she could see the small red dot at the corner of the tag. So it *had* been on sale. Still a lot of money, though, and the most expensive dress she'd ever owned.

He wanted her to model it for him, so she spun around once or twice, arms raised.

"Charming. It was made for you." He sounded breathless.

"Don't you think it's a little tight?"

"On you it's perfect."

"Well, thank you. I guess I'll change back now."

"Must you?"

"A dress like this should be for a special occasion."

"True enough. Hurry, though. We can't let much more time lapse before we contact the police."

Back in the restroom, she was glad to peel the thing off again. She stood there in her underwear for a moment, glad to be in a small, enclosed place. The room was windowless, utilitarian, just a sink and a toilet, but fairly clean since Piety herself took care of that chore. She closed her eyes. Guy. How could he? Jeffrey was pushing so hard to report him. If there had been an explanation, why hadn't Guy said so? She wished she hadn't gone away without her keys, her phone. All her touchstones had disappeared.

Deacon's policy allowed only a single forty-watt bulb in the ceiling fixtures of the restrooms. She'd never been in there when the front of the shop was darkened. Now, in the sullen light, an odd sliver of brightness caught her attention. It issued from a gap, an inch or so wide, where a pipe disappeared into the wall. She'd known it was there because it collected webs that had to be brushed away with a broom, but she'd never paid much attention. She put the toilet lid down, but it slipped out of her hand and hit the seat hard, the crack echoing through the shop.

When her nerves settled, she climbed on top to look through. A shaft of light brought out the higher surfaces of the kitchen, especially a metal table just below the pipe. They used it to store extra trays and other supplies too broad to fit on the shelves. The table had never been level; it rocked so much that the trays slid off if you piled them too high. It was empty now, but she could see it swaying, as if something heavy had just been removed from it. Something heavier than trays.

Dizzy, she climbed down and put her own clothes on as quickly as she could.

Was this paranoia? For the rest of her days, would she see every unsealed gap in an old wall as a peephole? Avoid every window? Caution was good; she'd learned that at her mother's knee. Security was better. Piety hated being unsettled, hated not knowing whether something was in her mind or reality. She wasn't sure about one damned thing she'd done all night. Crazy, she thought, I'm going crazy. She wanted to pound her head on the wall until she knocked this whole night right out of her memory. She tried one tentative bang against the wall, but it hurt too much. The rain drummed on the roof like a long-nailed hand, harder and harder; if only she could run out into it, let it wash all over her. The restroom opened into the shop, though, so she couldn't go outside without passing Jeffrey. She knew he'd stop her. Truth was, she was running out of options.

Chapter 30

"...the attempt to connect a bygone time with the very present that is flitting away from us."

—HAWTHORNE

The dog burst forth when Coral and Doane entered her cottage, trumpeting his frustration.

"Sorry," she told him. "The show's over now."

The dog seemed unconvinced. He began to circle the small rooms, black tongue pendulous, ears pricked.

"I should have let him out. Brown's afraid of him."

"What's his name?"

"Dickon."

"Ugly cuss. Smart?" Doane patted the dog as it passed. It acknowledged this with a nod and continued its circuit.

"Smarter than most people. I trust him."

A heavily weighted verb for a night like this one. Once uttered, she regretted it. No damage done, though. Here they were, she and Doane, safe in her cottage with the weather and other people locked out in the all-hell-broken-loose night. Again, and without effort, they were back as they'd been before they left the hotel.

It was strange and familiar at the same time. Where was her old contempt for the animal need for warmth, touch, companionship? How presumptuous she'd been, creating her own mute society, simulacrums that couldn't betray her. She'd tried to do the same with Guy. Weren't there legends and fables enough to warn her against that old sin? Perhaps, though, it was not unpardonable.

She recalled the crow law. Three powerful deeds, by her interpretation. But sending the photos to Jeffrey Brown's wife, evicting Guy, where had these gotten her?

In her ancestors' time, they'd thought the slain birds a fair price, that to prohibit marriage without the price of violence was justified in order to rid the community of scavengers. Consider the targets: unloved birds, devoid of the color and music common to their kind, useless for food. She could identify with them. They made a logical blood sacrifice, a reasonable brutality.

She eased deeper into Doane's arms. They leaned against each other, resting, balancing. She'd been right about three crows as three deeds to win your heart's desire, but she'd been going about it wrong. Vengeance wasn't what was required. The violence of centuries past had become history, the stuff of anecdotes.

The three birds should indeed represent threats to her existence, but what were those really? Coldness, immutable solitude, old grudges and regrets. Her crime lay in the failure to move forward, not backward. To let the past harden the present into granite. Telling her story to Doane, hearing his, and their reunion—that was the first deed, not the third. Two to go.

She was left with the problem of Jeffrey Brown. He'd play on this incident with Piety, spread rumors that a sex offender roamed Wonderstrand, call in debts from public officials to eliminate the problem. Who knew better than he how such matters worked? Awakening an old scandal would have the same effect as allowing him to make Guy a scapegoat: putting cottages into the public eye. Poor Guy, with his tender feelings, his bustling hope, his thirst for glory in a world of mammon and mud.

"What do we do now?" Doane asked.

"I have to look for Guy."

"Wouldn't he have headed off-Cape?"

She considered. "I don't think so. He's like us. He belongs here no matter what."

Doane stepped away, took her hand. "Let's go."

"Come on," she said to the dog.

A full-fledged nor'easter was upon them now. Armed with slickers and flashlights, they piled into the truck, counting on its four-wheel drive. After scouring the mostly unpaved streets of Wonderstrand, they'd found no sign of him.

"Where to now?"

"Let's drive south on Route 6 toward Orleans. That's where he worked, so he might know a place to hole up there." Just before the Eastham rotary, though, they found the road under water.

"It's too deep. This truck probably won't make it through, and Guy's car certainly couldn't."

"It's probably been flooded for awhile. Let's try the Bay side."

They didn't get far. Bridge Road, over the marshes, also lay under water.

"There's no other way into Orleans—or off Cape, for that matter. There are a lot of motels on Route 6 if we drive north. Maybe he went to one of them."

"No, he'd be afraid. He thinks the police are looking for him. Besides, who has vacancies in August?"

A gust sent the truck skidding against the curb.

"We'd better turn back," Doane said.

"I can't."

"Okay. But where else can we look?"

Suddenly she knew where Guy would be. "If you live on the Cape, where do you go if you're in turmoil and you need to think?"

"The beach."

"Of course."

"In this weather?"

She hesitated. "If you're running on pure emotion, yes, I think you might."

"The bay beaches are closest."

"Let's try."

First Encounter, Campground, Sunken Meadow, they tried as many as they could, but the roads to most of them were impassable; the few they reached revealed only foam flecked marshes and blowing sand. Coral wasn't surprised not to find Guy there. In his mood, the wilder eastern coast and the open sea would attract him.

Back on Route 6, they made a right turn down Nauset Road past the Visitor's Center toward the Eastham oceanside beaches. They had to travel slowly; the windshield wipers were nearly useless in the downpour. The truck, though, lit by the soft light of the dashboard, felt intimate, safe and dry. They didn't look at each other, both scanning the road, but they talked.

She told Doane of the day the planes hit the towers, how she couldn't stay in the cottage, had to escape that TV image of blue sky and white smoke. She'd gone to the sea. Many others had done the same. They stood on the sand in little knots, mostly twos and threes, some larger families, not speaking, just staring over the water as if somewhere on that horizon lay a different, happier world. For a brief time, Coral had felt connected to them.

"But there was one woman away from the others, young, holding a glass of white wine. I can still see the straw color of it in the crystal. She was laughing, talking on a cell. She'd just arrived on a vacation, and was rhapsodizing about the beach, the weather. Hadn't she heard? I wondered. Didn't she care? I couldn't look at her long, but I can't forget her."

Doane told her he'd had been traveling that day, stranded in an airport in the midwest, all flights grounded. He described an old man who had been sitting near him, weeping. "I bought him a sandwich and a cup of coffee, but he wouldn't eat. Eventually, medics came and took him away. No one else took that chair, though the airport was crowded. It was like the old man's grief stuck there and might add to their own. I couldn't take my eyes off that empty chair."

At Coast Guard Beach, the sea had claimed the driveway, blotting out the grasses, the fragile low dunes. The white hulk of the old station and its small parking lot stood like a far off island floating above the sheet of water. The tidal streams that crisscrossed the marshes, that ran with tadpoles in summer, now swelled to torrents.

"He can't have gotten through here. Let's try Nauset Light beach next. If he's not there, we'll try to get to Marconi. I don't think we'll get farther north, though, to Wellfleet and beyond—the road in that direction might be flooded at Blackfish Creek."

They crept a few dozen yards down Ocean View Drive. The wind on the exposed coastline rocked the truck, threatening to flip it like a turtle. Trees thrashed, groaning and crackling, looking as if they would step forward with on their twisted roots and barricade the road.

"We can't go this way. We'll have to double back and take the long way, down Cable Road."

Coral managed a u-turn, but the sense of being safe against the storm had evaporated. She gripped the wheel so hard her knuckles ached. Even the dog's muscles were locked with tension.

"What's that?" A car stood on the shoulder.

"It's Guy's!"

She slowed, put the truck in park, and Doane jumped out, but was back in an instant.

"He's not in there."

"He could walk to the beach from here."

"Let's go."

They were able to get into the deserted parking lot, close to the stairs down to the beach. There was no discussion. They raised the hoods of their raincoats and headed down. Even without the heavy flashlights she'd brought, they could make out the huge breakers clawing at the ocean cliffs, exposing the roots of trees, pulling clods of earth and rocks down into the roiling waters.

When the white beam of the lighthouse came around, they saw that the whole surface of the water was covered with whitecaps, like bleached cloths shaken from a thousand windows in the sea, a thousand ghosts churned up from their rest in the deep, surrendering.

From the platform midway down the stairs, they saw Guy on the narrow strip of remaining beach. Their shouts flew away into the storm. Doane started down, waving her back, but she gripped his arm and wouldn't let go, following right behind him. The dog wove past them, and was first to touch the last step, now covered with washed up sand and debris.

The water was so cold, drawn up from the ocean floor miles from shore. Even at the base of the steps, the waves splashed above their knees, buckling them. Guy was only steps away, but had lost his footing already. He seemed neither to hear nor see them. The dog leapt in, tried to paddle, but was washed back again and again. Then as they watched, a larger wave climbed on the back of another, and Guy disappeared.

They plunged in after him. Though they didn't know it until later, the stones in his pockets were pulling him down, while they managed to hold the surface. The sea was shallow, barely waist high when a wave receded, but it rose over their heads with each surge, making it impossible to stay upright. Saltwater stung Coral's nose and throat; freezing, so intense that it felt more like fire. Her skin numbed quickly; underneath, her bones and joints ached.

Coral's hand slipped from Doane's, and she watched in horror as he crashed hard against the cliff. Somehow he was able to edge the few yards back to the stair rail and hold on. He waved to show he was okay. Dickon tossed about, too, his fur providing some buoyancy. When she began to tread water, so did he.

She kept her legs and arms pumping, attempting a few forward strokes to the place she'd last seen Guy. Then a wave pulled her under. Instantly the roar of wind and water vanished, replaced by gentle bubbling, the sudden quiet in weird contrast to the currents that shoved and yanked as if they would pull her to pieces. Underwater, only her interior world remained, her heart pounding, the blood slowing in her extremities.

Even while her physical being focused on survival, a thought came with vivid clarity: this is how I've felt for years, only multiplied a thousandfold. Utter isolation. But now, the wonder of her reunion with Doane shone hot and bright. She stroked hard, pushing herself upward.

There was no way to tell if she was being dragged out to sea, or about to be smashed against the cliff as Doane had been, but she kicked as hard as she could. When she collided with a solid object, something soft, flesh, not rock, she grabbed onto it with fingers that just managed to close. She held tight, kept pumping. At last she burst above the surface. A rush of sound, the shriek and percussion of wind and rain poured forth. A voice shouting.

Doane. She filled her lungs with air, opened her eyes, blinked. The light-house beam brushed past, blurred, but illuminating what she grasped—Guy, unnaturally heavy, coughing, but alive. The turbulence pitched them under again and then above the surface so quickly she could barely catch a breath. The receding waves yanked them apart until she thought her arms would be jerked from their sockets, while the incoming hurled them into each other, threatening to knock the precious air out of her.

The next revolution of the lighthouse beam revealed the dog's head bobbing just behind her, a mouthful of her coat clamped between his teeth. Dickon pulled her like a demon, she pulled Guy, and then, won-drously, Doane was dragging the whole linked chain of them onto the steps. Each delicious inhalation was raw and wet, hoarse as a crow's call.

Coral, coughing and spitting, collapsed against the support of the stairway, holding it in the crook of her arm because her fingers were too numb. The dog shoved his bulk against her other side. Guy lay still a few stairs above. Doane was working on him, pumping at his chest, breathing into his mouth.

A long time seemed to pass; still Guy didn't stir.

Then suddenly seawater erupted from his mouth; his teeth rattled so loudly she could hear it above the weather. When at last he was breathing steadily, she and Doane propped him between them, Guy's arms raised in a limp T, and they began the long journey to the top of the stairs and back to the truck.

Water and Stones

Among the Puritans of the mainland colonies, suicide was far from unknown, despite the threat of eternal hellfire. Across the Bay, Cape Cod's citizens, perhaps less oppressed than those on the mainland, didn't see their first until 1677. The victim was the wife of a prominent citizen, a fact we might not find so shocking today.

The first recorded suicide in Wonderstrand didn't occur until 1698. This poor soul was buried in an unmarked grave in unconsecrated ground, just outside the only churchyard. The church itself no longer stands, but the cemetery remains, hedged with weeds only slightly higher than those in the holier ground within, still hosting a burial every few years. A popular rite of passage among local youths is the search for the mysterious suicide's grave. Supposedly, if you stand on it by the light of the moon, the ground will tremble beneath you, and your fondest wish will come true. No one has come forward to verify this.

In these enlightened times, Wonderstrand suicides are no longer consigned to eternal anonymity. In the not so distant past, a Wonderstrand teenager fatally overdosed in the Provinceland dunes and is said to harass the living who dare to play 1980s music within hearing distance of his gravesite by draining car and MP3 batteries. In one case, a Barry Manilow CD spun out of a dashboard like a Frisbee and split in two before the eyes of the offending couple. Then there was the elderly man who saw his mind and body fading, and chose to die by his own hand, on his own terms, causing an eruption of letters to the *local newspaper debating the morality of euthanasia. His tombstone is defaced every year or so by someone who believes only God should have authority in such matters. Those of the opposing view clean it off, beginning a new cycle of debate*

Most of the rest are the usual stories of pain and desperation, as common here as elsewhere. There's only one recorded case of a Wonderstrand resident's committing suicide by drowning. In such a watery place, one would expect it to have occurred in the sea, the bay, or a pond, but instead we must look to a smaller source of water, the well. Since Biblical times, wells have been known as places of great power and enchantment. Most of us have tossed a coin into a wishing well, half believing. Ornamental versions are easily available from mill shops all over the Cape and adorn many a front yard. As for functional wells, all Wonderstrand's water comes from these private sources, since a public system has yet to be installed. Some go back to the colonists; others are recent.

The date of the tragedy I'm about to describe happened around the end of the nineteenth century. I've never been able to pin down the exact place, but I believe the well still exists in Wonderstrand.

A young local man had suffered from inordinately bad luck all his life. While still a child, an infection from a bad case of chicken pox left him heavily scarred. Then a few years later, a neighbor's horse kicked him, breaking his nose and cheekbone and splitting his lip. Again, he did not heal well. His was not a pretty face, and the neighborhood children rarely let him forget it.

By the time he was twenty, he'd resigned himself to a solitary existence. He became a master fence builder, a trade that allowed him to spend his days relatively alone, for he could pound stakes and lift loads unassisted and stack stones so close, so balanced, that the walls he built were sure to survive for generations.

One day, as he was at work on a new base for a well in the neighborhood, he happened to glance inside. The well was uncovered, used mostly for livestock, and the water level happened to be high. He saw within i the reflection of his own face, but not the way it looked back at him from his shaving mirror. His nose, instead of being twisted cruelly to one side, was straight and fine as a statue's. His cheekbone, a lumpen mass like a blighted turnip, looked round and smooth. Peach skin seemed to have replaced his pits and mottles. Best of all, the purple, wormlike scar that divided his lip and rendered his rare smiles grotesque, had disappeared. He smiled at his reflection, and his mouth curved tantalizingly.

"We're one," it seemed to say.

He blinked. Looked again. The handsome face remained. He stood, found a trowel, and polished it on his jacket. Even in its worn surface, he could see his old face looking back at him. He began to weep.

He finished his work on the well, fortifying himself with many glances inside. The next day, and the next, after attending to his other jobs, he returned to the image.

"I'm you," it said.

During the days that followed, he took note of the people he met instead of lowering his eyes. Most had known him all his life, and were used to his face. He noticed how the kind ones looked to the man beneath the appearance, and the cruel or stupid addressed only the outside, regarding him with distaste. He was of an age when a man's blood runs hot, and he forced himself not to think on the local girls, the way they turned their heads when he passed.

He began to neglect his work, to spend more and more of his time at that well. Its owner was a fisherman, often away at sea, whose wife was busy with an infant and expecting another. They took little notice of the fence builder, gazing into the circle of water.

About this time, the beautiful daughter of the richest man in Wonderstrand returned from her finishing school in Boston. Never unkind, she greeted him warmly when they met at church the following Sunday. He'd loved her since childhood, from the time before his face was ruined, but knew she could have any man on Cape Cod and would never choose a wrecked creature like him. Now he remembered his face as it looked in the well. He offered his arm to walk her home. She accepted. A gentle *rain began to fall, so he slipped off his Sunday coat and held it over her head to shelter her. As they walked, she inquired about his work, mentioned some land of her father's that would soon be requiring his expertise. When they reached her house, he asked if he might call on her again soon. He bowed, and there beheld his face, his true face, reflected in the small puddle that had collected at her doorstep. Rising, he saw the pity in her eyes.*

With all the dignity he could muster, he parted from her and went straight to the well. He looked in.

"Come down," said the image. "Be me."

The fisherman's wife happened to be on her way to the outhouse when she saw him climb onto the steady rocks at the side of the well. At first, she wasn't sure what he was doing. Then she heard a splash. She ran to look in, but saw only a slight disturbance of the water. The rope she heaved down stayed slack. She shouted and shouted for a long time before anyone came to help.

It took them a long time to retrieve the body, and when they did, the water had altered it. They hardly recognized him.

Chapter 31

"For perchance the only time, since this so often empty and deceptive life of mortals began its course, an Illusion had seen and fully recognized itself."

—HAWTHORNE

"**D**on't think I haven't considered it, too" Coral told Guy. "Lots of times. You can always hang on to the option. That's what I do. If things get worse, it's your escape hatch. And there's always a chance things will get better." She cringed to speak the truism, yet found it no longer so ridiculous.

They were in Guy's bedroom, he dried off and under the covers, face to the wall, she wrapped in towels. Doane had gone back to her cottage for more blankets and a change of clothes for himself and Coral.

"I wish you'd left me there." Guy's voice was hoarse from coughing and vomiting saltwater.

She scrabbled for words. It had been so long since she'd tried to comfort anyone.

Dickon lay at their feet, also swathed in towels. He'd had to ride home in the back of the truck, for the cab wouldn't hold all four of them.

"Damn, that dog stinks when he's wet," she said finally.

Guy had nothing to add to this, and the silence in the room grew around them.

Coral could still feel the vastness of the waves, taste the ocean. Tomorrow her body would still ache from the struggle. Still, she felt at peace here with Guy and the dog, waiting for Doane. Maybe there was substance to the notion of the interconnectedness of all beings. She even wondered if the thing that happened when she locked eyes with people, when they told their secrets to her, might not be a manifestation of the transcendent. Maybe it *was* a kind of witchcraft, tapping into what our minds are still too puny to fathom.

The old instinct of avoidance stirred, but she said, "Tell me what happened tonight, before you ran off."

"It doesn't matter anymore."

"It does to me. And Piety deserves to know the truth."

He groaned, but rolled to face her. He began by addressing the wall, the pillow, the dog, anything but her, as he had when she'd first known him.

"Stop that. I'm over here."

His words came more freely then. It didn't take long. There were few surprises.

"I'm sorry," she said. For hadn't she made him as he was, sent him on his way?

Doane came back then with the dry clothes and blankets. "You go change first. I can wait," she told him. She pulled the damp towels off the dog and replaced them with a blanket. The animal lolled, perfectly comfortable now.

Then while she changed, Doane made coffee—there'd been none in Guy's kitchen, so she'd told Doane to bring some, plus a jug of water from the cupboard.

"He doesn't have water here?"

"Not like that. Bring that Myer's rum, too. It's in the top cupboard on the left."

She left Guy in bed with a steaming mug. "It's made with the water from my private well," she said, and saw the spark in his hollowed eyes.

She followed Doane to the kitchenette, where they could talk in private.

"Brown was behind the whole thing. Coming here at night, the window, all of it."

"I figured." Doane inclined his head toward Guy's room. "Think we ought to take him to a hospital?"

"We can't get to Hyannis in this weather. Besides, he's okay now physically. He'll probably sleep for awhile, but he wants to see Piety."

"What's with them? Is she his girlfriend?"

"Yes. But Brown's been lusting after her, too."

"Damn him to hell. I hope you don't think I was in on this. I wasn't, I swear."

How strange. The thought hadn't even occurred to her. She hardly recognized herself these last few hours.

"I know," she said.

"Piety should be told what Maulkin's done."

"Yes, but who knows where they've gone? And she might have Guy arrested when she finds out he's back, especially if Brown's there to tell her what to do. If I call her, he'll guess right away whom she's talking to."

"I meant to ask—why did you want me to wait when I started to tell her about Brown's history?"

"I didn't want to show our hand. Before you came to the hotel tonight, I was doing some research, checking into his business, his connections. When we confront him, it should be final."

"Confront him with what? I've tried. Photographs won't stop him; they backfired with his wife. And awakening the old scandal would have the same effect as allowing him to make Guy a scapegoat. Either way, it's bad for the cottages."

"We won't let that happen, and we'll spoil his little romance with Piety if she has any sense. But I want more. It'll take pressure from several sources, including financial. I can arrange that. I have contacts, too, my love. But I need more time."

Coral nodded. "If we tell Piety about Guy, will she still care?"

"I think," Doane said, "there should be no misunderstandings between them."

Chapter 32

"There is no good on earth; and sin is but a name. Come, devil;
for to thee is this world given."

—HAWTHORNE

Puffing a bit, Jeffrey Brown sat back. He pushed aside his cup, with its surfeit of cream and sugar. Couldn't deny he was getting a little fatter and slower than he ought to be. Lucky the clap of that toilet seat had given him fair warning. With a young woman like Piety by his side, he'd get back in shape soon enough. He ran his tongue over his bottom lip, recalling what he's just seen. How well she wore white, and how nicely the dress had revealed her body. He'd enjoyed choosing it for her. It would be great fun planning a house for the two of them, to his particular specifications.

She returned, again in her ordinary clothes, and folded the dress back into its box. "I think I'd like to go back home now."

"I understand. Travel will be slow in this weather, but we'll be more comfortable at my house."

"No, I mean back to my cottage."

"What? Why?"

"I just feel like being in my own space."

He decided to humor her. "Perhaps that would be best after all, to report the crime from the scene. Maulkin has absconded, and the other two will have gone about their own business. I'll stay with you of course." With his forefinger, he touched a button in the middle of her chest. "You missed one there."

She clutched the front of her shirt, then turned sideways to button it, hiding her bare skin from him. "You seem out of breath," she said.

"Do I? I don't think so."

She was silent on the return drive. The rain fell in perpendicular sheets until a mighty gust rose to twist it sideways. Bulky as it was, the SUV rocked under the forces pummeling it. The road was a blur. Small black shapes seem to ride the tempest, rolling through Brown's vision. Probably something blown on the wind, since he'd never noticed them before. A storm like this stirred up layers of filth and detritus long buried in gutters, gullies, the crotches of trees, under porches.

Piety let out a small cry when they reached the rotary. "It's flooded!"

"Never fear." He hit the gas harder. As he knew it would, the Escalade skimmed right through, spraying wings high above them on each side. It took more than a couple of feet of water to stop Jeffrey Goodman Brown.

Loose branches and humps of pinecones carpeted the driveway to the colony. The SUV crept along, lurching into potholes, splashing muddy water onto the front and rear windshields. As they passed by Guy's cottage, he thought he saw a light inside, insignificant behind the rain and debris. Was that a silhouette peering out, or merely a blur in his vision? Hard to tell. He was confident that Maulkin wouldn't have gone to ground there; the man was a fool but not insane. But the Rigby woman or Wakefield might be in there snooping. Well, let them. Piety didn't appear to have noticed, so no matter.

Near the spot where the path veered off toward Coral's cottage, a figure broke from the trees and toppled just in front of them, crunching under the tires. Piety pitched forward with a scream.

A broken heap lay behind them, blood red in the taillights. Brown rubbed his eyes. Appendages jutted from the pile, but of wood, not flesh.

He swore. "It's only one of those damned scarecrows. It had better not have damaged my tires." More of them loomed along the path, blown loose from their posts, their wooden arms jutting out, gesturing obscenely. He couldn't wait for the time when this land was purged of his cousin and her hellish effigies.

Piety sunk back into her seat. When he stopped at her door, she jumped out before he turned off the ignition. He followed. Her hair whipped about, strands of it slapping at his face when he leaned close so she could hear him.

"I'll go in first," he shouted. The cooler of oysters still stood outside where he'd left it, though it had blown over onto its side. He hoisted it up. No sense wasting them. He turned on all the lights while she stood waiting, holding the door half open, letting the rain puddle on the floor.

"You can come in. It's perfectly safe now."

A sharp gust pulled the door out of her hands, slamming it wide against the outer wall, jerking it back again. When she stepped over the threshold to get out of its way, he yanked the door shut behind her and locked it.

"There. All cozy." He pulled out his cell, checked the screen. "Let's get this call over with."

"No," she said.

"Hmm?" He found himself momentarily distracted by those floating black shapes in his vision. Odd that even inside, with all the lamps lit, they were still there. He needed a tissue, or some Visine. Perhaps glasses. When all this was settled, he'd make an appointment with an optometrist.

"I'm not going to say anything to the police."

He drew his attention back to her. Her set jaw showed she was serious. He would need to be firm. "Is this Piety?" he demanded. "The same woman who was frightened out of her wits when that fool stalked her?"

"Maybe. Maybe not."

"What's this mumbo-jumbo? You'll make that call," he said. No need to raise his voice. She quailed. A good sign.

Then, unexpectedly, she rallied. "What were you doing while I was changing?"

So he'd made a mistake back at Deacon's. Not a serious one. He should never have stinted on restroom bulbs, but a man can't plan for *every* detail. She couldn't have seen him, only suspected, and there could be no real confusion; the face she'd seen in her window tonight had been Maulkin's.

"Whatever do you mean?"

"Just tell me."

On the plus side, she'd felt good clothes against her skin, and knew who'd bought them for her.

"Were you looking at me through that pipe hole in the ladies' room?"

The spots in his vision mingled and separated like amoebae under a microscope.

"I'm not surprised that you would imagine such a thing, after the trauma you've suffered this evening, but for you to accuse me...."

"Did you get the idea from Guy? Or did he get it from you?"

"What idea? Have you gone mad?"

"I don't know."

The spots spread, dirtying his perception of her. Gnashing his teeth, he found he could restrain himself no longer.

"I'm an observant man. I know you, who and what you are. Ah, my own Piety. You lust for the good life, for ease and luxury. Isn't that so?"

She reddened.

Brown laughed. "A blush. Charming."

"I hate you both."

He grabbed her arm. "Of course you hate Maulkin. He looks, but he doesn't pay."

She uttered a little sound of disgust.

He took a step closer; she took one back, closer to the wall. He kept hold of her arm. "Sweet Piety. Your young knight isn't the paragon you imagined. So what? None of us is as naïve, or as young, as we once were." Another step. "It's time to be realistic."

She was pinned against the wall now. Hot little jolts raced along his groin, like spiders up a tree trunk. He pressed harder, drew his tongue along her neck.

Piety sucked in her breath, drawing her abdomen back from his.

"Didn't you enjoy the way that dress slipped over your shoulders?"

"You're sick."

"Ah. The whole world is sick."

He closed his eyes, the better to savor the sensations in his groin. The amoebae still swirled behind his eyelids, but not so distinctly.

Piety was shouting something. He didn't bother to listen. He slid his hands under her shirt. Rapture. He pressed his chest and belly against her to keep her pinned while he unbuckled his belt.

As he progressed to his trouser button and fly, there came a pounding of drums, like fists on wood, a counterpoint to his pulse. He cursed, straightened himself...

And she wrenched her body from beneath his. He fell forward heavily, hitting the wall with his nose and forehead. By the time the shock passed, she'd crossed the room and flung open the door.

The rain and wind swept in. The chill aggravated his smarting face; he shrank and withered.

"Get out! Get the fuck out!"

She must be talking to Wakefield, who had somehow materialized in the open doorway. But Wakefield didn't move.

"She wants you to leave," Wakefield shouted over the storm.

"Your interference isn't needed here." Brown sidled closer to Piety, tried to put his arm around her, but she sidestepped him.

"I said get out," she repeated.

She went to stand near Wakefield, who said something to her that Brown couldn't hear. She shook her head in refusal. Wakefield spoke again, and Piety clapped both hands to her mouth. What was he telling her? What tactic was this? Brown wanted to get between them, to get rid of Wakefield, but the floaters in his vision mingled, spread. For a moment, they blotted out everything, and when his sight cleared, he was alone.

He charged the door but couldn't follow. The floaters tricked him—he reached out for the doorknob but found nothing there but a dark spot. He roared with frustration. Hand over hand, he made his way to the refrigerator, seized a bottle, grunted to find it was wine. He closed his teeth around the cork, pulled, and spit it out. He drank. When the floaters cleared a little, he found her bed and lay down. The pillow smelled of her, of cinnamon and vanilla, of rebellion, perfidy. There he would wait for morning.

Chapter 33

"To make a story out of a scarecrow, giving it odd attributes. From different points of view, it should appear to change,—now an old man, now an old woman,—a gunner, a farmer, or the Old Nick."

—HAWTHORNE, STORY IDEA

Coral opened the door of Guy's cottage to Doane and Piety, who stopped just inside the threshold.

"Is it true?" Piety asked.

"He walked into the ocean. With stones in his pockets. In this storm," Coral said.

Piety twisted her head to the side as if she'd been struck.

"He's resting now. The seawater's out of his lungs and stomach.

"God." The voice was hardly audible, a true prayer.

"He wants to see you."

"I can't."

"Forget everything Brown said."

Piety waved the words and the name away. "I saw Guy spying on me. He knew—he *knew*—how I felt about that. I trusted him. Everybody's pretending to be something they're not."

"True. Most of the time we aren't even aware we're doing it."

Then Doane spoke. "Just hear what he has to say."

Still Piety didn't move.

"Look, I've been where you are," Coral said.

"And I should take you for a role model?"

"Come sit down," Coral said. "If you don't want to talk to Guy, then I've got a tale for you. Mine." She glanced at Doane. "All of it, from the beginning."

"Spare me."

Glaring at Piety, Doane moved closer to Coral. "You eager to go back to your own place? Spend some more time with Brown?"

Coral saw that the anger and impatience that had driven Doane away hadn't disappeared; rather it had been honed into power and confidence. Coral touched her forehead to his arm, felt the muscles relax.

Piety looked from one of them to the other, her red-rimmed eyes wide and blinking. "Wow. You two, huh?" She shook her head, as if to adjust the contents. "All right. Talk."

Coral told about herself, about Doane.

"Don't make a mistake," she finished.

"Like we did," Doane added.

In the empty space that followed, Coral felt a shift, a flutter in the air as if a bird had launched itself into the sky. No one else seemed to notice.

Piety stared at the floor for several minutes. Then she stood and went into Guy's room.

Coral and Doane waited at the kitchen table.

"Something happened between her and Brown, just before I got there," he said.

"It was bound to."

Some time later, Piety came out of Guy's room. "I'll stay with him. You guys don't have to."

"Brown's car's still in front of your place, so I'll leave the dog here. No one gets past him if he doesn't want them to. We'll be at my cottage."

Back home, Coral showered off the salt and sand from her immersion in the sea, aware of the steam, the smell of the soap, the hum of the taps, as she'd never been before. She felt so tired but so alive. When Doane knocked and asked permission to join her, she thought at first that the shower had gone cold, but that was only fear. She found she wanted him to feel the sluice of warm water more than she wanted to hide. They let it wash over their bodies.

"How can you love me now? My skin's all lined."

"Like the underside of a rose petal."

She saw herself reflected in his eyes, her face alight, her hair loose about her shoulders, which were still white and smooth.

"I could ask how you can love *me*," he said. "I used to be able to lift a stack of two-by-fours and never get a backache. Now I'm growing soft."

"No." She slid her hands down his shoulders, his arms. "And it wouldn't matter, anyway. Young bodies are built for the long years of toil ahead."

"No twenty year old could conceive a hunger like this," he said.

Oh, she loved him. Had always loved him. She knew, in every gesture, in the hand that lifted her chin when they kissed, in the untainted ease of their naked bodies, that he still loved her.

And all else fell away.

Neither spoke for a minute or two, then he went on. "We don't have to worry about saving up for the future, or finding ourselves, or propagating the species. Not our problems anymore."

"No. We're free."

Chapter 34

"My poor, dear, pretty Feathertop! There are thousands upon thousands of cox-combs and charlatans in the world, made up of just such a jumble of worn-out, forgotten, and good-for-nothing trash, as he was! Yet they live in fair repute, and never see themselves for what they are!"

—HAWTHORNE

What a storm it had been. Such high seas. Somewhere, a freakishly warm wind had swelled over a glacier; an island-sized lump broke off and plopped into the Arctic ocean, began to melt, and next thing anyone knew, houses' foundations buckled, piers collapsed, roads flooded, and freshwater wells broke down, blending with the murky water of marshes.

The tempest ended in a washed dawn, dazzling in its clarity. A breeze carried birdsong and the scent of raw wood from split trees. Scattered tomatoes, zucchinis, and flowers littered gardens. Here and there a patio umbrella, left raised, had turned inside out, throwing bare spokes skyward like thin arms. The day promised to be warm and bright.

In Wonderstrand Colony, three cottages stood occupied that morning. Two held couples, one a solitary man.

Jeffrey Goodman Brown woke alone in Piety's bed, but the storm's aftermath held no relief for him. The black spots in his vision had multiplied, thickening, eddying, turning into tiny winged things that darted through his field of vision. When he reached for his shoes, darkness blotted them out. Smoke-colored wraiths curtained off part the room; he bumped into a wall, mistaking it for the bathroom door. He cursed wood and plaster. Calling his doctor at home, waking him, Brown demanded and got an early appointment. He dreaded being behind the wheel of his car, but if he called for an ambulance, the EMT's might think he was mad, hallucinating. Perhaps he was, temporarily maddened by Piety's defection, the many cabals against him, and the tumult of the storm. Nevertheless, no officious stranger was going to see him in his weakened state. Certainly, Piety would not. He clamped his fingers around the steering wheel to control their shaking, and through ever-changing inkblots against the rising sun, inched the car through puddles, over fallen detritus, and out of the sleeping colony.

Piety slid closer to Guy, trying to warm him with her body, though he'd told her many times through the night that the ocean's chill had left him.

"Is it morning?" he asked.

She shifted onto her elbow. "Just rest."

"I just can't believe you're here with me."

"Well, I am."

"I've ruined everything. You, you're beautiful and good."

Beautiful and good? Piety saw only the avarice, the self consciousness, the insecurity that had kept her trapped so long. "Baby, I'm no better than you. I even understand why you went into the ocean. I'd probably have used pills, but to each his own. That's over, though. Now we're in it together."

With each other, they knew exactly where matters stood. That had been established over the course of the long night. Exhausted as they'd been, they'd made certain things clear. He'd fallen asleep with his hand in hers.

"The question is what to do now. Neither of us has a job or a place to live, and we've made a bigtime enemy."

Guy shook his head, sank into the pillow.

"Maybe the first thing is to get some breakfast into you. Can you eat?"

"There's not much here."

"Coral left some coffee last night. How about if I just warm that up?"

She found a loaf of half-stale bread, too, and made toast under the broiler, wishing his sparse kitchen contained butter instead a tub of margarine. He joined her in the kitchenette, dressed now, and they sat opposite each other at the small table, drinking the coal-black brew.

"This isn't so bad," she said. "It tastes awful, but it sure wakes you up."

Guy was sitting straighter, too.

"You know what? Jeffrey Brown doesn't scare me anymore." It became true as she uttered it. "If he's not out of my cottage by now, I'll call the police. I'll tell them what he did last night. It'll be he said/she said, but it'll embarrass him." Her voice trailed off as for the first time since she'd known him, she saw Guy angry. He clutched his mug like a rock he could throw.

"Really, there's not one thing I can prove," she went on. That's how it is with people like him. They get away with it. Just pick up a newspaper. Corporate thugs, war profiteers, crooked politicians—how often does anyone pin them down?"

"It happens sometimes." He swallowed the last of his coffee.

"You know what I think? People like that pollute the whole world, and everybody else has to counteract it. Sort of pour clear water into the pond until the scum rises to the top where it can be scooped off." This idea had never occurred to her before, but she believed it now absolutely.

"By whom?"

"Who knows? Anyway, we're the clear water, starting now. I'm moving out of that cottage. He owns it."

"Bring your stuff here." Guy hesitated. "But then I'm supposed to move out, too."

"Don't be crazy. Coral isn't going to evict you."

She saw that he was remembering a strong grasp in the dark sea. Last night, their prickly, solitary neighbor and Doane Wakefield had been heroes, no less. But the two of them together? Funny how wrong you could be about people.

After breakfast, Guy felt ready to confront Jeffrey Brown or any other dragons they encountered, but when they walked over, he and Piety found her cottage empty. The white dress Brown had bought her lay half spilled from its box; she kicked it behind a chair leaving a muddy footprint on the skirt.

They carried what she needed back to his place, making several trips.

"We'll come back for the rest later," he said.

"Leave it; it's junk. There's no room for it anyway. After this, we should get online and see what kind of jobs are out there. Next week's Labor Day, and a lot of college kids have gone back to school early, so the restaurants and hotels might need help for the rest of the season."

He hung the pile of clothes in his closet. "I've got a little money saved. It will keep us going for awhile."

"I feel all new and energized."

He felt a ribbon of ice curl down his back. "You didn't see strange lights in the sky last night, did you?"

"Huh?"

"I just wondered if you'd seen some kind of sign."

"That things have changed? After last night, I don't need signs and omens to tell me that."

Guy relaxed. "Present needs aside, what's your heart's desire?" He had to know. He'd find some way to give it to her.

She tilted her head, and the angle put her face in shadow. "Honest to God? I want to go back to school. To the community college or maybe even cross the bridge to one of the schools in Boston. Maybe I could work days and take classes at night or on weekends, but I don't know how I'd pay for it."

"Do you want to move to the city? Live somewhere else?"

She didn't hesitate. "Wonderstrand is right for you, and I want to stay with you."

How was he supposed to contain this kind of happiness? "This isn't the real world, though, is it?"

"Maybe. Maybe not. Who cares?"

He lifted her off her feet, wanting to whirl her around the room, but they kept colliding with transplanted boxes. One tumbled over, dislodging her collection of kitchen implements. When he put her down, she stepped on a rusty muffin tin, squashing it with a metallic crunch.

"So much for my dowry." She picked up the tin and tried to bend it back into shape. "You know what I've always kind of wanted to be? Don't laugh, okay? A pastry chef. Not doughnuts, never, never doughnuts, and not the kind of stuff that looks so pretty you're afraid to eat it, but good, substantial things, with fresh flour and butter and fruit."

"Perfect," Guy said. He saw the difference between her dream and his former delusion. Hers grew out of her real self, not some flashy illusion. But how to make it happen? They couldn't live by his writing. Guy had become too much of a realist to hope for that. The little tales of the past could be dug out of the sand and polished up; he might see his true self reflected in them, and his neighbors, and those generations who came before them. Was there a better way to spend a life? He couldn't think of any, not for him. But they couldn't eat tales, couldn't fill their gas tanks or pay bills with them. Maybe he could get his vending route back.

First things first. "There are lots of culinary schools in commuting distance," he said.

When Coral came by late that afternoon, she found them still planning. "You look better," she told Guy.

"Thank you." He addressed it to her, not the ceiling or floor, and she knew he wasn't referring to the compliment.

"I have some things to say. First, the cottage is yours as long as you want it. Piety's welcome here, too. Doane has plans for the rest of the property, and for Jeffrey Brown, but I can't talk about that yet. Why are you grinning?"

"Piety's going to study in Boston."

"Well. Good for her." Coral hoped she sounded as sincere as she felt; she wasn't yet used to friendly interaction.

Piety piped up. "There's this culinary arts school with a pastry chef program. It's set up so you can work and go to school at the same time."

"You have a good head on your shoulders. You'll manage just fine."

Piety turned pink.

Coral suppressed an eye roll. As badly as she'd underestimated this young woman, she could see that Piety would always be the blushing type. Well, so be it.

"Don't worry about the rent in the meantime."

Before they could speak, Coral continued. "There's something else I need to talk to you about." She pointed to Guy. "Alone."

They stepped outside. "The well's gone bad." What she'd drawn that day smelled of beached bones and blackened seaweed, and tasted of low tide, devoid of the power to refresh. She'd dumped it out into the puddles in the garden.

He seemed to take this calmly. "So you do drink it yourself? I always wondered."

"I was away from Wonderstrand for a long while. When I came back, my cottage was a wreck. Among other things, the water pump was broken. I remembered the old well. It hadn't been used in my lifetime, but it wasn't dry."

"I used to imagine bottling it for sale. How greedy I was."

"We won't be needing it now." She turned away then, as eager to get home as he was to get back to Piety.

Doane stood when she entered, inconveniencing Dickon, who lazed at his feet.

Two computer screens, his and hers, displayed type and numbers, as they had in varying patterns all day. His phone was still in his hand.

"Brown's working more dirty deals than I imagined. For one thing, he's been buying up foreclosed properties on credit, slipping the loans through. His finances are convoluted, but cracks are showing."

Coral nodded. "Guy and Piety are together for the long haul. She's going to cooking school. I told them they don't need to worry about rent."

"Good. Money's not a problem. I'll make sure we get the cottages free and clear, but that's only the beginning. I can reduce Jeffrey Goodman Brown to rubble. How far do you want to take this?"

She bent down to scratch the dog's head. "Does anyone care about the Wonderstrand Incubus anymore?"

"The victims do. That includes us."

"But enough to relive it? For so long it's been just sensationalism."

"I located one of the women from back then, the one you worked with in the inn in Chatham. Actually talked to her. Turns out she figured out that it was Jeffrey Brown, too."

"You're kidding."

"He approached her later, in the normal way, and something about him bothered her. She put two and two together, but she didn't have any proof, so she went back to Ohio. She said she was angry for years, at herself for not pursuing it and at him most of all. But it was eating her from the inside out and she had to stop. She's a minister now, Unitarian, I think she said."

"Is she?" Coral remembered her, curled on the floor, afraid to be near a window. So the girl who had cowered on the floor stood in front of a congregation and evoked the universe. "I'm glad."

"Yes, for her, but I'm not sure I can forgive. Or should."

"Brown is slippery; he'll find a way out of the net no matter what you do."

"Not this time."

"With the business dealings, maybe. But the Incubus story? His signed confession?"

And then she realized. The clothes she'd been wearing the night before were draped, still dripping seawater, over a rack in the tiny alcove off her kitchen where she did laundry. From deep in the pocket, she extracted a sodden clump of paper. It dissolved in her fingers. She held it out to show him.

Next, she went to the portrait of the hatchet-faced woman, slid it aside. A smell of wet lumber rushed out of the hidden compartment, and a trickle of rusty water slid down the wall. The plastic bag, torn and leaking, was slippery in her hands. Within was smoke-smelling liquid and a pitted, corroded pipe.

She stared at it in silence, and Doane came to join her.

"It was never watertight," she said.

The scarecrow nearest her wore a plaid flannel shirt. She put the ruined box down, dumped in the ball of wet paper. She pulled off the shirt, and wound it around and around the box until its shape was lost. This bundle she put in the kitchen trash can.

Doane watched, the muscles in his jaw rigid.

She returned to the room. "It's for the best."

Doane drew in a long breath.

Coral continued. "You and I have won. So have Guy, and Piety, and that woman in Ohio. See to it that Brown can't do any more damage. Make this colony solid and safe. Do that much. As for the rest, we said we were free."

"Is it enough?"

"We're alive in this moment, not that one."

"Then that's how we'll leave it."

Detached retinas, concluded the ophthalmologist to whom Jeffrey Goodman Brown was referred.

"Strange to have it affect both eyes at once." She typed something into her notebook.

"What the hell does that mean?"

"It's as you've described, first the floaters, then a shadow over part of the visual field. Blurring, too, just like you're experiencing."

"How could this happen to me?"

"Sometimes it's age related, but it can be spontaneous, too."

Brown tried to blink away the Rorschach blots over the doctor's face. "What are you going to do about it?"

"Without surgery, I'm afraid there could be permanent vision loss, so let's get it scheduled ASAP." She accompanied Brown to the outer office to make arrangements and sign forms.

WONDERSTRAND TALES | 311

Brown longed to tear down walls with his own hands, to wreak havoc, to howl his protest at the way fate had treated him, but fear made him follow his doctor's advice to rest, to stay off the roads. He tried to work from home, but his business cohorts became suddenly, inexplicably distant. Debts were called in, agreements cancelled. Soft touches became hard. Books were audited, and assets had to be sold at a loss. Employees gave notice. His house on Pleasant Bay seemed haunted with all he couldn't do or see. September entered warm and sweet, but not for him.

The surgery was not successful.

Loss of vision strikes so many who delight in seeing the shape of a child's hand, the road from the driver's seat, the tools they need to do their job. But Jeffrey Goodman Brown? He never looked for anything but corruption and subterfuge. To his dying day, all he would see was in himself, and that never clearly. Piety became a lost dream to him. As he saw less, he distrusted all around him more. His face settled into a perpetual and permanent scowl.

The one activity he enjoyed was composing his own life story, scrawled by hand onto broadly lined paper. What he'd written appeared to him only as vague marks on a lighter rectangle, but he was confident that he was capturing the essence of himself. Sometimes he'd unearth a memory so infuriating that he couldn't move beyond it—confrontations with his cousin, time wasted with his ex-wife, the persecution of his legitimate businesses, his betrayal by Piety. He'd skip over these incidents, and gradually the story he expected to require reams, diminished to pages, then to a handful of sentences, shrunk from book to obituary to the length of an epitaph on a tombstone. In the end, it contained no hopeful language, for his life was gloom.

On an apple-scented autumn morning, Doane approached Piety on the path between their cottages.

"You still want that bakery?"

"Sure, someday. I love my classes. I've learned so much about egg whites, you can't imagine. I'm actually pretty good with puff pastry already, and next week we're starting basic crèmes."

"The Deacon's Doughnuts building is for sale. Brown left a residue of lard and corn syrup for the cockroaches, but it's a good location, and the new owner would pay for redesigning."

"That would be you, right?"

He laughed. "I could have it ready for you in six months."

"My own place? Not just as counter help?"

"If you're interested."

"By then I'd have finished a lot of the coursework. I could work days and finish school at night."

"You'd still need help until you graduate."

"Oh, my God—I know half a dozen advanced students, even a couple of grads, who'd love to put it on their resumé. You really mean it?"

"I don't make offers I don't mean. Nor proposals I don't believe in."

"Sorry. Old habit." She knew she was blushing again, and she didn't care.

Piety had always pictured her inferiority like a tattoo, needled smack in the middle of her forehead. It had begun to fade when she'd told off Jeffrey Brown, in spite of how scared she'd been, in spite of his beribboned presents. When she'd made up her mind to trust Guy, it had dimmed even more. It was nearly invisible even to her after her first few days at culinary school. Now she knew the last shadow of it was lasered away. She didn't think there'd even be a scar.

"Another thing you might like to know," Doane continued. "Brown's office across the street is closed, too."

She cheered. "I have to tell Guy."

But Guy was busy elsewhere.

"That's very kind, but what would I be doing?" Guy asked. He'd been summoned to Coral's cottage.

"You'll be a property manager," she said. "Keeping watch over the place."

"Kind of like a scarecrow."

"It's an innocent and useful occupation."

Was she joking? Guy couldn't tell.

"You'll have plenty to do. It's time the bushes were pruned, the dead wood hauled away. There'll be some construction. Doane and I need more room, so we're building an addition to our cottage. To yours, too, if you like—what if the two of you have children? We're going to dismantle the cottage where Piety lived and reuse the wood. I like the weathered look. The two ruins are coming down, and we're going to rehab one of the empty cottages as studio and office space for ourselves."

"What about the other one?

"We'll fix it up a bit. Then we'll see. There may be others out there whom Wonderstrand would suit. Life needs some open questions. "

Who might these others be? Guy wondered. Probably someone else who appeared, at least at first, like a character out of an old book: recluses and dissemblers, the credulous and the canny, scapegrace spawn of Puritans, and wanderers with nowhere to lay their heads.

"So will you take the job? You have too much heart to bustle around out in the world."

"I will. With pleasure."

"Good. And by the way, when you're not busy as a scarecrow, you can be a scribe, telling Wonderstrand's tales. Better you, who love the place, than an outsider."

"I'd like that."

"The stories we tell about ourselves, to ourselves, are so different from what we see in the mirror, aren't they? But then you already know that." She stood up. "Go home to Piety now."

He was halfway out the door when she stopped him.

"We're all scarecrows, you know, made up of bits and pieces that happen to stick together at a particular time. Matter, which is just energy anyhow, consciousness, geography and all the rest. I've come to believe, though, that there's something more. The stick that forms the backbone."

"What would you call it?"

"You're the wordsmith, not me."

The first pumpkins preened themselves from doorsteps. Burning bush and poison ivy turned scarlet, and the white blossoms on the chokeberries turned to clusters of inky berries. Katydids rasped out their last love songs. All over the Cape and beyond, Coral's creations emerged from harvested gardens and appeared as the centerpieces of autumn displays.

Nothing remained to Coral and Doane now but joy, long suppressed. They had all they'd ever need. For her, no more sweaty days at the flea market. For him, no more stale hotel pillows, or meals in airports. It was like being children again, but with sex, a driver's license, and good liquor.

When the fancy struck, they had company, Guy and Piety. Piety brought boxes of muffins rich with nuts and apples, tiny cakes, delicious if sometimes a little lopsided, tarts filled with silky fillings, but never once anything resembling a doughnut. Coral's face and arms grew rounder, which Doane said suited her.

Most of their time, though, they spent alone. They sat beside the fire, talking, the windows open to bird calls. She told him about scarecrows, what went into them and who they were. He told her about his travels, his planning and building. The cottages would be snug and neat by winter.

On clear nights, they bundled up in blankets and lay on the beach, the Milky Way exploding above them. Sometimes they watched old monster movies until they fell asleep with the TV on, and didn't wake until afternoon. They could do anything they pleased. They bought wetsuits and plunged into a soft, lapping sea at midnight. They weren't young; she'd never again conceive a child in love, but the ocean lay vast around them. They followed the path of the waxing moon on the water until they were sure it never ended, then they swam back to shore.

Coral wore a leaf shaped emerald on her left hand, and Doane a feather cast in silver on his, but neither saw the need of any ceremony beyond their own. Dickon had a new bed with odorproof cushions, and once a week a van picked him up to take him to the groomer's. He came home fluffed and shining, and went to roll in the garden.

The well turned sweet again, but its water no longer brought illusion, only perfect relief from thirst. Whenever Coral wanted some, she had only to clap her hands and call the dog.

"Dickon! Another jug of water!"

And there it would be.

Bethiah's Child

Massachusetts is well known for its witch tales, and Cape Cod has plenty of its own:

Liza Tower Hill, Ould Betty, who aptly outsmarted Goodman Pease in the young days of the colony, Granny Squannit of the Nausets, and all the others. Best known may be Goodie Hallett, Black Bellamy's consort, who used to dance at Apple-tree hole near the cemetery in Eastham.

Wonderstrand, too, had its resident spaewife or wisewoman. In the first half of the eighteenth century, Bethiah Smith made her home in a rare cluster of woodland next to the marshes. At that time, much of the Cape had been deforested for houses, ships, and firewood, but her house stood in leafy shadow. Some said she warmed her hearth and boiled her pot with kindling pilfered from her neighbors, sparing her own; others maintained she used coals from some demonic source and had no need of firewood. A spinster, she was skilled in the uses of herbs and philters, and commonly consulted by townsmen and women who didn't deign to tip their hats or curtsey to her during daylight.

She kept a fat gray squirrel as a pet. Wagging tongues called it her familiar. They claimed it had one blue eye and one black, that it taught her the secrets of leaping from tree to roof to tree again without ever touching the ground, and that she used this skill to spy and steal. Some even swore that she had a bushy tail hidden under her skirts, the secret of her agility and balance.

Bethiah also kept two young servants, a girl with skin the color of cocoa and hair dark as midnight, and a boy with fair skin and hair red as autumn maples. Both were reputed to be her own offspring by pirates who sometimes came ashore to partake of the local ale.

The dark girl became pregnant by the eldest son of a prosperous local farmer and deacon of the church, the very man who owned the land where Wonderstrand Colony stands today. The lad refused to marry her, and neither she nor her infant survived childbirth. Not long afterward, Bethiah's red-haired boy was accused of stealing livestock from the same farm, and hanged. For three full seasons thereafter, a steady rain of plagues fell on the community. Huge acorns, hail the size of beach plums, and smooth round rocks shattered windows, cracked roofs, and splintered shingles.

The assault ended the following summer. Over forty by then, Bethiah gave birth to a girl child. She called the baby Coral, a name that reminded her of the warm South Seas described to her by many a seaman. The girl grew up to be strong limbed, flaxen haired, with eyes the color of May leaves, and possessed of a precocious, uncanny intelligence. Legend has it that when no more than sixteen, she dressed as a boy and served in Washington's army. Later, she became mistress to more than one of the signers of the Constitution. Be that as it may, the girl eventually returned to Wonderstrand with considerable gold in her pocket, and took up residence in her mother's house.

Bethiah had never forgiven the neighboring farmer's family for their treatment of her dark girl and ginger boy. She was furious when her beloved, fierce daughter began keeping company with William, their youngest son. Coral Smith laughed at Bethiah's warnings.

"I'm no lamb among wolves, Mother," she said. "I've marched and fought alongside men, eaten and starved with them, sent them to kingdom come when I needed to. I'll let no farm boy have the advantage of me."

And she did not. Before long, she tired of the spoiled youth. Jilted, humiliated, he came to the women's house one night armed with a knife, *determined to force the girl to come away with him. She refused to allow him inside the door, but against her mother's pleas, accompanied him outside into the shade of an old oak. Raised voices, his in passion, hers in laughter, rang over the marshes. Maddened, William lifted the knife to plunge it into her chest. But the witch, her mother, leaped upon him from above, as if she'd been lurking in the branches. In the struggle, it was Bethiah who felt the knife blade sink deep.*

What happened next varies with the teller. Some say the mother used her last strength to slit the throat of the attacker. Some say the girl seized the knife and killed her mother's murderer. In the end, the jury of brave men and true decided on the first version, swayed by the girl's beauty or fear of her mother's power even in death.

All sources agree on this: with her dying breath, Bethiah Smith uttered a curse upon the neighboring farm and the land where it stood. The turnips, corn, and asparagus shriveled; the soil brought forth tares instead of wheat. The cattle lay down in the fields and died; the chickens laid locusts instead of eggs.

The family, however, turned to other trades and thrived in commercial matters, as the mendacious often do. One curse they reportedly could not escape, however.

Everyone who slept on that land was doomed to see the world through a distorting haze. Under Bethiah's curse, all was altered or exaggerated. The mote they saw in one's neighbor's eye was more than a log; it was a whole forest, populated with beasts. Conversely, the log in one's own eye seemed a bridge to glory, or doom. A bit of luck became a license to throw caution to the winds; a penny found meant bounty was a birthright. They lived in dream or nightmare, never touching firm ground. A lover might see the beloved as true, though he or she shared the bed of a dozen others, or might condemn a partner as unfaithful when that person was reliable as the tides. Card players came to believe they couldn't lose, and forfeited their homes and families. Fisherman assured themselves their craft could survive swells that dwarfed the Nauset dunes, and drowned.

Today such curses seem merely quaint explanations for what's really simple psychology. But the legends live on in the area, as, in a sense, do all the characters. The marsh that divides Wonderstrand from the sea is still known as Bethiah's Swamp. Her daughter Coral, who in her lifetime married several husbands and gave birth to many children, is buried in Wonderstrand's small cemetery, where visitors can still read the lettering on her arched and skull-bedecked stone. Once or twice in a generation, one of those passersby might even bear the same name. I've met a local woman who does so now.

Was Bethiah's tale one of witchcraft, or merely of human failings? That depends on your opinion of Wonderstrand. I find in it the last vestige of primal Cape Cod, as it was before the tourist industry and the real estate booms and crashes, before Thoreau, Joseph Lincoln, the National Seashore. Maybe before the white man came, armed with guns and hellfire, when the tales were of Maushop and the Nauset people, of the spirits of sea and land. Others may regard Wonderstrand as a sad little pocket in the great theme park of Cape Cod, a locale that exists only for the sentimental. But then, few of us see anything in a cold, clear light.

Judge for yourself. Come to Wonderstrand. Look at your reflection in a grassless patch of marsh water. Watch it shift and waver as clouds pass over the sun. Plunge your hand in and see your face shatter into a thousand ripples and disappear. One illusion ends, another begins.

What if our Eurekas are our moments of greatest self-delusion, what Hawthorne described in his own final tale as, "a spectral illusion, and a cunning effect of light and shade"? Could our greatest joys be no more than scarecrows, propped up on pipe dreams and fantasies, stuffed with animal longing? If so, maybe our greatest tragedies are only so many marauding crows. We tell ourselves tales to keep them at bay.

—From *Wonderstrand Tales*, by Guy Thomas Maulkin

Author's Note

Everybody has his or her own Cape Cod; I've tried to write about mine. Commercialized, romanticized, criticized, idealized, to me it's a place still not quite part of the ordinary world. Though I might be driving down an overdeveloped highway or walking on a boardwalk manufactured from recycled plastic, I still can see ghosts emerging from the mist wearing eighteenth century clothing. Wonderstrand itself is an imagined locale culled from legends and history. Some of the locations mentioned do exist; I hope I've done them justice. No record exists of Nathaniel Hawthorne's having visited here, though he did take several mysterious journeys as a young man, listening to local tales and folklore, spinning them into his own work. I'd love to think he included Cape Cod among them.

Acknowledgments

My gratitude goes out to the following people. To Laurie Higgins and Debi Stetson for their crackerjack editing, as well as their friendship, support and encouragement. To William Kantar for showing me possibilities. To US Coast Guard Senior Chief Jason Holm, for his description of what it feels like to be underwater in heavy seas. Last and most, to Katie Dryden, who sometimes knows what I need before I do, and Howard Gostin for the long *danse macabre*—really, for everything. Just everything.

I'm also indebted to the following sources in researching and writing *Wonderstrand Tales*. Foremost, of course, were the works of Nathaniel Hawthorne, particularly *Mosses from an Old Manse* (which includes my primary inspiration, "Feathertop; a Moralized Legend"), *Nathaniel Hawthorne's Tales*, *The House of Seven Gables*, and *Passages from the American Notebooks*. Where I've used one of his timeless characters as a starting point for one of mine or lifted a word, phrase, or a theme of his, I intended it entirely as a tribute.

Three biographies were especially helpful, *Nathaniel Hawthorne in His Times*, by James R. Mellow, *Salem Is My Dwelling Place*, by Edwin Haviland

Miller, and *Hawthorne: A Life,* by Brenda Wineapple. For local history, I consulted *Eastham, Massachusetts 1651-1951,* by Donald G. Trayser, *Cape Cod Architecture,* by Clair Baisly, *Becoming Cape Cod,* by James C. O'Connell, and *Cape Cod,* by Henry David Thoreau. *The Narrow Land,* by Elizabeth Reynard, *A Treasury of New England Folklore,* by B.A. Botkin, and *Weird New England,* by Joseph A. Citro, provided Cape Cod follklore. Other valuable sources included *Scarecrows,* by Felder Rushing, *Scarecrows* by Colin Garret, *Opium,* by Martin Booth, *Bottlemania: How Water Went on Sale and Why We Bought It,* by Elizabeth Royte. Finally, I know of two other treatments of Hawthorne's "Feathertop": a children's book of the same name by Robert D. Sans Souci, and *Scarecrow,* a play by Percy MacKaye released on video by Kultur's Broadway Theatre Archive. Nice to know others loved this story as much as I did. I hope their work and mine bring more of today's readers to the original.

Made in the USA
Charleston, SC
29 August 2013